A
TREASURY
OF
CAT MYSTERIES

A TREASURY OF CAT MYSTERIES

Compiled by
Martin H. Greenberg

Carroll & Graf Publishers, Inc.
New York

First Carroll & Graf edition 1998

Carroll & Graf Publishers, Inc.
19 West 21st Street
New York, NY 10010

Library of Congress Cataloging-in-Publication data is available.
ISBN: 0-7867-0541-8

Manufactured in the United States of America

The following acknowledgments constitute an extension of this
copyright page.

"SuSu and the 8:30 Ghost" by Lilian Jackson Braun. Copyright ©
1964 by Lilian Jackson Braun. Reprinted by permission of the
Berkley Publishing Group, Inc.

"Ginger's Waterloo" by Peter Lovesey. Copyright © 1991 by
Peter Lovesey. Reprinted by permission of the author.

"Nine Lives to Live" by Sharyn McCrumb. Copyright © 1992 by
Sharyn McCrumb. Reprinted by permission of the author.

"Bedeviled" by Bill Pronzini. Copyright © 1991 by Bill
Pronzini. Reprinted by permission of the author.

"The Maggody Files: Hillbilly Cat" by Joan Hess. Copyright ©
1992 by Joan Hess. Reprinted by permission of the author.

"Enduring As Dust" by Bruce Holland Rogers. Copyright © 1993
by Bruce Holland Rogers. Reprinted by permission of the
author.

"Buster" by Bill Crider. Copyright © 1991 by Bill Crider.
Reprinted by permission of the author.

"Where the Cat Came In" by Mat Coward. Copyright © 1998 by
Mat Coward.

Contents

Contents

Introduction

WITHOUT A DOUBT, CATS ARE one of the great mysteries of the animal kingdom. Aloof, inscrutable, mystifying, they live their lives according to a schedule only they know, which usually leaves little time for their owners. When they do deign to mingle with those who feed them, it is on the cat's terms, make no mistake. One supercilious glance from them can reduce the most rational of people to nervous wrecks, wondering what they may have done to deserve such scorn.

And yet, there is a sense of wonder and joy to be found in cats as there is in few other animals. When a cat is happy, there can be no doubt, as they will indubitably let you know. Their obvious intelligence and marvelous grace are only two in a long list of endearing traits. To watch a kitten explore his world is to see unbounded enthusiasm coupled with an insatiable curiosity. It is no wonder that humans identify so strongly with cats, as they embody both the good and evil sides of mankind.

In this way, cats and mysteries go hand in paw. Humans feed, pamper, play with, and care for their cats perhaps in the hopes of unraveling some of the timeless mysteries that lie behind their sometimes smug, sometimes worshipful eyes. The cats themselves, however, don't seem to be inclined to let these secrets go lightly. Occassionally they'll deign to give their owners a slight glimpse into that mystical world, only to close the door again before revealing too much. In their own way, cats are an everyday mystery to be puzzled over, exasperated by, and, most of all, enjoyed.

The mysteries collected in this book are all centered upon that most mystical of animals, the cat. Outstanding mystery authors such as Ruth Rendell, Bill Pronzini, and Peter Lovesey, along with many others, reveal not nine but twenty-one lives of the otherwise ordinary housecat. From an old man's love for his only friend in the world, and the risks he takes to get that friend back, to a cat that helps solve a thirty-year-old mystery involving the King of Rock and Roll, felines in all their glory are represented here. So make sure your feline companion is comfortably settled near you, turn the page, and enter a world where detectives and criminals walk on four feet instead of two.

MARTIN H. GREENBERG
Green Bay, Wisconsin

A
Treasury
of
Cat Mysteries

SuSu and the 8:30 Ghost

Lilian Jackson Braun

WHEN MY SISTER AND I returned from vacation and learned that our eccentric neighbor in the wheelchair had been removed to a mental hospital, we were sorry but hardly surprised. He was a strange man, not easy to like, and no one in our apartment building seemed concerned about his departure—except our Siamese cat. The friendship between SuSu and Mr. Van was so close it was alarming.

If it had not been for SuSu we would never have made the man's acquaintance, for we were not too friendly with our neighbors. The building was very large and full of odd characters who, we thought, were best ignored. On the other hand, our old apartment had advantages: large rooms, moderate rent, and a thrilling view of the river. There was also a small waterfront park at the foot of the street, and it was there that we first noticed Mr. Van.

One Sunday afternoon my sister Gertrude and I were walking SuSu in the park, which was barely more than a strip of grass alongside an old wharf. Barges and tugs sometimes docked there, and SuSu—wary of these monsters—preferred to stay away from the water's edge. It was one of the last nice days in November. Soon the river would freeze over, icy winds would blow, and the park would be deserted for the winter.

SuSu loved to chew grass, and she was chewing industriously when something diverted her attention and drew her toward the river. Tugging at her leash, she insisted on moving across the grass to the boardwalk, where a middle-aged man sat in a most unusual wheelchair.

It was made almost entirely of cast iron, like the base of an old-fashioned sewing machine, and it was upholstered in worn plush.

With its high back and elaborate ironwork, it looked like a mobile throne, and the man who occupied the regal wheelchair presided with the imperious air of a monarch. It conflicted absurdly with his shabby clothing.

To our surprise this was the attraction that lured SuSu. She chirped at the man, and he leaned over and stroked her fur.

"She recognizes me," he explained to us, speaking with a haughty accent that sounded vaguely Teutonic. "I was-s-s a cat myself in a former existence."

I rolled my eyes at Gertrude, but she accepted the man's statement without blinking.

He was far from attractive, having a sharply pointed chin, ears set too high on his head, and eyes that were mere slits, and when he smiled he was even less appealing. Nevertheless, SuSu found him irresistible. She rubbed against his ankles, and he scratched her in the right places. They made a most unlikely pair—SuSu with her luxurious blond fur, looking fastidious and expensive, and the man in the wheelchair, with his rusty coat and moth-eaten lap robe.

In the course of a fragmentary conversation with Mr. Van we learned that he and the companion who manipulated his wheelchair had just moved into a large apartment on our floor, and I wondered why the two of them needed so many rooms. As for the companion, it was hard to decide whether he was a mute or just unsociable. He was a short thick man with a round knob of a head screwed tight to his shoulders and a flicker of something unpleasant in his eyes. He stood behind the wheel-chair in sullen silence.

On the way back to the apartment Gertrude said: "How do you like our new neighbor?"

"I prefer cats before they're reincarnated as people," I said.

"But he's rather interesting," said my sister in the gentle way that she had.

A few evenings later we were having coffee after dinner, and SuSu—having finished her own meal—was washing up in the downglow of a lamp. As we watched her graceful movements, we saw her hesitate with one paw in midair. She held it there and listened. Then a new and different sound came from her throat, like a melodic gurgling. A minute later she was trotting to our front door with intense purpose. There she sat, watching and waiting and listening, although we ourselves could hear nothing.

It was a full two minutes before our doorbell rang. I went to open the door and was somewhat unhappy to see Mr. Van sitting there in his lordly wheelchair.

SuSu leaped into his lap—an unprecedented overture for her to make—and after he had kneaded her ears and scratched her chin, he smiled a thin-lipped, slit-eyed smile at me and said: "*Goeden avond.* I was-s-s unpacking some crates, and I found something I would like to give you."

With a flourish he handed me a small framed picture, whereupon I was more or less obliged to invite him in. He wheeled his ponderous chair into the apartment with some difficulty, the rubber tires making deep gouges in the pile of the carpet.

"How do you manage that heavy chair alone?" I asked. "It must weigh a ton."

"But it is-s-s a work of art," said Mr. Van, rubbing appreciative hands over the plush upholstery and lacy ironwork and wheels.

Gertrude had jumped up and poured him a cup of coffee, and he said: "I wish you would teach that man of mine to make coffee. He makes the worst *zootje* I have ever tasted. In Holland we like our coffee *sterk* with a little chicory. But that fellow, he is-s-s a *smeerlap*. I would not put up with him for two minutes if I could get around by myself."

SuSu was rubbing her head on the Hollander's vest buttons, and he smiled with pleasure, showing small square teeth.

"Do you have this magnetic attraction for all cats?" I asked with a slight edge to my voice. SuSu was now in raptures because he was twisting the scruff of her neck.

"It is-s-s only natural," he said. "I can read their thoughts, and they read mine of course. Do you know that cats are mind readers? You walk to the refrigerator to get a beer, and the cat she will not budge, but walk to the refrigerator to get out her dinner, and what happens? Before you touch the handle of the door she will come bouncing into the kitchen from anyplace she happens to be. Your thought waves reached her even though she seemed to be asleep."

Gertrude agreed it was probably true.

"Of course it is-s-s true," said Mr. Van, sitting tall. "Everything I say is-s-s true. Cats know more than you suspect. They can not only read your mind, they can plant ideas in your head. And they can sense something that is-s-s about to happen."

My sister said: "You must be right. SuSu knew you were coming here tonight, long before you rang the bell."

"Of course I am right. I am always right," said Mr. Van. "My grandmother in Vlissingen had a tomcat called Zwartje just before she died, and for years after the funeral my grandmother came back to pet the cat. Every night Zwartje stood in front of the chair where Grootmoeder used to sit, and he would stretch and purr although there was-s-s no one there. Every night at half past eight."

After that visit with Mr. Van I referred to him as Grandmother's Ghost, for he too made a habit of appearing at eight-thirty several times a week. (For Gertrude's coffee, I guessed.)

He would say: "I was-s-s feeling lonesome for my little sweetheart," and SuSu would make an extravagant fuss over the man. It pleased me that he never stayed long, although Gertrude usually encouraged him to linger.

The little framed picture he had given us was not exactly to my taste. It was a silhouette of three figures—a man in frock coat and top hat, a woman in hoopskirt and sunbonnet, and a cat carrying his tail like a lance. To satisfy my sister, however, I hung the picture, but only over the kitchen sink.

One evening Gertrude, who is a librarian, came home in great excitement. "There's a signature on that silhouette," she said, "and I looked it up at the library. Augustin Edouart was a famous artist, and our silhouette is over a hundred years old. It might be valuable."

"I doubt it," I said. "We used to cut silhouettes like that in the third grade."

Eventually, at my sister's urging, I took the object to an antique shop, and the dealer said it was a good one, probably worth several hundred dollars.

When Gertrude heard this, she said: "If the dealer quoted hundreds, it's probably worth thousands. I think we should give it back to Mr. Van. The poor man doesn't know what he's giving away."

I agreed he could probably sell it and buy himself a decent wheelchair.

At eight-thirty that evening SuSu began to gurgle and prance.

"Here comes Grandmother's Ghost," I said, and shortly afterward the doorbell rang.

"Mr. Van," I said after Gertrude had poured the coffee, "remember that silhouette you gave us? I've found out it's valuable, and you must take it back."

"Of course it is-s-s valuable," he said. "Would I give it to you if it was-s-s nothing but *rommel?*"

"Do you know something about antiques?"

"My dear Mevrouw, I have a million dollars' worth of antiques in my apartment. Tomorrow evening you ladies must come and see my treasures. I will get rid of that *smeerlap*, and the three of us will enjoy a cup of coffee."

"By the way, what is a *smeerlap?*" I asked.

"It is-s-s not very nice," said Mr. Van. "If somebody called me a *smeerlap*, I would punch him in the nose. . . . Bring my little sweetheart when you come, ladies. She will find some fascinating objects to explore."

Our cat seemed to know what he was saying.

"SuSu will enjoy it," said Gertrude. "She's locked up in this apartment all winter."

"Knit her a sweater and take her to the park in winter," said the Hollander in the commanding tone that always irritated me. "I often bundle up in a blanket and go to the park in the evening. It is-s-s good for insomnia."

"SuSu is not troubled with insomnia," I informed him. "She sleeps twenty hours a day."

Mr. Van looked at me with scorn. "You are wrong. Cats never sleep. You think they are sleeping, but cats are the most wakeful creatures on earth. That is-s-s one of their secrets."

After he had gone, I said to Gertrude: "I know you like the fellow, but you must admit he's off his rocker."

"He's just a little eccentric."

"If he has a million dollars' worth of antiques, which I doubt, why is he living in this run-down building? And why doesn't he buy a wheelchair that's easier to operate?"

"Because he's a Dutchman, I suppose," was Gertrude's explanation.

"And how about all those ridiculous things he says about cats?"

"I'm beginning to think they're true."

"And who is the fellow who lives with him? Is he a servant, or a nurse, or a keeper, or what? I see him coming and going on the elevator, but he never speaks—not one word. He doesn't even seem to have a name, and Mr. Van treats him like a slave. I'm not sure we should go tomorrow night. The whole situation is too strange."

Nevertheless, we went. The Hollander's apartment was jammed with furniture and bric-a-brac, and he shouted at his companion: "Move that *rommel* so the ladies can sit down."

Sullenly the fellow removed some paintings and tapestries from the seat of a carved sofa.

"Now get out of here!" Mr. Van shouted at him. "Get yourself a beer," and he threw the man some money with less grace than one would throw a dog a bone.

While SuSu explored the premises we drank our coffee, and then Mr. Van showed us his treasures, propelling his wheelchair through a maze of furniture. He pointed out Chippendale-this and Affleck-that and Newport-something-else. They were treasures to him, but to me they were musty relics of a dead past.

"I am in the antique business," Mr. Van explained. "Before I was-s-s chained to this wheelchair, I had a shop and exhibited at the major shows. Then . . . I was-s-s in a bad auto accident, and now I sell from the apartment. By appointment only."

"Can you do that successfully?" Gertrude asked.

"And why not? The museum people know me, and collectors come here from all over the country. I buy. I sell. And my man Frank does the legwork. He is-s-s the perfect assistant for an antique dealer—strong in the back, weak in the head."

"Where did you find him?"

"On a junk heap. I have taught him enough to be useful to me, but not enough to be useful to himself. A smart arrangement, eh?" Mr. Van winked. "He is-s-s a *smeerlap*, but I am helpless without him. . . . Hoo! Look at my little sweetheart. She has-s-s found a prize!"

SuSu was sniffing at a silver bowl with two handles.

Mr. Van nodded approvingly. "It is a caudle cup made by Jeremiah Dummer of Boston in the late seventeenth century—for a certain lady in Salem. They said she was-s-s a witch. Look at my little sweetheart. She knows!"

I coughed and said: "Yes, indeed. You're lucky to have Frank."

"You think I do not know it?" Mr. Van said in a snappish tone. "That is-s-s why I keep him poor. If I gave him wages, he would get ideas. A *smeerlap* with ideas—there is-s-s nothing worse."

"How long ago was your accident?"

"Five years, and it was-s-s that idiot's fault. He did it! He did this to me!" The man's voice rose to a shout, and his face turned red as he pounded the arms of his wheelchair with his fist. Then SuSu rubbed against his ankles, and he stroked her and began to calm down. "Yes, five years in this miserable chair. We were driving to an antique show in the station wagon. Sixty miles an hour—and he went through a red light and hit a truck. A gravel truck!"

Gertrude put both hands to her face. "How terrible, Mr. Van!"

"I remember packing the wagon for that trip. I was-s-s complaining all the time about sore arches. Hah! What I would give for some sore arches today yet!"

"Wasn't Frank hurt?"

Mr. Van made an impatient gesture. "His-s-s head only. They picked Waterford crystal out of that blockhead for six hours. He has-s-s been *gek* ever since." He tapped his temple.

"Where did you find this unusual wheelchair?" I asked.

"My dear Mevrouw, never ask a dealer where he found something. It was-s-s made for a railroad millionaire in 1872. It has-s-s the original plush. If you must spend your life in a wheelchair, have one that gives some pleasure. And now we come to the purpose of tonight's visit. Ladies, I want you to do something for me."

He wheeled himself to a desk, and Gertrude and I exchanged anxious glances.

"Here in this desk is-s-s a new will I have written, and I need witnesses. I am leaving a few choice items to museums. Everything else is-s-s to be sold and the proceeds used to establish a foundation."

"What about Frank?" asked Gertrude, who is always genuinely concerned about others.

"Bah! Nothing for that *smeerlap!* . . . But before you ladies sign the papers, there is-s-s one thing I must write down. What is-s-s the full name of my little sweetheart?"

We both hesitated, and finally I said: "Her registered name is Superior Suda of Siam."

"Good! I will make it the Superior Suda Foundation. That gives me pleasure. Making a will is-s-s a dismal business, like a wheelchair, so give yourself some pleasure."

"What—ah—will be the purpose of the foundation?" I asked.

Mr. Van blessed us with one of his ambiguous smiles. "It will sponsor research," he said. "I want universities to study the highly developed mental perception of the domestic feline and apply the knowledge to the improvement of the human mind. Ladies, there is-s-s nothing better I could do with my fortune. Man is-s-s eons behind the smallest fireside grimalkin." He gave us a canny look, and his eyes narrowed. "I am in a position to know."

We witnessed the man's signature. What else could we do? A few days later we left on vacation and never saw Mr. Van again.

Gertrude and I always went south for three weeks in winter, taking SuSu with us. When we returned, the sorry news about our eccentric neighbor was thrown at us without ceremony.

We met Frank on the elevator as we were taking our luggage upstairs, and for the first time he spoke. That in itself was a shock.

He said simply, without any polite preliminaries: "They took him away."

"What's that? What did you say?" we both clamored at once.

"They took him away." It was surprising to find that the voice of this muscular man was high-pitched and rasping.

"What happened to Mr. Van?" my sister demanded.

"He cracked up. His folks come from Pennsylvania and took him back home. He's in a nut hospital."

I saw Gertrude wince, and she said: "Is it serious?"

Frank shrugged.

"What will happen to all his antiques?"

"His folks told me to dump the junk."

"But they're valuable things, aren't they?"

"Nah. Junk. He give everybody that guff about museums and all." Frank shrugged again and tapped his head. "He was *gek*."

In stunned wonderment my sister and I reached our apartment, and I could hardly wait to say it: "I told you your Dutchman was unbalanced."

"Such a pity," she murmured.

"What do you think of the sudden change in Frank? He acts like a free man. It must have been terrible living with that old Scrooge."

"I'll miss Mr. Van," Gertrude said softly. "He was very interesting. SuSu will miss him, too."

But SuSu, we observed later that evening, was not willing to relinquish her friend in the wheelchair as easily as we had done.

We were unpacking the vacation luggage after dinner when SuSu staged her demonstration. She started to gurgle and prance, exactly as she had done all winter whenever Mr. Van was approaching our door. Gertrude and I watched her, waiting for the bell to ring. When SuSu trotted expectantly to the door, we followed. She was behaving in an extraordinary manner. She craned her neck, made weaving motions with her head, rolled over on her back, and stretched luxuriously, all the while purring her heart out; but the doorbell never rang.

Looking at my watch, I said: "It's eight-thirty. SuSu remembers."

"It's quite touching, isn't it?" Gertrude remarked.

That was not the end of SuSu's demonstrations. Almost every night at half past eight she performed the same ritual.

I recalled how SuSu had continued to sleep in the guest room long after we had moved her bed to another place. "Cats hate to give up a habit. But she'll forget Mr. Van's visits after a while."

SuSu did not forget. A few weeks passed. Then we had a foretaste of spring and a sudden thaw. People went without coats prematurely, convertibles cruised with the tops down, and a few hopeful fishermen appeared on the wharf at the foot of our street, although the river was still patched with ice.

On one of these warm evenings we walked SuSu down to the park for her first spring outing, expecting her to go after last year's dried weeds with snapping jaws. Instead, she tugged at her leash, pulling toward the boardwalk. Out of curiosity we let her have her way, and there on the edge of the wharf she staged her weird performance once more—gurgling, arching her back, craning her neck with joy.

"She's doing it again," I said. "I wonder what the reason could be."

Gertrude said, almost in a whisper: "Remember what Mr. Van said about cats and ghosts?"

"Look at that animal! You'd swear she was rubbing against someone's ankles. I wish she'd stop. It makes me uneasy."

"I wonder," said my sister very slowly, "if Mr. Van is really in a mental hospital."

"What do you mean?"

"Or is he—down there?" Gertrude pointed uncertainly over the edge of the wharf. "I think Mr. Van is dead, and SuSu knows."

"That's too fantastic," I said. "*Really*, Gertrude!"

"I think Frank pushed the poor man off the wharf, wheelchair and all—perhaps one dark night when Mr. Van couldn't sleep and insisted on being wheeled to the park."

"You're not serious, Gertrude."

"Can't you see it? . . . A cold night. The riverfront deserted. Mr. Van trussed in his wheelchair with a blanket. Why, that chair would sink like lead! What a terrible thing! That icy water. That poor helpless man."

"I just can't—"

"Now Frank is free, and he has all those antiques, and nobody cares enough to ask questions. He can sell them and be set up for life."

"And he tears up the will," I suggested, succumbing to Gertrude's fantasy.

"Do you know what a Newport blockfront is worth? I've been looking it up in the library. A chest like the one we saw in Mr. Van's apartment was sold for hundreds of thousands at an auction on the East Coast."

"But what about the relatives in Pennsylvania?"

"I'm sure Mr. Van had no relatives—in Pennsylvania or anywhere else."

"Well, what do you propose we should do?" I said in exasperation. "Report it to the manager of the building? Notify the police? Tell them we think the man has been murdered because our cat sees his ghost every night at eight-thirty? We'd look like a couple of middle-aged ladies who are getting a little *gek*."

As a matter of fact, I was beginning to worry about Gertrude's obsession—that is, until I read the morning paper a few days later.

I skimmed through it at the breakfast table, and there—at the bottom of page seven—one small item leaped off the paper at me. Could I believe my eyes?

"Listen to this," I said to my sister. "The body of an unidentified man has been washed up on a downriver island. Police say the body had apparently been held underwater for several weeks by the ice. . . . About fifty-five years old and crippled. . . . No one fitting that description has been reported to the Missing Persons Bureau."

For a moment my sister stared at the coffeepot. Then she left the breakfast table and went to the telephone.

"Now all the police have to do," she said with a quiver in her voice, "is to look for an antique wheelchair in the river at the foot of the street. Cast iron. With the original plush." She blinked at the phone several times. "Would you dial?" she asked me. "I can't see the numbers."

Ginger's Waterloo

Peter Lovesey

*This story was drafted by my son, Phil, who commutes
by train to London, and I'd like to record my thanks to
him.—P. L.*

AND THIS IS HOW BAD things can happen.

I stood on the new station, in the new suit for the new job,
with no idea whose ground I was invading. The regular com-
muters were streaming along the platform for the 8.16 to Waterloo.

A glance at the flipping metal digital clock told me I had
eight minutes before the train pulled in. Bad news. I would have
preferred to get straight on to a waiting one without having to
negotiate this minefield.

Grey clouds hung indolently over Shipley. Rain was threatening. Only threatening. A pity, this. Even a light drizzle would
have forced a hasty rearrangement under Shipley's station can-
opy. The two uncovered ends of the platform would then have
been given up except by the few willing to unfurl their tightly
rolled umbrellas.

But the rain held off. Since Joyce and I had moved to 19, Winter Gardens three weeks previously, the sun had not once broken through. The weather here was as implacable as the inhabitants. Still, I tried telling myself, this was October, a time of the year when it was unfair to judge the potential of any town. Joyce, an unfailing optimist, was sure our small square of rear garden would be a sun-trap in summers to come.

I'd ventured along the platform to the less populated end and found a space. Enough room here to swing a cat, I thought. Yes, that insensitive phrase truly came into my head that Monday morning just minutes before I met Colin.

This end was where the singles hung out. Or loners, if you like; anyway, the people who preferred their own company to anyone else's. Executive briefcases, broadsheet newspapers and definitely no eye contact. Naked without a *Times* of my own, I positioned myself the requisite eighteen inches from the platform edge, pretending to be completely absorbed in the billboard opposite, an advert for cigarettes.

At the edge of my field of vision I noticed another minute flip down on the station clock. Five more to go. The man on my left saw my eyes move. He flinched and closed his paper a little in case I sneaked a glimpse of the headlines. Probably he was relishing the arrival of whoever it was who usually stood where I had taken up position. The space had asked to be filled—a sure sign it already had an owner. I expected hot breath on the back of my neck any second.

I actually felt homesick for Barton Vales Station. The tree-lined car park, Joe punching tickets and apologizing to every passenger for late-running trains. The sound of birds, not buses. But that was gone now. I couldn't even imagine it existing any longer. Surely Barton Vales had ceased to be, out of respect, the minute I left?

I'd exchanged that rustic idyll for a City job with the biggest insurance company in Europe. In no time at all, I'd promised Joyce, we'd reap the benefits.

Four minutes. I read the health warning on the cigarette ad. Didn't smoke myself.

Then Colin came into my life.

"I shouldn't stand there if I were you."

Ignore. Ignore. Read the health warning again.

"You're in the wrong place, mate."

Jesus, he's definitely talking to me, I thought. And this was worse than I'd imagined. I'm no snob, but the accent wasn't the sort you expected on the 8.16 to London.

"I can always spot a new face."

His face, and a gust of garlic breath, invaded me from my right. I stared ahead like a guardsman. No paper to hide behind. I cursed myself for walking past the newsstand.

"I mean you, mate."

A note of aggression in the voice. Because I'm a coward, I responded by sliding my eyes a fraction his way.

Fatal.

Eye contact. He was in.

"This is a gap, see?"

I didn't need telling.

The others around me relaxed and started to read the share prices again. They weren't being spoken to. I was.

"The carriages all stop at certain places, right?" The stocky, scruffy figure pointed a denimed arm at the sign 6 which hung directly above my head. "There won't be no door here when it comes. You'll be stood facing the gap between the carriages."

I nodded and tried to appear grateful for the information.

He stabbed a finger at several of the people around me and said, embarrassingly in the circumstances, "These clever buggers here, see, they've got it sorted. They're stood ready by the doors, ain't they? You won't get a look in, mate."

I remained as deadpan as I could, allowing how acutely uncomfortable I felt. Just go away now, please.

"Straight up," he said. "I tell no lies. They've got it down to inches here, mate. Worst station on the line. Cut-throat. You're new to the game, I can see—a butterboy."

Brilliant. New job, my first day on the 8.16, and I'd found the loudmouth.

"Don't take offence, squire. I like your style."

Perhaps it was the compliment that did it. Or just relief that he wasn't about to turn nasty.

Stupidly, I felt compelled to respond. "It's coming, I think."

"Bang on time, for once."

"Unusual, is it?"

"Unheard of, these days. Better expect a hold-up at Clapham Junction."

A joke. I rewarded it with a grin.

The 8.16 cruised in, brakes squealing, and the melee started. Doors opened and released a few sleepy-eyed shop assistants and schoolteachers to a day's work in Shipley, while the London-bound lot plunged in and planted cold-trousered rears on still-warm seats.

"This way, mate," my newfound friend bawled in my right ear, grabbing my sleeve. "Always space in a smoker."

Now, I have never smoked in my life—nor do I intend to. I had until that day avoided smoking compartments in restaurants and trains. I travel on the lower decks of buses, avoiding any contact with the noxious weed. But that day, that Monday, because I was too weak to antagonize the loudmouth, I clambered in with him.

Tobacco stung my nostrils. We sat opposite each other, squeezed on the ends of seats of three.

"Good to get some cloth under your bum, eh? Never failed to find a seat in a smoker before it pulls out. Standing-room only in the other carriages. By the way," he continued, offering a muscular hand, "mine's Colin. What's yours?"

My cynical old Dad once told me that friends are like fish. Kept too long, they begin to smell. Three weeks after our first encounter, Colin stank.

That may sound mean, but I hadn't sought him out in the first place. We had, by now, become regulars. I deeply regretted my initial wish to blend into Shipley's status quo. I was discovering it had unforeseen consequences. I just couldn't fend Colin off. Every morning I endured him for the twenty-seven minutes from Shipley to Waterloo. I'd arrive at the terminus with my paper unread and tightly curled, my hands black from the newsprint, my face aching from the polite smile as he talked at me.

You see, there was no escape from his conversation. He enjoyed a chat, he told me. There wasn't much chatting in his work as a contract-plumber on the new Nomura building in the City. He must have been the only tradesman on the train. I've nothing against plumbers, but Colin was redefining my limits of tolerance. My new suit reeked of stale tobacco. The smoke clung to my hair. My eyeballs, soft from sleep, stung from the exhaled poison from Colin's roll-ups.

As the days passed, my frustration increased. Frankly it was becoming intolerable. Colin's outspokenness was acutely embarrassing. At the beginning, I'd been willing to put up with it just to avoid a scene, even tried to persuade myself that it was amusing. By now it was confirmed as uncouth and insupportable. My fellow-travellers, well-bred to the core, said nothing, but rolled their eyes at each other and rustled their papers during particularly unpleasant harangues.

So what held me back? What prevented me from avoiding him? Why didn't I step smartly into a different carriage—a nonsmoker—to enjoy some privacy and my paper?

Cowardice. I didn't dare provoke him. My dread of an ugly outburst grew daily in me like a cancer, stronger than the rage I felt at the daily imposition.

"Take women, for instance. Take my wife. Are you listening, Davey?"

How I loathed his distortion of my name. Why didn't I correct him? I suppose it was better he called me that, than David, which I reserved for friends who were, frankly, more my type. Oh God, not again! He was about to come out with it once more.

"I said take my wife, and I wish you would." Followed by the quick look round to see who was smiling. "No, wouldn't wish that on Adolf Hitler. I mean, I don't know about your missus, Davey boy, and believe me I don't want to pry, but, like, it's different once they get that ring on their finger. Your sex bomb turns into a couch potato, know what I mean?"

I just nodded, aware that every woman in the carriage expected me to put a stop to his boorish talk. As I didn't, they could only assume I was another bigot. If only the voice weren't so loud, so coarse.

"Take Louise, right? She's got her life to lead, the same as you or me. She's out all day and comes back knackered. We're both knackered, right? Now, I'm no chauvinist."

You could have fooled me, I thought—and so, no doubt, thought everyone else in the carriage.

"No, very liberated I am. I do my share. I don't mind washing up. And I'll open a tin for the cat. It was my cat in the first place. I just think, as a bloke, I'm entitled to some sort of dinner on the table. Nothing fancy, just meat and two veg, maybe. I mean, marriage is supposed to be a partnership, am I right?"

Here it came again, as familiar now as Vauxhall Bridge flying by. The wife-and-cat diatribe. Colin felt left out. Couldn't stand the wife all woosey over the cat.

"Don't get me wrong, Davey. I've nothing against cats. I grew up with cats. And Ginger, well, she's affectionate. It's her nature. She's looking for attention, like they do. She wants fussing up, but there are limits. I get home, like, and all I see is Louise and Ginger all over each other. Okay, so Louise hasn't seen her all day, but I need my dinner. The cat gets fed. I see to that. And I'm bloody starving."

A silence. Time for my lines. Wearily, like an actor in a long run, I said, "Why not make yourself a sandwich?"

"Ain't the food for a hungry fella, is it, Davey, eh? Ain't the food to send vigour coursing through these veins, is it? No, not a pesky sandwich."

A pause. I hadn't been listening. Missed my cue. Fortunately the script was unchanging.

"I always enjoy a takeaway myself," I said too late and too flatly, watching the silver rails collide and cross in rhythmical patterns beneath me.

"Ah, now you *are* talking, Davey. Don't mind a bit of foreign myself. Louise, God bless her, just laps up that Chinky grub. Ever tried that chicken chop-suey thing? Hey, it's no wonder they're all walking round like this . . . I say, Davey, like this, eh?"

Dreading this, I looked up to see his fingers at the outer

corners of his eyes, pulling the skin sideways. A goofy mouth, bottom lip pulled under top teeth, completed the hideous parody.

"Fu Manchu, ain't I? Numburrhh flifty-two wi plawn balls and flied ri. Ginger likes a bite of the old sweet and sour, you know. They're canny creatures, females, whatever bloody species they are. Listen to this. I reckon Ginger has twigged that if she plays with Louise for half an hour when she comes in, then there's no meal for me. So it's off down the takeaway. I bring back the sweet and sour, and Ginger gets her portion, see?"

"I see."

But I didn't want to see. I sincerely hoped the mental images of Colin's crass domestic life, his apathetic wife and his manipulative cat, would be erased from my mind, replaced by something more uplifting.

The airbrakes swished and hissed under our feet, the points clattering repeatedly, a sombre drumming into Waterloo, and work. Very likely I was the only passenger arriving there with a sense of release. Each day I longed to leave that train, to step into anonymity, knowing that our captive audience was dispersing. The appalling Colin would disappear, too, bound for his plumbing contract.

And now I have to explain something, and it's not easy, so bear with me.

Between the train and the ticket-barrier, I talked to Colin each morning. I felt the pressure to respond to the diatribe he'd given me all the way from Shipley. I'd said very little in the train. Now, with no one else eavesdropping, I could humour the man. I didn't want to part on bad terms. I've already admitted to being a coward. I'm also a humbug. So I pretended to share his opinions.

"I couldn't agree with you more, old man," I'd find myself saying as I eyed the approach of the ticket collector's gate.

"Yeah?" he'd say.

"Women. And cats. They need training. They don't like it, but it's got to be done."

"Just what I said, Davey. You and me, we think alike. Not like these wimps, eh?"

"Absolutely not, Colin."

"Your meal always on the table, then?"

"Every day, Colin—or else." An absolute lie, but strangely exhilarating to plant a fictional seed of my own chauvinistic home life in his head.

"You got it well sussed, Davey." He put a comradely hand on my shoulder. "So what would you do, then, about Louise and Ginger?"

"Well, Colin," I said, raising my voice to compete with the Tannoy. "It's a matter of priorities. Who wears the trousers?" We had reached the gate. That morning I paused to finish the conversation. "Just talk to Louise. Tell her you expect certain standards. She has to know you're boss. You'll be fine after that."

"Talk to her? You reckon?"

"They love it, Colin, they love it."

"Yeah?"

"See you, then."

He looked grateful, if doubtful. "Yeah, Davey. Tomorrow, eh?"

And I left him and stepped out briskly to the sanctuary of the Underground, where nobody talked. There was just the drone of the trains that whisked me away from the station, and my shame.

In those few weeks I had made a good start with my insurance giant. I rose to the challenges my new post offered. Moving from small claims to the juicier stuff proved stimulating. I had my own office, too—a distinct improvement on the ghastly impersonality of the open-plan system I had endured before. The others in my group proved a lively lot and were quick to invite me to join them for pub-lunches in shoulder-to-shoulder London bars, where the outrages of previous claims (mostly apocryphal, I'm sure) were cheerfully discussed.

My Group Head, Mr. Law, was less approachable, a bit of a stickler for procedures (we speculated over lunch one day that he was probably into bondage in his sex life), but scrupulously fair. He dispensed advice without ever knocking my small-claims background. He even referred to it as a useful training-ground that had developed my attention to detail, a definite asset in my present post.

"You see, Walters," he told me in confidence, "we all have to start somewhere. I've studied every one of your reports. You don't miss anything. The others here . . . well, there's a tendency to rush things. Successful broking, Walters, begins with a sharp eye. You seem to have it. Indeed, I have a feeling you could go far."

Naturally, this conversation sent my confidence soaring, with its hint that I was ahead of the others in the group. I cast myself as the young hopeful, sure of promotion. That four years in the sticks sorting small claims was bearing fruit. So I had nothing to fear, one evening when I had volunteered to work late, when Mr. Law called me into his office.

"Ah, Walters. Still enjoying the work here?"

"Tremendously, Mr. Law."

"Good, good. Sit down, please. Just an informal chat. I see from the records you reside in Shipley, yes?"

"Yes, sir," I replied, a trifle uncertain what bearing this might have on my promotion prospects.

"Never been to Shipley myself," he continued, his back to me as he stared at the lighted cityscape eighteen floors below.

Feeling the need to contribute something, I volunteered, "It suits me, Mr. Law. Suits me fine. At this stage in my career. Good amenities. Convenient for London." I was slipping smoothly into the staccato-style speech Mr. Law himself used, the businesslike delivery that fitted me for the role of Deputy Group Head.

He continued to survey the trail of antlike humanity on its way home. "My sister moved there not long ago. She's an artist. Abstract stuff. I don't understand it at all. It sells, I'm told. I haven't seen much of her lately. Don't care much for the man she married. We're not a marrying family."

He turned from the window quite suddenly and looked at me. "Walters, I need help."

Christ. Now I was out of my depth. I had a hideous feeling it was going to be personal. Was he, perhaps, infatuated with one of the secretaries? I could see myself as a go-between pandering to Mr. Law's perverted tastes.

What relief, then, as he continued, without mention of whips and handcuffs, "I'm down your way at sissie's next week. Tuesday. Duty visit. Her first exhibition. The preview. Sure to run late. The last train leaves at eleven-oh-five—too early for me. Have to use their sofa-bed. Inevitably I shall travel up by train on Wednesday. You're a good timekeeper, Walters. Always in by nine-thirty. Tell me, which train do you catch from Shipley?"

"The eight-sixteen," I told him.

"In that case I'll look out for you on Shipley Station on Wednesday morning."

"Splendid."

"Shall we say ten past, just to be sure?"

"Fine, Mr. Law," I said, without a thought of Colin.

But I was sharply reminded the next time I saw him, on the Monday.

"Cha, mate."

"Hello, Colin."

"Didn't do no good, what you told me last week," he announced, attaching the verbal tow-rope that would drag me once again up the cat-and-wife alley.

"Really?" I responded without interest.

"Louise has taken it bad. I gave her a rollicking like you said, and she walked out."

"Left you?" I said, more concerned. I didn't want to be responsible for a broken marriage.

"Not for keeps. She's not that daft. Just pushed off, God knows where. She did the same Friday, Saturday and Sunday. She's got a pal, I reckon."

"Maybe." I tried to sound casual, as he had. From his tone, it hadn't dawned on him yet that the pal might be a boyfriend.

Then he added, "Doesn't come home until after I've gone to bed."

"What do you do?"

"Sit around all evening with Ginger for company."

The train was approaching. I had something more urgent on my mind than Colin's domestic crisis. Wednesday was too close.

"You, er, working all this week, Colin?"

"Sure thing, mate."

"Wednesday?"

"Same as ever."

We were seated in the smoker as usual. I wondered frantically how I might disentangle myself from the routine for one day. In a perfect world, I would just ignore Colin on Wednesday and travel up with Mr. Law. But our arrangement was too entrenched for that. Colin regarded me as a soulmate. I'd got in too deep, particularly in our conversations between train and ticket barrier at Waterloo.

What if the two met? I shuddered at the prospect of Mr. Law being subjected to Colin's inane monologue all the way to London. In my mind's eye I could see my Group Head grimly enduring the barrage, and later adding a note to my personal file: *Showed early promise, but betrayed a lack of discrimination in the company he keeps. Might be better employed, after all, in some limited capacity. Small claims, perhaps?*

The nightmare was interrupted.

"Louise and I, we go back years. Then wallop. Ginger's on the scene. Don't ask me how. She sort of adopted us both. Mind you, I didn't object at first. It was good company for Louise. Me, too. Let's be honest. But now Louise ignores me, it's hurtful, Davey, and I'm getting flaming mad with her. I blame the cat. I shouldn't, but I do."

"Well, yes."

"She could be jealous of Ginger. Is it possible? Do you think she's jealous of Ginger?"

I caught eyes observing me, peering over the tops of the *Times* like snipers in the trenches at the Somme. "I wouldn't know."

Then, unexpectedly, came an impassioned plea, made all the more ludicrous by the presence of the other passengers: "I couldn't bear to lose Louise. I want her back. I want my Louise back, Davey. That's all." He was on the verge of tears.

I looked at the thick-set plumber and mentally commanded him to snap out of this. Pitiful though he was, my major concern was my own predicament. For God's sake, he was just someone I met in the train each morning.

"Help me, Davey. You have an answer, don't you?"

Oh, this was great entertainment for the others. A highlight in the saga, like the murder of a well-known soap-opera character to push up the ratings at Christmas.

Vauxhall came up. We were just a few minutes from Waterloo. I had to settle this today. It couldn't be allowed to run on, not into Wednesday.

"I'll need to think," I told him. "Take it easy while I consider the matter."

Believe me, my brain worked overtime.

Colin watched me, mercifully silent until we reached the terminus.

On the platform, away from the eavesdroppers, I gave him the advice he'd begged for. I tried to sound calm. "From all you've told me, it's obvious that Ginger is a problem. She came between you and Louise, and now you want to get back on the old footing with your wife and you can't. It won't work. The solution to me, an outsider, is this. Get rid of Ginger."

His eyes widened. "But how, Davey, how?"

For once we were walking quite slowly along the platform, and anyone who travelled with us must have got far ahead, out of earshot.

Speaking as if to a child, I said, "Any way you choose. In a sack, isn't that the way it's done? Tie the top and drop it in a river. No more Ginger."

"But what about Louise? She's not going to like this."

"She's out every evening, isn't she?"

"Well, yes, but . . ."

"How will she know? Cats run away, Colin."

"True, but it seems kind of—"

I lost my patience with him. "Do what you bloody want. You asked for advice and I gave it to you."

I heard him say, "I'll think about it, Davey," as I marched on and gave up my ticket.

Colin wasn't on the train next morning and my hopes were raised for Wednesday. I got to the station early, really early. I had a dozen possible strategies in mind and just one purpose: to keep Colin and Mr. Law apart. I bought a copy of the *Financial Times*, to impress my boss, and stood by the station entrance. Mr. Law, being tall, would be easy to spot.

"What you doing here, Davey?"

God, no! Colin had caught me on the blind side.

"Er, Colin, I, er . . ." But I didn't have to fumble long for an excuse.

He was keen to tell me something. "Done it, mate. Like you said. Monday night. Louise and me, it's all made up, at least for now, anyway."

"Ah."

"Look," he went on, "Don't take offence, Davey, but I'm going to sit by myself this morning, okay?"

"Fine," I said, trying to sound just a little despondent as the tidal wave of relief crashed over me.

"Ah, there you are, Walters."

The worst possible outcome. Mr. Law, bang on 8.10, and just ten seconds too early for me. Colin was lingering.

"You're not offended, are you, Davey? Listen, why don't you come round for a drink tonight? I'll be fine by then. You can meet Louise. You know, put some names to faces, mate?"

My toes curled. I was caught between two conversations.

"Is it always so crowded?" from Law.

"Just for an hour, eh?" from Colin.

"Eight-sixteen on schedule, I hope?" Law.

"Forty-seven, Cramer Way. The green door. About seven." Colin.

"Yes, Colin. I'll do my best."

"Champion!" And Colin was away.

My toes uncurled.

"A friend?" enquired Law.

"I wouldn't put it so strongly as that, Mr. Law. Actually

he's a local plumber. The fellow gave me some advice about installing central heating. Seems to think I want to get to know him better, which I don't."

"Ah, I know the sort."

The 8.16 arrived dead on time. It hadn't let me down. Moreover, Mr. Law and I stepped into a non-smoking carriage and found two empty seats. I glowed with satisfaction.

I was so relieved at how the day had turned out that I decided that evening to take up Colin's invitation. I needed a drink. And Colin's decision to travel alone had given me the break I needed. I was willing to show some gratitude. We would drink to our futures.

I might even get to like travelling in Colin's company now that the cat-and-wife saga had come to an end. We'd have something different to talk about. Football, perhaps. Or television. But I would avoid any more marriage counselling.

Forty-seven, Cramer Way was fronted by the green door Colin had mentioned. A council-built house with a carport and a white van standing there. I pushed the doorbell.

"Davey—come in, mate." Colin reached out and grasped my arm. He was towel-drying his hair. "Just had a shower. The brick-dust gets everywhere. Come through to the kitchen."

The kitchen was a tip. I stood, conspicuous in my coat, surveying unwashed pans and piles of aluminium takeaway trays. And he'd brought me in here from choice.

A beer was offered. "You don't mind drinking from the can? I don't have a glass handy. Give us your coat, Davey. Louise'll be through that door any minute."

I took a sip of beer, grateful that it came from a sealed container. My eyes travelled around the cramped room and spotted a grease-spattered photograph standing on the fridge. Colin's wedding. The couple stood on what I recognized as Shipley Library's steps, confetti scattered over an ill-fitting suit and summer dress and jacket. She looked attractive, face vibrant with the occasion. Colin's remark about the couch potato came back to me. I felt uncomfortable knowing so much about Louise before I met her.

"The wedding snap," said Colin, opening a can. "Don't times bleeding change, eh?"

I passed no comment.

"Hey up," he said. "Here she comes now, bang on cue."

I turned to face the front door, first placing my can on the kitchen table. It didn't seem right to be drinking when the lady of the house arrived.

But nothing happened. The door didn't open. I looked towards Colin and saw that he was watching the back door. That, also, remained closed—apart from one small section. The bottom left-hand panel. The cat-flap.

It opened.

"Louise, my little beauty!" Colin cried as he swept the creature into his arms, a small, white cat. "Look, we've got a visitor. Remember I told you about Davey, the man on the train?"

I froze.

"Davey told me what to do with Ginger."

Louise purred approvingly in Colin's arms.

Stroking her head, Colin said to me, "Honestly, Davey, I could cheerfully have killed you as well the other night. Do you know how difficult it is tying a live woman into a sack?"

Nine Lives to Live

Sharyn McCrumb

IT HAD SEEMED LIKE A good idea at the time. Of course, Philip Danby had only been joking, but he had said it in a serious tone in order to humor those idiot New Age clients who actually seemed to believe in the stuff. "I want to come back as a cat," he'd said, smiling facetiously into the candlelight at the Eskeridge dinner table. He had to hold his breath to keep from laughing as the others babbled about reincarnation. The women wanted to come back blonder and thinner, and the men wanted to be everything from Dallas Cowboys to oak trees. *Oak trees?* And he had to keep a straight face through it all, hoping these dodos would give the firm some business.

The things he had to put up with to humor clients. His partner, Giles Eskeridge, seemed to have no difficulties in that quarter, however. Giles often said that rich and crazy went together; therefore, architects who wanted a lucrative business had to be prepared to put up with eccentrics. They also had to put up with long hours, obstinate building contractors, and capricious zoning boards. Perhaps that was why Danby had plumped for life as a cat next time. As he had explained to his dinner companions that night, "Cats are independent. They don't have to kowtow to anybody; they sleep sixteen hours a day; and yet they get fed and sheltered and even loved—just for being their contrary little selves. It sounds like a good deal to me."

Julie Eskeridge tapped him playfully on the cheek. "You'd better take care to be a pretty, pedigreed kitty, Philip," she laughed. "Because life isn't so pleasant for an ugly old alley cat!"

"I'll keep that in mind," he told her. "In fifty years or so."

It had been more like fifty days. The fact that Giles had wanted to come back as a shark should have tipped him off. When they found out that they'd just built a three-million-dollar building on top of a toxic landfill, the contractor was happy to keep his mouth shut about it for a mere ten grand, and Giles was perfectly prepared to bury the evidence to protect the firm from lawsuits and EPA fines. Looking back on it, Danby realized that he should not have insisted that they report the landfill to the authorities. In particular, he should not have insisted on it at 6:00 P.M. at the building site with no one present but himself and Giles. That was literally a fatal error. Before you could say "philosophical differences," Giles had picked up a shovel lying near the offending trench, and with one brisk swing, he had sent the matter to a higher court. As he pitched headlong into the reeking evidence, Danby's last thought was a flicker of cold anger at the injustice of it all.

His next thought was that he was watching a black-and-white movie, while his brain seemed intent upon sorting out a flood of olfactory sensations. *Furniture polish . . . stale coffee . . . sweaty socks . . . Prell Shampoo . . . potting soil . . .* He shook his head, trying to clear his thoughts. Where was he? The apparent answer to that was: lying on a gray sofa inside the black-and-white movie, because everywhere he looked he saw the same colorless vista. A concussion, maybe? The memory of Giles Eskeridge swinging a shovel came back in a flash. Danby decided to call the police before Giles turned up to try again. He stood up, and promptly fell off the sofa.

Of course, he landed on his feet.

All four of them.

Idly, to keep from thinking anything more ominous for the moment, Danby wondered what *else* the New Age clients had been right about. Was Stonehenge a flying saucer landing pad? Did crystals lower cholesterol? He was in no position to doubt anything just now. He sat twitching his plume of a tail and wishing he hadn't been so flippant about the afterlife at the Eskeridge dinner party. He didn't even particularly like cats. He also wished that he could get his paws on Giles in retribution for the shovel incident. First he would bite Giles's neck, snapping his spine, and then he would let him escape for a few seconds. Then he'd sneak up behind him and pounce. Then bat him into a corner. Danby began to purr in happy contemplation.

The sight of a coffee table looming a foot above his head brought the problem into perspective. At present Danby weighed approximately fifteen furry pounds, and he was unsure of his exact whereabouts. Under those circumstances avenging his murder would be difficult. On the other hand, he didn't have any other pressing business, apart from an eight-hour nap which he felt in need of. First things first, though. Danby wanted to know what he looked like, and then he needed to find out where the kitchen was, and whether Sweaty Socks and Prell Shampoo had left anything edible on the counter tops. There would be time enough for philosophical thoughts and revenge plans when he was cleaning his whiskers.

The living room was enough to make an architect shudder. Clunky early American sofas and clutter. He was glad he couldn't see the color scheme. There was a mirror above the sofa, though, and he hopped up on the cheap upholstery to take a look at his new self. The face that looked back at him was definitely feline, and so malevolent that Danby wondered how anyone could mistake cats for pets. The yellow (or possibly green) almond eyes glowered at him from a massive triangular face, tiger-striped, and surrounded by a ruff of gray-brown fur. Just visible beneath the ruff was a dark leather collar equipped with a little brass bell. That would explain the ringing in his ears. The rest of his body seemed massive, even allowing for the fur, and the great plumed tail swayed rhythmically as he watched. He resisted a silly urge to swat at the reflected movement. So he was a tortoiseshell, or tabby, or whatever they called those brown striped cats, and his hair was long. And he was still male. He didn't need to check beneath his tail to confirm that. Besides, the reek of ammonia in the vicinity of the sofa suggested that he was not shy about proclaiming his masculinity in various corners of his domain.

No doubt it would have interested those New Age clowns to learn that he was not a kitten, but a fully-grown cat. Apparently the arrival had been instantaneous as well. He had always been given to understand that the afterlife would provide some kind of preliminary orientation before assigning him a new identity. A deity resembling John Denver, in rimless glasses and a Sierra Club tee shirt, should have been on hand with some paperwork regarding his case, and in a nonthreatening conference, they would decide what his karma entitled him to become. At least, that's what the New Agers had led him to believe. But it hadn't been like that at all. One minute he had been tumbling into a sewage pit, and the next: he had a craving for Meow Mix. Just like that. He wondered what sort of consciousness had been flickering inside that narrow skull prior to his arrival. Probably not much. A brain with the wattage of a lightning bug could control most of the items on the feline agenda: eat, sleep, snack, doze, dine, nap, and so on. Speaking of eating . . .

He made it to the floor in two moderate bounds, and jingled toward the kitchen, conveniently signposted by the smell of lemon-scented dishwashing soap and stale coffee. The floor could do with a good sweeping, too, he thought, noting with distaste the gritty feel of tracked-in dirt on his velvet paws.

The cat dish, tucked in a corner beside the sink cabinet, confirmed his worst fears about the inhabitants' instinct for tackiness. Two plastic bowls were inserted into a plywood cat model, painted white, and decorated with a cartoonish cat-face. If his food hadn't been at stake, Danby would have sprayed *that* as an indication of his professional judgment. As it was, he summoned a regal sneer, and bent down to inspect the of-

fering. The water wasn't fresh; there were bits of dry cat food
floating in it. Did they expect him to drink *that?* Perhaps he
ought to dump it out so that they'd take the hint. And the dry
cat food hadn't been stored in an airtight container, either. He
sniffed contemptuously: the cheap brand, mostly cereal. He
supposed he'd have to go out and kill something just to keep
his ribs from crashing together. Better check out the counters
for other options. It took considerable force to launch his bulk
from floor to counter top, and for a moment he teetered on the
edge of the sink, fighting to regain his balance, while his bell
tolled ominously, but once he righted himself, he strolled onto
the counter with an expression of nonchalance suggesting that
his dignity had never been imperiled. He found two breakfast
plates stacked in the sink. The top one was a trove of con-
gealing egg yolk and bits of buttered toast. He finished it off,
licking off every scrap of egg with his rough tongue, and thinking what a favor he was doing the people by cleaning the plate
for them.

While he was on the sink, he peeked out the kitchen window
to see if he could figure out where he was. The lawn outside
was thick and luxurious, and a spreading oak tree grew beside
a low stone wall. Well, it wasn't Albuquerque. Probably not
California, either, considering the healthy appearance of the
grass. Maybe he was still in Maryland. It certainly looked like
home. Perhaps the transmigration of souls has a limited geographic range, like AM radio stations. After a few moments
consideration, while he washed an offending forepaw, it occurred to Danby to look at the wall phone above the counter.
The numbers made sense to him, so apparently he hadn't lost
the ability to read. Sure enough, the telephone area code was
301. He wasn't far from where he started. Theoretically, at
least, Giles was within reach. He must mull that over, from the
vantage point of the window sill, where the afternoon sun was
marvelously warm, and soothing . . . zzzzz.

Danby awakened several hours later to a braying female voice
calling out, "Tigger! Get down from there this minute! Are you
glad Mommy's home, sweetie?"

Danby opened one eye, and regarded the woman with an insolent stare. *Tigger?* Was there no limit to the indignities he must bear? A fresh wave of Prell Shampoo told him that the self-proclaimed "Mommy" was chatelaine of this bourgeois bungalow. And didn't she look the part, too, with her polyester pants suit and her cascading chins! She set a grocery bag and a stack of letters on the counter top, and held out her arms to him. "And is my snook-ums ready for din-din?" she cooed.

He favored her with an extravagant yawn, followed by his most forbidding Mongol glare, but his hostility was wasted on the besotted Mrs. . . . (he glanced down at the pile of letters) . . . Sherrod. She continued to beam at him as if he had fawned at her feet. As it was, he was so busy studying the address on the Sherrod junk mail that he barely glanced at her. He hadn't left town! His tail twitched triumphantly. Morning Glory Lane was not familiar to him, but he'd be willing to bet that it was a street in Sussex Garden Estates, just off the by-pass. That was a couple of miles from Giles Eskeridge's mock-Tudor monstrosity, but with a little luck and some common sense about traffic he could walk there in a couple of hours. If he cut through the fields, he might be able to score a mouse or two on the way.

Spurred on by the thought of a fresh, tasty dinner that would beg for its life, Danby/Tigger trotted to the back door and began to meow piteously, putting his forepaws as far up the screen door as he could reach.

"Now, Tigger!" said Mrs. Sherrod in her most arch tone. "You know perfectly well that there's a litter box in the bathroom. You just want to get outdoors so that you can tomcat around, don't you?" With that she began to put away groceries, humming tunelessly to herself.

Danby fixed a venomous stare at her retreating figure, and then turned his attention back to the problem at hand. Or rather, at paw. That was just the trouble: Look, Ma, no hands! Still, he thought, there ought to be a way. Because it was warm outside, the outer door was open, leaving only the metal storm door between himself and freedom. Its latch was the straight-handled kind that you pushed down to open the door. Danby considered the factors: door handle three feet above floor; latch opens on downward pressure; one fifteen-pound cat intent upon going out. With a vertical bound that Michael Jordan would have envied, Danby catapulted himself upward and caught onto the handle, which obligingly twisted downward, as the door swung open at the weight of the feline cannonball. By the time gravity took over and returned him to the ground, he was claw-deep in scratchy, sweet-smelling grass.

As he loped off toward the street, he could hear a plaintive voice wailing, "Ti-iii-ggerr!" It almost drowned out the jingling of that damned little bell around his neck.

Twenty minutes later Danby was sunning himself on a rock in an abandoned field, recovering from the exertion of moving faster than a stroll. In the distance he could hear the drone of cars from the interstate, as the smell of gasoline wafted in on a gentle breeze. As he had trotted through the neighborhood, he'd read street signs, so he had a better idea of his whereabouts now. Windsor Forest, that pretentious little sub-urb that Giles called home, was only a few miles away, and once he crossed the interstate, he could take a short cut through the woods. He hoped that La Sherrod wouldn't put out an all-points bulletin for her missing kitty. He didn't want any SPCA interruptions once he reached his destination. He ought to ditch the collar as well, he thought. He couldn't very well pose as a stray with a little bell under his chin.

Fortunately, the collar was loose, probably because the ruff around his head made his neck look twice as large. Once he determined that, it took only a few minutes of concentrated effort to work the collar forward with his paws until it slipped over his ears. After that, a shake of the head—jingle! jingle!—rid him of Tigger's identity. He wondered how many pets who "just disappeared one day" had acquired new identities and went off on more pressing business.

He managed to reach the by-pass before five o'clock, thus avoiding the commuter traffic of rush hour. Since he under-stood automobiles, it was a relatively simple matter for Danby to cross the highway during a lull between cars. He didn't see what the possums found so difficult about road crossing. Sure enough, there was a ripe gray corpse on the white line, a mute testimony to the dangers of indecision on highways. He took a perfunctory sniff, but the roadkill was too far gone to interest anything except the buzzards.

Once across the road, Danby stuck to the fields, making sure that he paralleled the road that led to Windsor Forest. His attention was occasionally diverted by a flock of birds overhead, or an enticing rustle in the grass that might have been a field mouse, but he kept going. If he didn't reach the Eskeridge house by nightfall, he would have to wait until morning to get himself noticed.

In order to get at Giles, Danby reasoned that he would first have to charm Julie Eskeridge. He wondered if she were susceptible to needy animals. He couldn't remember whether they had a cat or not. An unspayed female would be nice, he thought; a Siamese, perhaps, with big blue eyes and a sexy voice.

Danby reasoned that he wouldn't have too much trouble finding Giles's house. He had been there often enough as a guest. Besides, the firm had designed and built several of the overwrought mansions in the spacious subdivision. Danby had once suggested that they buy Palladian windows by the gross, since every nouveau riche homebuilder insisted on having a brace of them, no matter what style of house he had commissioned. Giles had not been amused by Danby's observation. He seldom was. What Giles lacked in humor, he also lacked in scruples and moral restraint, but he compensated for these deficiencies with a highly-developed instinct for making and holding onto money. While he'd lacked Danby's talent in design and execution, he had a genius for turning up wealthy clients, and for persuading these tasteless yobbos to spend a fortune on their showpiece homes. Danby did draw the line at carving up antique Sheraton sideboards to use as bathroom sink cabinets, though. When he also drew the line at environmental crime, Giles had apparently found his conscience an expensive luxury that the firm could not afford. Hence, the shallow grave at the new construction site, and Danby's new lease on life. It was really quite unfair of Giles, Danby reflected. They'd been friends since college, and after Danby's parents died, he had left a will leaving his share of the business to Giles. And how had Giles repaid this friendship? With the blunt end of a shovel. Danby stopped to sharpen his claws on the bark of a handy pine tree. Really, he thought, Giles deserved no mercy whatsoever. Which was just as well, because, catlike, Danby possessed none.

The sun was low behind the surrounding pines by the time Danby arrived at the Eskeridges' mock-Tudor home. He had been delayed en route by the scent of another cat, a neutered orange male. (Even to his color-blind eyes, an orange cat was recognizable. It might be the shade of gray, or the configuration of white at the throat and chest.) He had hunted up this fellow feline, and made considerable efforts to communicate, but as far as he could tell, there was no higher intelligence flickering behind its blank green eyes. There was no intelligence at all, as far as Danby was concerned; he'd as soon try talking to a shrub. Finally tiring of the eunuch's unblinking stare, he'd stalked off, forgoing more social experiments in favor of his mission.

He sat for a long time under the forsythia hedge in Giles's front yard, studying the house for signs of life. He refused to be distracted by a cluster of sparrows cavorting on the birdbath, but he realized that unless a meal was forthcoming soon, he would be reduced to foraging. The idea of hurling his bulk at a few ounces of twittering songbird made his scowl even more forbidding than usual. He licked a front paw and glowered at the silent house.

After twenty minutes or so, he heard the distant hum of a car engine, and smelled gasoline fumes. Danby peered out from the hedge in time to see Julie Eskeridge's Mercedes rounding the corner from Windsor Way. With a few hasty licks to smooth down his ruff, Danby sauntered toward the driveway, just as the car pulled in. Now for the hard part: how do you impress Julie Eskeridge without a checkbook?

*   *   *

He had never noticed before how much Giles's wife resembled a giraffe. He blinked at the sight of her huge feet swinging out of the car perilously close to his nose. They were followed by two replicas of the Alaska pipeline, both encased in nylon. Better not jump up on her; one claw on the stockings, and he'd have an enemy for life. Julie was one of those people who air-kissed because she couldn't bear to spoil her make-up. Instead of trying to attract her attention at the car (where she could have skewered him with one spike heel), Danby loped to the steps of the side porch, and began meowing piteously. As Julie approached the steps, he looked up at her with wide-eyed supplication, waiting to be admired.

"Shoo, cat!" said Julie, nudging him aside with her foot.

As the door slammed in his face, Danby realized that he had badly miscalculated. He had also neglected to devise a backup plan. A fine mess he was in now. It wasn't enough that he was murdered, and reassigned to cathood—now he was also homeless.

He was still hanging around the steps twenty minutes later when Giles came home, mainly because he couldn't think of an alternate plan just yet. When he saw Giles's black sports car pull up behind Julie's Mercedes, Danby's first impulse was to run, but then he realized that, while Giles might see him, he certainly wouldn't recognize him as his old business partner. Besides, he was curious to see how an uncaught murderer looked. Would Giles be haggard with grief and remorse? Furtive, as he listened for police sirens in the distance?

Giles Eskeridge was whistling. He climbed out of his car, suntanned and smiling, with his lips pursed in a cheerfully tuneless whistle. Danby trotted forward to confront his murderer with his haughtiest scowl of indignation. The reaction was not quite what he expected.

Giles saw the huge, fluffy cat, and immediately knelt down, calling, "Here, kitty, kitty!"

Danby looked at him as if he had been propositioned.

"Aren't you a beauty!" said Giles, holding out his hand to

the strange cat. "I'll bet you're a pedigreed animal, aren't you, fella? Are you lost, boy?"

Much as it pained him to associate with a remorseless killer, Danby sidled over to the outstretched hand, and allowed his ears to be scratched. He reasoned that Giles's interest in him was his one chance to gain entry to the house. It was obvious that Julie wasn't a cat fancier. Who would have taken heartless old Giles for an animal lover? Probably similarity of temperament, Danby decided.

He allowed himself to be picked up, and carried into the house, while Giles stroked his back and told him what a pretty fellow he was. This was an indignity, but still an improvement over Giles's behavior toward him during their last encounter. Once inside, Giles called out to Julie, "Look what I've got, honey!"

She came in from the kitchen, scowling. "That nasty cat!" she said. "Put him right back outside!"

At this point Danby concentrated all his energies toward making himself purr. It was something like snoring, he decided, but it had the desired effect on his intended victim, for at once Giles made for his den, and plumped down in an armchair, arranging Danby in his lap, with more petting and praise. "He's a wonderful cat, Julie," Giles told his wife. "I'll bet he's a pure-bred Maine Coon. Probably worth a couple of hundred bucks."

"So are my wool carpets," Mrs. Eskeridge replied. "So are my new sofas! And who's going to clean up his messes?"

That was Danby's cue. He had already thought out the piece de resistance in his campaign of endearment. With a trill that meant "This way, folks!", Danby hopped off his ex-partner's lap, and trotted to the downstairs bathroom. He had used it often enough at dinner parties, and he knew that the door was left ajar. He had been saving up for this moment. With Giles and his missus watching from the doorway, Danby hopped up on the toilet seat, twitched his elegant plumed tail, and proceeded to use the toilet in the correct manner.

He felt a strange tingling in his paws, and he longed to scratch at something and cover it up, but he ignored these urges, and basked instead in the effusive praise from his self-

appointed champion. Why couldn't Giles have been that enthusiastic over his design for the Jenner building? Danby
thought resentfully. Some people's sense of values were so
warped. Meanwhile, though, he might as well savor the Eskeridges' transports of joy over his bowel control; there weren't
too many ways for cats to demonstrate superior intelligence.
He couldn't quote a little Shakespeare or identify the dinner
wine. Fortunately, among felines toilet training passed for genius, and even Julie was impressed with his accomplishments.
After that, there was no question of Giles turning him out into
the cruel world. Instead, they carried him back to the kitchen,
and opened a can of tuna fish for his dining pleasure. He had
to eat it in a bowl on the floor, but the bowl was Royal Doul-
ton, which was some consolation. And while he ate, he could
still hear Giles in the background, raving about what a wonderful cat he was. He was in.

"No collar, Julie. Someone must have abandoned him on the
highway. What shall we call him?"

"Varmint," his wife suggested. She was a hard sell.

Giles ignored her lack of enthusiasm for his newfound prod-
igy. "I think I'll call him Merlin. He's a wizard of a cat."

Merlin? Danby looked up with a mouthful of tuna. Oh well,
he thought, Merlin and tuna were better than Tigger and cheap
dry cat food. You couldn't have everything.

After that, he quickly became a full-fledged member of the
household, with a newly-purchased plastic feeding bowl, a catnip mouse toy, and another little collar with another damned
bell. Danby resisted the urge to bite Giles's thumb off while he
was attaching this loathsome neckpiece over his ruff, but he
restrained himself. By now he was accustomed to the accom-
paniment of a maniacal jingling with every step he took. What
was it with human beings and bells?

Of course, that spoiled his plans for songbird hunting outdoors. He'd have to travel faster than the speed of sound to
catch a sparrow now. Not that he got out much, anyhow. Giles
seemed to think that he might wander off again, so he was
generally careful to keep Danby housebound.

That was all right with Danby, though. It gave him an excellent opportunity to become familiar with the house, and with the routine of its inhabitants—all useful information for someone planning revenge. So far he (the old Danby, that is) had not been mentioned in the Eskeridge conversations. He wondered what story Giles was giving out about his disappearance. Apparently the body had not been found. It was up to him to punish the guilty, then.

Danby welcomed the days when both Giles and Julie left the house. Then he would forgo his morning, mid-morning, and early afternoon naps in order to investigate each room of his domain, looking for lethal opportunities: medicine bottles, perhaps, or perhaps a small electrical appliance that he could push into the bathtub.

So far, though, he had not attempted to stage any accidents, for fear that the wrong Eskeridge would fall victim to his snare. He didn't like Julie any more than she liked him, but he had no reason to kill her. The whole business needed careful study. He could afford to take his time analyzing the opportunities for revenge. The food was good, the job of house cat was undemanding, and he rather enjoyed the irony of being doted on by his intended victim. Giles was certainly better as an owner than he was as a partner.

An evening conversation between Giles and Julie convinced him that he must accelerate his efforts. They were sitting in the den, after a meal of baked chicken. They wouldn't give him the bones, though. Giles kept insisting that they'd splinter in his stomach and kill him. Danby was lying on the hearth rug, pretending to be asleep until they forgot about him, at which time he would sneak back into the kitchen and raid the garbage. He'd given up smoking, hadn't he? And although he'd lapped up a bit of Giles's Scotch one night, he seemed to have lost the taste for it. How much prudence could he stand?

"If you're absolutely set on keeping this cat, Giles," said Julie Eskeridge, examining her newly-polished talons, "I suppose I'll have to be the one to take him to the vet."

"The vet. I hadn't thought about it. Of course, he'll have to have shots, won't he?" murmured Giles, still studying the newspaper. "Rabies, and so on."

"And while we're at it, we might as well have him neutered," said Julie. "Otherwise, he'll start spraying the drapes and all."

Danby rocketed to full alert. To keep them from suspecting his comprehension, he centered his attention on the cleaning of a perfectly tidy front paw. It was time to step up the pace on his plans for revenge, or he'd be meowing in soprano. And forget the scruples about innocent bystanders: now it was a matter of self-defense.

That night he waited until the house was dark and quiet. Giles and Julie usually went to bed about eleven-thirty, turning off all the lights, which didn't faze him in the least. He rather enjoyed skulking about the silent house using his infrared vision, although he rather missed late-night television. He had once considered turning the set on with his paw, but that seemed too precocious, even for a cat named Merlin. Danby didn't want to end up in somebody's behavior lab with wires coming out of his head.

He examined his collection of cat toys, stowed by Julie in his cat basket, because she hated clutter. He had a mouse-shaped catnip toy, a rubber fish, and a little red ball. Giles bought the ball under the ludicrous impression that Danby could be induced to play catch. When he'd rolled it across the floor, Danby lay down and gave him an insolent stare. He had enjoyed the next quarter of an hour, watching Giles on his hands and knees, batting the ball, and trying to teach Danby to fetch, but finally Giles gave up, and the ball had been tucked in the cat basket ever since. Danby picked it up with his teeth, and carried it upstairs. Giles and Julie came down the right side of the staircase, didn't they? That's where the banister was. He set the ball carefully on the third step, in the approximate place that a human foot would touch the stair. A tripwire would be more reliable, but Danby couldn't manage the technology involved.

What else could he devise for the Eskeridges' peril? He couldn't poison their food, and since they'd provided him with a flea collar, he couldn't even hope to get bubonic plague started in the household. Attacking them with tooth and claw seemed foolhardy, even if they were sleeping. The one he wasn't biting could always fight him off, and a fifteen-pound cat can be killed with relative ease by any human determined to do it. Even if they didn't kill him on the spot, they'd get rid of him immediately, and then he'd lose his chance forever. It was too risky.

It had to be stealth, then. Danby inspected the house, looking for lethal opportunities. There weren't any electrical appliances close to the bathtub, and besides, Giles took showers. In another life Danby might have been able to rewire the electric razor to shock its user, but such a feat was well beyond his present level of dexterity. No wonder human beings had taken over the earth; they were so damned hard to kill.

Even his efforts to enlist help in the task had proved fruitless. On one of his rare excursions out of the house (Giles went golfing, and he slipped out without Julie's noticing), Danby had roamed the neighborhood, looking for . . . well . . . pussy. Instead he'd found dimwitted tomcats, and a Doberman pinscher, who was definitely Somebody. Danby had kept conversation to a minimum, not quite liking the look of the beast's prominent fangs. Danby suspected that the Doberman had previously been an IRS agent. Of course, the dog had *said* that it had been a serial killer, but that was just to lull Danby into a false sense of security. Anyhow, much as the dog approved of Danby's plan to kill his humans, he wasn't interested in forming a conspiracy. Why should he go to the gas chamber to solve someone else's problem?

Danby himself had similar qualms about doing anything too drastic—such as setting fire to the house. He didn't want to stage an accident that would include himself among the victims. After puttering about the darkened house for a wearying few hours, he stretched out on the sofa in the den to take a quick nap before resuming his plotting. He'd be able to think better after he rested.

The next thing Danby felt was a ruthless grip on his collar, dragging him forward. He opened his eyes to find that it was morning, and that the hand at his throat belonged to Julie Eskeridge, who was trying to stuff him into a metal cat carrier. He tried to dig his claws into the sofa, but it was too late. Before he could blink, he had been hoisted along by his tail, and shoved into the box. He barely got his tail out of the way before the door slammed shut behind him. Danby crouched in the plastic carrier, peeking out the side slits, and trying to figure out what to do next. Obviously the rubber ball on the steps had been a dismal failure as a murder weapon. Why couldn't he have come back as a mountain lion?

Danby fumed about the slings and arrows of outrageous fortune all the way out to the car. It didn't help to remember where he was going, and what was scheduled to be done with him shortly thereafter. Julie Eskeridge set the cat carrier on the back seat and slammed the door. When she started the car, Danby howled in protest.

"Be quiet back there!" Julie called out. "There's nothing you can do about it."

We'll see about that, thought Danby, turning to peer out the door of his cage. The steel bars of the door were about an inch apart, and there was no mesh or other obstruction between them. He found that he could easily slide one paw sideways out of the cage. Now, if he could just get a look at the workings of the latch, there was a slight chance that he could extricate himself. He lay down on his side and squinted up at the metal catch. It seemed to be a glorified bolt. To lock the carrier, a metal bar was slid into a socket and then rotated downward to latch. If he could push the bar back up and then slide it back . . .

It wasn't easy to maneuver with the car changing speed and turning corners. Danby felt himself getting quite dizzy with the effort of concentrating as the carrier gently rocked. But finally, when the car reached the interstate and sped along smoothly, he succeeded in positioning his paw at the right place on the bar, and easing it upward. Another three minutes of tense probing allowed him to slide the bar a fraction of an inch, and then another. The bolt was now clear of the latch. There was no getting out of the car, of course. Julie had rolled up the windows, and they were going sixty miles an hour. Danby spent a full minute pondering the implications of his dilemma. But no matter which way he looked at the problem, the alternative was always the same: do something desperate or go under the knife. It wasn't as if dying had been such a big deal, after all. There was always next time.

Quickly, before the fear could stop him, Danby hurled his furry bulk against the door of the cat carrier, landing in the floor of the backseat with a solid thump. He sprang back up on the seat, and launched himself into the air with a heartfelt snarl, landing precariously on Julie Eskeridge's right shoulder, and digging his claws in to keep from falling.

The last things he remembered were Julie's screams and the feel of the car swerving out of control.

When Danby opened his eyes, the world was still playing in black and white. He could hear muffled voices, and smell a jumble of scents: blood, gasoline, smoke. He struggled to get up, and found that he was still less than a foot off the ground. Still furry. Still the Eskeridges' cat. In the distance he could see the crumpled wreckage of Julie's car.

A familiar voice was droning on above him. "He must have been thrown free of the cat carrier during the wreck, Officer. That's definitely Merlin, though. My poor wife was taking him to the vet."

A burly policeman was standing next to Giles, nodding sympathetically. "I guess it's true what they say about cats, sir. Having nine lives, I mean. I'm very sorry about your wife. She wasn't so lucky."

Giles hung his head. "No. It's been a great strain. First my business partner disappears, and now I lose my wife." He stooped and picked up Danby. "At least I have my beautiful kitty-cat for consolation. Come on, boy. Let's go home."

Danby's malevolent yellow stare did not waver. He allowed himself to be carried away to Giles's waiting car without protest. He could wait. Cats were good at waiting. And life with Giles wasn't so bad, now that Julie wouldn't be around to harass him. Danby would enjoy a spell of being doted on by an indulgent human; fed gourmet cat food; and given the run of the house. Meanwhile, he could continue to leave the occasional ball on the stairs, and think of other ways to toy with Giles, while he waited to see if the police ever turned up to ask Giles about his missing partner. If not, Danby could work on more ways to kill humans. Sooner or later he would succeed. Cats are endlessly patient at stalking their prey.

"It's just you and me, now, fella," said Giles, placing his cat on the seat beside him.

And after he killed Giles, perhaps he could go in search of the building contractor that Giles bribed to keep his dirty secret. He certainly deserved to die. And that nasty woman Danby used to live next door to, who used to complain about his stereo and his crabgrass. And perhaps the surly headwaiter at *Chantage*. Stray cats can turn up anywhere.

Danby began to purr.

Bedeviled

Bill Pronzini

"YOUNG MAN," MRS. ABBOTT SAID to me, "do you believe in ghosts?"

The "young man" surprised me almost as much as the question. But then, when you're eighty, fifty-eight looks pretty damn young. "Ghosts?"

"Crossovers. Visitors from the Other Side."

"Well, let's say I'm skeptical."

"I've always been skeptical myself. But I just can't help wondering if it might be Carl who is deviling me."

"Carl?"

"My late husband. Carl's ghost, you see."

Beside me on the sofa, Addie Crenshaw sighed and rolled her eyes in my direction. Then she smiled tolerantly across at Mrs. Abbott in her Boston rocker. "Nonsense," she said. "Carl has been gone ten years, Margaret. Why would his ghost come back *now*?"

"Well, it could be he's angry with me."

"Angry?"

"I'm not sure I did all I could for him when he was ill. He

46

may blame me for his death; he always did have a tendency to hold a grudge. And surely the dead know when the living's time is near. Suppose he has crossed over to give me a sample of what our reunion on the Other Side will be like?"

There was a small silence.

Mrs. Crenshaw, who was Margaret Abbott's neighbor, friend, watchdog, and benefactor, and who was also my client, shifted her long, lean body and said patiently, "Margaret, ghosts can't ring the telephone in the middle of the night. Or break windows. Or dig up rose bushes."

"Perhaps if they're motivated enough . . ."

"Not under any circumstances. They can't put poison in cat food, either. You know they can't do *that*."

"Poor Harold," Mrs. Abbott said. "Carl wasn't fond of cats, you know. In fact, he used to throw rocks at them."

"It wasn't Carl. You and I both know perfectly well who is responsible."

"We do?"

"Of course we do. The Petersons."

"Who, dear?"

"The Petersons. Those real estate people."

"Oh, I don't think so. Why would they poison Harold?"

"Because they're vermin. They're greedy swine."

"Addie, don't be silly. People can't be vermin or swine."

"Can't they?" Mrs. Crenshaw said. "Can't they just?"

I put my cup and saucer down on the coffee table, just hard enough to rattle one against the other, and cleared my throat. The three of us had been sitting here for ten minutes, in the old-fashioned living room of Margaret Abbott's Parkside home, drinking coffee and dancing around the issue that had brought us together. All the dancing was making me uncomfortable; it was time for me to take a firm grip on the proceedings.

"Ladies," I said, "suppose we concern ourselves with facts, not speculation. That'll make my job a whole lot easier."

"I've already told you the facts," Mrs. Crenshaw said. "Margaret and I both have."

"Let's go over them again anyway. I want to make sure I

have everything clear in my mind. This late-night harassment started two weeks ago, is that right? On a Saturday night?"

"Saturday morning, actually," Mrs. Abbott said. "It was just three A.M. when the phone rang. I know because I looked at my bedside clock." She was tiny and frail and she couldn't get around very well without a walker, and Mrs. Crenshaw had warned me that she was inclined to be "a little dotty," but there was nothing wrong with her memory. "I thought someone must have died. That is usually why the telephone rings at such an hour."

"But no one was on the line."

"Well, someone was breathing."

"But whoever it was didn't say anything."

"No. I said hello several times and he hung up."

"The other three calls came at the same hour?"

"Approximately, yes. Four mornings in a row."

"And he didn't say a word until the last one."

"Two words. I heard them clearly."

" 'Drop dead.' "

"It sounds silly but it wasn't. It was very disturbing."

"I'm sure it was. Can you remember anything distinctive about the voice?"

"Well, it was a man's voice. I'm certain of that."

"But you didn't recognize it."

"No. It was muffled, as if it were coming from . . . well, from the Other Side."

Mrs. Crenshaw started to say something, but I got words out first. "Then the calls stopped and two days later somebody broke the back porch window. Late at night again."

"With a rock," Mrs. Abbott said, nodding. "Charley came and fixed it."

"Charley. That would be your nephew, Charley Doyle."

"Yes. Fixing windows is his business. He's a glazier."

"And after that, someone spray-painted the back and side walls of the house."

"Filthy words," Mrs. Abbott said, "dozens of them. It was a terrible mess. Addie and Leonard . . . Leonard is Addie's brother, you know."

"Yes, ma'am."

"They cleaned it up. It took them an entire day. Then my rose bushes . . . oh, I cried when I saw what had been done to them. I loved my roses. Pink floribundas and dark red and orange teas." She wagged her white head sadly. "He didn't like roses any more than he did cats."

"Who didn't?"

"Carl. My late husband. And he sometimes had a foul mouth. He knew all those words that were painted on the house."

"Margaret," Mrs. Crenshaw said firmly, "it wasn't Carl. There is no such thing as a ghost, there simply isn't."

"Well, all right. But I do wonder, Addie. I really do."

"About the poison incident," I said. "That was the most recent thing, two nights ago?"

"Poor Harold almost died," Mrs. Abbott said. "If Addie and Leonard hadn't rushed him to the vet, he would have."

"Arsenic," Mrs. Crenshaw said. "That's what the vet said it was. Arsenic in Harold's food bowl."

"Which is kept inside or outside the house?"

"Oh, inside," Mrs. Abbott said. "On the back porch. Harold isn't allowed outside. Not the way people drive their cars nowadays."

"So whoever put the poison in the cat's bowl had to get inside the house to do it."

"Breaking and entering," Mrs. Crenshaw said. "That was the final straw."

"Were there any signs of forced entry?"

"Leonard and I couldn't find any."

Mrs. Abbott said abruptly, "Oh, there he is now. He must have heard us talking about him."

I looked where she was looking, behind me. There was nobody there. "Leonard?"

"No, Harold. Harold, dear, come and meet the nice gentleman Addie brought to help us."

The cat that came sauntering around the sofa was a rotund and middle-aged orange tabby, with a great swaying paunch that brushed the carpet as he moved. He plunked himself down five feet from where I was, paying no attention to any of us, and began to lick his shoulder. For a cat that had been sick as a dog two days ago, he looked pretty fit.

"Mrs. Abbott," I said, "who has a key to this house?"

She blinked at me behind her glasses. "Key?"

"Besides you and Mrs. Crenshaw, I mean."

"Why, Charley has one, of course."

"Any other member of your family?"

"Charley is my only living relative."

"Is there anyone else who . . . *uff!*"

An orange blur came flying through the air and a pair of meaty forepaws almost destroyed what was left of my manly pride. The pain made me writhe a little but the movement didn't dislodge Harold; he had all four claws anchored to various portions of my lap. I thought an evil thought that had to do with retribution, but it died in shame when he commenced a noisy purring. Like a fool I put forth a tentative hand and petted him. He tolerated that for all of five seconds; then he bit me on the soft webbing between my thumb and forefinger. Then he jumped down and streaked wildly out of the room.

"He likes you," Mrs. Abbott said.

I looked at her.

"Oh, he does," she said. "It's just his way with strangers. When Harold nips you it's a sign of affection."

I looked down at my hand. The sign of affection was bleeding.

It was one of those cases, all right. I'd sensed it as soon as Addie Crenshaw walked into my office that morning, and I'd known it for sure two minutes after she started talking. City bureaucracy, real estate squabbles, nocturnal prowlings, poisoned cats, a half-dotty old lady—off-the-wall stuff, with seriocomic overtones. The police weren't keen on investigating the more recent developments and I didn't blame them. Neither was I. So I said no.

But Addie Crenshaw was not someone who listened to no when she wanted to hear yes. She pleaded, she cajoled, she gave me the kind of sad, anxious, worried, reproving looks matronly women in their fifties cultivate to an art form—the kind calculated to make you feel heartless and ashamed of yourself and to melt your resistance faster than fire melts wax. I hung in there for a while, fighting to preserve my better judgment . . . until she started to cry. Then I went all soft-hearted and soft-headed and gave in.

According to Mrs. Crenshaw, Margaret Abbott's woes had begun three months ago, when Allan and Doris Peterson and the city of San Francisco contrived to steal Mrs. Abbott's house and property. The word "steal" was hers, not mine. It seemed the Petersons, who owned a real estate firm in the Outer Richmond district, had bought the Abbott property at a city-held auction where it was being sold for nonpayment of property taxes dating back to the death of Mrs. Abbott's husband in 1981. She wouldn't vacate the premises, so they'd sought to have her legally evicted. Sheriff's deputies refused to carry out the eviction notice, however, after a Sheriff's Department administrator went out to talk to her and came to the conclusion that she was the innocent victim of circumstances and cold-hearted bureaucracy.

Margaret Abbott's husband had always handled the couple's finances; she was an old-fashioned sheltered housewife who knew nothing at all about such matters as property taxes. She hadn't heeded notices of delinquency mailed to her by the city tax collector because she didn't understand what they were. When the tax collector received no response from her, he ordered her property put up for auction without first making an effort to contact her personally. House and property were subsequently sold to the Petersons for $186,000, less than half of what they were worth on the current real estate market. Mrs. Abbott hadn't even been told that an auction was being held.

Armed with this information, the Sheriff's Department administrator went to the mayor and to the local newspapers on her behalf. The mayor got the Board of Supervisors to approve city funds to reimburse the Petersons, so as to allow Mrs. Abbott to keep her home. But the Petersons refused to accept the reimbursement; they wanted the property and the fat killing they'd make when they sold it. They hired an attorney, which

prompted Mrs. Crenshaw to step in and enlist the help of lawyers from Legal Aid for the Elderly. A stay of the eviction order
was obtained and the matter was put before a Superior Court
judge, who ruled in favor of Margaret Abbott. She was not
only entitled to her property, he decided, but to a tax waiver
from the city because she lived on a fixed income. The Petersons
might have tried to take the case to a higher court, except for
the fact that negative media attention was harming their business. So, Mrs. Crenshaw said, "They crawled back into the
woodwork. But not for long, if you ask me."

It was Addie Crenshaw's contention that the Petersons had
commenced the nocturnal "reign of terror" against Mrs. Abbott out of "just plain vindictive meanness. And maybe because
they think that if they drive Margaret crazy or straight into her
grave, they can get their greedy claws on her property after
all." How could they hope to do that? I'd asked. She didn't
know, she said, but if there was a way, "Those two slimeballs
have found it out."

That explanation didn't make much sense to me. But based
on what I'd been told so far, I couldn't think of a better one.
Margaret Abbott lived on a quiet street in a quiet residential
neighborhood; she seldom left the house anymore, got on fine
with her neighbors and her nephew, hadn't an enemy in the
world nor any money or valuables other than her house and
property that anybody could be after. If not the Petersons, then
who would want to bedevil a harmless old woman? And why?

Well, I could probably rule out Harold the psychotic cat and
the ghost of Mrs. Abbott's late husband. If old Carl's shade
really was lurking around here somewhere, Addie Crenshaw
would just have to get herself another soft-headed detective. I
don't do ghosts. I definitely do not do ghosts.

Mrs. Crenshaw and I left Margaret Abbott in her Boston rocker
and went to have a look around the premises, starting with the
rear porch.

A close-up examination of the back door revealed no marks
on the locking plate or any other indication of forced entry.
But the lock itself was of the push-button variety: anybody with

half an ounce of ingenuity could pop it open in ten seconds flat. The cat's three bowls—water, dried food, wet food—were over next to the washer and dryer, ten feet from the door. Easy enough for someone to slip in here late at night and dose one of the bowls with arsenic.

Outside, then, into the rear yard. It was a cold autumn day, clear and windy—the kind of day that makes you think of football games and the good smell of burning leaves and how much you looked forward to All Hallows Eve when you were a kid. The wind had laid a coating of dead leaves over a small patch of lawn and flower beds that were otherwise neatly tended; Mrs. Crenshaw had told me her brother, Leonard, took care of Mrs. Abbott's yardwork. The yard itself was enclosed by fences, no gate in any of them and with neighboring houses on two sides; but beyond the back fence, which was low and easily climbable, was a kids' playground. I walked across the lawn, around on the north side of the house, and found another trespasser's delight: a brick path that was open all the way to the street.

I went down the path a ways, looking at the side wall of the house. Mrs. Crenshaw and her brother had done a good job of eradicating the words that had been spray-painted there, except for the shadow of a *bullsh* that was half hidden behind a hedge.

In the adjacent yard on that side, a man in a sweatshirt had been raking leaves fallen from a pair of white birches. He'd stopped when he saw Mrs. Crenshaw and me, and now he came over to the fence. He was about fifty, thin, balding, long-jawed. He nodded to me, said to Mrs. Crenshaw, "How's Margaret holding up, Addie?"

"Fair, the poor thing. Now she thinks it might be ghosts."

"Ghosts?"

"Her late husband come back to torment her."

"Uh-oh. Sounds like she's ready for the loony bin."

"Not yet she isn't. Not if this man"—she patted my arm—"and I have anything to say about it. He's a detective and he is going to put a stop to what's been going on."

"Detective?"

"Private investigator. I hired him."

"What can a private eye do that the police can't?"

"I told you, Ev. Put a stop to what's been going on."

Mrs. Crenshaw introduced us. The thin guy's name was Everett Mihalik.

He asked me, "So how you gonna do it? You got some plan in mind?"

People always want to know how a detective works. They think there is some special methodology that sets private cops apart from public cops and even farther apart from those in other public-service professions. Another byproduct of the mystique created by Hammett and Chandler and nurtured—and badly distorted—by films and TV.

I told Mihalik the truth. "No, I don't have a plan. Just hard work and perseverance and I hope a little luck." And of course it disappointed him, as I'd known it would.

"Well, you ask me," he said, "it's kids. Street punks."

"What reason would they have?"

"They need a reason nowadays?"

"Any particular kids you have in mind?"

"Nah. But this neighborhood's not like it used to be. Full of minorities now, kids looking for trouble. They hang out at Ocean Beach and the zoo."

"Uh-huh." I asked Mrs. Crenshaw, "There been any other cases of malicious mischief around here recently?"

"Not that I heard about."

"So Margaret's the first," Mihalik said. "They start with one person, then they move on to somebody else. Me, for instance. Or you, Addie." He shook his head. "I'm telling you, it's those goddamn punks hang out at Ocean Beach and the zoo."

Maybe, I thought. But I didn't believe it. The things that had been done to Margaret Abbott didn't follow the patterns of simple malicious mischief, didn't feel random to me. They felt calculated to a specific purpose. Find that purpose and I'd find the person or persons responsible.

Addie Crenshaw lived half a block to the west, just off Ulloa. This was a former blue-collar Caucasian neighborhood, built in the thirties on what had once been a windswept stretch of sand dunes. The parcels were small, the houses of mixed architectural styles and detached from one another, unlike the ugly shoulder-to-shoulder row houses farther inland. Built cheap and bought cheap fifty years ago, but now worth small fortunes thanks to San Francisco's overinflated real estate market and a steady influx of Asian families, both American-and foreign-born, with money to spend and a desire for a piece of the city. Original owners like Margaret Abbott, and people who had lived here for decades like Addie Crenshaw, were now the exceptions rather than the norm.

The Crenshaw house was of stucco and similar in type and size, if not in color, to the one owned by Mrs. Abbott. It was painted a garish brown with orange-yellow trim, which made me think of a gigantic and artfully sculpted grilled-cheese sandwich. The garage door was up and a slope-shouldered man in a Giants baseball cap was doing something at a workbench inside. Mrs. Crenshaw ushered me in that way.

The slope-shouldered man was Leonard Crenshaw. A few years older than his sister and on the dour side, he had evidently lived here for a number of years, though the house belonged to Mrs. Crenshaw; Leonard had moved in after her husband died, she'd told me, to help out with chores and to keep her company. If he had a job or profession, she hadn't confided what it was.

"Don't mind telling you," he said to me, "I think Addie made a mistake hiring you."

"Why is that, Mr. Crenshaw?"

"Always sticking her nose in other people's business. Been like that her whole life. Nosy and bossy."

"Better than putting my head in the sand like an ostrich," Mrs. Crenshaw said. She didn't seem upset or annoyed by her brother's comments. I had the impression this was an old sibling disagreement, one that went back a lot of years through a lot of different incidents.

"Can't just live her life and let others live theirs," Leonard said. "It's Charley Doyle should be taking care of his aunt and her problems, spending his money on a fancy detective."

Fancy detective, I thought. Leonard, if you only knew.

"Charley Doyle can barely take care of himself," Mrs. Crenshaw said. "He has two brain cells and one of those works only about half the time. All he cares about is gambling and liquor and cheap women."

"A heavy gambler, is he?" I asked.

"Oh, I don't think so. He's too lazy and too stupid. Besides, he plays poker with Ev Mihalik and Ev is so tight he squeaks."

Leonard said, "You know what's going to happen to you, Addie, talking about people behind their backs that way? You'll spend eternity hanging by your tongue, that's what."

"Oh, put a sock in it, Leonard."

"Telling tales about people, hiring detectives. Next thing you know, *our* phone'll start ringing in the middle of the night, somebody'll bust one of *our* windows."

"Nonsense."

"Is it? Stir things up, you're bound to make 'em worse. For everybody. You mark my words."

Mrs. Crenshaw and I went upstairs and she provided me with work and home addresses for Charley Doyle and the address of the real estate agency owned by the Petersons. "Don't mind Leonard," she said then. "He's not as much of a curmudgeon as he pretends to be. This crazy business with Margaret has him almost as upset as it has me."

"I try not to be judgmental, Mrs. Crenshaw."

"So do I," she said. "Now you go give those Petersons hell, you hear? A taste of their own medicine, the dirty swine."

The impressive-sounding Peterson Realty Company, Inc. was in fact a storefront hole-in-the-wall on Balboa near Forty-sixth, within hailing distance of the Great Highway and Ocean Beach.

Coming to this part of the city always gave me pangs of nostalgia. It was where Playland-at-the-Beach used to be, and Playland—a ten-acre amusement park in the grand old style— had been where I'd spent a good portion of my youth. Funhouses, shooting galleries, games of chance, the Big Dipper roller coaster swooping down out of the misty dark, laughing girls with windcolor in their cheeks and sparkle in their eyes

. . . and all of it wrapped in thick ocean fogs that added an element of mystery to the general excitement. All gone now; closed nearly twenty years ago and then allowed to sit abandoned for several more before it was torn down; nothing left of it except bright ghost-images in the memories of graybeards like me. Condo and rental apartment buildings occupied the space these days: Beachfront Luxury Living, Spectacular Views. Yeah, sure. Luxuriously cold gray weather and spectacular weekend views of Ocean Beach and its parking areas jammed with rowdy teenagers and beer-guzzling adult children.

It made me sad, thinking about it. Getting old. Sure sign of it when you started lamenting the dead past, glorifying it as if it were some kind of flawless Valhalla when you knew damned well it hadn't been. Maybe so, maybe so—but nobody could convince me Beachfront Luxury Living condos were better than Playland and the Big Dipper, or that some of the dead past wasn't a hell of a lot better than most of the half-dead present.

There were two desks inside the Peterson Realty Company offices, each of them occupied. The man was dark, forty, dressed to the nines, with a smiley demeanor and earnest eyes that locked onto yours and hung on as if they couldn't bear to let go. The woman was a few years younger, ash-blonde, just as smiley but not quite as determinedly earnest or slick. Allan and Doris Peterson. Nice attractive couple, all right. Just the kind you'd expect to find in the front row at a city-held tax auction.

They were friendly and effusive until I told them who I was and that I was investigating the harassment of Margaret Abbott. No more smiles then; unveiling of the true colors. Allan Peterson said, with more than a little nastiness, "That Crenshaw woman hired you, I suppose. Damn her; she's out to get us."

"I don't think so, Mr. Peterson. All she wants is to get to the bottom of the trouble."

"Well, my God," Doris Peterson said, "why come to us about that? We don't have anything to do with it. What earthly good would it do us to harass the old woman? We've already lost her property, thanks to that bleeding-heart judge."

"I'm not here to accuse you of anything," I said. "I just want to ask you a few questions."

"We don't have anything to say to you. We don't know anything, we don't want to know anything."

"And furthermore, you don't give a damn. Right?"

"You said that, I didn't. Anyway, why should we?"

Peterson said, "If you or that Crenshaw woman try to imply that we're involved, or even that we're in any way exploiters of the chronologically gifted, we'll sue. I mean that—we'll sue."

"Exploiters of the what?" I said.

"You heard me. The chronologically gifted."

Christ, I thought. Old people hadn't been old people—or elderly people—for some time, but I hadn't realized that they were no longer even senior citizens. Now they were "the chronologically gifted"—the most asinine example of newspeak I had yet encountered. The ungifted ad agency types who coined such euphemisms ought to be excessed, transitioned, offered voluntary severance, or provided with immediate career-change opportunities. Or better yet, subjected to permanent chronological interruption.

So much for the Petersons. A waste of time coming here; all it had accomplished was to confirm Addie Crenshaw's low opinion of them. I would be happy if it turned out they had something to do with the nocturnal prowling, but hell, where was their motive? Assholes, yes; childishly vindictive bedevilers, no. And unfortunately there is no law against being an asshole in today's society. If there was, five percent of the population would be in jail and another ten percent would be on the cusp.

Charley Doyle's place of employment was a glass-service outfit in Daly City. But it was already shut down for the weekend when I got there; glaziers, like plumbers and other union tradesmen, work four-or four-and-a-half-day weeks. So I drove back into San Francisco via Mission Street, to the run-down apartment building in Visitacion Valley where Doyle resided. He wasn't there either. The second neighbor I talked to said he hung out in a tavern called Fat Leland's, on Geneva Avenue, and that was where I finally ran him down.

He was sitting in a booth with half a dozen bottles of beer and a hefty, big-chested blonde who reminded me of a woman my partner, Eberhardt, mistakenly came close to marrying a few years ago. They were all over each other, rubbing and groping and swapping beer-and-cigarette-flavored saliva. They didn't like it when I sat down across from them; and Doyle liked it even less when I told him who I was and why I was there.

"I don't know nothing about it," he said. He was a big guy with a beer belly and dim little eyes. Two brain cells, Addie Crenshaw had said. Right. "What you want to bother me for?"

"I thought you might have an idea of who's behind the trouble."

"Not me. Old Lady Crenshaw thinks it's them real estate people that tried to steal my aunt's house. Why don't you go talk to them?"

"I already did. They deny any involvement."

"Lying bastards," he said.

"Maybe. You been out to see your aunt lately?"

"Not since I fixed her busted window. Why?"

"Well, you're her only relative. She could use some moral support."

"She's got the Crenshaws to take care of her. She don't need me hanging around."

"No, I guess she doesn't at that. Tell me, do you stand to inherit her entire estate?"

"Huh?"

"Do you get her house and property when she dies?"

His dim little eyes got brighter. "Yeah, that's right. So what? You think it's me doing that stuff to her?"

"I'm just asking questions, Mr. Doyle."

"Yeah, well, I don't like your questions. You can't pin it on me. Last Saturday night, when them rose bushes of hers was dug up, I was in Reno with a couple of buddies. And last Wednesday, when that damn cat got poisoned, me and Mildred here was together the whole night at her place." He nudged the blonde with a dirty elbow. "Wasn't we, kid?"

Mildred giggled, belched, said, "Whoops, excuse me," and

giggled again. Then she frowned and said, "What'd you ask me, honey?"

"Wednesday night," Doyle said. "We was together all night, wasn't we? At your place?"

"Sure," Mildred said, "all night." Another giggle. "You're a real man, Charley, that's what you are."

I left the two of them pawing and drooling on each other— one of those perfect matches you hear about but seldom encounter in the flesh. Cupid triumphant. Four brain cells joined against the world.

Even though it was too late in the day to get much background checking done, I drove down to my office on O'Farrell and put in a couple of calls to start the wheels turning. Credit information and possible arrest records on the Petersons and Charley Doyle, for openers. I had nothing else to go on, and you never know what a routine check might turn up.

At five-thirty I quit the office and drove home to Pacific Heights. Poker game tonight at Eberhardt's; beer and pizza and smelly pipe smoke and lousy jokes. I was looking forward to it. Kerry says all-male poker games are "bonding rituals with their roots in ancient pagan society." I love her anyway.

While I was changing clothes I wondered if maybe, after the game, I ought to run an all-night stakeout on Margaret Abbott's home. It had been two days since the last incident; if the pattern held, another was due any time. But I talked myself out of it. I hate stakeouts, particularly all-night stakeouts. And with two easy ways to get onto her property, front and back, I could cover only one of the possibilities at a time from my car. Of course I could run the stakeout from inside her house, but that wouldn't do much good if the perp stayed outside. Besides, I was not quite ready to spend one or more nights on Mrs. Abbott's couch, and I doubted that she was ready for it either.

So I went to the poker game with a clear conscience, and won eleven dollars and forty cents, most of it on a straight flush to Eberhardt's kings full, and drove back home at midnight and had a pretty good night's sleep. Until the telephone bell jarred me awake at seven-fifteen on Saturday morning. Addie Crenshaw was on the other end.

"He broke into Margaret's house again last night," she said.

"Damn!" I sat up and shook the sleep cobwebs out of my head. "What'd he do this time?"

"Walked right into her bedroom, bold as brass."

"He didn't harm her?"

"No. Just scared her."

"So she's all right?"

"Better than most women her age would be."

"Did she get a good look at him?"

"No. Wouldn't have even if all the lights had been on."

"Why not?"

"He was wearing a sheet."

"He was . . . what?"

"A sheet," Mrs. Crenshaw said grimly, "wearing a white sheet and making noises like a ghost."

When I got to the Abbott house forty-five minutes later I found a reception committee of three on the front porch: Addie and Leonard Crenshaw and Everett Mihalik, talking animatedly among themselves. Leonard was saying as I came up the walk ". . . should have called the police instead. They're the ones who should be investigating this."

"What can they do?" his sister said. "There aren't any signs of breaking and entering this time either. Nothing damaged, nothing stolen. Just Margaret's word that a man in a sheet was there in the first place. They'd probably say she imagined the whole thing."

"Well, maybe she did," Mihalik said. "I mean, all that non-sense about her dead husband coming back to haunt her . . ."

"Ev, she didn't say it was a ghost she saw. She said it was a man dressed up in a sheet pretending to be a ghost. There's a big difference."

"She still could've imagined it."

Mrs. Crenshaw appealed to me. "It happened, I'm sure it did. She may be a bit dotty, but she's not senile."

I nodded. "Is she up to talking about it?"

"I told her you were coming. She's waiting."

"Guess you don't need me," Mihalik said. A gust of icy wind swept over the porch and he rubbed at a red-stained hand, then winced, and said, "Brr, it's cold out here. Come on, Leonard, I've got a pot of fresh coffee made."

"No thanks," Leonard said, "I got work to do." He gave me a brief disapproving look and then said pointedly to his sister, "Just remember, Addie—chickens always come home to roost."

Mrs. Crenshaw and I went into the house. Margaret Abbott was sitting in her Boston rocker, a shawl over her lap and Harold, the orange tabby, sprawled out asleep on the shawl. She looked tired, and the rouge she'd applied to her cheeks was like bloody splotches on too-white parchment. Still, she seemed to be in good spirits. And she showed no reluctance at discussing her latest ordeal.

"It's really rather amusing," she said, "now that I look back on it. A grown man wearing a sheet and moaning and groaning like Casper with a tummy ache."

"You're sure it was a man?"

"Oh yes. Definitely a man."

"You didn't recognize his voice?"

"Well, he didn't speak. Just moaned and groaned."

"Did you say anything to him?"

"I believe I asked what he thought he was doing in my bedroom. Yes, and I said that he had better not have hurt Harold."

"Harold?"

"It was Harold crying that woke me, you see."

"Not the man entering your bedroom?"

"No. Harold crying. Yowling, actually, as if he'd been hurt. Usually he sleeps on the bed with me, and I think he must have heard the man come into the house and gone to investigate. You know how cats are."

"Yes, ma'am."

"The intruder must have stepped on him or kicked him," Mrs. Abbott said, "to make him yowl like that. Poor Harold, he's been through so much. Haven't you, dear?" She stroked the cat, who started to purr lustily.

"Then what happened?" I asked. "After you woke up."

"Well, I saw a flickery sort of light in the hallway. At first I couldn't imagine what it was."

"Flashlight," Mrs. Crenshaw said.

"Yes. It came closer, right into the doorway. Then it switched off and the intruder walked right up to the foot of my bed and began moaning and groaning and jumping around." She smiled wanly. "Really, it was rather funny."

"How long did he keep up his act?"

"Not long. Just until I spoke to him."

"Then he ran out?"

"Still moaning and groaning, yes. I suppose he wanted me to think he was the ghost of my late husband. As if I wouldn't know a man from a spirit. Or Carl, in or out of a sheet."

I sat quiet for a little time, thinking, remembering some things. I was pretty sure then that I knew the why behind this whole screwy business. I was also pretty sure I knew the who. One more question, of Mrs. Crenshaw this time, and I would go find out for sure.

Everett Mihalik was doing some repair work on his front stoop: down on one knee, using a trowel and a tray of wet cement. But as soon as he saw me approaching he put the trowel down and got to his feet.

"How'd it go with Margaret?" he asked.

"Just fine. Mind answering a couple of questions, Mr. Mihalik?"

"Sure, if I can."

"When I got here this morning, you were on Mrs. Abbott's porch. Had you been inside the house?"

"No. Wasn't any need for me to go in."

"When was the last time you were inside her house?"

"I don't remember exactly. A while."

"More than a few days?"

"A lot longer than that. Why?"

"Do you own a cat?"

"A cat?" Now he was frowning. "What does a cat have to do with anything?"

"Quite a bit. You don't own one, do you?"

"No."

"Then how did you get that bite on your hand?"

"My—?" He looked at his left hand, at the iodine-daubed bite mark just above the thumb. I'd noticed it earlier, when he'd winced while rubbing his reddened hand, but the significance of it hadn't registered until I'd talked with Mrs. Abbott.

"Fresh bite," I said. "Can't be more than a few hours old." I held out my own bitten hand for him to see. "Fresher than mine, and it's only about twenty hours old. Similar marks, too. Looks like they were done by the same cat—Mrs. Abbott's cat, Harold."

Mihalik licked his lips and said nothing.

"Harold is an indoor cat, never allowed outside. And he likes to nip strangers when they aren't expecting it. Somebody comes into his house in the middle of the night, he'd not only go to investigate, he'd be even more inclined to take himself a little nip—especially if the intruder happened to try to pat him to keep him quiet. Mrs. Abbott was woken up last night by Harold yowling; she thought it was because the intruder stepped on him or kicked him, but that wasn't it at all. It was the intruder swatting him after being bitten that made him yell."

"You can't prove it was Harold bit me," Mihalik said. "It was another cat, a neighborhood stray. . . ."

"Harold," I said, "and the police lab people *can* prove it. Test the bites on my hand and yours, test Harold's teeth and saliva . . . they can prove it, all right."

He shook his head, but not as if he were denying my words. As if he were trying to deny the fact that he was caught. "You think I'm the one been doing all that stuff to Margaret?"

"I know you are. Dressing up in that sheet last night, pretending to be a ghost, was a stupid idea in more ways than one. Only one person besides Addie Crenshaw and me knew of Mrs. Abbott's fancy about her dead husband's ghost. You, Mihalik. Mrs. Crenshaw mentioned it when we talked to you yesterday afternoon. She didn't mention it to anybody else, not even her brother; she told me so just a few minutes ago."

Another headshake. "What reason would I have for hassling an old lady like Margaret?"

"The obvious one—money. A cut of the proceeds from the sale of her property after she was dead or declared incompetent."

"That don't make sense. I'm not a relative of hers. . . ."

"No, but Charley Doyle is. And you and Charley are buddies; Mrs. Crenshaw told me you play poker together regularly. Charley's not very bright and just as greedy as you are. Your brainchild, wasn't it, Mihalik? Inspired by that auction fiasco. Hey, Charley, why wait until your aunt dies of natural causes; that might take years. Give her a heart attack or drive her into an institution, get control of her property right away. Then sell it to the Petersons or some other real estate speculator for a nice quick profit. And you earn your cut by doing all the dirty work while Charley sets up alibis to keep himself in the clear."

Mihalik stood tensed now, as if he were thinking about jumping me or maybe just trying to run. But he didn't do either one. After a few seconds he went all loose and saggy, as though somebody had cut his strings; he took a stumbling step backward and sank down on the stairs and put his head in his hands.

"I never done anything wrong before in my life," he said. "Never. But the bills been piling up, it's so goddamn hard to live these days, and they been talking about laying people off where I work and I was afraid I'd lose my house . . . ah, God, I don't know. I don't know." He lifted his head and gave me a moist, beseeching look. "I never meant that Margaret should die. You got to believe that. Just force her out of there so Charley could take over the house, that's all. I like her, I never meant to hurt her."

Three brain cells to Charley Doyle's two. Half-wits and knaves, fools and assholes—more of each than ever before, proliferating like weeds in what had once been a pristine garden. It's a hell of a world we live in, I thought. A hell of a mess we're making of the garden.

*   *   *

I went to see Mrs. Abbott again later that day, after Everett Mihalik and Charley Doyle had been arrested and I'd finished making my statement at the Hall of Justice. Addie and Leonard Crenshaw were both there. All three were still a little shaken at the betrayal of a neighbor and a relative, but relief was the dominant emotion. Even Leonard was less dour than usual.

A celebration was called for, Mrs. Crenshaw said, and so we had one: coffee and apple strudel. Harold joined in too. Mrs. Abbott had some "special kitty treats" for him and she insisted that I give him one; he was, after all, something of a hero in his own right. So I got down on one knee and gave him one.

In gratitude and affection, he bit me. Different hand, same place.

The Maggody Files: Hillbilly Cat

Joan Hess

I WAS REDUCED TO WHITTLING away the morning, and trying to convince myself that I was in some obscure way whittling away at the length of my sentence in Maggody, Arkansas (pop. 755). Outside the red-bricked PD, the early morning rain came down steadily, and, as Ruby Bee Hanks (proprietress of a bar and grill of the same name, and, incidentally, my mother) would say, it was turning a mite crumpy. I figured the local criminal elements would be daunted enough to stay home, presuming they were smart enough to come in out of the rain in the first place. This isn't to say they rampaged when the sun shone. Mostly they ran the stoplight, fussed and cussed at their neighbors, stole such precious commodities as superior huntin' dawgs, and occasionally raced away from the self-service station without paying for gas. There'd been some isolated violence during my tenure, but every last person in town still based their historical perspective on before-or-after Hiram Buchanon's barn burned to the ground.

I suppose I ought to mention that my sentence was self-imposed, in that I scampered home from Manhattan to lick my wounds after a nasty divorce. In that I was the only person stupid enough to apply for the job, I was not only the Chief of Police, but also the entirety of the department. For a while I'd had a deputy, who just happened to be the mayor's cousin, but he'd gotten himself in trouble over his unrequited love for a bosomy barmaid. Now I had a beeper.

That October morning I had a block of balsa wood that was harder than granite, and a pocket knife that was duller than most of the population. I also had some bizarre dreams of converting the wood into something that remotely resembled a duck—a marshland mallard, to be precise. Those loyal souls who're schooled in the local lore know I tried this a while back, with zero success. Same wood, for the record, and thus far, same rate of success.

So I had my feet on the corner of my desk, my cane-bottomed chair propped back against the wall, and an unholy mess of wood shavings scattered all over the place when the door opened. The man who came in wore a black plastic raincoat and was wrestling with a brightly striped umbrella more suited to a swanky golf course (in Maggody, we don't approve of golf—or any other sissified sport in which grown men wear shorts). He appeared to be forty or so, with a good ol' boy belly and the short, wavy hair of a used car salesman.

Strangers come into the PD maybe three times a year, usually to ask directions or to sell me subscriptions to magazines like *Field and Stream* or *Sports Illustrated*. I guess it's never occurred to any of them that some of us backwoods cops might prefer *Cosmopolitan*.

He finally gave up on the umbrella and set it in a corner to drip. Flashing two rows of pearly white teeth at me, he said, "Hey, honey, some weather, isn't it? Is the chief in?"

"It sure is some weather," I said politely, "and the chief is definitely in." I did not add that the chief was mildly insulted, but by no means incensed or inclined to explain further.

This time I got a wink. "Could I have a word with him?"

"You're having a word with *her* at this very moment," I said as I dropped my duck in a drawer and crossed my arms, idly wondering how long it'd take him to work it out. He didn't look downright stupid like the clannish Buchanons, who're obliged to operate solely on animal instinct, but he had squinty eyes, flaccid lips, and minutes earlier had lost a battle to an umbrella.

"Sorry, honey." His shrug indicated he wasn't altogether overwhelmed with remorse. "I'm Nelson Mullein from down near Pine Bluff. The woman at the hardware store said the chief's name was Arly, and I sort of assumed I was looking for a fellow. My mistake."

"How may I help you, Mr. Mullein?" I said.

"Call me Nelson, please. My great-grandaunts live here in Maggody, out on County 102 on the other side of the low-water bridge. Everybody's always called them the Banebury girls, although Miss Columbine is seventy-eight and Miss Lark-spur's seventy-six."

"I know who they are."

"Thought you might." He sat down on the chair across from my desk and took out a cigar. When he caught my glare, he replaced it in his pocket, licked his lips, and made a production of grimacing and sighing so I'd appreciate how carefully he was choosing his words. "The thing is," he said slowly, "I'm worried about them. As I said, they're old and they live in that big, ramshackle house by themselves. It ain't in the ghetto, but it's a far cry from suburbia. Neither one of them can see worth a damn. Miss Larkspur took a fall last year while she was climbing out of the tub, and her hip healed so poorly she's still using a walker. Miss Columbine is wheezier than a leaky balloon."

"So I should arrest them for being old and frail?"

"Of course not," he said, massaging his rubbery jowls. "I was hoping you could talk some sense into them, that's all, 'cause I sure as hell can't, even though I'm their only relative. It hurts me to see them living the way they do. They're as poor as church mice. When I went out there yesterday, it was colder inside than it was outside, and the only heat was from a wood fire in a potbelly stove. Seems they couldn't pay the gas bill last month and it was shut off. I took care of that immediately and told the gas company to bill me in the future. If Miss Columbine finds out, she'll have a fit, but I didn't know what else to do."

He sounded so genuinely concerned that I forgave him for calling me "honey," and tried to recall what little I knew about the Banebury girls. They'd been reclusive even when I was a kid, although they occasionally drove through town in a glossy black Lincoln Continental, nodding regally at the peasants. One summer night twenty or so years ago, they'd caught a gang of us skinny-dipping at the far side of the field behind their house. Miss Columbine had been outraged. After she'd carried on for a good ten minutes, Miss Larkspur persuaded her not to report the incident to our parents and we grabbed our clothes and hightailed it. We stayed well downstream the rest of the summer. We avoided their house at Halloween, but only because it was isolated and not worth the risk of having to listen to a lecture on hooliganism in exchange for a stale popcorn ball.

"I understand your concern," I said. "I'm afraid I don't know them well enough to have any influence."

"They told me they still drive. Miss Columbine has macular degeneration, which means her peripheral vision's fine but she can't see anything in front of her. Miss Larkspur's legally blind, but that works out just fine—she navigates. I asked them how on earth either had a driver's license, and damned if they didn't show 'em to me. The date was 1974."

I winced. "Maybe once or twice a year, they drive half a mile to church at a speed of no more than ten miles an hour. When they come down the middle of the road, everybody in town knows to pull over, all the way into a ditch if need be, and the children have been taught to do their rubberneckin' from their yards. It's actually kind of a glitzy local event that's discussed for days afterwards. I realize it's illegal, but I'm not about to go out there and tell them they can't drive anymore."

"Yeah, I know," he said, "but I'm going to lose a lot of sleep if I don't do something for them. I'm staying at a motel in Farberville. This morning I got on the phone and found out about a retirement facility for the elderly. I went out and looked at it, and it's more like a boardinghouse than one of those smelly nursing homes. Everybody has a private bedroom, and meals are provided in a nice, warm dining room. There was a domino game going on while I was there, and a couple of the women were watching a soap opera. There's a van to take them shopping or to doctor appointments. It's kind of expensive, but I think I can swing it by using their social security checks and setting up an income from the sale of the house and property. I had a real estate agent drive by it this morning, and he thought he could get eight, maybe ten, thousand dollars."

"And when you presented this, they said . . . ?"

"Miss Columbine's a hardheaded woman, and she liked to scorch my ears," he admitted ruefully. "I felt like I was ten years old and been caught with a toad in the pocket of my choir robe. Miss Larkspur was interested at first, and asked some questions, but when they found out they couldn't take Eppie, the discussion was over, and before I knew what hit me, I was out on the porch shivering like a hound dog in a blizzard."

"Eppie?"

"Their cat. In spite of the sweet-sounding name, it's an obese yellow tomcat with one eye and a tattered ear. It's mangy and mean and moth-eaten, and that's being charitable. But they won't even consider giving it away, and the residence home forbids pets because of a health department regulation. I went ahead and put down a deposit, but the director said she can't hold the rooms for more than a few days and she expects to be filled real soon. I hate to say it, but it's now or never." He spread his hands and gave me a beseeching look. "Do you think you or anybody else in town can talk them into at least taking a look at this place?"

I suspected I would have more luck with my balsa wood than with the Banebury sisters, but I promised Nelson I'd give it a shot and wrote down the telephone number of his motel room. After a display of effusively moist gratitude, he left.

I decided the matter could wait until after lunch. The Banebury sisters had been going about their business nearly four score years, after all, I told myself righteously as I darted through the drizzle to my car and headed for Ruby Bee's Bar & Grill.

"So what's this about Miss Columbine and Miss Larkspur being dragged off to an old folks' home?" Ruby Bee demanded as I walked across the tiny dance floor. It was too early for the noon crowd, and only one booth was occupied by a pair of truck drivers working on blue plate specials and a pitcher of beer.

"And who'd pay ten thousand dollars for that old shack?" Estelle Oppers added from her favorite stool at the end of the bar, convenient to the pretzels and the rest room.

I wasn't particularly amazed by the questions. Maggody has a very sturdy grapevine, and it definitely curls through the barroom on its way from one end of town to the other. That was one of the reasons I'd left the day after I graduated, and eventually took refuge in the anonymity of Manhattan, where one can caper in the nude on the street and no one so much as bothers with a second look. In Maggody, you can hear about what you did before you're finished planning to do it.

"To think they'd give up their cat!" Ruby Bee continued, her hands on her hips and her eyes flashing as if I'd suggested we drown dear Eppie in Boone Creek. Beneath her unnaturally blond hair, her face was screwed up with indignation. "It ain't much to look at, but they've had it for fourteen years and some folks just don't understand how attached they are."

I opened my mouth to offer a mild rebuttal, but Estelle leapt in with the agility of a trout going after a mayfly. "Furthermore, I think it's mighty suspicious, him coming to town all of a sudden to disrupt their lives. I always say, when there's old ladies and a cat, the nephew's up to no good. Just last week I read a story about how the nephew tried to trick his aunt so he could steal all her money."

I chose a stool at the opposite end of the bar. "From what Nelson told me, they don't have any money."

"I still say he's up to no good," Estelle said mulishly, which is pretty much the way she said everything.

Ruby Bee took a dishrag and began to wipe the pristine surface of the bar. "I reckon that much is true, but Eula said she happened to see him in the hardware store, and he had a real oily look about him, like a carnival roustabout. She said she wouldn't have been surprised if he had tattoos under his clothes. He was asking all kinds of questions, too."

"Like what?" I said, peering at the pies under glass domes and ascertaining there was a good-sized piece of cherry left.

"Well, he wanted to know where to go to have all their utility bills sent to him, on account of he didn't think they had enough money to pay 'em. He also wanted to know if he could arrange for groceries to be delivered to their house every week, but Eula stepped in and explained that the church auxiliary already sees to that."

I shook my head and made a clucking noise. "The man's clearly a scoundrel, a cad, a veritable devil in disguise. How about meatloaf, mashed potatoes and gravy, and cherry pie with ice cream?"

Ruby Bee was not in her maternal mode. "And wasn't there an old movie about a smarmy nephew trying to put his sweet old aunts in some sort of insane asylum?" she asked Estelle.

"That was because they were poisoning folks. I don't recollect anyone accusing the Banebury girls of anything like that. Miss Columbine's got a sharp tongue, but she's got her wits about her. I wish I could say the same thing about Miss Larkspur. She can be kind of silly and forgetful, but she ain't got a mean bone in her body. Now if the cat was stalking me on a dark street, I'd be looking over my shoulder and fearing for my life. He lost his eye in a fight with old Shep Humes's pit bull. When Shep tried to pull 'em apart, he liked to lose both of his eyes and a couple of fingers, and he said he cain't remember when he heard a gawdawful racket like that night."

"Meatloaf?" I said optimistically. "Mashed potatoes?"

Still wiping the bar, Ruby Bee worked her way towards Estelle. "The real estate agent says he can sell that place for ten thousand dollars?"

"He didn't sound real sure of it, and Eilene said Earl said the fellow didn't think the house was worth a dollar. It was the forty acres he thought might sell." Estelle popped a pretzel

in her mouth and chewed it pensively. "I took them a basket
of cookies last year just before Christmas, and the house is in
such sad shape that I thought to myself, I'm gonna sit right
down and cry. The plaster's crumbling off the walls, and there
was more than one window taped with cardboard. It's a matter
of time before the house falls down on 'em."

Aware I was about to go down for the third time, I said,
"Meatloaf?"

Ruby Bee leaned across the bar, and in a melodramatic whisper that most likely was audible in the next county, said, "Do
you think they're misers with a fortune buried in jars in the
back yard? If this Mullein fellow knows it, then he'd want to
get rid of them and have all the time he needs to dig up the
yard searching for the money."

"Them?" Estelle cackled. "There was some family money
when their daddy owned the feed store, but he lost so much
money when that fancy co-op opened in Starley City that he
lost the store and upped and died within the year. After that,
Miss Larkspur had to take piano students and Miss Columbine
did mending until they went on social security. Now how are
they supposed to have acquired this fortune? Are you accusing
them of putting on ski masks and robbing liquor stores?"

"For pity's sake, I was just thinking out loud," Ruby Bee
retorted.

"The next thing, you'll be saying you saw them on that television show about unsolved crimes."

"At least some of us have better things to do than read silly
mystery stories about nephews and cats," Ruby Bee said disdainfully. "I wouldn't be surprised if you didn't have a whole
book filled with them."

"So what if I do?" Estelle slapped the bar hard enough to
tump the pretzels.

It seemed the only thing being served was food for thought.
I drove to the Dairee Dee-Lishus and ate a chilidog in my car
while I fiddled with the radio in search of anything but whiny
country music. I was doing so to avoid thinking about the conversation at Ruby Bee's. Nelson Mullein wasn't my type, but
that didn't automatically relegate him to the slime pool. He

had good reason to be worried about his great-grandaunts. Hell, now I was worried about them, too.

Then again, I thought as I drove out County 102 and eased across the low-water bridge, Estelle had a point. There was something almost eerie about the combination of old ladies, cats, and ne'er-do-well nephews (although, as far as I knew, Nelson was doing well at whatever he did; I hadn't asked). But we were missing the key element in the plot, and that was the fortune that kicked in the greed factor. Based on what Estelle had said, the Banebury girls were just as poor as Nelson had claimed.

The appearance of the house confirmed it. It was a squatty old farmhouse that had once been white, but was weathered to a lifeless gray. What shingles remained on the roof were mossy, and the chimney had collapsed. A window on the second floor was covered with cardboard; broken glass was scattered on the porch. The detached garage across the weedy yard had fared no better.

Avoiding puddles, I hurried to the front door and knocked, keenly and uncomfortably aware of the icy rain slithering under my collar. I was about to knock a second time when the door opened a few cautious inches.

"I'm Arly Hanks," I said, trying not to let my teeth chatter too loudly. "Do you mind if I come in for a little visit?"

"I reckon you can." Miss Columbine stepped back and gestured for me to enter. To my astonishment, she looked almost exactly the same as she had the night she stood on the bank of Boone Creek and bawled us out. Her hair was white and pinned up in tight braids, her nose was sharp, her cheekbones prominent above concave cheeks. Her head was tilted at an angle, and I remembered what Nelson had said about her vision.

"Thanks," I murmured as I rubbed my hands together.

"Hanks, did you say? You're Ruby Bee's gal," she said in the same steely voice. "Now that you're growed up, are you keeping your clothes on when you take a moonlight swim?"

I was reduced to an adolescent, "Yes, ma'am."

"Do we have a visitor?" Miss Larkspur came into the living

room, utilizing an aluminum walker to take each awkward step. "First Nelson and now this girl. I swear, I don't know when we've had so much company, Columbine."

The twenty years had been less compassionate to Miss Larkspur. Her eyes were so clouded and her skin so translucent that she looked as if she'd been embalmed. Her body was bent, one shoulder hunched and the other undefined. The fingers that gripped the walker were swollen and misshapen.

"I'm Arly Hanks," I told her.

"Gracious, girl, I know who you are. I heard about how you came back to Maggody after all those years in the big city. I don't blame you one bit. Columbine and I went to visit kin in Memphis when we were youngsters, and I knew then and there that I'd never be able to live in a place like that. There were so many cars and carriages and streetcars that we feared for our very lives, didn't we?"

"Yes, I seem to recall that we did, Larkspur."

"Shall I put on the tea kettle?"

Miss Columbine smiled sadly. "That's all right, sister; I'll see to it. Why don't you sit down with our company while I fix a tray? Be sure and introduce her to Eppie."

The room was scantily furnished with ugly, battered furniture and a rug worn so badly that the wooden floor was visible. It smelled of decay, and no doubt for a very good reason. Plaster had fallen in several places, exposing the joists and yellowed newspaper that served as insulation. Although it was warmer than outside, it was a good twenty degrees below what I considered comfortable. Both sisters wore shawls. I hoped they had thermal underwear beneath their plain, dark dresses.

I waited until Miss Larkspur had made it across the room and was seated on a sofa. I sat across from her and said, "I met Nelson this morning. He seems concerned about you and your sister."

"So he says," she said without interest. She leaned forward and clapped her hands. "Eppie? Are you hiding? It's quite safe to come out. This girl won't hurt you. She'd like the chance to admire you."

An enormous cat stalked from behind the sofa, his single

amber eye regarding me malevolently and his tail swishing as
if he considered it a weapon. He was everything Nelson had
described, and worse. He paused to rake his claws across the
carpet, then leapt into Miss Larkspur's lap and settled down to
the convey to me how very deeply he resented my presence.
Had I been a less rational person, I would have wondered if he
knew I was there to promote Nelson's plan. Had I been, as I
said.

"Isn't he a pretty kitty?" cooed Miss Larkspur. "He acts so
big and tough, but him's just a snuggly teddy bear."

"Very pretty," I said, resisting an urge to lapse into baby-
talk and tweak Eppie's whiskers. He would have taken my
hand off in a flash. Or my arm.

Miss Columbine came into the room, carrying a tray with
three cups and saucers and a ceramic teapot. There were more
chips than rosebuds, but I was delighted to take a cup of hot
tea and cradle it in my hands. "Did Nelson send you?" she said
as she served her sister and sat down beside her. Eppie snuggled
between them to continue his surly surveillance.

"He came by the PD this morning and asked me to speak to
you," I admitted.

"Nelson is a ninny," she said with a tight frown. "Always
has been, always will be. When he came during the summers,
I had to watch him like a hawk to make sure he wasn't tor-
menting the cat or stealing pennies from the sugar bowl. His
grandmother, our youngest sister, married poor white trash,
and although she never said a word against them, we were all
of a mind that she regretted it to her dying day." She paused
to take a sip of tea, and the cup rattled against the saucer as
she replaced it. "I suppose Nelson's riled up on account of our
Sunday drives, although it seems to me reporting us to the police is extreme. Did you come out here to arrest us?"

Miss Larkspur giggled. "What would Papa say if he were
here to see us being arrested? Can't you imagine the look on
his face, Columbine? He'd be fit to be tied, and he'd most likely
throw this nice young thing right out the door."

"I didn't come out here to arrest you," I said hastily, "and
I didn't come to talk about your driving. As long as you don't

run anybody down, stay on this road, and never ever go on the highway, it's okay with me."

"But not with Nelson." Miss Columbine sighed as she finished her tea. "He wants us to give up our home, our car, our beloved Eppie, and go live in a stranger's house with a bunch of old folks. Who knows what other fool rules they'd have in a house where they don't allow pets?"

"But, Columbine," Miss Larkspur said, her face puckering wistfully, "Nelson says they serve nice meals and have tea with sandwiches and pound cake every afternoon. I can't recollect when I last tasted pound cake—unless it was at Mama's last birthday party. She died of influenza back in September of fifty-eight, not three weeks after Papa brought the new car all the way from Memphis, Tennessee." She took a tissue from her cuff and dabbed her eyes. "Papa died the next year, some say on account of losing the store, but I always thought he was heartsick over poor—"

"Larkspur, you're rambling like a wild turkey," Columbine said sternly but with affection. "This girl doesn't want to hear our family history. Frankly, I don't find it that interesting. I think we'd better hear what she has to say so she can be on her way." She stroked Eppie's head, and the cat obligingly growled at yours truly.

"Is Eppie the only reason you won't consider this retirement house?" I asked. I realized it was not such an easy question and plunged ahead. "You don't have to make a decision until you've visited. I'm sure Nelson would be delighted to take you there at tea time."

"Do you think he would?" Miss Larkspur clasped her hands together and her cloudy eyes sparkled briefly.

Miss Columbine shook her head. "We cannot visit under false pretenses, Larkspur, and come what may, we will not abandon Eppie after all these years. When the Good Lord sees fit to take him from us, we'll think about moving to town."

The object of discussion stretched his front legs and squirmed until he was on his back, his claws digging into their legs demandingly. When Miss Columbine rubbed his bloated belly, he purred with all the delicacy of a truck changing gears.

"Thank you for tea," I said, rising. "I'll let myself out." I was almost at the front door when I stopped and turned back to them. "You won't be driving until Easter, will you?"

"Not until Easter," Miss Columbine said firmly.

I returned to the PD, dried myself off with a handful of paper towels, and called Nelson at the motel to report my failure.

"It's the cat, isn't it?" he said. "They're willing to live in squalor because they won't give up that sorry excuse for a cat. You know, honey, I'm beginning to wonder if they haven't wandered too far out in left field to know what's good for them. I guess I'd better talk to a lawyer when I get back to Pine Bluff."

"You're going to force them to move?"

"I feel so bad, honey, but I don't know what else to do and it's for their own good."

"What's in it for you, Nelson?"

"Nothing." He banged down the receiver.

"My shoe's full of water," Ruby Bee grumbled as she did her best to avoid getting smacked in the face by a bunch of soggy leaves. It wasn't all that easy, since she had to keep her flashlight trained on the ground in case of snakes or other critters. The worst of it was that Estelle had hustled her out the door on this harebrained mission without giving her a chance to change clothes, and now her best blue dress was splattered with mud and her matching blue suede shoes might as well go straight into the garbage can. "Doncha think it's time to stop acting like overgrown Girl Scouts and just drive up to the door, knock real politely, and ask our questions in the living room?"

Estelle was in the lead, mostly because she had the better flashlight. "At least it's stopped raining, Miss Moanie Mouth. You're carrying on like we had to go miles and miles, but it ain't more than two hundred feet to begin with and we're within spittin' distance already."

"I'd be within spittin' distance of my bed if we'd dropped in and asked them." Ruby Bee stepped over a log and right into a puddle, this time filling her other shoe with cold water and forcing her to bite her tongue to keep from blurting out some-

thing unseemly. However, she figured she'd better pay more
attention to the job at hand, which was sneaking up on the
Banebury girls' garage through the woods behind it.

"I told you so," Estelle said as she flashed her light on the
backside of the building. "Now turn out your light and stay
real close. If that door's not locked, we'll be inside quicker than
a preacher says his prayers at night."

The proverbial preacher would have had time to bless a lot
of folks. The door wasn't locked, but it was warped something
awful and it took a good five minutes of puffing and grunting
to get it open far enough for them to slip inside.

Ruby Bee stopped to catch her breath. "I still don't see why
you're so dadburned worried about them seeing us. They're
both blind as bats."

"Hush!" Estelle played her light over the black sedan.
"Lordy, they made 'em big in those days, didn't they? You
could put one of those little Japanese cars in the trunk of this
one, and have enough room left for a table and four chairs.
And look at all that chrome!"

"This ain't the showroom of a car dealership," Ruby Bee
said in the snippety voice that always irritated Estelle, which
was exactly what she intended for it to do, what with her ruined shoes and toes nigh onto frozen. "If you want to stand
there and admire it all night, that's fine, but I for one have
other plans. I'll see if it says the model on the back, and you
try the interior."

She was shining her light on the license plate and calculating
how many years it had been since it expired when Estelle
screamed. Before she could say a word, Estelle dashed out the
door, the beam from the flashlight bobbling like a ping-pong
ball. Mystified but not willing to linger on her own, Ruby Bee
followed as fast as she dared, and only when she caught Estelle
halfway through the woods did she learn what had caused the
undignified retreat.

According to Estelle, there'd been a giant rat right in the
front seat of the car, its lone amber eye glaring like the devil's
own. Ruby Bee snorted in disbelief, but she didn't go back to
have a look for herself.

*   *   *

The next morning, sweet inspiration slapped me up the side of the head like a two by four. It had to be the car. I lunged for the telephone so hastily that my poor duck fell to the floor, and called Plover, a state cop with whom I occasionally went to a movie or had dinner. "What do you know about antique cars?" I demanded, bypassing pleasantries.

"They're old. Some of them are real old."

"Did you forget to jump start your brain this morning? I need to find out the current value of a particular car, and I assumed you were up on something macho like this."

He let out a long-suffering sort of sigh. "I can put gas in one at the self-service pump, and I know how to drive it. That's the extent of my so-called macho knowledge."

"Jesus, Plover," I said with a sigh of my own, "you'd better get yourself a frilly pink skirt and a pair of high heel sneakers. While you're doing that, let me talk to someone in the barracks with balls who knows about cars, okay?"

He hung up on what I thought was a very witty remark. State cops were not renowned for their humor, I told myself as I flipped open the telephone directory and hunted up the number of the Lincoln dealer in Farberville. The man who answered was a helluva lot more congenial, possibly (and mistakenly) in hopes he was dealing with a potential buyer.

Alas, he was no better informed than Plover about the current market value of a '58 Lincoln Continental, but his attitude was much brighter and he promised to call me back as soon as possible.

Rather than waste the time patting myself on the back, I called Plover, apologized for my smart-mouthed remark, and explained what I surmised was going on. "It's the car he's after," I concluded. "The house and land are close to worthless, but this old Lincoln could be a collector's dream."

"Maybe," he said without conviction, "but you can't arrest him for anything. I don't know if what he tried to do constitutes fraud, but in any case, he failed. He can't get his hands on the car until they die."

"Or he has them declared incompetent," I said. "I suppose

I could let him know that I'm aware of his scheme, and that I'll testify on their behalf if he tries anything further."

We chatted aimlessly for a while, agreed to a dinner date in a few days, and hung up. I was preparing to dial the number of Nelson's motel room when the phone rang.

The dealer had my information. I grabbed a pencil and wrote down a few numbers, thanked him, and replaced the receiver with a scowl of disappointment. If the car was in mint condition (aka in its original wrapper), it might bring close to ten thousand dollars. The amounts then plummeted: sixty-five hundred for very good, less than five thousand for good, and on down to four hundred fifty as a source for parts.

It wasn't the car, after all, but simply a case of letting myself listen to the suspicious minds in Ruby Bee's Bar & Grill. I picked up the balsa wood and turned my attention to its little webbed feet.

It normally doesn't get dark until five-thirty or so, but the heavy clouds had snuffed out the sunset. I decided to call it a day (not much of one, though) and find out if Ruby Bee was in a more hospitable mood. I had locked the back door and switched off the light when the telephone rang. After a short debate centering around meatloaf versus professional obligations, I reluctantly picked up the receiver.

"Arly! You got to do something! Somebody's gonna get killed if you don't do something!"

"Calm down, Estelle," I said, regretting that I hadn't heeded the plea from my stomach. "What's the problem?"

"I'm so dadburned all shook up I can barely talk!"

I'd had too much experience with her to be overcome with alarm. "Give it your best shot."

"It's the Banebury girls! They just drove by my house, moving real smartly down the middle of the road, and no headlights! I was close enough to my driveway to whip in and get out of their way, but I'm thanking my lucky stars I saw 'em before they ran me over with that bulldozer of a car."

I dropped the receiver, grabbed my car keys, and ran out to the side of the highway. I saw nothing coming from the south, but if they were driving without lights, I wouldn't be the only one not to see them coming . . . relentlessly, in a great black death machine.

"Damn!" I muttered as I got in my car, manuevered around, and headed down the highway to the turnoff for County 102. Miss Columbine couldn't see anything in front of her, and Miss Larkspur was legally blind. A dynamite duo. I muttered a lot more things, none of them acceptable within my mother's earshot.

It was supper time, and the highway was blessedly empty. I squealed around the corner and stopped, letting my lights shine down the narrow road. The wet pavement glistened like a snakeskin. They had passed Estelle's house at least three or four minutes ago. Presuming they were not in a ditch, they would arrive at the intersection any minute. Maybe Nelson had a justifiable reason to have them declared incompetent, I thought as I gripped the steering wheel and peered into the darkness. I hadn't seen any bunnies hopping outside my window, and if there were chocolate eggs hidden in the PD, I hadn't found them.

It occurred to me that I was in more than minimal danger, parked as I was in their path. However, I couldn't let them go on their merry way. A conscientious cop would have forbidden them to drive and confiscated the keys. I'd practically given them my blessing.

My headlights caught the glint of a massive black hood bearing down on me. With a yelp, I changed the beam to high, fumbled with a switch until the blue light on the roof began to rotate, grabbed a flashlight, and jumped out of my car. I waved the light back and forth as the monster bore down on me, and I had some sharp insights into the last thoughts of potential roadkill.

All I could see was the reflection on the chrome as the car came at me, slowly yet determinedly. The blue light splashed on the windshield, as did my flashlight. "Miss Columbine!" I yelled. "Miss Larkspur! You've got to stop!" I retreated behind my car and continued yelling.

The car shuddered, then, at the last moment, stopped a good

six inches from my bumper (and a six-hour session with the mayor, trying to explain the bill from the body shop).

I pried my teeth off my lower lip, switched off the flashlight, and went to the driver's window. Miss Columbine sat rigidly behind the wheel, but Miss Larkspur leaned forward and, with a little wave, said, "It's Arly, isn't it? How are you, dear?"

"Much better than I was a minute ago," I said. "I thought we agreed that you wouldn't be driving until this spring, Miss Columbine. A day later you're not only out, but at night without headlights."

"When you're blind," she said tartly, "darkness is not a factor. This is an emergency. Since we don't have a telephone, we had no choice but to drive for help."

"That's right," said Miss Larkspur. "Eppie has been catnapped. We're beside ourselves with worry. He likes to roam around the yard during the afternoon, but this evening he did not come to the back door to demand his supper. Columbine and I searched as best we could, but poor Eppie has disappeared. It's not like him, not at all."

"Larkspur is correct," Miss Columbine added. Despite her gruff voice and expressionless face, a tear trickled down her cheek. She wiped it away and tilted her head to look at me. "I am loath to go jumping to conclusions, but in this case, it's hard not to."

"I agree," I said, gazing bleakly at the darkness surrounding us. It may not have been a factor for them, but it sure as hell was for me. "Let's go back to your place and I'll try to find Eppie. Maybe he's already on the porch, waiting to be fed. I'll move my car off the road, and then, if you don't object, I think it's safer for me to drive your car back for you."

A few minutes later I was sitting in the cracked leather upholstery of the driver's seat, trying to figure out the controls on the elaborate wooden dashboard. There was ample room for three of us in the front seat, and possibly a hitchhiker or two. Once I'd found first gear, I turned around in the church parking lot, took a deep breath, and let 'er fly.

"This is a daunting machine," I said.

Giggling, Miss Larkspur put her hand on my arm and said,

"Papa brought it all the way from Memphis, as I told you. He'd gone there on account of Cousin Pearl being at the hospital, and we were flabbergasted when he drove up a week later in a shiny new car. This was after he'd lost the store, you see, and we didn't even own a car. We felt real badly about him going all the way to Memphis on the bus, but he and Cousin Pearl were kissin' cousins, and she was dying in the Baptist Hospital, so—"

"The Methodist Hospital," Miss Columbine corrected her. "I swear, some days you go on and on like you ain't got a brain in your head. Papa must have told us a hundred times how he met that polite young soldier whose mother was dying in the room right next to Cousin Pearl's."

"I suppose so," Miss Larkspur conceded, "but Cousin Pearl was a Baptist."

I pulled into the rutted driveway beside their house. The garage door was open, so I eased the car inside, turned off the ignition, and leaned back to offer a small prayer. "Why don't you wait in the house? I'll have a look out back."

"I can't believe our own kin would do such a thing," Miss Columbine said as she took Miss Larkspur's arm. I took the other and we moved slowly toward the back porch.

I believed it, and I had a pretty good idea why he'd done it. Once they were inside, I went back to the car, looked at the contents of the glove compartment to confirm my suspicions, and set off across the field. I'd had enough sense to bring my flashlight, but it was still treacherously wet and rough and I wasn't in the mood to end up with my feet in the air and my fanny in the mud. I could think of a much better candidate.

I froze as my light caught a glittery orb moving toward me in an erratic pattern. It came closer, and at last I made out Eppie's silhouette as he bounded past me in the direction of the house. His yowl of rage shattered the silence for a heart-stopping moment, then he was gone and I was once again alone in the field with a twenty-year-old memory of the path that led to Boone Creek.

Long before I arrived at the bank, I heard a stream of curses and expletives way too colorful for my sensitive ears. I followed the sound and stopped at a prudent distance to shine my light on Nelson Mullein. He was not a pretty picture as he futilely attempted to slither up the muddy incline, snatching at clumps of weeds that uprooted in his hands. He was soaked to the skin. His face was distorted not only by a swath of mud across one cheek, but also by angry red scratches, some of which were oozing blood.

"Who is it?" he said, blinking into the light.

"It's traditional to take your clothes off when you skinny-dip in the creek."

"It's you, the lady cop." He snatched at a branch, but it broke and he slid back to the edge of the inky water. "Can you give me a hand, honey? It's like trying to climb an oil slick, and I'm about to freeze to death."

"Oh, my goodness," I said as I scanned the ground with the light until it rested on a shapeless brown mound nearby. "Could that be a gunny sack? Why, I do believe it is. I hope you didn't put Eppie in it in an unsuccessful attempt to drown him in the creek."

"I've never seen that before in my life. I came down here to search for the cat. The damn thing was up in that tree, me-owing in a right pitiful fashion, but when I tried to coax him down, I lost my footing and fell into the water. Why don't you try to find a sturdy branch so I can get up the bank?"

I squatted next to the gunny sack. "This ol' thing's nearly ripped to shreds. I guess Eppie didn't take kindly to the idea of being sent to Cat Heaven before his time. By the way, I know about the car, Mr. Mullein."

"That jalopy?" he said uneasily. He stopped skittering in the mud and wiped his face. "I reckoned on getting six, maybe seven thousand for it from an ol' boy what lives in Pine Bluff. That, along with the proceeds from the sale of the property, ought to be more than enough to keep my great-grandaunts from living the way they do, bless their brave souls."

"It ought to be more than enough for them to have the house remodeled and pay for a full-time housekeeper," I said as I rose, the gunny sack dangling between my thumb and forefinger. "I'm taking this along as evidence. If you ever again so much as set one foot in Maggody, I'll tell those brave souls what you tried to do. You may be their only relative, but someone might suggest they leave what's going to be in the range of half a million dollars to a rest home for cats!"

"You can't abandon me like this." He gave me a view of his pearly white teeth, but it was more of a snarl than a smile. "Don't be cruel like that, honey."

"Watch me." Ignoring his sputters, I took my tattered treasure and walked back across the field to the house. Miss Columbine took me into the living room, where her sister had swaddled Eppie in a towel.

"Him was just being a naughty kitty," she said, stroking the cat's remaining ear and nuzzling his head.

I accepted a cup of tea, and once we were settled as before, said, "That polite young soldier gave your papa the car, didn't he?"

Miss Columbine nodded. "Papa didn't know what to think, but the boy was insistent about how he'd gone from rags to riches and how it made him feel good to be able to give folks presents. Papa finally agreed, saying it was only on account of how excited Mama would be."

"It was charity, of course," Miss Larkspur added, "but the boy said he wanted to do it because of Papa's kindness in the waiting room. The boy even told Papa that he was a hillbilly cat himself, and never forgot the little town in Mississippi where he was born."

Eppie growled ominously, but I avoided meeting his hostile eye and said, "He was called the Hillbilly Cat, back in the earliest stage of his career. The original paperwork's in the glove compartment, and his signature is on the bill of sale and registration form." I explained how much the car would bring and agreed to supervise the sale for them. "This means, of course, that you won't be driving anymore," I added.

"But how will we get to church on Easter morning?" Miss Larkspur asked.

Miss Columbine smiled. "I reckon we can afford a limousine, Larkspur. Let's heat up some nice warm milk for Eppie. He's still shivering from his . . . adventure outside."

"Now that we'll be together, will you promise to never run away again?" Miss Larkspur gently scolded the cat.

He looked at her, then at me on the off chance I'd try to pet him and he could express his animosity with his claws.

I waved at him from the doorway, told the ladies I'd be in touch after I talked with the Lincoln dealer, and wished them a pleasant evening. I walked down the road to my car, and I was nearly there before I realized Eppie was a nickname. Once he'd been the Hillbilly Cat, and his death had broken hearts all around the world. But in the Banebury household, Elvis Presley was alive and well—and still the King.

"Give me that shovel," Estelle hissed. "All you're doing is poking the dirt like you think this is a mine field."

Ruby Bee eased the blade into the muddy soil, mindful of the splatters on the hem of her coat and the caked mud that made her shoes feel like combat boots. "Hold your horses," she hissed back, "I heard a clink. I don't want to break the jar and ruin the money."

Estelle hurried over and knelt down to dig with her fingers. "Ain't the Banebury girls gonna be excited when we find their Papa's buried treasure! I reckon we could find as much as a thousand dollars before the night is out." She daintily blotted her forehead with her wrist. "It's a darn shame about the car, but if it ain't worth much, then it ain't. It's kinda funny how that man at the Lincoln dealership rattled off the prices like he had 'em written out in front of him and was wishing somebody'd call to inquire. Of course I wasn't expecting to hear anything different. Everybody knows just because a car's old doesn't mean it's valuable."

A lot of responses went through Ruby Bee's mind, none of them kindly. She held them back, though, and it was just as well when Estelle finally produced a chunk of brick, dropped it back in the hole, stood up, and pointed her finger like she thought she was the high and mighty leader of an expedition.

"Start digging over there, Ruby Bee," she said, "and don't worry about them seeing us from inside the house. I told you time and again, they're both blind."

Enduring As Dust

Bruce Holland Rogers

I DRIVE PAST THE DEPARTMENT of Agriculture every morning on my way to work, and every morning I slow to a crawl so that I can absorb the safe and solid feel of that building as I go by. The north side of Agriculture stretches for two uninterrupted city blocks. The massive walls look as thick as any castle's. Inside, the place is a warren of offices and suboffices, a cozy organizational hierarchy set in stone. I've often thought to myself that if an H-bomb went off right over the Mall, then the White House, the Capitol, the memorials and the reflecting pools would all be blown to ash and steam, but in the midst of the wreckage and the settling dust, there would stand the Department of Agriculture, and the work inside its walls would go securely on.

I don't have that kind of security. The building that houses the Coordinating Administration for Productivity is smaller than our agency's name. The roof leaks. The walls are thin and haven't been painted since the Great Depression.

That I am here is my own fault. Twenty years ago, when I worked for the Bureau of Reclamation, I realized that the glory

89

days of public dam building were over. I imagined that a big RIF wave was coming to the bureau, and I was afraid that I'd be one of those drowned in the Reduction In Force. So I went looking for another agency.

When I found the Coordinating Administration for Productivity, I thought I had found the safest place in Washington to park my career. I'd ask CAP staffers what their agency did.

"We advise other agencies," they would say.

"We coordinate private and public concerns."

"We review productivity."

"We revise strategies."

"We provide oversight."

"But clearly, clearly, we could always do more."

In other words, nobody knew. From the top down, no one could tell me precisely what the administrative mission was. And I thought to myself, I want to be a part of this. No one will ever be able to suggest that we are no longer needed, that it's time for all of us to clear out our desks, that our job is done, because no one knows what our job is.

But I was wrong about the Bureau of Reclamation. It hasn't had a major project for two decades, doesn't have any planned, and yet endures, and will continue to endure, through fiscal year after fiscal year, time without end. It is too big to die.

The Coordinating Administration for Productivity, on the other hand, employs just thirty civil servants. We're always on the bubble. With a stroke of the pen, we could vanish from next year's budget. All it would take is for someone to notice us long enough to erase us. And so, as I soon learned, there was an administrative mission statement after all: Don't Get Noticed.

That's why we never complained to GSA about the condition of our building, why we turned the other cheek when FDA employees started parking in our lot and eventually took it over. That's also why no one ever confronted the secretaries about the cats named Dust. And above all, that is why I was so nervous on the morning that our chief administrator called an "urgent meeting."

I sat waiting outside of the administrator's office with Susana de Vega, the assistant administrator, and Tom Willis, Susana's deputy. "I don't like this," Tom said. "I don't like this one damn bit."

Susana hissed at him and looked at the administrator's secretary. But Roxie wasn't listening to us. She was talking, through an open window, to the cat on the fire escape. The cat was a gray tom with the tattered ears of a streetfighter. He backed up warily as Roxie put the food bowl down. "Relax, Dust," she said. "I'm not going to hurt you."

It was January, a few days before the presidential inauguration, and the air coming in through the window was cold, but nobody asked Roxie to close it.

"When has Cooper ever called an *urgent* meeting?" Tom continued in a lower voice. "Hell, how many times has he called a meeting of any damn kind? He's up to something. He's got to throw his goddam Schedule-C weight around while he still has it to throw."

Throwing his weight around didn't sound like Bill Cooper, but I didn't bother to say so. After all, Cooper was a political appointee on his way out, so whether he threw his weight around or not, Tom's underlying point was correct: Cooper was a loose cannon. He had nothing to lose. Intentionally or not, he might blow us up.

Roxie waited to see if the cat would consent to having his chin scratched, but Dust held his ground until the window was closed. Even then, he approached the food warily, as if checking for booby traps.

Susana told Tom to relax. "Two weeks," she reminded him. "Three at the outside."

"And then god only knows what we'll be getting," Tom said, pulling at his chin. "I hate politics."

Roxie's intercom buzzed, and without turning away from the cat she told us, "You can go in now."

I followed Susana and Tom in, and found Cooper nestled deeply in his executive chair, looking as friendly and harmless as he ever had. His slightly drooping eyelids made him seem, as always, half asleep. He waved us into our seats, and as I sat down, I realized how little he had done to personalize his office in the twelve years of his tenure. Everything in the room was government issue. There weren't any family pictures or the usual paperweights made by children or grandchildren. In fact, there wasn't anything on the surface of his desk at all. It was as if Cooper had been anticipating, from the day he moved in, the day when he would have to move out.

There was *some* decoration in the room, a pen and ink drawing on the wall behind Cooper, but that had been there for as long as I had been with the CAP. It showed an Oriental-looking wooden building next to a plot of empty ground, and I knew from having looked once, maybe fifteen years ago, that the drawing wasn't just hung on the wall. The frame had been nailed into the paneling, making it a permanent installation.

"People," Cooper said from deep inside his chair, "we have a problem." He let that last word hang in the air as he searched for what to say next.

Susana, Tom and I leaned forward in our chairs.

"An impropriety," he went on.

We leaned a little more.

"A mystery."

We watched expectantly as Cooper opened his desk drawer and took out a sheet of paper. He studied it for a long time, and then said, "You people know my management style. I've been hands-off. I've always let you people handle the details," by which he meant that he didn't know what we did all day and didn't care, so long as we told him that everything was running smoothly. He tapped the sheet of paper and said, "But here is something that demands my attention, and I want it cleared up while I'm still in charge."

And then he read from the letter in his hand. The writer represented something called the Five-State Cotton Consortium, and he had come to Washington to get advice on federal funding for his organization. He had taken an employee of the Coordinating Administration for Productivity to lunch, picking her brain about the special appropriations process as well as various grant sources. The woman had been very helpful, and the letter writer just wanted Cooper to know that at least one member of his staff was really on the ball. The helpful staffer's name was Kim Semper.

At the sound of that name, I felt ice form in the pit of my stomach. I stared straight ahead, keeping my expression as plain as I could manage. I knew some of what Cooper was going to say next, but I tried to look genuinely surprised when he told us what had happened after he received the letter.

"I wanted to touch base with Ms. Semper and make sure that the citizen hadn't actually paid for her lunch. You people know as well as I do that we don't want any conflict of interest cases."

"Of course not," said Susana. "But I don't see how there could be any such conflict. We don't actually make funding decisions."

"We don't?" Cooper said, and then he recovered to say, "No, of course not. But you people will agree that we wouldn't want even the *appearance* of impropriety. And anyway, that doesn't matter. What matters is that in my search for Kim Semper, I came up empty. We don't have an employee by that name."

Trying to sound more convincing than I felt, I said, "Maybe it's a mistake, Bill. Maybe the letter writer had the name wrong, or sent the letter to the wrong agency."

"Hell, yes!" Tom said with too much enthusiasm. "It's just some damn case of mistaken identity!"

But Cooper wasn't going to be turned easily. "I called the citizen," he told us. "No mistake. Someone is posing as an officer of our agency, a criminal offense."

I said, "Doesn't there have to be intent to defraud for this to be a crime?"

Cooper frowned. "The citizen did buy lunch for this Kim Semper. She benefitted materially." He shook the letter at me. "This is a serious matter."

"And one we'll get to the bottom of," Susana promised.

"I want it done before my departure," Cooper said. "I don't want to saddle my successor with any difficulties," by which he meant that he didn't want to leave behind any dirty laundry that might embarrass him when he was no longer in a position to have it covered up.

Susana said again, "We'll get to the bottom of it."

Cooper nodded at Tom. "I want a single point of responsibility on this, so the personnel director will head up the investigation."

With Cooper still looking at him, Tom looked at me expectantly, and I felt compelled to speak up. "That would be me," I said. "Tom's your deputy assistant."

"Of course," Cooper said, covering. He turned to me. "And you'll report to him." Then he added, "You aren't too busy to take care of this matter, I assume."

"It'll be tight," I said, thinking of the Russian novel I'd been wading through for the last week, "but I'll squeeze it in."

Outside of Cooper's office, Susana patted Tom's shoulder, then mine, and said with complete ambiguity, "You know what to do." Then she disappeared down the hall, into her own office.

Roxie's cat was gone, but Roxie had something else to distract her now. She was reading a GPO publication called, *Small Business Administration Seed Projects: Program Announcement and Guidelines*. She didn't even look up when Tom hissed at me, "Sit on it!"

"What?"

"You know damn well what I mean," Tom said through his teeth. "I don't know what this Kim Semper thing is all about, and I don't want to know! This is just the kind of problem that could blow us out of the goddam water!"

I said, "Are you telling me to ignore an assignment from the chief administrator?"

I could see in Tom's eyes the recognition that he had already been too specific. "Not at all," he said in a normal voice, loud enough for Roxie to overhear if she were listening. "I'm telling you to handle this in the most appropriate fashion." Then he, too, bailed out, heading for his own office.

I found my secretary, Vera, trying to type with a calico cat in her lap. The cat was purring and affectionately digging its claws into Vera's knee.

"Damn it, Vera," I said, surprising myself, "the memo specifies feeding only. Everybody knows that. You are not supposed to have the cat inside the building!"

"You hear that, Dust?" Vera said as she rubbed behind the cat's ears. "It's back out into the cold with you." But she made no move to get up.

"Hold my calls," I growled. I went into my office and closed the door, wishing that I had a copy of the legendary memo so that I could read chapter and verse to Vera. It was bad enough that the secretaries had distorted the wording of the memo, issued well over twenty years ago, that had allowed them to feed a stray cat named Dust, "and only a cat named Dust." It seemed like every so often, they had to push beyond even the most liberal limits of that allowance, and no manager was willing to make an issue of it, lest it turn into a civil service grievance that would bring an OPM investigation crashing down around our ears.

I didn't stew about the cat for long. I still had Kim Semper on my mind. It took me a few minutes to find the key to my file cabinet, but once I had the drawer open, there weren't many folders to search through before I found what I wanted. I untaped the file folder marked PRIVATE and pulled out the letter. It was addressed to me and sported an eleven-year-old date. "After failing to determine just who her supervisor is," the text began, "I have decided to write to you, the Director of Personnel, to commend one of your administrators, Miss Kim Semper." The story from there was pretty much the same: a citizen had come to Washington looking for information, had stumbled across the Coordinating Administration for Productivity, and had ended up buying Semper's lunch in exchange for her insights on the intricacies of doing business in the Beltway. Though he had been unable to contact her subsequently, her advice had been a big help to him.

After checking the personnel files, I had called the letter writer to tell him that he'd been mistaken, that there was no Kim Semper here at the CAP. Maybe, I suggested, he had gone to some other agency and confused the names? But he was sure that it was the CAP that he had consulted, and he described our building right down to the tiny, nearly unreadable gray lettering that announced the agency's name on the front door.

In a government agency, a mystery, any mystery, is a potential bomb. If you're not sure of what something is, then you assume that it's going to blow up in your face if you mess with it. At the CAP, where everything was uncertain and shaky to begin with, the unknown seemed even more dangerous. So I had buried the letter.

Now maybe it was coming back to haunt me. I wondered if I should cover my tail by Xeroxing my letter and bringing Cooper a copy right now. "Hey, Bill. I had to check my files on this, to make sure, but would you believe . . ." Maybe that would be good damage control.

But maybe not. After all, Cooper seemed to think this was an urgent matter. I had known about it for eleven years and done nothing. And my letter was so old that I probably didn't have to worry about it hurting me if I didn't bring up its existence. By now, the writer himself might not even remember sending it to me. Perhaps the man was even dead. If I kept my mouth shut, it was just possible that no one would ever know about my Kim Semper letter. And if that was what I wanted, then it would help my cause to do just what Tom had urged: To sit on the investigation, to ignore Kim Semper until the executive branch resignations worked their way down, layer by layer, from the new president's cabinet to our agency, and Cooper was on his way.

Either option, hiding the letter or revealing it, had its dangers. No matter how I played it out in my mind, I couldn't see the safe bet. I returned to what I'd been doing before the meeting with Cooper, and I should have been able to concentrate on it. Napoleon was watching this Polish general, who wanted to impress him, trying to swim some cavalry across a Russian river, but the horses were drowning and everything was a mess. It was exciting, but it didn't hold my attention. I read the same page over and over, distracted with worry.

At the end of the day, there was no cat in Vera's lap, but there was a skinny little tabby begging on the fire escape. At her desk, Vera was pouring some cat food into a bowl labeled, "Dust."

"Sorry I snapped earlier," I said.

"Bad day?" Vera said, opening the window.

"The worst," I told her, noticing the stack of outgoing mail on her desk. "Is that something I asked you to do?"

"Oh, I'm just getting some information for the staff library," she said.

I nodded, trying to think of something managerial to say. "You're self-directed, Vera. I like to see that."

"Oh, I've always been that way," she told me. "I can't stand to be idle." She opened the window to feed the cat and said, "Here you go, Dust."

Cooper called another meeting for Thursday of the next week. It was the day after the inauguration, and he must have felt the ticking clock. Before the meeting, Tom called me.

"How's your investigation coming?" he said.

"Slowly."

"Good. That's damn good. See you in the old man's office."

For once there wasn't a cat on Roxie's fire escape. Cooper's door was open, and I walked right in. Susana and Tom were already there, and Cooper motioned me to a seat. Cooper didn't waste any time.

"What have you got?"

I opened my notebook. "First, I double-checked the personnel files, not just the current ones, but going back twenty-five years." I looked at Cooper grimly. "No one by the name of Kim Semper has ever worked for the Coordinating Administration for Productivity."

"Yes, yes," Cooper said. "What else?"

"I called over to the Office of Personnel Management. There is not now, nor has there ever been, anywhere in the civil service system, an employee named Kim Semper." I closed the notebook and put on the face of a man who has done his job well.

Cooper stared at me. I pretended to look back at him earnestly, but my focus was actually on the framed pen and ink behind him. If I had to give it a title, I decided, it would be, "Japanese Shed With Empty Lot."

At last Cooper said, "Is that all?"

"Well, Bill, I haven't been able to give this my full attention."

"It's been a week, a *week* since I brought this up to you people."

"And a hellish week it's been," I said, looking to Tom for help.

"That's true," Tom jumped in. "The inauguration has stirred things up. We've had an unusually, ah, unusually heavy run of requests." Cooper frowned, and I could see Tom's hands tighten on the side of his chair. He was hoping, I knew, that Cooper wouldn't say, "Requests for what? From whom?"

Susana saved us both by saying, "I'm ashamed of the two of you! Don't you have any sense of priorities? And, Tom, you're supposed to be supervising this investigation. That means staying on top of it, making sure it's progressing." She turned to Cooper. "We'll have something substantial next week, Bill."

"I don't know, people," Cooper said. "Realistically, something like this is out of your purview. Maybe it calls for an outside investigator."

Cooper was almost certainly bluffing. Any dirt at the bottom of this would cling to him like tar if we brought in the consul general's office. He wanted to keep this internal as much as we did.

Even so, Susana paled. She played it cool, but it was a strain on her. "Why don't you see what we come up with in seven working days? Then you can decide."

Minutes later, in the hallway, Tom said, "So what now?"

"Don't look at me," Susana told him without breaking stride. "I pulled your bacon out of the fire, boys. Don't ask me to think for you, too." Then over her shoulder, she added, "You'd just better appear to be making progress by our next little get-together."

Before he left me standing alone in the hallway, Tom said, "You heard the lady, Ace. Let's see some goddam action."

In my office, with the door closed behind me, I finished another chapter of the Russian novel and then got right on the case. I cleared space on the floor and laid out the personnel files for the last eleven years. It made sense to assume that "Kim Semper" was an insider, or had an inside confederate who could arrange her lunchtime meetings. And I knew that Ms. Semper had been working this free-lunch scam since at least the date of my letter. I figured that I could at least narrow down my suspect pool by weeding out anyone who hadn't been with the CAP for that long.

Unfortunately, this didn't narrow things much. Even Cooper, by virtue of three straight presidential victories for his party, had been with the CAP for longer than that.

So what did I really have to go on? Just two letters of praise for Kim Semper, dated eleven years apart. The letter writers themselves had met Kim Semper, but there were good reasons for not calling them for more information. After all, I wanted to keep my letter buried to preserve my plausible deniability. And Cooper's letter writer had already been contacted once about Kim Semper. If I called again and grilled him, he might resent it, and I could use up his good will before I even knew what questions to ask. Also, he might get the impression that the Coordinating Administration for Productivity didn't have its act together, and who knew where that could lead? I didn't want a citizen complaining to his congressional rep.

What I needed was another source, but there wasn't one.

Or was there?

I arranged the personnel files on the floor to look like an organizational hierarchy. If someone were to send a letter praising an employee of the CAP, where might that letter go?

To the top, of course. That was Cooper.

And to the Director of Personnel. That was me.

But what about the space between these two? What about the Assistant Administrator and her Deputy? That is, what about Susana and Tom?

Outside of Susana's office, her administrative assistant, Peter, was preparing to feed a black cat on the fire escape. Almost as soon as he opened the window, Peter sneezed.

"Susana in?"

"Yes," Peter said, "but she's unavailable." He set the cat

bowl down and closed the window. Then he sneezed again.

"If you're so allergic," I said, "how come you're feeding the kitty?"

"Oh, I like cats, even if they do make my eyes swell shut." He laughed. "Anyway, feeding Dust is the corporate culture around here, right? When in Rome . . ."

From the other side of Susana's door, I could hear the steady beat of music.

I watched the stray cat as it ate. "I'm surprised, with all the cats on our fire escapes, that it isn't just one continuous cat fight out there."

"They're smart animals," Peter said. "Once they have a routine, they stay out of each other's way."

I nodded, but I wasn't really paying attention. Over the beat of the music, I could hear a female voice that wasn't Susana's counting *one-and-two-and-three-and—*

I went to her door and put my hand on the knob.

"I told you," Peter said. "Susana's unavailable. If you want to make an appointment . . ."

"This can't wait," I said. I opened the door.

Susana was in a leotard, and I caught her in the middle of a leg lift. She froze while the three women on the workout tape kept on exercising and counting without her.

"I told Peter I wasn't to be disturbed," she said, still holding her leg up like some varicolored flamingo.

"This won't take but a minute," I said. "In fact, you can go right on with your important government business while we talk."

She stopped the tape and glared at me. "What do you want?"

"To get to the bottom of this Kim Semper thing. And if that's what you really want too, then you can't be throwing me curve balls."

"What are you talking about?" She pushed the audiovisual cart between two file cabinets and threw a dust cover over it.

"I'm talking, Susana, about sitting on information. Or call it withholding evidence. I want your correspondence file on Kim Semper."

Susana circled behind her desk and sat down. Ordinarily, that would have been a good gesture, a way of reminding me that she was, after all, the assistant admin, and this was her turf I had invaded. But it was a hard move to pull off in a leotard. "Just what makes you think I even have such a file?"

That was practically a confession. I fought down a smile. "I'm on your side," I reminded her. "But we've got to show some progress on this. Cooper is on his last official breath. Dying men are unpredictable. But if we hold all the cards, how dangerous can he be?"

She stared over my head, no doubt thinking the same thoughts I had about my own Kim Semper letter. How would Cooper react to knowing that she'd had these letters in her files all along?

"You've got the file where, Susana? In your desk? In one of those cabinets? If I close my eyes," I said, closing them, "then I'll be able to honestly tell Cooper that I don't know *exactly* where my information came from. It was just sort of dropped into my lap."

It took her a minute of rummaging, and then a folder fell into my hands. I opened my eyes. The three letters ranged from two to ten years old.

"Read them in your own office," she said. "And next time, knock."

On my way out, I noticed that Peter was reading something called *America's Industrial Future: A Report of the Presidential Colloquium on U.S. Manufacturing Productivity for the Year 2020 and Beyond*. A thing like that wouldn't ordinarily stick in my mind, except that Tom's secretary, Janet, was reading the same report. She was also holding a mottled white and tan cat in her lap. I didn't bother to confront her about it—that was Tom's fight, if he wanted to fight it. I just knocked on Tom's door and stepped into his office.

He swept a magazine from his desk and into a drawer, but he wasn't fast enough to keep me from noting the cover feature: THE GIRLS OF THE PAC TEN. "What the hell do you want?" he growled.

"A hell of a lot more than I'm getting," I barked back.

"Damn little you've done to help this investigation along, Willis. Enough bullshit. I'm up to here with bullshit. I want your goddam Kim Semper correspondence file."

"Like hell." Tom glowered, but a little quiver of uncertainty ran across his lowered eyebrows. He wasn't used to being on the receiving end of such bluster.

"Cut the crap, Tom. This goddam Semper bullshit will toss us all on our asses if we don't give Cooper something to chew on. So give."

A little timidly, he said, "I don't know what you're . . ."

"Like hell," I said, waving de Vega's letters. "Susana came across, and I'd sure as hell hate to tell Cooper that you're the one stalling his goddam investigation."

He bit his lip and took a file cabinet key from his desk drawer. "Jesus," he said. "I've never seen you like this."

"You better hope like hell you never see it again," I said, which was probably overdoing things, but I was on a roll.

As I read it in my office, the first of Tom's letters cheered me considerably. One was twenty years old, which altered my suspect list quite a bit. From my array of files on the floor, I removed anyone who hadn't been with the CAP for the last two decades. That left just myself, Tom Willis, and Tom's secretary Janet. I picked up Janet's file and smiled. Kim Semper, I thought, you have met your match.

And then I read Tom's other letter, the most recent one of all, excepting Cooper's. It praised *Mr.* Kim Semper, for *his* dedication to public service.

No, I thought. This can't be right.

Unless there was more than one Kim Semper.

I sat down behind my desk. Hard. And I thought about the cat named Dust, who came in a dozen variations, but who, by long tradition, was always Dust, was always considered to be the same cat, because the ancient memo had allowed for the feeding of a cat named Dust, "and only a cat named Dust."

I picked up the phone and dialed the number of the man who had written to praise Mr. Semper. "Mr. Davis," I said when I had him on the line, "one of our employees is in line for a service award, and I just want to make sure it's going to the right person. You wrote a letter to us about a Mr. Kim Semper. Now, we've got a Kim Semple on our staff, and a Tim Kemper, but no Kim Semper. Could you do me the favor of describing the man who was so helpful?"

As lame stories go, this one worked pretty well. It sounded plausible, and it didn't make the CAP look bad. And it brought results. Davis was only happy to make sure Semper or Semple or Kemper got his due. The description fit Peter to a T.

I tried the next most recent letter, but the number had been disconnected. The next one back from that—I changed Tim Kemper to Lynn—brought me a good description of Roxie. The third call, the one that cinched it, paid off with a description that could only be my own Vera.

That's when I buzzed Vera into my office.

"I want a copy of the cat memo," I told her.

"The cat memo?"

"Don't fence with me. If you don't have a copy of it yourself, you know how to get one. I want it within the hour." Then I lowered my voice conspiratorially. "Vera, I don't have anything against cats. Trust me on that."

She had a copy in my hands in five minutes. When I looked at the date, I whistled. Dust the cat had been on this officially sanctioned meal ticket for more than forty years, much longer than I had supposed. The memo also named the secretary who had first started feeding Dust. After a phone call to OPM, I was on my way to Silver Spring, Maryland.

The house I stopped in front of was modest, but nonetheless stood out from all the other clapboard houses on that street. There were abstract, Oriental-looking sculptures in the garden. The white stones around the plum trees had been raked into tidy rows, and there was a fountain bubbling near the walkway to the front door.

A white-haired woman holding a gravel rake came around the side of the house, moving with a grace that belied her eighty years.

"Mrs. Taida?" I said. She looked up and waved me impatiently into the garden. As I opened the gate, I said, "I'm the one who called you, Mrs. Taida. From the Coordinating Administration for Productivity."

"Yes, of course," she said. As I approached, she riveted me with her gaze. Her eyes were blue as arctic ice.

"You are Janet Taida, yes?"

"You expected me to look more Japanese," she said. "Taida was my husband's name. Sakutaro Taida. The artist." She waved at the sculptures.

"I see," I said, then reached into my pocket for the photocopied memo. "Mrs. Taida, I want to talk to you about the cat named Dust."

"Of course you do," she said. "Come inside and I'll make some tea."

The house was furnished in the traditional Japanese style, with furniture that was close to the floor. While Mrs. Taida started the water boiling in the kitchen, I looked at the artwork hanging on the walls. There were paintings and drawings that seemed vaguely familiar, somehow, but it wasn't until I saw the big pen and ink on the far wall that I knew what I was looking at.

"There's a drawing like this in the administrator's office," I said when Mrs. Taida came into the room with the teapot.

"A drawing *almost* like that one," Mrs. Taida said. She waved toward a cushion. "Won't you sit down?" she commanded. She poured the tea. "That's a Shinto temple. It has two parts, two buildings. But only one stands at a time. Every twenty years, one is torn down and the other is rebuilt. They are both present, always. But the manifestation changes."

"The drawing at work shows the other phase," I said, "when the other building is standing and this one has been torn down."

Mrs. Taida nodded. A white long-haired cat padded into the room.

"Dust?" I said.

Taking up her teacup, Mrs. Taida shook her head. "No, there's only one Dust."

I laughed. "But like the temple, many manifestations." I unfolded the memo. "This memo, the Dust memo, mentions you by name, Mrs. Taida. You started it, didn't you? You were the administrator's secretary when the secretaries received their sanction to keep caring for, as it says here, 'a cat named Dust.' "

"Once we began to feed one, it was very hard to turn the others away. So I read the memo very carefully."

"Mrs. Taida, cats are one thing, but . . ."

"I know. Cats are one thing, but Kim Semper is far more serious, right?" She lowered her teacup. "Let me explain something to you," she said. "The Coordinating Administration for Productivity was commissioned over fifty years ago. They had a clear wartime purpose, which they completed, and then the agency began to drift. Your tea is getting cold."

She waited until I had picked it up and taken a sip.

"A government agency develops a culture, and it attracts people who are comfortable with that culture. After its wartime years the CAP attracted ostriches."

I opened my mouth, but she held up her hand.

"You can't deny it," she said. "For forty years, the CAP has been managed by men and women who wanted to rule over a quiet little fiefdom where nothing much happened."

She sipped her own tea.

"Do you have any idea what it's like to be a secretary under conditions like that?" She shook her head. "Nothing happens. There's too little to do, and the day just crawls by. You can't have any idea how hard it was, at the end of the war and with a Japanese husband, to get a government job. And then to have to sit on my hands all day, doing nothing . . ."

"Mrs. Taida . . ."

"I am not finished speaking," she said with authority, and I felt my face flush. "As I was saying, working at the CAP was like being a sailor on a rudderless ship. Have some more tea."

I held out my cup, as commanded.

"What endures in a government agency?" she asked as she poured again. "The management? The support staff? Job titles shift. Duties change. But the culture remains. It's like the tradition of a secretary feeding a stray cat at ten in the morning. The secretary may retire, but another will come, and if there's a tradition of feeding the stray cat at ten, then the person who takes the job will likely be someone who likes cats anyway. The cat may die or move on, but another will appear before long. The feeding goes on, even if who is fed and by whom changes over time."

She put the teapot down. "Administrators come and go, but the culture endures. And Kim Semper endures. When a citizen calls the agency for help, he isn't referred to management. No one at that level knows anything. No, the citizen is referred to Kim Semper. And for the pleasure of the work itself, of knowing things and being helpful, the secretaries do the job of the Coordinating Administration for Productivity. And they do a very good job. How many of those people who are helped by Kim Semper bother to write letters, do you suppose? And how many of the letters that are written actually end up in the hands of CAP administrators? Kim Semper provides good answers to hard questions about productivity and legislative action. I gave the CAP a rudder, you see. It operates from the galley, not the bridge."

"There's the question of ethics," I said. "There's the matter of lunches paid for by citizens, of benefit derived by fraud."

She looked at me long and hard. It was a look that said everything there was to say about collecting a GS-13 salary working for an agency where the managers were fuzzy about how they should fill their days. She didn't have to say a word.

"Well, what am I supposed to do then?" I said. "Now that I know the truth, what do I say when the administrator asks for my report?"

"You didn't get to where you are today without knowing how to stall," Mrs. Taida said. "You do what you do best, and let the secretaries do what *they* do best."

"What about *after* Cooper is gone?" I said. "This is a bomb just waiting to go off. This is the kind of thing that can sink a little agency like ours."

"The Coordinating Administration for Productivity is a fifty-year-old bureaucracy," Mrs. Taida said, "with a little secret that no one has discovered for forty years. You're the only one who threatens the status quo." She picked up our teacups and the pot. "If you don't rock the boat, I'm sure the CAP, along with Dust and Kim Semper, will endure for time without end. And now, if you don't mind, I have things to do."

I drove back to the office slowly. I knew what I had to do, but I didn't know exactly how to get it done. At least, not until I got as far as the Department of Agriculture. There, I pulled into the right lane and slowed to a crawl.

Size, I thought. The thing that comforts me about the Department of Agriculture is its size. It is big and white and easy to get lost in. That's what safety is.

I drove back and got right to work. It was a big job. I enlisted Vera and Roxie, along with Janet, Peter, and some of the secretaries from downstairs. I didn't explain in great detail what we were doing or why it was important. They understood. In a week, we had generated the very thing that Bill Cooper had called for.

"Results," I announced, shouldering between Susana and Tom to drop my report onto Cooper's desk. It landed with a thud. Cooper blinked slowly, then opened the heavy white binding to the first page. *A Report on Personnel and Operational Dislocation at the Coordinating Administration for Productivity*, it read. "Everything you need to know about Kim Semper is in there."

Cooper nodded. "It's, ah, impressive. You people really knocked yourselves out."

"Yes, sir," I said. "I can't take all the credit. Susana and Tom were instrumental, really."

Neither of them looked up. They were still staring at the report.

Cooper began to scan the executive summary, but his eyes began to glaze when he got to the paragraph about operational location as a time-and institution-based function not contingent upon the identity of the individual operator. "So can you summarize the contents for me?"

"Well," I said, "it's a bit involved. But you can get the gist of it in the summary that you're reading."

Cooper kept thumbing through the summary. It went on for ninety-three pages.

"To really get a complete sense of the situation," I said, "you'll need to read the complete report. Right, Susana?"

She nodded. "Of course."

"Tom?"

"You bet your ass. It's all there, though. Every damn bit of it." He said it with pride, as though he really had made some contribution.

"It took a thousand pages to get it said, Bill. And it really takes a thousand to make sense of it all. So, you see, I can't just give it to you in a sentence."

"I see," Cooper said, nodding, and he was still nodding, still looking at the four-inch volume, when Susana and Tom and I left the room.

"You're a goddam genius is what you are," Tom said. And Susana told me, "Good work."

And when Cooper cleared out for good, he left the report behind. It's there still, taking up space on his successor's desk. Sometimes when I see it sitting there, I think to myself that a bomb could go off in that room, and everything would be blown to hell but that plastic-bound, metal-spined, ten-pound volume of unreadable prose. It wouldn't suffer so much as a singed page.

It gives me a safe and solid feeling.

Buster

Bill Crider

WHEN THE PHONE RANG, HACK Jensen, the dispatcher at the Blacklin County Jail, picked it up on the first jingle.

"Sheriff's office," he said. "Hack speaking." He listened for a second. "Yes'm," he said. "Yes'm, Miss Onie. Yes'm." Every time he said "Yes'm," he nodded his head. "Yes'm. I'll tell him right now. Don't you do anything. He'll be out there before you know it."

Because of the dispatcher's respectful tone, Sheriff Dan Rhodes, sitting at his desk on the other side of the room, didn't need to hear Miss Onie's name to know that Hack was speaking to someone even older than himself. Hack was somewhere in his middle seventies, but Miss Onie was well over eighty.

Hack said "Yes'm" one more time and hung up the phone. He turned to Rhodes. "That was Miss Onie Calder. She says you better get out to her house quick. Says somebody's killed Buster."

Miss Onie lived in a two-story house on the far northwest side of Clearview, an area of town that had once been fashionable but that was now occupied mostly by tumbledown old homes with weeds growing high in the yards and trees that had not been trimmed for years. Her house was different from the others in the neighborhood only because it was bigger.

Rhodes parked the county car in front and walked up to the door. There were weeds springing up through the cracks in the sidewalk, and a young hackberry tree was pushing through a place on the edge of the porch where several boards were missing. There were high wooden columns on the porch, and their paint was cracked and flaking away, like the paint on the outside walls and window frames.

Rhodes banged on the screen door with the heel of his hand. The door rattled in the frame, making a considerable noise. When Miss Onie didn't appear immediately, he kept on banging. He knew that her hearing wasn't particularly good.

The door behind the screen was half wood and half glass, and Rhodes could see into the hallway. After a minute or so, he saw movement in the house and someone approached the door.

"Is that you, Dan Rhodes?" Miss Onie called out in a high, thin voice.

"Yes, ma'am," Rhodes said. "It's me."

He heard the sound of a deadbolt being pushed back and the door opened. Miss Onie stood behind the screen. She was about five feet tall and must have weighed a good hundred and sixty. She wore thick glasses and had her gray hair piled up in a bun.

She pushed on the screen and Rhodes moved out of the way. "Come on in," she said. "Buster's in the kitchen."

Rhodes went in the house and Miss Onie closed the door behind him. The place was a fire chief's nightmare.

To Rhodes' right, there was a stairway leading up to the second floor. The steps were piled high with old newspapers and magazines, some of them bundled together and tied with string, some of them simply sitting in loose stacks. Rhodes recognized the distinctive yellow spines of hundreds of issues of *National Geographic*.

The hallway was like the stair, and Rhodes had to turn sideways to make his way down it. There were stacks of newspapers, magazines, and other paper items. Rhodes saw a copy of the Clearview newspaper dated November 5, 1943, on top of one stack. On the top of another was a 1953 calendar from Calder's grocery.

Rhodes hadn't thought of that particular store for years. It had closed sometime around 1960, when Miss Onie's husband had died, but Rhodes could suddenly remember buying baseball cards there when he was a kid. He could still remember the smell of the gum that came with the cards.

The gum was flat, pink, and brittle, and he wished that he had about six pieces of it right now, strapped in front of his nose. The smell in Miss Onie's house was incredible.

Part of the reason was that Miss Onie never opened the windows of her house. Winter or summer, spring or fall, the windows remained tightly closed. So the smell had built up over the years. It was a combination of mustiness, age, and cats.

It was the cat smell that was the strongest, and it was clear to Rhodes why that was so.

Cats were everywhere.

There were yellow cats, gray cats, and black cats. There were calico cats and patchwork cats. There were big cats and middlesized cats, along with a few kittens. There were tomcats and pussycats. There were cats that had a vaguely oriental look and cats that looked like they had just come in out of the alley.

Rhodes didn't try to count them. There must have been forty or fifty of them.

They scratched at the fraying carpet on the stairs and at the peeling wallpaper. They seethed around Rhodes' legs, purring and meowing, bumping their heads against him, rubbing against his ankles. They walked down the hallway atop the magazines and papers. They peered at him from between the balustrades of the stairway. Cat hair floated in the air all around him and danced in front of his eyes.

He sneezed.

"Bless you," Miss Onie said.

Then they were in the kitchen, which was relatively free of clutter, except for a mound of cereal boxes that reached nearly to the ceiling in one corner and a line of bowls of dry cat food alternating with bowls of water along the baseboard.

On the cracked Formica top of the cabinet by the sink there was a package of something wrapped in foil. Pinkish liquid ran from the foil, and there were two cats on the counter lapping at the liquid with their tongues.

"Naugh-ty boys!" Miss Onie said, shooing them with her hands. They jumped lightly from the counter, landed on the floor, and mingled with the other cats.

"You know better than to play with Mama's lunch," Miss Onie said. She turned and looked at Rhodes. "Pork chops," she said.

Rhodes looked at the cat hair wafting all around and settling on the foil and wondered if he would ever eat pork chops again.

"Where's Buster?" he said.

"Over there," Miss Onie said, pointing at her kitchen table.

The table was made of oak and might have been attractive if it had ever been polished. On its dull surface lay the body of a huge ash-colored tom. The cat was stiff as a poker, its eyes open and glassy. As Rhodes looked at it, two other cats—not the same two who had been at the pork chops—levitated themselves up onto the table. They sniffed at Buster's mortal remains without much enthusiasm and then jumped silently back to the floor.

"Poisoned," Miss Onie said. She brushed at her cheek, where there was a red patch of a rash of some kind.

Rhodes wasn't surprised to see the rash. He found himself itching in all sorts of unlikely places, and he refrained from scratching only with a powerful effort of will.

"You're sure about that?" he said. "That Buster was poisoned, I mean?"

"It was that Ralph Ramsdell," Miss Onie said. "He's the one done it, because of Tuggle bein' such a bully. But that's not my fault. I can't help it if one of the boys is a little rowdy, can I? You know what they say."

"No," Rhodes said. "Maybe you better tell me."

"Boys will be boys," Miss Onie said, looking down at Buster. "That's what they say." She brushed at her eyes.

"Buster was such a good boy, too, nothin' at all like Tuggle, so I don't see why Ralph Ramsdell—"

"Maybe you better tell me about Tuggle," Rhodes said.

"Oh. Well, he just came here a few weeks back." Miss Onie looked around at the cats churning around the kitchen, some of them meowing, some of them purring, some of them not making a sound. "I swear, I don't know why cats keep comin' here. Just seems like this place attracts them, somehow."

"I guess some places are like that," Rhodes said. He sneezed.

"Bless you. I guess so. Anyway, Tuggle came here in bad shape. He'd been declawed on his front paws, couldn't climb a tree or anything. I thought he'd be happy here with the boys, but he's a real roisterer, that one. Goes out all the time, picks fights with the neighbor cats, especially that big orange one that belongs to Ralph Ramsdell. It's a real sight to see, the way he does. He can't fight with his front paws, but he rolls on his back and just works those other cats over with his hind feet. The fur flies, let me tell you."

Rhodes was about to ask how Tuggle could get out when a dark blur smashed through the bottom of the kitchen door and shot through the room.

Rhodes looked at the door and saw that a flap built into it was still swinging.

"Tuggle!" Miss Onie said to the fleeing cat, now being pursued out of the room by about half the population of the kitchen. "Is that mean Mr. Ramsdell shootin' at you again?"

"Shooting?" Rhodes said.

"He's got him one of those BB guns," Miss Onie said. "He likes to use it on the boys. But he didn't stop Tuggle with it, and that's when he started putting out the poison. I want him stopped, and I want him arrested for the murder of Buster!"

"I'll see what I can do," Rhodes said.

Rhodes stepped off Miss Onie's back porch and sneezed. Then he took a deep breath of the crisp fall air. It was quite a relief.

He looked across the back yard at Ralph Ramsdell's detached garage. Ramsdell's house faced the street that ran perpendicular to the one running in front of Miss Onie's house;

the garage was between the two houses and to the back.

Rhodes walked over to the garage. The fall sun felt good on his back.

"You in there, Mr. Ramsdell?" he said when he was nearly to the garage.

"Who wants to know?"

Rhodes stopped just outside the garage. "This is the Sheriff, Mr. Ramsdell. Dan Rhodes."

A short, skinny man came out of the shadows, walking along the side of what looked like a 1949 or 1950 Dodge that was backed into the garage.

"What can I do for you, Sheriff?" the man said. He was wearing a pair of jeans faded almost white, a blue work shirt, and a pair of black suspenders.

"I wanted to ask you about Miss Onie's cats," Rhodes said.

"Sonsabitches come over here botherin' Al," Ramsdell said. "All the time. Can't leave him alone. He come in the other day, bleedin' like a stuck pig. Damn left ear split right down the middle. I never woulda thought so much blood could come from a split ear."

"Al's your cat?" Rhodes said.

"Short for Alley. Anyway, those damn cats been pickin' on him for a couple of weeks. I told her if it didn't stop—"

"By 'her' you mean Miss Onie."

"That's the only 'her' around here. Anyway, I told her that if it didn't stop, I was goin' to Wal-Mart and buy me a gun. I warned her, Sheriff, fair and square. But it didn't stop, so I got me the gun."

"You want to show it to me?" Rhodes said.

Ramsdell turned and walked back into the garage. While he was gone, Rhodes heard a car door slam. He turned and looked out at the street. A black Ford Ranger was parked there, and a man was walking toward Miss Onie's house.

Then Ramsdell was back, carrying a small rifle.

"Here it is," he said. "Just a BB gun."

Rhodes put out his hand, and Ramsdell gave him the gun. It was a Crossman Powermaster 760.

"Single shot," Ramsdell said. "You got to pump it ever' time you shoot it."

"Did you just use it?"

"Damn sure did. That big tabby come over here lookin' for trouble, and he found it. Shot him right square in the butt. I'll teach him to come over here tryin' to beat up on my cat."

"Where is your cat, by the way?" Rhodes said.

"In the garage," Ramsdell said. "He likes to sleep on top of the car."

"I don't guess you ever thought about using anything more lethal than a BB gun on Miss Onie's cats, did you?"

"Hell no," Ramsdell said. "What do you mean by that?"

"Miss Onie says you poisoned Buster."

"Who the hell is Buster?"

"One of her cats."

"Well, I didn't poison whatshisname, Buster, nor nobody else. I got me a BB gun, but you can't kill a cat with a BB gun. Hell, Sheriff, I don't want to kill 'em. I *like* cats. I just want to keep 'em off poor old Al. A BB won't hurt 'em, maybe sting a little is all."

There was a soft thump, and Rhodes looked into the garage. An orange cat was walking along the hood of the old Dodge. Ramsdell reached out and rubbed the cat's head. The cat started to purr.

"This here's Al," Ramsdell said. "Look here. You can see where those damn cats split his ear."

Rhodes looked. The ear was split, all right.

"I sure wouldn't want anything happenin' to Al," Ramsdell said. "He's about all the company I got."

"And you wouldn't hurt anyone else's cats, either?" Rhodes said.

Ramsdell sighed. "I sure wouldn't," he said.

"That Ralph Ramsdell's a liar and the truth's not in him," Miss Onie said.

She had the pork chops sizzling in a heavy black pan, and the cats were milling around and yowling. It had been stuffy in the room earlier, despite the cool fall weather outside. Now, with the pork chops smoking in the pan, it was even worse. Miss Onie had rolled up the sleeves of her dress.

There was a young man with dark hair sitting at the table. Buster was gone.

"This is my nephew, Robert Calder," Miss Onie said over her shoulder when Rhodes entered the kitchen. "Robert, this is Sheriff Rhodes."

Robert got up and extended his hand. Rhodes shook it.

"Glad to meet you, Robert," Rhodes said, releasing the nephew's hand. "What happened to Buster?"

"Oh, I took him outside," Robert said. "Couldn't have him cluttering up the kitchen, not when somebody's fixing lunch and all."

"Where is he?" Rhodes said.

"Out in my truck," Robert said, smiling. "Don't worry, Sheriff. I won't dump him on public property."

"Dump him!" Miss Onie said, turning from the stove, a two-pronged cooking fork in her hand. Rhodes noticed that there was a large purple bruise on her left arm. "I thought you said you were going to give him a decent burial."

"I am, Aunt Onie," Robert said. Noticing that Rhodes was looking at the bruise, he added in a lower voice, "Aunt Onie fell down last week. I've been trying to get her to hire someone to stay here with her, but she won't hear of it."

"I didn't fall down, and don't you say so," Miss Onie said. "I just bumped into the cabinet. And I don't need anybody here pesterin' me in my own house. Sheriff, did you arrest that Ralph Ramsdell?"

"Not yet," Rhodes said. "He didn't seem like the kind of man to go around poisoning cats."

Miss Onie shook her head. "Well, he is. Anybody'd shoot at a cat with a BB gun would just as soon poison him as not. And you'd better do something about it."

"He has a cat of his own," Rhodes said. "He likes cats."

"Ha," Miss Onie said. "He just got that cat to chase mice. He doesn't like mice, either."

"I don't guess you have much of a problem with mice, yourself," Rhodes said, looking at the swarming cats.

"Robert takes care of that," Miss Onie said. She turned back to the stove and prodded at the pork chops. "Got to cook these things well done, or you might get that disease, tricky-nosis. I've had some of the symptoms, lately. Been meanin' to get myself checked by the doctor."

"Now, Aunt Onie," Robert said. "You know you don't have trichinosis."

"Ha. Shows what little you know about it. Wouldn't be ea-tin' these pork chops right now if I had anything else in the house."

One of the cats, a mostly white calico, stood on its hind legs and pawed at Miss Onie's apron. "You stop that, Sassy," Miss Onie said. "You can't have any pork chops." She swung the cooking fork down, and the cat dropped to the floor and sat looking up at her.

"I got plenty for visitors, though," Miss Onie said to Rhodes and Robert. "Either of you want me to set you a plate?"

"No thanks," Rhodes said. He wasn't so much afraid of getting trichinosis as of getting a hair ball. "I have to be getting back to the jail."

"I have to go, too," Robert said.

"You better not leave here without arrestin' that Ralph Ramsdell, Sheriff," Miss Onie said.

"I'll have to do a little more investigation first," Rhodes said. "I'll just leave by the back door."

He let himself out and once more took a deep breath of the clean air. Then he walked out to the black pickup that was parked by the side street to wait for Robert.

"Poor old Buster. Stiff as a poker."

Rhodes turned and saw Robert Calder standing beside him, looking down at the carcass of the cat that lay in the pickup bed.

"Not that Aunt Onie will miss one cat, more or less," Calder said. "Lord knows what she sees in them."

"They keep her company, I guess," Rhodes said, thinking of what Ramsdell had said.

"They do that. But, Lord, the smell in there. I think she's

getting a little senile, to tell the truth. Falling down and not wanting to admit it, talking to those cats like they could understand her. It's not normal, Sheriff."

"That's a mighty big house," Rhodes said. "Does Miss Onie live in all of it?"

Calder leaned forward, resting his arms on the side of the pickup bed. "Just a few rooms. The rest of the place is closed off."

"What about the cats? Do they have the run of the place?"

"Nope. They can go in and out through the flap in the back door, but they don't get into any of the upstairs rooms."

"What's in the rest of the place?" Rhodes said. "I mean, is it like the downstairs?"

Robert laughed. "Just about. I guess Aunt Onie never threw away a thing in her life, or Uncle Josh, either, when he was alive. What anybody'd want with all that old junk is a mystery to me. Cereal boxes, newspapers, magazines. God knows what-all she's got in there."

"Nothing will get chewed up by mice, though," Rhodes said. "Not with all those cats around. But then, from what Miss Onie said, I don't guess she holds with having the cats keep down the mouse population."

Robert looked for a moment as if he didn't quite know what Rhodes was talking about. Then he smiled. "Oh. You mean what she said about me taking care of the mice. I just bought some mouse bait for her. Since she doesn't let the cats out of those downstairs rooms, she has to use something else for the upstairs. You know how those old houses are. Mice come in about this time of year, looking for a warm place to stay."

Rhodes didn't really know, not ever having lived in one, but he could imagine. He reached into the pickup bed and poked Buster's stiff carcass with his index finger.

"I'll just take the deceased with me," he said.

"You don't have to do that, Sheriff," Robert said. "I'll take care of it."

Rhodes picked Buster up. "Can't let you do that," he said. "You never know. Buster might be evidence. I'll see that he gets a good burial." He stuck the stiff body under his arm.

"What about Ramsdell?" Robert said. "What are you going to do about him?"

"We'll see," Rhodes said.

He forgot all about Ramsdell when he got back to the jail, however, because there had been what the newspapers liked to call a "daring daylight robbery" of a convenience store.

" 'Cept this one was a little different," Hack said.

Lawton, the jailer, was leaning against the wall, eager to join in. "That's the truth, Sheriff. There ain't never been one like this."

That was the way it always went. Hack and Lawton would talk around the subject for as long as they could, trying to make Rhodes ask about the specifics of the crime. He resisted as long as he could.

"Teenagers," Hack said. "You never know what they'll think of next."

"*I* know what they'll think of next," Lawton said. "Same thing they always think of. You prob'ly think about it a lot too, seein' as you're sweet on Miz McGee the way you are."

Hack's face got red. "You take that back," he said.

"I didn't mean anything by it," Lawton said. "Besides, you were the one that brought it up."

"I wasn't talkin' about *that*. I was talkin' about the way teenagers come up with these new ways to steal things."

"Well, it was a new one all right," Lawton said, nodding.

"All right," Rhodes said. He couldn't stand it any longer. "What was new about it?"

"The turtle," Hack said, getting it said before Lawton could.

"They stole a turtle?" Rhodes said.

"Nope," Lawton said. "They used one as a weapon."

"You're making this up," Rhodes said.

"Not a bit of it," Hack said. "They went in the Quik-Sak carryin' a snappin' turtle. Big ol' mossback, accordin' to the clerk. Must've weighed twenty, thirty pounds. Said if the clerk didn't empty the register, they'd get the turtle to bite off his fingers."

"Coulda done it, too," Lawton said. "I seen one of them

things once, he bit a tree limb right half in two. That thing must've been three inches around."

"I don't doubt it," Hack said. "I remember one time—"

"Never mind that," Rhodes said. "What about the robbery?"

"Oh," Hack said. "Well, natcherly the clerk gave 'em all the money in the register. Wasn't but about thirty bucks. Ruth Grady responded to the call, and she ought to be able to catch 'em. They drove off in an old Chevy, and the clerk got the license number."

"But did he get it right?" Rhodes said. He'd dealt with eye-witness reports of license numbers before.

"I expect he did," Hack said. "Anyway, Ruth'll know whether she stops the right car or not."

"Yeah," Lawton said. "Not too many people carry snappin' turtles around with 'em nowadays."

"They took the turtle with them?" Rhodes said.

"Sure they did," Hack said. "You don't think they'd leave a dangerous weapon like that lyin' around, do you?"

Rhodes shook his head. "No," he said. "I don't guess they would."

"I almost hate to tell you," Herman Talbert said. "You sure you don't know where they are?"

Talbert was the owner of Clearview's only baseball card shop. Rhodes had stopped by to talk about the old cards he'd thought of that morning in Miss Onie's house.

"I don't have any idea," Rhodes said. "I traded a lot of them for comic books, I think."

"You don't have the comic books, either, I bet," Talbert said. He was young and enthusiastic, with brush-cut black hair and eyes that sparkled behind his glasses. "They might be worth more than the baseball cards."

"Read them to pieces," Rhodes said. "No cards, no comics."

Talbert shook his head in sympathy. "Happens all the time. That's why they're worth so much. A 1952 Topps Mantle card, now, in like-new condition, that would be worth in the neighborhood of ten thousand dollars all by itself."

Rhodes whistled. He'd had no idea.

Talbert picked up a slick magazine with a photo of Bo Jackson on the front from on top of his counter. Below the glass Rhodes could see colorful cards in plastic protectors with small price stickers on them.

Talbert opened the magazine and located the page he was looking for. He ran his finger down a list and said, "According to this month's Beckett, that Mantle card would go for eight thousand. Of course, you'd have to find someone willing to pay that much."

"How hard would that be?" Rhodes said.

"Not as hard as you might think. Of course none of the others from that year are worth near that much, except maybe the Willie Mays."

"What if somebody found a whole box of cards from that year?" Rhodes said.

"You mean just a box of loose cards? That would depend on their condition."

"No," Rhodes said. "I mean a box of unopened cards, still in the packages, gum and all."

"Holey moley," Talbert said. "I have no idea. A lot. A whole lot." He looked at Rhodes over the tops of his glasses. "You don't know where to find anything like that do you?"

"No," Rhodes said. But he wasn't sure he was telling the truth.

"Warfarin," Dr. Slick said. "That's what killed Buster."

Rhodes had not given Buster's body a burial of any kind. He had taken it to Slick, one of Blacklin County's veterinarians, for an autopsy.

"Warfarin," Rhodes said. "Pretty easy to get hold of."

Dr. Slick nodded. "Sure is. Used in a lot of rat bait."

"How fast would it work on a cat?" Rhodes said.

"Not too fast, unless he got a lot of it at one time. Cats wouldn't normally eat enough of it. You leave it out for rats and mice and they eat it over a period of time. It doesn't work instantly."

"So it wouldn't be the kind of thing you'd use to kill a cat," Rhodes said.

"Nope. There's lots of better things for that."

"That's what I thought," Rhodes said.

Robert Calder lived in a run-down house not too far from his aunt's. He was in his driveway looking under the hood of his pickup when Rhodes stopped by late that afternoon.

He looked up when Rhodes approached and wiped his hands on a red rag that had been hanging out of the pocket of his jeans.

"Hey, Sheriff," he said. "What can I do for you?"

"I want to talk to you about your aunt," Rhodes said.

Calder turned around and slammed down the hood of the truck. "Brake fluid was low," he said, turning back to Rhodes. He wiped his hands again. "What about my aunt?"

"She didn't fall," Rhodes said.

The sun was going down and there were long shadows across the scraggly lawn. It was much cooler than it had been in the morning, and Rhodes thought they might have a freeze that night.

Calder stood there looking at Rhodes, but he didn't say anything.

"You told me Miss Onie got that bruise on her arm from a fall," Rhodes said. "She didn't. She bumped into the cabinet, just like she said."

Calder tossed the red rag on the pickup hood. "She has a little trouble remembering, like I told you."

"A little," Rhodes said. "That's why she writes things down."

"What things?" Calder said.

"Things like falls, or bumping into cabinets. She does that so that if she wakes up hurting one morning, she'll know whether she needs to worry or not."

"I don't get it," Calder said. "You mean she keeps a diary?"

"Sort of. She showed me where she wrote it down."

Rhodes pulled a small spiral notebook from his back pocket

and flipped back its yellow cover. He flicked back the pages until he came to the one he was looking for.

"Here it is. 'November fifth. Bumped into kitchen cabinet. Left arm.' "

"Maybe she didn't fall, then," Calder said. "I thought she did."

"Then there's that rash on her face," Rhodes said.

"I didn't see any rash," Calder said.

"Not to mention the trichinosis."

"I don't know what you're getting at, Sheriff. My aunt doesn't have trichinosis."

"I know it," Rhodes said. "She's being poisoned."

Calder leaned back against the hood of the pickup. "You've lost me, Sheriff. Trichinosis, diaries, rashes. I don't think I can do anything for you, after all."

"You might tell me why you dropped by your aunt's house every day at meal times."

Calder pushed himself away from the pickup and started walking toward his house. "I go by to check on her, make sure she's all right. You know how it is, an old lady living alone. Something could happen, and she'd need help."

Rhodes followed him. "I asked Miss Onie about Buster, too. He ate table scraps. He was the only cat that did. He refused to eat the dry food, and Miss Onie humored him even if she didn't think table scraps were good for him."

"I didn't know that," Calder said. He had reached his front door.

"I didn't think so," Rhodes said. "Anyway that rat poison you'd been putting in the food, Buster got too much of it. It's a good thing he did. Otherwise you might have gotten away with killing Miss Onie."

Calder turned. "Sheriff, why would I want to do that? Why would anyone want to do that?"

"Baseball cards," Rhodes said. "Cereal boxes. Dixie cup tops. Comic books. Old coffee cans. Miss Onie's got all of them. The upstairs is knee-deep in them. She and her husband kept everything from the store that didn't sell. They couldn't bear to part with anything, so they just stacked it away. She took me on a little tour about an hour ago. It's all still there. And it's all worth a lot of money."

"Even the cereal boxes?" Calder said.

"Even them. People will collect anything."

"I could have had any of it for the asking," Calder said.

"No you couldn't," Rhodes said. "Miss Onie said you did ask. She told you it was all in her will."

"That damn will."

"I have to agree with you on that one," Rhodes said. "I never did understand anyone who would leave everything to a bunch of cats."

"Everything," Calder said, shaking his head. "The house to be left just as it was. Sheriff, it was a pure waste."

"Maybe," Rhodes said. "But that was no reason to kill anyone. You could have challenged the will in court when the time came."

"I wasn't going to kill anyone." Calder opened the screen door and reached inside.

Rhodes's hand clamped around Calder's wrist as Calder tried to bring the shotgun out and up.

"You won't be needing that," Rhodes said. "You don't want more trouble than you've already got."

Calder relaxed his grip and let go of the shotgun. "I guess you're right. Besides, I don't think you can get a conviction."

"We'll see," Rhodes said. "You never know what a jury will do. They might think killing that cat is worth fifty years."

"I never meant to kill any cat."

"That part, I believe," Rhodes said.

Almost as soon as they got Calder booked and printed, Ruth Grady came in with the two suspects from the convenience store robbery.

"Caught up with them on the old Obert Road," she said. "You'll have to send somebody for their car."

"I'll drive you out there after we've got these two taken care of," Rhodes said. "You can drive it back."

"No sir, not me."

"Why not?" Rhodes said.

Hack laughed. "I bet I know. Snappin' turtle."

"That's right," Ruth said. "I never saw anything like that, not close up. It looks like something out of a book on dinosaurs. *I'm* not getting in that car."

"You better not shoot it," Hack said. "We got us a sheriff who can solve animal murders real quick."

Ruth looked at Rhodes. "What's he talking about?"

"Never mind," Rhodes said.

Where the Cat Came In

Mat Coward

I WAS LOCKED IN. JUST me, the cat and twenty thousand pounds in cash.

I took a deep breath, and did what I always do when I'm in a hole. I panicked. I find it helps to get it out of the way right off—clears the mind, leaves one better able to cope with the long hard slog of extrication.

So I took my head in both hands and beat it against various available surfaces—walls, doors, floor—as if attempting to gain entry to an unusually coy coconut, while the cat, taking its cue from me, ran up and down the walls and across the ceiling with its ears stretched back along its body like those fins you see on old American cars.

Coconut panic; aerodynamic panic. Each to his own. Yeah, we can do you vanilla, but you'll have to call back.

I'm what the Crime Prevention people term a "creeper"—a burglar who creeps into your house on a hot afternoon when you leave the back door open for the breeze while you're upstairs making love to your sister-in-law—and I was just having a little look around the snooker room when I heard a sound that pretty much froze my blood.

There are a number of sounds that'll do that, obviously, to a man in my line of business. Shotguns tumescing, sirens approaching, hairy baritones asking "What the hell do you think you're doing with my wife's panties?" right in my ear when I'd thought I was all alone. But this particular noise was more blood-freezing than any of those. It was the faint, but preternaturally penetrating *bleep-whurr-clunk* of a top-of-the-range, state-of-the-art security system being activated by a departing householder.

I was locked in. Me, the cat, the cash.

A creeper isn't a cat burglar, isn't a safecracker, doesn't really carry much in the way of specialised equipment, doesn't possess any particular skills. The ability to move about very quietly is an advantage, and of course one does require guts. That's not boasting, it's just true: I make my living strolling into people's houses in broad daylight and stealing their valuables from literally under their noses. Well, OK, not *literally* under their noses, but literally behind their backs, as often as not.

I once had a VCR out of a bloke's living-room while the bloke himself was snoring on the sofa with a beer can in his hand. The beer can could have dropped from his grip at any moment and he would have woken up, but the VCR was brand new, an expensive make, and I had to have it.

I had it, got clean away, and whenever the guy finally did wake up, he must have thought the bad fairies had been. This was about two o'clock in the afternoon, and that kind of thing takes guts. I even ejected the video he'd been watching and left it on the arm of the sofa for him, because it was rented and he'd have got into all sorts of form-filling hassle if I'd taken it away. Besides, he'd fallen asleep halfway through the film, and he'd want to know how it ended. I thought, like, maybe he could take it round to his neighbour's place and finish watching it on her machine and it would turn out she was a pretty widow and years later they'd place an ad in the local paper publicly thanking the burglar who brought love to two lonely people. . . .

My point being, creeping takes guts. But it doesn't take any fancy equipment or magical tricks of the trade. No breaking-in, so no breaking-in tools. And thus no breaking-out tools.

The house I was in was a big one. I like stealing from big houses, not only because they are demographically more likely to have something in them worth robbing (I'm a cash and jewellery man myself, given the choice; aren't we all, given the choice?), but also because, when stealing from the rich, I can fool myself that I'm not a common creeper at all, but some sort of brothel-soled Robin Hood.

(Point worth remarking: just because you know you're fooling yourself, doesn't mean you're not fooling yourself.)

I don't do much scouting out. What's the point? It would only increase my chances of being seen and described. Instead, I get up in the mornings, put on a decent suit and a prosperous tie (because your average creeper is a fourteen-year-old boy with his arse hanging out of his trousers), prepare my excuse, and head out to where the rich folk roost. (I never go anywhere, do anything, without having my excuse prepared and practised. Something I learned at school. Probably the only thing I learned at school).

And in I go. Upstairs, downstairs, it doesn't matter; places like that have something worth nicking in just about every room. I once found a very nice gold ring sitting in a soapdish in a downstairs loo.

On this particular day, in this particular house, I started in the basement. Rich people, for some weird reason, love to own facilities that they never use. A swimming pool with no water in it, a squash court with no scuff marks, a sunbed still in its plastic wrap, that sort of thing. Maybe when I'm rich I'll understand this better. Maybe when I'm rich I'll buy a Jacuzzi and forget to plumb it in.

Anyway, snooker rooms are favourites in this category. Almost every rich house has a snooker room, and it's always in the basement, and it's very rarely used except as a place to dump stuff. And, interestingly, to keep valuables. It's like the fat wallets reckon that since they never go down there, the burglars won't bother either. (Does this puzzle you? Because it puzzles me. You never meet a rich person with a brain, right? So how did they get to be rich in the first place?)

As I crept down the stairs to the converted basement, I could hear noises of habitation coming from somewhere above, and I kept half an ear open to that while I scanned the snooker room. Didn't have to scan very thoroughly, as it turned out, because right there on the virgin baize table itself, more or less the first thing I noticed as I entered the room, was a large, bulgy canvas bag.

Some times you just *know*, and I'm telling you—if that bag had contained anything other than used tenners, I'd have eaten it: zip, luggage tags and all.

I opened the bag and looked inside. My stomach remained empty of canvas even as my heart filled up with joy: twenty thousand pounds was my guess. Could have been more, I was always a conservative guesser.

A month's wages, probably, for the guy who owned the house. A day's wages, if he was even more crooked than most rich people. For me, the biggest single haul of my entire creeping career. By a country mile.

I had the dosh bag in my left hand, and was preparing to decamp, when I heard hurried footsteps clatter down the main stairs, from the upstairs to the hall; heard the front door open and close; and finally heard the aforementioned *bleep-whurr-clunk*. Which was, if you'll forgive the heavily laboured irony, where we came in, right? I was locked in. The creeper, the feline, the readies.

I didn't really do that panic bit that I mentioned earlier. I mean, I did it, but only internally. Externally, what I did was stand very still, stiller than you have ever stood in your life, and listen. I detected no furthers sounds of humanity, which was pretty cold comfort under the circumstances.

There was no point searching for an open window. All the doors and windows had been locked automatically at the moment of *bleep-whurr-clunk*. That's the whole idea of the system; saves you having to troll round your big house checking every little entry point every time you go out. Great break-through for obsessive-neurotics, and fat wallets in a rush.

Once the doors and windows have been locked using the electronic "key", they cannot be opened, from inside or out, except with that same key.

In other words, the only way I was going to get out of this house was to wait until the owner got back, and talk my way out. Well, I still had my excuse ready. I just had to hope the owner hadn't left on a Caribbean cruise. Meanwhile, I needed to use the loo (what I lack in glamour, I make up for in candour, right?).

I located it, went in, enjoyed the amenities, and when I re-emerged found myself looking at a tall, blonde woman in her late thirties, who I was quite sure hadn't been there a couple of minutes earlier. At least she'd waited until I'd emptied my bladder before confronting me, which showed good breeding, I thought. She was rather attractive in a stern sort of way, and one thing I knew about her from the start: she was a better creeper than I was, since she'd heard me and I hadn't heard her.

"OK, who the hell are you, and what the bloody hell do you think you're doing in this house?" Heaven knows what made me say such a thing. I should have played my excuse and left. But her sudden appearance had caught me on the hop; well, zipping my fly, in point of fact.

She made the obvious reply: "I live here, this is my house! Who are *you*, more to the point?" Her accent was American, and matched her big white teeth.

Something about the way she said it—something about the way she looked at me, calm and considering, not scared or angry—made me say: "You're not the lady of the house, lady. I happen to know that lady very well, and she doesn't look a bit like you."

She sighed theatrically, and said "Oh, why pretend? I guess I know who you are, and I guess you can guess who I am. Right?"

This whole thing was getting a little wacky for my taste, so I said nothing.

"And I guess," she continued guessing, "that you have as much right as I have to be here." I said nothing again, so she spelled it out for me. "I'm Simon's *mistress*, OK? Christina." We shook hands. "And you'd be Pete, right?" I nodded. "Justine's *toy-boy*. Well, my, what a family, huh?"

I felt *toy boy* lacked the dignity of *mistress*, but I didn't get huffy. Instead I got down to the main business. "So, Christina, do you have a key to get us out of here?"

She sighed again. Theatrically, again. "Look, Pete, I'm going to level with you. This is going to sound crazy, but you have to trust me."

"OK," I said.

"I think Simon wants to kill me," she said.

"OK," I said. "What makes you think that?"

"Long story," she said, "but basically, I don't have the key, we're trapped in here, and I think he's going to burn the place down. Isn't that horrible?"

"It is," I agreed. "Why would he do that?"

Yet another sigh. "I did a foolish thing. I threatened to tell his wife about us. I realise now that he never intended to leave her—because of the money, you know."

"Sure," I said. "So what about the phone? We could ring for help."

Christina shook her head. "Not working. That's where he said he was going, just now, to report the fault. And he doesn't allow mobile phones in the house, because he says they give you cancer."

"So where's the wife now?" I said. "I mean, of course, *Justine*, my beloved."

"Shopping," said Christina.

"Great. Then maybe she'll get home before—"

"Abroad," said Christina.

"Shopping abroad? Oh, right. Pity." Should Pete have known about that, I wondered. And then I wondered a bit more, and finally I said: "One thing I don't understand."

"Yes?"

"The cat."

"Cat?" said Christina.

I pointed at the cat.

"Oh, yeah," she said. "That's old Mouser. Yeah."

"So what's she doing sitting in the hall inside a carrying basket?"

"Long story," said Christina. "Basically, she has an appointment with the veterinarian. She's supposed to be there right now, poor little kitty."

"And instead Simon's going to burn her to death? Just to get rid of a troublesome mistress?"

"I guess it all adds to the authenticity. Besides, Mouser's not Simon's cat. It's Justine's cat, and he hates it. Kind of like transference, you know?"

"So what do we do now?" I said, genuinely curious.

"OK," she said. "I'm thinking, there has to be a spare key here somewhere, right? If we can find it before Simon does whatever he's planning to do . . . I think that's our only chance."

"What are we waiting for?" I said. "I'll take upstairs, you do the living-room."

As soon as I entered the main bedroom, I started screaming. I screamed like a girl in a horror film, and within seconds I could hear Christina's valiant steps running up the stairs to save me.

The minute she poked her head around the door behind which I was hiding, I hit her as hard as I could with a ski stick (still in its plastic wrapper, naturally). Even so, she managed to squeeze off four incredibly loud shots from her big handgun before succumbing.

"That's a good idea," I told her, as she lay on the floor. She wasn't dead, but she certainly looked tired. "Shoot the windows out, why didn't I think of that?"

My scream had been a ruse, planned mere seconds in advance, but it came out more authentic than I'd anticipated, because I'd never before seen a garrotted corpse. Not until the moment I burst into that bedroom and saw the lady of the house lying on her bed, corporeal proof that you can't take it with you when you go. She looked horrible.

I'd been expecting something of the sort, because by then I knew for certain that Christina was neither the wife nor the mistress. Nor yet the cleaning lady. She was, though, hired help of a kind.

While I was searching Christina for the key, I worked out the rest of the story. Or at least, a version that made sense to me.

(See, I can come up with some pretty good stories myself, like that thing with the VCR, how I stole that VCR from under that sleeping man's nose. Not really true. I did steal the video, yes, but the man wasn't asleep, he was dead, had been for days according to my nose, and I could've made all the noise I liked. Or, to look at it another way, if he *had* woken up, a burglary charge would've been the least of my worries.)

Obviously, Christina was a freelance killer, hired by this delightful Simon character. That's what the twenty grand was for. He lets her in, they murder the unfaithful wife, then Simon drives off, leaving the coast clear for Pete, the toy boy, to arrive for his rendezvous with Justine.

Presumably, Christina would have taken care of him, then fired the place, making it all look like a tragic accident. When I showed up, she must have thought I was Pete, taking my cue a bit early. She didn't have time to wonder how I got in—she was too busy making sure I didn't find the body in the bedroom.

Which meant she had to have a key to let herself out. So where was it? Believe me, I searched every fair inch of her recumbent loveliness before giving up.

Then it hit me. Why hadn't she shown me the gun right off? Why the "let's look for the key" ruse? Because the gun was somewhere else, and she had to go and fetch it. And that's where the key would be.

Sure enough, in the dining room, at the other end of the house from the snooker room steps, I found the tools of Christina's trade, neatly assembled in an expensive leather evening bag. Lipstick, paracetamol, spare ammo, spare key.

That was when I heard the cop sirens. I told you those gun-shots had been loud.

I had a decision to make and it had to be made quickly. The cat was in his cat basket in the hall, and the cash was in its cash bag down in the snooker room, and it was pretty clear I couldn't hope to collect both of them and still pass Go before the cops, or the toy boy, or both, arrived. Hard choice, huh? Not really.

I skittered down the hall, scooped up the cat, keyed the security system, and disappeared through the back door, without so much as a sad look back in the direction of the money.

After all, I owed that cat my life. If Christina hadn't lied about knowing "Mouser," I might not have figured out who she was, and she'd have killed me at her convenience. Besides, me and Leo (*Mouser, indeed!*), we've been partners a long time.

I mentioned excuses earlier. Well, here's mine, and it's a damn good one, which has got me out of trouble on more than one occasion:

I get caught creeping round someone's basement, and the householder, reasonably enough, wants to know what I'm up to; I act all embarrassed, and say, "I'm so sorry, but you see I was walking Leo to the vet and somehow he escaped from his basket and ran in here, and I just wanted to get him back before he disgraced himself on your lovely carpet."

So you see, my hard choice wasn't hard at all. Twenty thousand quid may be a lot of money, but a good excuse is worth its weight in diamonds.

(There, now: I bet you'd been wondering where the cat came into it, hadn't you?)

Photo Opportunity

Larry Segriff

THERE WAS A BRANCH POKING me in the face, but I couldn't squirm enough to get away from it. What made it worse was that I probably didn't even have to be in the bushes. We'd done this enough times and never had any problems, but still, I guess one of the reasons we'd made it for so long was that we didn't take any chances we didn't have to.

I heard his low whistle then and relaxed. A few minutes longer and I could move. Grinning, I flipped the little lever and opened the cage. Tom streaked out, not even bothering to stretch. He knew what was coming. He was ready.

On the other side of the yard, Jamie was letting Tiger out. I grinned again, careful to keep my teeth from showing. The fun was about to begin.

I could feel them drawing closer to each other. Both cats were black as night, impossible to see in the nearly total darkness, but this was an old, familiar routine for all of us.

"Three . . . two . . . one," I counted silently. Right on cue, an explosion of sound rent the night.

Cat fight. At one o'clock in the morning, it was guaranteed to piss people off.

Tom and Tiger were giving it all they had, their yowls and screams sounding ferocious even to me. Within minutes, lights were going on all around us. Tom and Tiger gave it a little bit longer, separating for a moment and then coming together again even louder than before. They split, then, each one vanishing once again into the darkness, finding his own way back to his waiting cage.

They were well trained, those cats. I smiled a third time as I bolted Tom in, but even as I did so I was taking careful note of which houses stayed dark. Later, when things quieted down, those were the ones Jamie and I would hit.

"Holy shit!" Jamie's voice cut across the silence of the room, but his words could just as easily have been mine.

This was the third house we'd entered since Tom and Tiger had done their thing. It was going on toward three o'clock in the morning. At this rate, we might have time to hit two more. A good night for us, if they all turned out like the first ones.

Now, though, we had to pause in our work and just stare at the photographs lining one wall of this den. It was dark in there, but our penlights were sufficient to illuminate an entire strata of our nation's history: there were maybe three dozen framed photographs, all showing the same guy, and all showing him with one or more political figure from the last twenty years. There were four different presidents, from both political parties, and more senators and congressmen than you could shake a federal indictment at.

"Jesus," I whispered. "Who is this guy?"

Jamie moved in closer, and in the shadows I could see him nod. "Yeah, I remember him. He was a big wheel in the Senate for a long time. Probably still would be if they hadn't passed all those term limitations."

This had me worried. I mean, D.C. was one of the cities on our circuit—we took our traveling cat fight to more than a dozen places before repeating, as a rule—and we'd broken into the homes of senators, congressmen, and even future presidents before. It was just that this was the first time I'd known about it while we were doing it.

"Should we leave?" I asked.

Jamie just turned and grinned at me. "Nah. Like I said, I remember this guy. If anybody deserves a visit from us, it's him."

"Are you sure you got all the alarms? He probably knows people in the defense industry."

That grin again. Jamie was nothing if not confident. "I'm sure."

It was a silly question, I guess. Jamie had about a dozen different ways to kill the power to an entire neighborhood. Sometimes, he did something to the electrical substation. Other times, like tonight, he took a bird that Tiger had killed—Tom was lousy at catching birds—and used it to short out a transformer. All things that looked accidental. On top of that, he also turned off the power at each house that we entered, and disconnected their phone lines, too.

He was cautious, competent, and thorough, and I shouldn't have been worried. I just didn't know enough about it to know if his precautions were enough. The electronics bit was his responsibility. I was lucky to know there was a difference between a green wire and a red one. Damned if I knew what that difference was. My job was to get us in after he'd done his thing. Well, that and finding all the best hiding places. I had something of a knack for that.

"What if he's home?" I asked. "He's pretty old. You can see that in these pictures. What if he didn't hear our boys out there? What if he gets up to pee and sees us?"

Jamie just shrugged. "What if he does? It's not like it hasn't happened before."

"Yeah." That was true, and we'd always gotten away. I didn't like it, though. Not like Jamie did. "But—"

"Christ," he interrupted me. "You're such a worrier anymore. Let's just do our thing and get out, all right?"

"Yeah. It's just that this guy is such a celebrity and all. I guess I'm a little intimidated."

He flashed me that famous grin again. "This guy's a crook,

just like us. Now stop worrying about it, will ya? Where should I look?"

"The desk," I said, finally turning away from the rogues' gallery on the wall. "Lower right-hand drawer. Nine times out of ten, they'll have something there."

"Right. Now you do something, too."

I nodded, but he was turning away and didn't see me.

I started in on the bookcases. They lined every wall except the one with the photos. I didn't stay with them for long, though. Even in the dark, with only my penlight to guide me, I could tell that the books had never been read. They were free of dust, and all neatly aligned on their shelves, but they had that feel of newness to them. Leather bindings, like these, pick up oil when they're handled. They develop a certain texture, like well-worn gloves. These had probably been delivered by the case, and only handled when they were loaded onto the shelves.

All, that is, except for one shelf. This was near the desk, and down low to the floor. Handy for a guy sitting in that leather chair, and not conspicuous. They were paperbacks, not leather-bound books, and they'd been read a lot. Curious, I pulled one out and looked at it.

The Story of O. Flicking my light across the broken spines, I quickly saw a couple of other titles I recognized: *Fanny Hill* and the collected works of Anaïs Nin. There was even one large, metal-bound book that was just called, *Sex*. I grinned to myself in the dark. The old pervert, I thought.

I put the book back and went over to see what Jamie had found. He had the right-hand drawer out, and I tsked softly when I saw how he'd gouged the wood to force the lock. He should have had me open it. He knew how I hated to see things vandalized.

To make matters worse, the drawer had been empty, at least as far as we were concerned. There were some papers and stuff in there, and what looked like a large, leather-bound account-ant's book, but nothing of interest to us.

I tsked again, shook my head, and turned back to the photos

on the wall. Something about them was calling to me, and I
wanted to know what.

Slowly I reached out and removed one that was near the
center. It had this same guy—Clark, I suddenly remembered
was his name—posing with a former president. One I'd liked,
sort of.

The frame was nothing special, just a postmodern black and
silver plastic thing done up to look like chrome and ebony. Or
maybe it was supposed to be silver and jet. In the dim glow of
my penlight, it just looked cheap.

The glass was nonglare and heavy. In fact, as I looked at the
picture, it seemed to me that the whole thing was slightly
deeper than normal. Turning it over, I slid the back out and
removed both the picture itself and the padding.

Jamie came up about then. "What're you doing?" he asked
in a low voice. "Looking for autographs?"

He'd never understood how I could find things the way I
did. For that matter, I'd never understood it, either. He kidded
me about it a lot, but he never, ever interfered.

The photo was a regular eight-by-ten glossy. There was an
inscription on the front, but I'd been able to see that without
taking the frame down. The back was unmarked.

Disappointed, I started to put everything back, ignoring Jamie's snort of derision—he'd have just tossed it on the floor—
when I noticed that the cardboard backing was really two
pieces stuck together. There was a slight gap between them that
I might easily have missed, but Jamie's penlight had picked it
up.

Slowly, I separated the two pieces. Sandwiched between
them were several more eight by tens—four of them—of that
same former president. These were much older, however, showing him a good twenty years younger than the photo in front,
and they weren't nearly as professionally done. They were quite
clear, however, leaving no doubt as to what the former president was doing, or who he was doing it to.

"Holy shit," I said. "Jamie, do you know what we have
here?"

"Yeah," he said. "A golden opportunity."

I nodded. "Let's see what else this guy's got."

It turned out that every photo on the wall held secrets. Some were surprising. Some were almost comical. All were valuable.

"Jesus," Jamie whispered when we were all through. "This guy had dirt on everybody."

"Seems like it," I agreed.

"No wonder he's got so much money."

"Nah." I shook my head. "I seem to recall reading that he was born into a rich family. I don't think he was blackmailing these people for money."

"What, then?"

"Come here." I took the stack of glossies over to the desk and got out the leather-bound ledger Jamie had found earlier. Flipping it open at random, I glanced at the figures and started nodding.

"What?" Jamie asked.

"Look." I pointed at the first column. "These numbers are probably file numbers, or a coded reference for the people in the photos. We could probably figure it out, if we wanted, because these," I shifted my finger over to the remaining two columns of figures, "will tell us."

Jamie bent down and looked. "HR141," he read out loud, "S242. They don't make any sense to me."

"Me either," I said, "at least not for sure, but my guess is that these are legislative bills from both the House and the Senate. I'll bet you that each one of these represents a certain vote."

"Sure," he interrupted me. "One column is for yes votes, the other for no."

I nodded. "That's the way I see it."

Jamie reached out and flipped a few of the pages. He let out a low whistle as we saw just how many votes over the past couple of decades this guy had probably influenced.

"Explains a lot, doesn't it?" I asked.

He only nodded.

"What do you think we should do with them?" he asked.

"Use 'em. Hell, if nothing else, maybe we can force them to legalize burglary."

We grinned at that. Not too much later, Jamie went off to search the rest of the house. I should have gone with him, if only to keep the damage to a minimum, but I had a feeling there was something else in that den. Something I was missing.

I couldn't find it. I could hear Jamie as his search took him from room to room, but, unlike him, I was getting no closer to what I sought. Finally, in frustration, I went out to the truck and got Tom.

I had a knack for finding things. He had a nose for it. I swear, that cat could smell money, among other things. Over the years, he'd led me to a lot of well-hidden secrets.

Both cages were nestled in the back of the carryall, along with the half-dozen or so oversized backpacks we brought with us to carry things. We always kept the truck at least a block away from the houses we hit. We tended to hit upscale neighborhoods, and the people who lived there tended to inform the cops when they were going to be gone for any length of time. A strange vehicle sitting in a supposedly empty driveway or in front of a vacationer's home was like a red flag to the patrolling officers. That was why we had the backpacks—so we could carry things relatively inconspicuously, and it was also why we always had to limit what we took to smaller, more portable items.

We could get away with carrying hiking gear down the street, even at three in the morning, but even the dumbest cop was bound to be suspicious if we were carrying framed artwork or expensive stereo equipment.

The bags we'd filled from the first two houses were near the cages, and I took a moment to look at them and smile. The cash we'd found would see us through a lot of lean times, and the jewels—even at the rates we had to pay to Three-Finger Mike—would buy a lot of beer.

Still smiling, I unlatched Tom's cage. "Come on, boy," I said. "There's work to do."

Tiger was at the door of his cage, and I could see his tail twitching. He hated to be left out of anything that included Tom. I grinned, and after a moment opened his cage, too.

"All right, Tiger. You can come, too." As far as I knew, he

was no good at finding things, but at least he'd never gotten in the way.

The cats paced me as we walked, Tom on my right, Tiger on my left, and they stayed in perfect formation. I'd seen them do that before, but I still had to smile as I watched them.

My good mood didn't last, however.

I decided to walk around Clark's house once, just to try and get its layout firmly in my head. I was still convinced I was missing something, and if Tom couldn't find it, I wanted to be able to figure it out.

There was a silver sedan parked out on the street in front of the house. It was the only car parked out in the open like that, but I didn't pay it much attention. Over the years, Jamie and I had both learned to spot cop cars, marked and unmarked, and this one didn't send up any red flags for me. As I glanced over at it, however, I saw a match flare dimly within, and suddenly things didn't look so good.

As soon as I could, I cut between a couple of houses and started working my way back to Jamie. It was time to call it a night.

We didn't make it. I got back inside Clark's house all right, and found Jamie up on the second floor. When I told him what I'd seen, he agreed with me that we should leave, but then we'd learned years ago that anytime either of us felt uncomfortable we would knock off. The way we figured it, there were lots of houses to hit. No need to press our luck.

Besides, he'd made a pretty good haul. His backpack was full, but I didn't get a chance to ask what he'd found.

We were going down the stairs, Tom and Tiger invisible shadows at our sides, when a couple of figures stepped out of the darkness below. There wasn't much light coming in through the windows, but what there was glinted off the metal in their hands.

Shit, I thought.

Beside me, Jamie, who could sometimes think pretty quickly, snapped his fingers once. The men below us didn't say anything, so we continued moving slowly down the stairs.

When we reached the bottom, the two of them stepped back,

out of range of any sudden lunges on our part, and motioned for us to precede them into the den. We didn't want to, but neither of us could see a way to avoid it.

We went.

My backpack was over by the desk, looking pretty empty. I wondered if the photos were still in it. They were all that I'd managed to stuff in there, those and that leather-bound ledger Jamie had found.

The men behind us gestured for us to go over by the desk. Once we were there, one of them spoke for the first time.

"You steal from Missah Clark, no? What you find?"

They were shorter than us, though their guns made them look much larger, and in the dim light I could see they were Asiatic, but that's all I knew about them.

Beside me, Jamie shrugged. "The usual. Some cash, a bit of jewelry, that sort of thing."

The other one hissed and said something in a fluent, sibilant language. The first one nodded and said, "We care nothing for that. You find pictures, you tell us, hey?"

"Pictures?" Jamie said, sounding puzzled. I let him talk. He was a better actor than I. Besides, he was the one with the plan. I had to let him set it up.

The second one spoke again, and again I didn't catch a word of it. I only knew he didn't sound happy.

"Yes," the first one said. "Pictures. Very—how do you say it?—*valuable* pictures. You give them to us, yes?"

"Who are you?" Jamie was playing a dangerous game, but it was for a reason. I thought I knew what that reason was, and I felt the skin on the back of my neck crawl as he gambled with our lives.

More fluid speech. The first one nodded, then said, "Let us say, we represent a foreign interest. These pictures will help us ease certain, ah, difficulties, between our governments. They will make for a better trade agreement, you see? It is no different than how these pictures have been used before, no? So, now you give them to us, and everybody win, okay?"

"Okay," Jamie said. "They're in my backpack. If I move slowly, can I get them out without being shot?"

All of a sudden, I was no longer sure what his game was. Sometimes—often, in fact—we found guns in houses like this. Had he found one upstairs? Was his whole intent merely to fish it out? God, I hoped not. I didn't think I would survive such a move.

Our friend was speaking again, the one I couldn't understand. We all listened, and then his partner said, "Of course. But, as you say, move very slowly."

Jamie nodded, slipped the pack off his shoulders, and started to kneel. It was then that he snapped his fingers again, and Tom and Tiger made their move.

He must have been waiting for them to sidle along the edges of the room, sticking to the shadows. Whether he knew they were in position, or whether he was merely hoping he'd given them enough time, I didn't know. I heard him snap his fingers and I started diving toward the floor.

The cats were quiet. They only made noise when we wanted them to. Out of the corner of my eye, I saw two black streaks launch themselves from the side, twin arrows aimed at those glinting gun hands.

Tiger was on my side, pitted against the one who'd spoken to us, and I saw his jaws lacerate the wrist. Blood spurted as the gun dropped to the floor, and I knew that both the artery and the tendons had been slashed.

Way to go, Tiger, I thought. Instinctively, I started moving toward the fallen gun.

Tom wasn't so lucky. He hit the Asian's gun, not the wrist, and for a moment I saw him hanging from the barrel by his jaws, his claws frantically searching for fingers or hand or anything.

He didn't find it.

Jamie was throwing his backpack; I was leaping for the gun; Tom was squirming for his life. None of us was in time. The barrel dipped, pulled down by the cat's weight, and then the gun went off. Even in the dark I could see how his side exploded outward, and I cried out in reaction.

A moment later Jamie's backpack hit the smaller man and then his partner's gun was in my hand. It almost seemed to rise of its own accord, turning to bear down on the man who'd killed my cat.

I fired once, but my anger made me jerk the trigger instead of squeezing it. My shot went wide, hitting him high in the shoulder, hurting him badly but not killing him as I'd intended.

That one shot was all I had in me. I tossed the gun at Jamie, and then went over to where Tom lay motionless on the floor. Tiger was already there, sniffing at his partner in crime, and letting out soft, plaintive mews.

Amazingly, Tom was still alive. Using my penlight, I could see that his side was badly torn, but perhaps not as badly as I'd first thought.

I turned toward Jamie. "We have to go," I said. "We've got to get him to a vet."

"But—" he started, making a single, small motion with his gun to indicate the room around us: the photos, his bulging backpack, the foreign agents. There was a fortune there, waiting for us, if we knew how to use it. And if we had time enough to grab it.

I didn't say anything. I knew what he meant, but in my mind there was no choice to make.

He held my gaze for one heartbeat, then another, before he nodded.

As gently as I could, I scooped up my cat and headed for the door. I think Jamie might have looked back once, in curiosity or regret. I didn't.

Together, then, we vanished into the night.

Bubastis

Michael Stotter

"How long has he been dead?"

The coroner looked up at the speaker peering over his glasses that had slipped down his nose.

"If you'd give me one minute, Frank." The coroner removed the thermometer and read the temperature. "At a rough guestimate, I'd say at least twelve hours."

Detective Chief Superintendent Frank Hunter looked at his watch, squinting in the gloom of the room. The curtains were closed, only allowing filtered sunlight into the room. "That would be around one in the morning."

"If you say so," the coroner said.

"Any obvious signs?"

The coroner rose to his feet, a knee bone clicking audibly as he did so. He winced. "Bloody rheumatism!" He wiped the thermometer carefully before putting it away. He pushed his spectacles into place and gave Hunter's question a minute's thought before answering: "None obvious at this point in time, Frank. But the prelim suggests he died of a heart attack. Rigor mortis has come and gone, you can see that by the way he still

146

grips the poker. And before you ask, yes, I'll get the autopsy report to you as soon as humanly possible."

Frank smiled. "Thanks, Ian, I owe you one."

"Hmm. Make it a double!"

Ian stepped over the body and left the room.

The call had come Hunter's way just over an hour ago, phoned in by a very worried neighbour. Life was normally pretty quiet in the village of Finchingfield. The village was in the county of Essex just fifty miles from London, and a mere stones throw from the M11 motorway. Far enough away to attract those who wanted a little peace and quiet in their life and still commute into London, which only took an hour on the British Rail service into Liverpool Street. There were still some unspoilt houses to be had, none of the mock-Tudor rubbish or neo-Georgian country manors. Good, solidly built homes designed for living in and not gracing the pages of *Country Life* or even *Essex*.

But the tranquillity of a rare balmy August evening, when the scent of Evening Primroses wafted in the air, had been shattered by incomprehensible screaming and shouting (according to Michelle Rose, the neighbour who phoned the police) coming from the late Robin Hewitt's home.

Mrs. Rose explained to Hunter and Inspector Helen MacLaughlin that she had left the comfort of her home and went to investigate. Her spouse, who was high up in a merchant bank in the City, was still away at a seminar and her children were at boarding school. That left Mrs. Rose on her own with no one else to support her to knock on Hewitt's door. She wasn't really surprised to find it opened, not wide but off the latch. So calling out Hewitt's name, she let herself into the house.

Michelle Rose wasn't a small woman but she wasn't large. An air of competence exuded from her borne from years as a special needs teacher. She said she entered the library and found Hewitt dead on the floor. Then she immediately phoned the local police station.

Within the hour the usual police hordes descended on Hewitt's house. The scene of crime officers now worked the room methodically, taking pictures, gathering samples of carpet and clothing fibres, and digging out everything from under the dead man's fingernails. Forensics had dusted everywhere for fingerprints. Although there was a dead body, there were no signs of forcible entry or that Hewitt had been assaulted, his death was a mystery.

"And you saw no one else?" Hunter asked.

They had moved out of the library into the kitchen and sat at a large breakfast table surrounded by units made of natural oak. Each had a cup of freshly made tea in front of them, thoughtfully provided by Inspector Helen MacLaughlin. She drank hers whilst standing with her back to them, looking out of the window across the manicured lawn with its borders of wild flowers and more formal planting of rose bushes with rows of African marigolds interplanted with salvias and silver leaf shrubs.

"Not that I can recall," Michelle replied. She flicked a loose lock of hair behind her ear.

"Are you sure?"

"As much as I can be, Inspector," she bristled slightly at the question.

Hunter chose to ignore his demotion. "What I'm wondering, Michelle. May I call you Michelle?" She nodded. "What I was wondering was if Mr. Hewitt was in the habit of leaving his front door open. Especially with a house full of fine artefacts."

Michelle gazed back in the direction of the library where large display cabinets contained the main collection of Hewitt's Egyptian treasure.

She said, "In a small village there are very few secrets that remain guarded. It's a well-known fact that Hewitt spent weeks, sometimes months away from his house gathering many of his archaeological artefacts from around the world."

"An archaeologist?" Helen MacLaughlin said turning around.

"Not quite, Inspector." Was everyone an inspector to her? "An antiquities expert. His speciality was collecting artefacts from the Middle Kingdom period of Ancient Egypt."

"The Middle Kingdom? If my schoolgirl memory serves, that

was that around 1600 BC, wasn't it? Are you interested as well?" Helen asked.

"A good guess. The period was from 2040 to 1648 BC, actually. I'm not that keen. We spent many evenings discussing the subject Robin and I. Well, if the truth be told, Robin lectured and I listened. Though it was not as boring as it seems."

"I see," Hunter said. "The artefacts in the library. Would you know if any were missing?"

"Possibly. I'm not sure."

Helen nodded. "If you wouldn't mind checking?"

Hunter let the women go by themselves. He had the urge to have a cigarette but quelled it for the time being. He finished his tea and placed the cup and saucer on the draining board. He noticed a tin of unopened cat food on the side, the tin opener lying alongside. He looked around for the cat bowl. It was on the floor in the corner. In fact, there were three double bowls. He waited for the women to come back.

Helen shook her head.

"Michelle," he began, "did Mr. Hewitt own cats?"

"The cats! Oh my, where are they Inspector?"

He ignored the question. "Was he in a habit of letting them out?"

"Not without good reason. They were Persian cats you see. Very fickle and a little nasty at times."

Hunter looked at her, waiting for her to continue.

"I would say jealous was a better word. Isis gave me a couple of nasty scratches. But Toth and Ra were okay with me."

Helen smiled. "All named after Egyptian deities." She explained for Hunter's benefit.

"Thank you, Inspector MacLaughlin," Hunter said. "Let's get back to the door, Michelle."

"Well, Inspector," Michelle said, "we don't have that inner-city mentality in our little community. That's why Robin's—I mean Mr. Hewitt's—death is such a shock."

Hunter looked at the woman, her hand wrapped around the blue and white china cup, nails nicely varnished and well manicured, talking lightly about Hewitt's demise. *If she's in shock then I'm a monkey's uncle*, he thought.

"There are no neighbours from hell in Finchingfield then, Michelle? Into cat-napping?"

She was taken aback by Hunter's flippant remark. They made eye contact and locked stares for a moment. He was suddenly filled with a cold numbness throughout his body. But as quickly as the sensation came it vanished. Michelle Rose dropped her hands into her lap, the tea forgotten. Helen saw the exchange and was agitated by it. She stepped forward as if her bodily presence would stop the confrontation.

"Michelle," she began, "What we're trying to ascertain is; was Mr. Hewitt in the habit of leaving his door unlocked?"

"No."

"Thank you."

Michelle looked at Helen and said, "Are you finished with me? May I go?"

"Yes, but be available to give an officer a formal statement. Leave your details with the constable at the front door on your way out."

Both police officers watched Michelle Rose leave the room and move out of ear shot.

"What the hell was that all about?" Helen asked.

"What?"

"Frank, that bloody look she gave you."

"You noticed it?"

"Christ sake, it would have frozen a snowball in hell."

Hunter stood up and pushed his hands into his pockets. "That came out of the blue. Scared the hell out of me."

"Right!" Hunter exclaimed clapping his hands together. "This seems to be a two pint problem. Let's adjourn and compare notes."

"Lead on, Macduff."

Hunter and MacLaughlin were seated in the restaurant section of the Finch Inn which sat on the top of the street next to the church. Like all roads led to Rome, all main roads in the area led to the village of Finchingfield and its pond. This tourist gathering point was fed by the River Plant and the brook kept the houses at a respectable distance as it tended to flood. The white painted Finch Inn was a stone's throw from the pond and had been around in one form or another since the mid sixteenth century. They chose to eat inside rather than in the pub garden, away from the swings and children.

Both had opted for the homemade pie, steak cooked in beer, with a pint of Courage beer for Hunter and a glass of draught cider for MacLauglin. Being mid-week the tourist trade was slow but there were enough locals to create an amiable atmosphere. The officers ate their meal in silence, both reflecting on the case. When the plates had been removed, their glasses refilled, they relaxed a little before embarking on their own post-mortem of events.

"So," Hunter said, "what's your opinion?"

"Ian reckons heart attack."

"Never saw one with a face like that, though."

"Yes, it was a bit strange."

"Like he was frightened to death."

"Come off it, Frank."

"Honestly. The bloke looked absolutely terrified about something."

Helen turned her face to the window. She absently brushed her mousey coloured hair out of her eyes, thinking on what her senior officer said.

"The poker."

"Ah! Wondered when your were going to get to that." Hunter couldn't hide his smirk.

"Middle of August. It's hot. There's no fire and he's got a poker in his hand."

"Go on."

"Why would he be holding a poker?"

"Why would you hold a poker?" He turned the question around.

"For protection."

"Against what?"

"Or whom."

"Exactly."

They looked at each other and Hunter took a long swig of his beer. Helen looked around the pub. The chief superintendent went to the bar and ordered another round.

Hunter returned with the drinks. Helen saw the look on his face.

"What's up?" she asked.

"Don't know. But I need to take another look at Hewitt's place." He looked at his watch. "The forensics boys should be done in a half hour, I'm going back."

"What's with the " 'I'm'?"

"Helen, I want you to get all the gen you can on Hewitt. Go back to the fort and get on to Custom and Excise and see if they've got anything on him."

"Such as?"

"Import export license. How many trips to Egypt in the last year. You know the stuff."

She leaned across the table, she was frowning. "And what will you be doing?"

Hunter gave her a weak smile. "Taking a closer look at Hewitt's place. I got a feeling that the answer is right there. Our Mrs. Rose says that there are no artefacts gone from the library, right? But three cats have disappeared."

"They might have got out whilst the door was opened."

"True enough. Cats and dogs may be independent but they still like the easy life of being fed and pampered. Our moggies didn't have their last supper."

Helen nodded. She'd worked long enough with Hunter to allow the man to follow his hunches.

Hunter flashed his ID to the constable positioned at the front door and entered the house. He made for the library. Hewitt's body had been removed and the scene of crime officers had done their job. All that was left was a taped outline of Hewitt's body where it once lay. Hunter moved to the display cabinets. Behind the locked glass doors were glass shelves holding various artefacts. Some were labelled, others not.

There were fragments of alabaster bowls; samples of papyrus, one or two very exotic scarab necklaces, statues of gods and goddesses. Hunter recognised Isis wearing a headdress of horns encompassing the sun. His attention was caught by what

he thought was a boomerang. He read the display card: Ivory
Magic Knife 1850 BC. It was engraved with animals, a lion, a
panther and what looked like a hippopotamus holding a knife.

Alongside one cabinet was a stone sarcophagus. He moved
in for a closer inspection. It appeared to be sealed, the engrav-
ing on the outside was faded. Hunter wondered if there was a
mummy entombed in its coffin inside. In another corner of the
room was a bronze casket with two feline figures on the lid,
one seated, the other standing. Hunter thought that the answers
he was seeking weren't to be found there.

His mobile phone rang and he answered it.

"Frank, it's Ian. Thought you might want to know this right
away." The coroner was excited.

"Go on, Ian, I'm listening."

"Our dead man. Wasn't a heart attack as I first thought. We
found some wounds around his arms and legs."

"Scratches?"

"How? Well, yes."

"Cat scratches?"

"You're in the wrong job, old son. Wouldn't definitely say
pussycat, but feline, though not recent. Now it wasn't the
scratches that killed him but some sort of blood poisoning.
Pound to a pinch of salt it entered the blood system through
the scratches. I'm waiting for the toxicology report to come
back. I've asked for it PDQ, and I'll get back to you as soon
as humanly."

"Right, cheers, Ian."

Hunter put the mobile phone away.

"Cats. Everything keeps coming back to cats." He needed to
say it aloud so that he could fully understand it himself.

He spent the next two and a half hours searching the house
from top to bottom. He wasn't sure what he was looking for
but one thing he was certain about was that a man who had
three cats didn't appear to have many cat associated goodies;
no scratching poles, squeaking plastic mice or balls on a rope.
He ended up back in the kitchen.

He decided a shot of coffee was needed to clear his mind.
Opening and shutting various cabinets he found the ingredients

for fresh coffee and prepared himself a jug. Taking the cream from the fridge, he saw the cork notice board. The calendar was showing the right month—August—and Hewitt had circled two dates: the 28th and 29th. The 28th being today. Was there any significance?

He poured his coffee and took it outside to the patio area. It was a hot evening and Hunter shrugged out of his jacket, throwing it over the back of a chair. He occupied another. He sat with his feet up on the table, resting the coffee cup on his growing belly, and watched the tree tops sway in the wind. After a few minutes he got bored and turned his attention to the garden.

The lawn dog-legged to the left where the ground began to rise slightly. He thought he saw something move in the undergrowth. Curiosity getting the better of him, he got to his feet and walked down to the end of the garden. Something told him to approach with caution. Instincts again said that he should go wide of the dog-leg. Which he did. A couple of yards in front of him were two Persian cats sitting upright as though they were on guard. Were either of them Ra, Isis or Toth? They looked at him but didn't move. On his guard he edged forward. A hissing noise from his right brought him to a dead stop. He moved only his head to see what it was. The third Persian cat, jet black with yellow piercing eyes, glared opprobriously at him.

Hunter slowly back away. He had nothing on him to protect himself. The black cat came out from the undergrowth and stood in the middle of the path. The other two cats looked at it, then at Hunter. He continued moving backward. The cats remained where they were. Suddenly his mobile phone sprang into life and rang. The noise startled the cats and they ran into the bushes. Hunter jabbed the send button.

"Hello!"

"Frank, it's Helen."

"Bloody life-saver you are." He began to jog down the garden.

"Eh? Look, news on Hewitt. According to Scotland Yard's Art and Antiquities Unit they have a file on him. In 1995 he was caught at Cairo Airport with some artefacts trying to get them out of the country disguised as something he bought from a bazaar. He got away with that. Then in 1996 he tried to sell, get this, some cat mummies to the British Museum Egyptology department. They were suspicious and found they were stolen from a cat graveyard near Bubastis. Somehow he got away with it again. He's well known in the antiquities trade and much sought after."

"So he's not the lilly-white boy Mrs. Rose would have him pegged as," he said reaching the patio.

"That's the other thing. There's no Mrs. Rose."

"What?"

"There's no one registered at that house. It's been vacant for six months. The owners, a Mr. and Mrs. Davies, are out of the country. No letting agent has it on their books."

"You have been a busy girl."

"The wonderful world of the Internet, granddad."

"Okay, get down here as soon as you can." He broke the connection.

Looking over his shoulder, he watched the trio of cats reappear. They started for the house but stopped. All three sat down, ears cocked towards the house. He quickly stepped into the kitchen.

"Cats, Cairo and a mysterious woman. Sounds like a TV plot."

"It does, doesn't it, Inspector Hunter."

Michelle Rose had silently entered the kitchen. Hunter looked up not really surprised to see her.

"The cats. You've come for the cats, Michelle?"

She nodded.

"What's your interest in them?"

"Ah, you haven't worked that out yet, then?"

"Me? I'm just an ignorant policeman. I think Inspector MacLaughlin may do in time."

"Yes, I'm sure she would. She much more intuitive than yourself." She moved gracefully into the room and stood on the other side of the kitchen table. "Females often are. But I suppose we can't all be perfect, can we?"

"You're not who you claim to be, Michelle. Why would you lie?"

"My dear inspector, you wouldn't believe me if I told you."

"Try me."

She wagged her finger at him slowly. "Now, now. But I will tell you a story about a robbery. In Istabl Antar in Middle Egypt grave robbers found a cemetery and ransacked it, taking all what they thought was worthy. But they left behind a treasure far beyond what they could ever imagine. Hewitt found it and smuggled it out of Egypt. It was not his to keep. I was sent to retrieve it but the fool had already meddled with it."

Hunter groaned. "Not an ancient curse?"

"You are not very wise to be so sceptical. He hadn't fully done his homework and released Pakhet's spirit at the wrong time. This time in the Egyptian calendar is the Festival of Bastet when no lions can be hunted. Pakhet is a lioness goddess, half cat and half female. Naturally Hewitt's cats thought that Pakhet was an enemy. I did tell you they were jealous."

"Hold on. You're telling me that an Egyptian lioness goddess came back to life and killed Hewitt because he had endangered her to his own cats."

"That and his own feeble cat cemetery he was preparing at the end of the garden."

Hunter shook his head to clear it. "Now Michelle, or whatever your name is, if you forgive my French, that's a load of crap."

"Inspector . . ."

"Detective Chief Inspector!"

Michelle moved around the table to stand only three feet away. "Whatever. Believe what you want but believe the truth."

She looked deep into his eyes and again he felt the strange cold numbness. This close to her he noticed that her eyes had changed colour, a peculiar hazel with pitch black pupils that were the wrong shape. She held his gaze for a minute before releasing him. He took an involuntarily step back and then she was moving away from him.

She trailed her hand across the kitchen table saying, "The name of the house, Inspector." Then she was gone.

Hunter took several moments to gather himself. His mind was befuddled but his eyes weren't clouded. Three lines of deep furrows crossed the table. The same area where Michelle had run her hand. He walked out of the house to the front door. The constable stood his guard. Hunter wanted to ask what direction Rose had gone but knew it was futile. He stopped on the garden path and turned to look at the nameplate. Engraved on a slab of polished wood was written: BUBASTIS.

Too Many Tomcats

B. J. Mull

IT WAS A LITTLE AFTER 10 p.m. when Ernie and Marie Finley climbed the steps of their modest white stucco house, after a Saturday evening out. Ernie was a small man, about five foot five, with a mustache and thinning brown hair; he had his key chain in his hands, searching for the right one in the dark. Marie, who was twenty pounds heavier than her husband, her dyed-black hair piled on top of her head adding to her five foot ten frame, stood next to him on the porch, biting her lower lip to keep from snapping, "Can't you hurry up!", which would have spoiled a perfect evening.

They had gone to a new French restaurant, Le Perroquet, and not once during the leisurely meal had Marie thought of their little Sarah, left at home with a babysitter. Later, they went to a movie—a comedy—where she was comfortably distracted during the feature. But as soon as the end credits began to roll, anxiety began to roll over her, and she couldn't wait to get out of the theater and get home. She suddenly felt heartsick being away from Sarah.

When Ernie suggested they stop for ice cream, Marie had

said quickly, "No. I'm trying to lose weight." (Never mind the four-course dinner topped off with cherries flambe.) Her husband just smiled; she knew he understood. That's what she loved most about him.

Ernie finally got the key in the lock and opened the front door and they both stepped inside.

Everything in the livingroom was purple—or shades of purple, from lavender to dusty rose. Ernie had gotten the idea several years ago when the middle-aged couple was trying to conceive. He'd read somewhere that the color purple sparked passion, and so he set about redecorating the house. It wasn't easy finding a purple couch.

The television—the only furnishing in the front room that wasn't purple—was on, volume low. Across from the TV, on the purple couch, sat the babysitter, a neighborhood girl named Misty. She was a pretty, pretty plump teen-ager, with flawless, cream-colored skin and short blonde hair cut like the Dutch Boy on the paint can. She looked up from a magazine as Ernie and Marie entered.

"Is Sarah asleep?" Marie asked in a whisper.

The babysitter nodded.

Marie sat down next to her on the couch. "Tell me about your evening."

Misty sighed; this was not her first visit to the Finleys. "Well," she said, "first off, right after you left, she started lookin' for you. Going from room to room, crying. . . ."

Marie looked sharply at Ernie, who stood next to the couch. "I *knew* we shouldn't have gone out," she told him. She turned back to the sitter. "Then what?" she asked.

"Then I played the tape of cartoons you rented, and she sat on my lap and watched for awhile . . . she seemed to like the ones about Garfield, best . . . but then she got bored and started lookin' for you again."

"Did you give her the cookies I left on the counter?" Marie asked.

"She wouldn't eat them. But she did drink the milk. I warmed it up like you showed me. After that, I put her to bed and shut the door and she cried herself to sleep."

Marie sat silently, her hands clasped tightly in her lap, feeling like a terrible parent.

Misty stood. "Well, if that's all, I better go. See you next Saturday night?"

Marie looked up anxiously at Ernie, who was getting money out of his wallet to pay the girl.

"No," he said softly, looking back at Marie. "We won't be needing you." He handed Misty the money. "I'll drive you home."

After they left, Marie tip-toed down the lavender carpeted hallway to Sarah's room. The door was shut and she quietly turned the knob and slowly opened the door.

Moonlight poured in through a window and fell across the tiny bed in the center of the room where Sarah lay sleeping, her pink tummy gently rising and falling. Marie smiled, filled with love and joy as she moved toward the little form.

Sarah must have heard Marie because she woke and jumped from the bed into Marie's arms. Marie fell to her knees, hugging the kitten tightly to her chest, kissing the animal all about its furry white face.

"Mommy's home," she purred. "Mommy's home."

The little kitten purred back.

"Now go to sleep," she said, and returned the kitten to the bed, which was really a doll's bed.

They had gotten the pink, plastic bed—which came with a little matching dresser and night stand—shortly after bringing the kitten home from the Humane Society. Ernie spotted the doll set in the window of Ingram's Department Store, and bought it as a joke. But Marie immediately cleared out the extra bedroom and put the little furniture in. At first, she placed the tiny dresser over against one wall, the bed against the other wall, and the night stand by the window. But that looked silly. So she moved everything to the center of the room, where it was now. Recently, she added a poster of Garfield to the wall, and one of a kitten hanging by its front paws from a limb, with the words: Hang In There.

Marie quietly left Sarah's room, closing the door gently, and walked down the hallway to the kitchen, where she found Ernie sitting at the round oak table. He had a serious expression on his face. She suspected he was upset with her for canceling the babysitter.

Marie pulled out a chair and sat next to him.

"I'm sorry about our Saturday night dates," she began, "but I'm just a wreck whenever I have to leave Sarah."

"I know," he said.

"We'll be able to go out again soon," Marie promised, "when she's a little bit older."

"That's fine."

Ernie's face remained somber, so Marie leaned toward her husband and asked, "Then . . . what's wrong?"

"It's time to have her spayed, Marie," he said.

Marie pulled back, horrified. "Oh, no. Not that."

"Now, Marie," Ernie said sternly, as if he were talking to a child, "we discussed this before we got Sarah, and you agreed."

"I know," she said, desperation building in her voice, "but I *hate* the idea. It's so. . . . so *inhumane*. Can't we just keep her inside the house all the time?"

Ernie shook his head. "You know she'll get out. . . . it happened last week . . . and there are just too many tomcats in the neighborhood to risk that."

Marie felt tears welling in her eyes. "I don't want anybody cutting her open. . . . She's too little to have that done. It's not the right time. We'll spay her later, I promise."

"It *is* the right time," Ernie argued. "She's four and a half months old and that's when the vet said to bring her in. The longer we wait, the harder it will be on Sarah."

Marie sat expressionless, but the rage was building up within her like lava in a volcano.

"I've already scheduled an appointment for Monday with Dr. Harden," Ernie continued. "He was very gentle with Sarah when we took her to him from the Humane Society. You said so yourself."

Marie said nothing.

"He'll be very careful."

And now Marie exploded. "How would *you* like being neutered? How would you like never being able to have children?"

Ernie's face fell; there was hurt in his eyes.

"I'm sorry," Marie said softly. "I didn't mean it like that. It's not entirely your fault we don't have our 2.5 quota."

Ernie took one of her hands in his and spoke earnestly. "Marie, if we don't have her spayed, and one of the toms gets her, and she has kittens, would you be able to give the babies away? I don't think so. Nor would I. And this house is too small for a lot of cats—even 2.5—having even more kittens we wouldn't have the heart to give away."

Marie was silent for a few moments, then she sighed. "All right, Ernie, we'll have her spayed. But I don't like it one bit. Not one little bit."

Dr. Tom Harden, dark-haired, thirty-five years old, his blue eyes setting off well-chiseled features, washed his hands at the stainless steel sink in the operating room of his veterinarian hospital.

In the center of the room, on a shiny chrome table, lay the Finley's kitten, stretched out on its back, still under the anesthesia, its belly yellow from the iodine he had just spread on the closed incisions.

The operation had gone well, but then, why shouldn't it? He was, after all, one of the best damn vets in the whole state, if not the whole United States—even if the rest of the country was denied his expertise because he was stuck in a backwater town in the middle of nowhere.

A backwater town, however, did have its advantages. Like low cost of living, inexpensive housing, no traffic jams, short lines at the bank. . . . And a bevy of lovely, lonely women. Juicy tomatoes just ripe for the pickin' and a very low incidence of sexually transmitted disease. He'd sampled plenty of the local harvest in this sleepy river town.

It didn't matter that he was married. With children. It was the hunter/gatherer's inalienable right to eat from bush to bush to satisfy his hunger. Of course, his wife didn't see it that way. So after the first time she caught him, he'd been careful ever since.

Dr. Harden picked up the kitten and took it over to one of

the cages and placed the slumbering animal inside, in the doll's bed the Finleys had brought along.

Was that couple *weird*! Really sick in the head, clinically, certifiable. Treating the kitten, which they called Sarah, like it was their child. He'd met some pretty neurotic people in his line of work, but they took the cake.

Furthermore, much to his annoyance, the Finleys had insisted on staying and keeping vigil in the reception area until the operation was over. Now he would have to go out and talk to them, as if he didn't have enough to do.

He left the operating room and went through a connecting door to the front of the building which was half office, half reception area, the two being separated by a high counter. As he passed through the office, the receptionist, Heather—a pretty young thing just out of high school—looked up from her typewriter and gave him a coy smile.

My God, she was luscious. With her long slender legs, curvaceous body, and wild blond hair, Heather was a Barbie doll come to life. . . . Too bad their relationship had to come to an end. This was one tomato that would need to die on the vine.

He entered the reception area, with its brown paneled walls, red vinyl chairs, and green tiled floor which Mr. Finley was pacing like an expectant father; the man reminded Dr. Harden of somebody . . . who? Ah! Mr. Whipple from the old toilet-paper commercials!

Mrs. Finley, who must have been half again her husband's size—and could probably hurt her husband if she wanted to—sat with her hands clenched tightly in her lap, worry lines etched across her forehead. The woman's hair, piled on her head in huge looping curls as if wrapped around soup cans, looked purple under the fluorescent ceiling lights.

Harden put on his kindly doctor face as he approached the couple.

The moment Mrs. Finley spotted him, she jumped up from her chair and rushed toward him.

"Oh, doctor," she said anxiously, "how is Sarah?"

"She's just fine," he told her with a smile.

Mr. Finley, joining his wife, asked, "Can we see her now?"

"I don't think that would be wise. She's resting."

"Oh, please," the woman said, pitifully. "Can't we see her for just a minute?"

"No," Dr. Harden said firmly. "I don't want her disturbed." Then patronizingly he added, "Why don't you folks run along home. You can see her in the morning."

Mr. Finley nodded, uncertainly, and turned to go, but the missus stood her ground. "Why can't we take Sarah with us?" the stupid woman asked. "The operation's over."

"Because you can't," Harden snapped, making Mrs. Finley frown, so he quickly explained, "We need to keep her overnight, for observation."

Which was ridiculous. No one checked on the animals during the night, the beasts were on their own; but Mrs. Finley seemed to accept these conventional words, and it was the clinic's policy to keep pets overnight after even a simple operation, mostly to justify higher charges.

Dr. Harden watched the pair go out the front door. The whole conversation had been ridiculous, he thought. In fact, going through with the operation at all had been ridiculous. Because in the morning the cat would be dead.

As he walked back into the office area, Heather rose from her desk and came to him, putting her arms around his waist, looking up into his face, with open, inviting lips.

"Did you tell her yet?" she asked.

"Who?"

"Who do you think?"

"No. I'm waiting for the right time."

Heather drew back, patted her tummy with one hand, and said, "Well you'd better tell her soon because I'm beginning to show. And I want a last name for our child *before* its born."

He gave her a half-hearted smile. "I'll tell her this weekend."

Heather smiled back, her arms around him again. "I know you will, so I won't have to." Then she said cheerfully, "Oh, by the way, my father said he'll put in the new waterheater on Sunday. I told him to use the key under the mat to let himself in."

Dr. Harden nodded numbly.

"Excuse me." A voice said.

Harden quickly pushed the girl away, and turned to see Mrs. Finley standing at the counter. She had something in her hands.

"The pillow fell out of the bed in the car," the woman said as she held out a little square white piece of fluff. "Would you please see that Sarah gets it?"

"Yes," Dr. Harden said tersely, his face red with both embarrassment and rage. "Just leave it on the counter."

Mrs. Finley nodded and thanked him and left. This time for good, he hoped.

Heather returned to his side. "I don't think she heard us," the girl said quietly.

He gave her a disgusted look, but Heather just shrugged. "And even if she did, it doesn't matter; people get married and divorced all the time." And she returned to her work at the desk.

Harden, feeling sick to his stomach, left the office area and went down a short hall to his private office, stepping over a bucket filled with rainwater from a recent downpour. He entered the room and shut the door, then slumped down in the leather chair behind his desk.

The building needed a new roof, and a sprinkler system to bring it up to code. Then there was the foundation that cracked. And equipment that should be replaced.

But he didn't have enough money for all that.

He did, however, have insurance. Insurance that would give him a brand new building and state-of-the-art equipment . . . if ever there were a disaster.

He'd been planning it for weeks, for just the right time. Which seemed like tonight because he didn't want many animals to die—his mission in life was to attend to the needs of God's creatures, after all—and there was only one animal being boarded in the building.

The Finleys would just have to get themselves another "baby." And it would serve those lunatics right, treating a cat better than a person.

He supposed he could have let the couple take their pet home with them, but that break from standard operating procedure might have tipped Heather. Lately she must have sensed his coolness, and everything needed to seem normal. And if no animals were present during the accident, that might raise suspicion. That's why he went ahead with the kitten's operation.

His original plan, which spread through his brain like the seeping gas of the faulty water heater, had been to destroy only the building. But recently, since he found out he was to be a father again, the plan took on an added element: Heather.

He'd read somewhere about an incident, a freakish accident, where leaking gas from a water heater filled a room, and the simple act of flipping on a nearby light switch was enough to spark an explosion that had blown up the house.

He'd return late tonight, and put out the pilot light and open the gas line, and let the back room fill with propane fumes.

At eight in the morning, Heather would enter the back room to feed the animals as she always did, turn on the lights and KA-BOOM!, creatures great and small would wing their way to heaven.

He smiled, leaning back in his office chair, hands hooked behind his head, elbows fanned out.

After all, why not kill two "burdens" with one stone?

Marie Finley couldn't sleep. She lay in bed and heard the hall clock strike one, then two. Next to her, Ernie was gently snoring.

How could he sleep so peacefully, she thought, *when their baby lay in a cold, dark cage?*

Quietly she slipped out of bed and wandered down the hall to Sarah's room, where the door stood open. She looked in.

Moonlight shown in past the curtains casting long shadows from the branches of a magnolia tree across the small, forlorn-looking doll furniture in the center of the room, particularly without Sarah's little bed. Marie felt tears spring to her eyes; she missed Sarah so much. She entered the room and sat down on the lavender carpeted floor, taking the place of the bed.

She thought about Dr. Harden. She didn't like that man very much. Maybe Ernie hadn't noticed, but the doctor talked down to them, like they were just children to be dealt with; even though his mouth smiled, there was contempt in his eyes.

And there was another thing she didn't like about the vet: he was a womanizer. She'd overheard the conversation between him and his pregnant secretary when she went back to deliver the pillow.

Marie, still seated on the floor, her hands folded primly in her pajamaed lap, sighed. The bad rumors about the doctor she'd heard in the locker room after her water aerobics class must be true.

His poor wife—Jenny was her name. She was an attractive woman, so why would he want to stray? Marie couldn't understand it. She'd seen Jenny recently at the grocery store, looking sad and weary, with her two small, well-behaved children, in tow.

Her thoughts turned back to Sarah. She doubted very much if Dr. Harden—or his pregnant girlfriend—would be checking on Sarah during the night, who had probably woken up from the anesthesia by now, scared, wondering why she was stuck in a cage, wondering what she had done to deserve being put there, mewing and mewing for her mother and father. . . .

Marie sat up straighter as an awful thought crossed her mind. What if something had gone wrong during the operation? What if there had been complications caused by the doctor's malpractice, and he was hiding it from them?

What if Sarah weren't even *alive*? What if she'd died during the operation, and that devious doctor didn't want to tell them? Why else wouldn't he let them see her?

Marie stood up, caught in the clutches of terror, which was squeezing the very breath out of her. Maybe *that* explained the sense of foreboding she'd had on the ride home from the animal clinic, and why she couldn't now get to sleep.

Marie bolted from the room and went quickly back down the hall to her bedroom. She'd made up her mind. She was going out to that animal hospital right now! She didn't care if it was the middle of the night. Hadn't the secretary said there was a key under the doormat?

Quietly, she slipped out of her nightgown and into a cotton

housedress. Across the room, Ernie slept soundly, his chest rising and falling.

She wouldn't wake him to discuss the matter; he would only
try to dissuade her. Besides, everyone knows that a mother
knows best.

A three-quarter moon hung high in the sky, illuminating the
way through the back-country road. Soon, Marie pulled her
car into the gravel parking lot of the animal hospital, and got
out, quietly shutting the car door. The building was dark and
silent. The only noise was the rustling of the leaves in the trees
from a cool summer night breeze.

She found the key under the rubber front door mat and let
herself in.

The place smelled funny. But then, animal hospitals always
did. She didn't know how anyone could stand to work in one.
But after a moment the bad smell went away, or anyway she
got used to it.

Then cautiously she moved through the dark reception room
and into the office area and down the hallway to the back,
when the animals were kept.

She opened the door and stood there a minute, feeling a little
dizzy. It was hard to see in the dark. Marie's hand moved to
the nearby light switch. Her fingers were on it, ready to flick
the switch, when she suddenly pulled her hand back. The lights
might attract someone's attention. And she didn't want that.
She could be caught for breaking and entering, though she
didn't at all see it that way.

With her eyes now accustomed to the dark, she moved ahead
toward the cages, where her feet bumped into a metal bucket,
tipping it over, water spilling onto the cement floor making an
awful clatter. She froze.

Then from one of the cages came a pitiful sound, tiny and
frightened, and Marie ran toward it, recognizing the cry of her
baby. She quickly unlatched the cage door and reached in and
withdrew Sarah and held the animal to her chest.

"You're alive. . . . You're alive," Marie sobbed with joy.

But the kitten felt limp in her hands, and Marie's joy was
replaced with fear as she realized that Sarah was really sick.

And suddenly Marie felt sick, too, stomach nauseous, head pounding.

"Let's get out of here," she told the kitten, and she snatched the little bed out of the cage and ran from the room, shutting the door behind them.

In the outer office she scribbled a note on a piece of typing paper, leaving it on the desk, and that's when she saw the little pillow, still left on the counter. Harden hadn't even bothered to give it to Sarah. That thoughtless bastard.

She left the building, locking the front door, returning the key to its place under the mat. In the car, on the way home, she glanced anxiously at Sarah who rested in the bed, her head on the pillow. The kitten seemed to be doing better, even giving Marie a mew or two.

Marie felt better, too, breathing the fresh country air coming in the car window. The nausea and dizziness were gone, but replaced by indignation and fury. They were never, ever going to go back there!

Dr. Harden had never slept so good, knowing that in the morning all his troubles would be gone. He was especially cheerful at the breakfast table, where his pretty wife, Jenny, served him pancakes and sausage. He must have been too cheerful, though, because she gave him a suspicious look. So he launched into a tirade about that stupid, lazy secretary of his who he'd like to replace. Jenny, cutting the link sausage with a knife, gave him another funny look that he couldn't quite interpret. He promised himself that if all went as planned, he would stay faithful to his wife.

For a while, anyway.

As he ate his breakfast, he thought the fire department or police might call, telling him that his building had blown up, but the phone didn't ring. He looked at his watch. It was a little too soon, really. Heather didn't show up for work until eight. Then it would be another few minutes before she went into the back to feed the Finley's cat.

He stalled around until eight, then left the house and got into his car for the ten minute drive.

He took his time along the winding country road, the morning overcast and cool, eyes fixed on the horizon, looking for signs of destruction.

Then around the bend, the animal hospital came into view, still standing. He slammed on his brakes, coming to a halt the middle of the road, not knowing what to do.

Had Heather not shown up for work? No, her car was parked in the lot. He needed to wait a few more minutes. But where? Not in the middle of the road. And if he retreated, some other car coming along might see him, and blow a hole in his story.

He decided to forge ahead and play the hero who arrived just as the building exploded. The hero who tried in vain to save his secretary and the lone animal inside, but was driven back by the heat and flames. He smiled, liking that idea.

He parked his car at the far end of the lot and sat and waited, feeling safe inside. But at eight-thirty, when nothing had happened, he disgustedly threw open the car door and got out and stomped toward the front door.

Inside, he found Heather at her desk, hanging up the phone.

"There you are," she said. "I just called the gas company . . . I think there's some sort of leak, so I opened the windows."

"You opened the windows?!" he repeated, realizing his plan had just dissipated with the gas.

"Well, yes," she replied. "Do you want the place to blow up? You look terrible . . . Is anything the matter?"

"No," he snapped, then asked, "Why didn't you go in the back to feed the cat?"

"Because I didn't *have* to," she said irritably. "Mrs. Finley came and got it in the middle of the night." She waved a piece of paper in his face, "She left me a note. . . . Say, what's wrong with you?"

He didn't answer, but stomped down the hallway to the back.

He opened the door to the darkened room where the metal cages sat, all empty. The back door was ajar, held open with a tin bucket.

Goddamnit! he thought. *The bitch let all the gas out.*
And he flicked on the lights.
He was wrong.

Ernie Finley relaxed in his overstuffed lavender recliner as he read the evening newspaper. Marie, curled up on the purple couch across from him, was working on a needlepoint sampler of a cat, while Sarah frolicked on the carpet between them, batting about a little rose-colored pouch that contained cat-nip.

"Unbelievable," Ernie said, shaking his head, folding the paper and putting it down.

"What's that, dear?" Marie asked, her eyes still glued to the sampler.

"The accident at the veterinarian hospital," he answered.

"Oh, yes," she said, working the needle in the material. "I guess it destroyed the back half of the building."

Marie looked up from the sampler, and their eyes met. Ernie, feeling a lump in his throat, got out of his chair and sat next to her on the couch, taking one of her hands in his.

"Thank God you drove out there last night and saved our little girl," he said, his voice cracking with emotion.

Marie set the sampler aside. Patted his hand with hers. "Yes. I'm glad I listened to my inner voice."

"And if you hadn't left that note," Ernie went on, "the receptionist would have gotten hurt, instead of the doctor." He paused and shook his head. "I feel so sorry for him."

"I don't," Marie said archly.

Ernie looked at his wife, surprised by her coldness. "Marie, how can you say such a thing? The blast blew off his . . ." Ernie swallowed, unable to say the word. "He'll never be able to have more children."

"Well, he's already had his quota," she explained, and told him about the pregnant receptionist.

And he told her about a few others he'd heard about at the barber shop.

"So you see," Marie said, sticking the needle in the sampler, pulling the thread through, "everything's turned out for the good."

"I guess you're right, my dear," Ernie admitted. "You always are." He gave her a small peck of a kiss. "Anyway, there's one less tomcat in the neighborhood."

A Capital Cat Crime

Richard T. Chizmar

CLASSIFIED MATERIAL (File #33)

THE FOLLOWING TRANSCRIPT CONTAINS EXCERPTS from the tape-recorded interrogation of suspect Michael Lee Flowers, conducted on April 12, 1994. Interrogation duties handled by Special Agent Jay Ryan (#A3323) and Special Agent Frank Cavanaugh (#A4194). Side B of the first of two tapes (Files #31 and #32) begins with the following statements:

RYAN: State your name again.

FLOWERS: Michael Flowers.

RYAN: Age?

FLOWERS: Forty-one.

RYAN: Occupation?

FLOWERS: I told you . . . I'm unemployed . . . I used to be a sixth-grade teacher, but that was a long time ago.

RYAN: Residence?

FLOWERS: (*laughs*) Washington, D.C. Downtown mostly.

RYAN: Okay, then let's get back to where we were before the tape ended. I'd just started to ask you who else you'd shared this information with. Can you tell me now exactly how many people you told about the cats?

FLOWERS: Humph, that's kinda tough to answer. Maybe six . . . seven . . . ten people. A dozen if you count the two cops who caught me this morning.

RYAN: (*directed at Agent Cavanaugh*) Jesus, that many.

FLOWERS: I don't know for sure. Maybe more, maybe less. Spend a few years out on the street and you become a storyteller. Everyone out there's got a story to tell—

RYAN: Names. We'll need the names of every person you told in case we need to talk to them later. When we're finished here, we're going to give you some paper and a pen, and what we need for you to do is this: write down the names and where we can find each and every person you told about this. If the senator decides to press charges, it'll be a damned sight better for you, if we can verify your story. A couple of witnesses who'll swear you told them this same story *before* today's events will prove that you didn't make up the whole thing on the spot just to save your ass . . . or as an excuse for what you were doing to those poor cats.

FLOWERS: (*pounds fist on table*) Christ, a city full of the damned animals and I have to pick a senator's daughter's cat. (*Several seconds of silence.*) Do you really think he'll press charges?

RYAN: Relax, Mr. Flowers. It's like I said, if you cooperate with us, tell us the complete truth, we'll do our best to make sure there are no charges. Agent Cavanaugh has known the senator for many years; if anyone can take care of you, he can.

FLOWERS: Well . . . I can give you the names, but it won't be easy to find these guys. Most of them are like me; they have to move around a lot.

RYAN: That's okay. It's really just a precaution we're taking for your own protection. Hopefully we won't have to bother with any of them. Now, listen, what we need to do right now is go over your story one more time.

FLOWERS: And then can I get something to eat?

RYAN: (*nodding*) When we're finished here we'll get those names down on paper and then you can eat anything you want.

FLOWERS: Do I start from the beginning again?

RYAN: Yes, from the beginning. But this time, instead of listening to the entire story at once, we're going to run through the short version. We're going to ask you specific questions and we'd like for you to answer each question to the best of your ability. We understand that the day in question took place almost a year ago, but remember, we're looking for details here. The more you remember, the better. So take your time and think carefully about everything you say.

FLOWERS: Not really much more to remember, but I'll tell you again just the same.

RYAN: Okay, let's go back to that day again.

FLOWERS: One more time, huh? (*Clearing his throat*) Let's see . . . it was a Monday, the day after Easter. I remember that because my stomach was still full from the big dinner we'd had the night before at Patterson's Shelter over on L and Tenth. Fresh Virginia ham, potato salad, hot rolls, the works. It was one helluva feast. Don't remember the exact date—

CAVANAUGH: Did you have anything to drink that night?

FLOWERS: Don't drink alcohol. Never have. I told the police they could test me but—

CAVANAUGH: Drugs?

FLOWERS: Never have.

RYAN: Are you certain about that—?

FLOWERS:—was early in the morning, somewhere between six and seven. I remember it was raining. A breeze was blowing in from the Potomac and it was cold. Real cold for April. I had just come from the wall . . . the Vietnam Memorial, you know? I go there a couple of times every month to visit some old friends of mine. I spent one tour in Vietnam . . . and I know maybe fifteen, twenty of those names on that wall. I know too many of them. Also know that I was damned lucky to come home from there, so I go and see my friends as often as I can.

The workers and guards don't like it when we come around during the day, though, because the tourists don't like to see us close up. It's the same way all over this city. Go right ahead and live and die on our streets, but for Godsakes, don't come near our national monuments, and whatever you do, don't do it when someone else can see you. You're too dirty, you stink, you're animals, you're dangerous. They've got plenty of reasons. Not too many good ones, though. The volunteer workers are a whole lot nicer, but they don't start up until the summer.

Anyway, back to the story. After I finished at the war memorial, I cut across the recreation fields near the river and walked over to one of the abandoned row homes over on Preston. You know, the ones they closed down last winter? Some of us used to go there from time to time to play cards or to get out of the cold. The basement was too messed up to be of any good use and was usually flooded anyway, but the top floor wasn't so bad. Corner unit had a sofa and a table and some old chairs. We tried to keep the place in decent condition and keep it quiet so that not too many others would find out about it. But it didn't work. A few months ago, a bunch of crackheads burned the place down, fried themselves in the process.

So, anyway, that's where I was—on the top floor of that old rowhouse on Preston Street, reading a paperback next to the window—when it happened . . .

RYAN: There were how many men?

FLOWERS: There were two men and—

CAVANAUGH: And you're sure they didn't come together?

FLOWERS: Positive. I watched them pull up on opposite sides of the street. I only read for about an hour or so that morning, and then I got tired and put the book down on the windowsill, checked out the view. It was still pretty early and the rain was getting heavier, so the streets were empty. I know what you're thinking . . . Preston Street is never empty, but it was that morning.
Both cars pulled up within a few minutes of each other. First, one of those long dark sedans with blacked-out windows circled the block, then parked across the street. I couldn't tell how many people were inside, but the man got out of the back door, so there was at least someone else inside the car doing the driving. The man who got out was black. Black skin, black coat, black pants, black umbrella. That's the best look I got of him and that's all I can remember about the way he looked. That and the fact that he was tall, very tall. A minute or so later, a green van pulled up almost directly beneath my window, and the second man got out.

RYAN:—so you're certain that you never saw a third person?

FLOWERS: Yeah. I never saw the driver leave the limousine, and I don't think there was anyone else inside the van.

CAVANAUGH: Why do you say that?

FLOWERS: Well, the guy driving the van wasn't very big and he didn't look very strong, either. After he opened the van's back doors, he struggled with that box for quite some time before he got a good hold on it. The black guy was still standing across the street, and I just figured that if someone else was inside the van, the little guy would've asked them for some help—

FLOWERS:—almost had myself a heart attack when I heard their footsteps on the stairs. I thought for sure that they were coming all the way up to the top floor, and I swear, I've never been so scared in my entire life. I didn't know what was going down—big-time drugs, a payoff, something—but I didn't think they'd be real happy to find me waiting up there. So I crawled into the corner behind the sofa and tried my best to stay real quiet. When they stopped on the second floor, I thanked the Lord and sat perfectly still, praying that they'd take care of their business in a hurry and be on their way.

But what I'd forgotten about that particular corner was that there were two holes—one about four inches across and one about half that size—in the floor behind the sofa where pipes used to run up from the basement. Not only could I hear most of what they were saying, I could actually *see* a small portion of the room.

CAVANAUGH: You say you saw only one of the men clearly?

FLOWERS: That's right. The man who was driving the van stopped right in my line of sight, at a perfect angle for me to see through the big hole, and that's where he put the box down. They talked for a minute or so, they might've shook hands, and then he started pacing back and forth as they spoke . . . so I could only see him for a few seconds at a time before he disappeared from my sight, but I must have glimpsed his face twenty or thirty times.

RYAN: Okay, one more time, what did he look like?

FLOWERS: Well, he sure wasn't anything special to look at. That's what I remember most about him. He was no taller than me and probably just as skinny. And he had white hair. I remember that real well. I'd thought he was blond when I saw him outside, but it must have been the rain and the window glass, because his hair was as white as snow—

FLOWERS: Christ, I've already told you all of this!

RYAN: I know this is terribly repetitive, Mr. Flowers, but that's the idea here . . . to see if we can help you to remember something you forgot about the first time. Now, please be patient with us. This next part is extremely important. What else can you tell us about the box he was carrying?

FLOWERS: (*Several seconds of silence.*) I'm telling you the truth, I don't remember anything else. The box just about came up to the man's waist. It was covered with a cloth or a blanket or something, which the man removed once they were inside. The box or cage or whatever it was looked like it was made of glass and metal, and it looked like it must have been pretty heavy. When I saw it, I remember thinking: no wonder he'd had so much of a problem getting it out from the van. And when the man removed the blanket, I got a clear view of what was inside that box—

FLOWERS: That's right. There were cats inside the box. Nothing else, I'm certain. The glass looked thick and heavy and practically bombproof, but it was crystal clear. The box was divided right down the middle by a clear partition and there were two cats inside one section and a third cat inside the other. I saw them clear as day. No question about it. And all three cats looked the same; I remember thinking that they looked like Halloween cats because they were orange and black—

CAVANAUGH:—and you're absolutely certain you heard them use those exact words?

FLOWERS: I told you, I couldn't hear everything clearly because it was raining so damned hard and the rain was making too much noise on the roof. But I heard enough. Snatches of conversation here and there. Words. Sentences.

The black man spoke kind of softly, so I didn't hear him much. I don't think he was American, though. He spoke pretty good English, but the words came out slow and stiff, like it was a learned language. The man from the van had a surprisingly strong voice, though, and I could hear him talk the majority of the time. I think he might've been nervous because—

CAVANAUGH: But let's be perfectly clear here, you do submit that you heard them talk about some type of rabies and you heard them mention those particular countries by name?

FLOWERS: Yeah, I heard all of that. I swear to it. I didn't hear the specifics, but I heard a word here, a word there, and it all fit together. They were talking about some kind of disease, some kind of new rabies strain or virus or something or other, and how dangerous their business at hand was. I remember they kept pointing and leaning down and looking at the cats, and the man from the van made a big show of explaining that the single cat was pregnant. Then they started talking about all those medical terms and foreign countries and they lost me in a hurry-

CAVANAUGH: But you recognized the names of those countries, huh?

FLOWERS: Sure did. I taught history for two long years before switching over to social studies, so I knew exactly what countries they were talking about, knew where they were located too. But it all happened so fast . . . I just couldn't piece everything together . . . until I read that newspaper last month—

RYAN: And you came to this conclusion as soon as you read the newspaper article?

FLOWERS: No, not *the* newspaper article; there were many articles. You see, papers are easy to get around here, even for the homeless, because so many people throw them away, leave them in the park, on the subway, wherever they please.

I read the first article last month in the *Washington Post*. The second story a week later. Then, two more ran last week, in both the *Post* and the *Washington Times*. Each story almost identical. Two tiny countries across the Atlantic, nearly a quarter of Central America, even somewhere in Cuba for Christsakes . . . all suffering from the same deadly virus. Thousands dead, thousands more dying, scientists and doctors baffled. A disease of unprecedented danger and unknown origin, the officials claimed. And the names of those countries . . . well, I could have told you them almost a year ago. Jesus—

FLOWERS:—was scared and that's the how and the why I got caught this morning taking off with the senator's daughter's cat. I freely admit it . . . I was gonna take that cat somewhere and kill it. Just like I did to all the others. All I can think about now is that I knew all this time. All those people dead . . . and I knew.

I'm not sorry for what I did to those cats, either. I mean, maybe our cats *are* safe, maybe it was just those three in that glass box. Who knows? But, for Christsakes, Cuba's awful close to the coast of Florida . . . and, besides, what if—

CLASSIFIED MATERIAL (File #34)

Confidential Memorandum

To: Royce Larkin, Commander-in-Chief
From: Jay Ryan, Special Agent
Date: April 13, 1994

Matters regarding the Michael Lee Flowers Case as of 10:30 A.M.—Immediately following his interrogation, Flowers identified (from an employee file photo) government researcher Jeremy Blevins as the man he observed in the green van. Blevins was apprehended at 4:54 A.M. and remains under guard at CIA Headquarters. After listing the seven names and approximate locations of other persons he'd shared this information with, Flowers was sedated and efficiently terminated. Special agents were dispatched immediately and as of nine this morning, only one of the seven persons remains at large. We are continuing to question the two police officers who brought Flowers in, although we have their full cooperation and the full cooperation of their home district. At this time, they appear to present no problem to this investigation. The senator is unaware of any problem other than that of the homeless catnapper. Please post further instructions at your convenience.

(The rather unusual structure of this tale evolved from two wonderful short stories—"The Interrogation" by Dean R. Koontz and "Love Letters" by Thomas F. Monteleone. I'd like to thank both authors for the inspiration.)

Tea and 'Biscuit

Jon L. Breen

DO HAVE A CUP OF tea, and I'll tell you a story.

My nephew Jerry Brogan sometimes accuses me of trying to escape reality. That is, of course, absurd. No one my age would think such a thing possible. Reality will always come after you, whether in the form of the unavoidable processes of aging or the more dramatic form of finding a dead body on the grounds of your own home, as I did some years ago when jockey Hector Gates was murdered there. I solved that one, with some help from Jerry, and yet when he has become involved in other puzzles of a criminal nature, he has never called on me, despite my deep knowledge of detection from a lifetime of reading about it. Am I trying to evade reality or is Jerry trying to shield me from it?

I should introduce myself before I go on. My name is Olivia Barchester, widow these many years of the late Colonel Glyndon Barchester, who campaigned Vengeful and other fine thoroughbreds on California tracks. I myself raced Vicar's Roses, among others, after my husband's death.

Odd to say I raced them. I never saw any of my own horses

in person, since I never went to the track after the Colonel died, but they ran in my colors. So if a trainer or a jockey's agent can say, "I hooked the favorite at the head of the stretch and beat him a nose at the wire," I suppose I can say I raced Vicar's Roses.

While I won't admit to evading reality, I do take the prerogative of one who is fairly advanced in years and comfortably off (say old and rich if you must) and control my environment to the greatest extent possible. I don't consider myself a recluse, but I see little need to leave my home and my books. After my husband's death, I decided to follow racing to the extent possible on television. More recently, I decided not to watch live races on television. That decision came after Go for Wand's tragic death in the Belmont stretch the day of the 1990 Breeder's Cup. Now I videotape the races on my VCR and watch them at my leisure the evening of the day they are run, relying on Jerry to let me know if anything tragic occurred that I can shield myself from seeing. Self-indulgent, I'll admit, but I can enjoy a race so much more when I know all the runners and their jockeys will reach home safely.

Now I must introduce you to my black cat Seabiscuit, a handsome fellow from a rather distinguished litter who has been my companion for the past fifteen years. All of Seabiscuit's siblings were named for notable one-word racehorses—Stymie, Citation, Equipoise, Swaps, Nashua, Regret. They were born on the backstretch to a stable pet from the barn of an English trainer who insisted, contrary to American superstition, black cats were *good* luck.

There are many cats in racetrack stable areas, though most of them are strays, semi-wild. They are seldom pets for racehorses. Goats are more often cast in that role, for their calming effect on the highstrung thoroughbred.

Thus it is hardly surprising that, while most of Seabiscuit's litter found homes with persons connected to racing, only one followed in his mother's footsteps as a stable mascot. That brings me, you'll be relieved, to the subject of my story.

On a coolish fall evening, toward the end of the annual Surfside Meadows meeting where my nephew Jerry works as track announcer, I was visited by an old acquaintance, trainer Walter Cribbage. I brought him into my library, where Seabiscuit was lying by the fire and I had been engrossed in a vintage Agatha Christie novel from my extensive collection. I offered Walter a choice of beverage. I was sipping tea, but he opted for a straight bourbon, an indication of his troubled state of mind.

Walter is of my generation, thus nearing eighty, but he still has a trim figure and an erect, almost military carriage, and he still is up early mornings seeing to his string of horses. On this particular evening, we began by exchanging good-natured banter in the old way, but it seemed a bit forced on his part. He was clearly worried about something, and I was relieved when he got to the point of his visit.

"Olivia, Exterminator died this morning."

Remembering the post-World War I gelding, I said, "I should think he died years ago."

"Not the horse. The cat. He lived in my stable all these years. He came from the same litter as Seabiscuit. Remember?"

"Oh, of course. I am sorry to hear it. Still, fifteen is a good age for a cat, and one cannot hope—"

"That litter is notably long-lived, Olivia. Citation and Stymie are both still around. And he didn't die of old age, Olivia. He was murdered. Poisoned."

"Oh, dear. But why? Some superstitious backstretch worker, I suppose."

"He survived fifteen years without superstition getting the better of him. I think I know why he was killed. I have a horse in my barn named Band Wagon."

"Walter, as I think you know very well, that was one of the last horses I bred. Odd to say I bred him—I wasn't there in the shed after all—but I did plan the mating of his parents, Red Band and Hay Ride."

"I thought you'd be concerned about his welfare."

"Most certainly. You're doing very well with him, I understand. Jerry tells me he may be favored for the Surfside Handicap. But I'm sorry he doesn't belong to my friends the Burnsides any more."

Walter made a face. "As one who has to deal with the cur-

rent owners, Mr. and Mrs. Preston Fremont and son, I sometimes share your sorrow. Still, if the Burnsides still had him, I
wouldn't have got the chance to train him, would I? I got him
just over a year ago. He was a bad actor and had never run
up to his potential. Since I've had him, he's gotten better and
better, and I don't take a smidgen of the credit. He fell in love
with Exterminator. As long as that black cat was around the
barn, he was as calm and as kind as can be. He started training
well and racing better. That black cat made him a stakes horse.
Now he's gone into a tailspin, not eating well, acting up. In
the state he's in now, I don't think he'd win a ten-thousand-
dollar claimer, let alone the Surfside Handicap."

Very sad, of course, for my last good horse to fall on bad
days, but how could I help? After considerable hemming and
hawing, Walter finally got to the point.

"Olivia, I have a big favor to ask of you. I want to borrow
Seabiscuit."

"Borrow Seabiscuit? You must be joking."

Hearing his name twice in quick succession, Seabiscuit woke
from his slumber and strolled over to sit by my chair, happily
oblivious to the significance of our conversation.

"He and Exterminator are virtually identical," Walter continued. "Maybe having him around the barn would bring Band
Wagon back into form."

I shook my head. "Walter, I'd like to help you, but I can't
believe you'd ask me that. To begin with, cats, even much
younger ones than Seabiscuit, don't always adjust well to new
surroundings. He has grown accustomed to this house and
these grounds, a quiet and predictable environment." I reached
down to scratch Seabiscuit's ear, and he appreciatively rubbed
his head against my palm. "Put him in the middle of the furor
of the backstretch at his age, and who knows how he would
react? Second, cats as much as horses have very distinct personalities. There is no reason to think Seabiscuit could establish
that same special bond with Band Wagon simply because he
and Exterminator are closely related. And finally, Walter, you
are asking Seabiscuit to fill in where his brother has already

been poisoned. You think I would consider putting him in that situation?"

Walter looked crestfallen. "You're quite right, of course. I never should have asked. But I don't know what else to do."

It was at that moment that Jerry phoned to assure me that the day's racing at Surfside, as well as ESPN's coverage of a midwestern stake, had passed without a hitch and was safe for me to watch. Not sharing my nephew's tendency to keep a mystery to himself, I invited him to join Walter and me for a discussion of the problem. He seemed to treat it as a command appearance, though of course it was nothing of the kind. He turned up at my door within minutes.

When he had settled his considerable bulk into an easy chair and accepted a cup of tea and a scone, Jerry listened closely to Walter's story and said rather archly, "It reminds me of the curious incident of Barnbuster's goat."

Walter seemed to brighten slightly. "Barnbuster had no goat."

"That was the curious incident."

"Really," I said, "while nothing delights me more than Sherlockian allusions, I haven't any idea what you two are talking about."

"Don't you remember a horse called Barnbuster a few years ago? He only lived up to his name when his pet goat Mary Poppins wasn't around. The owner-trainer was down on his luck and forced to sell the horse. He got a good price based on the horse's record, but he cleverly withheld Mary P. Barnbuster proved unmanageable for his new owner, and the original owner was able to buy him back for considerably less than he'd been paid for him. Reunited with his nanny, Barnbuster resumed his winning ways."

Walter chuckled at what was obviously a familiar story, then turned grim again. "Doesn't apply to my situation."

"Not exactly, no, but I wouldn't rule out the former owners. Could they be looking for a way to get Band Wagon back cheap? Or maybe seeking revenge against the new owners?"

I was scandalized. "Jerry, what a suggestion! You've known Matthew and Helen Burnside all your life."

"A lot of people probably knew Jack the Ripper all *his* life, too."

"Do be serious! He's just talking this way to irritate me, Walter."

"All right, all right. I don't really suspect the Burnsides, okay?"

"Besides, they've been living on Maui for over a year," I had to add.

"Then let's see what else we can figure out," Jerry said, truly applying himself to the problem for the first time. "How do you know Exterminator was poisoned?"

"The vet recognized the symptoms," Walter said, "and it wasn't the first time someone had tried to kill him. A week or two before, I discovered someone had put a rubber band around the poor cat's stomach. It was eating into his flesh, and there was nothing he could have done about it. It surely would have killed him eventually, and very painfully. I got it off him, and saved his life."

"What a terrible thing to do to an innocent animal," I said, more thankful than ever I had declined to loan Seabiscuit. He cooperated reluctantly as I protectively gathered him into my lap.

"Any new stable employees?" Jerry asked.

"They've all worked for me for years."

"Any of them unusually superstitious?"

"Perhaps, but not about black cats."

Annoyingly, Jerry resumed his anecdotal posture. "It's not always just black cats. I once knew a hotwalker who was heavily into numerology. To him, *any* cat was bad luck in a barn. You take a horse's four legs and add them to a cat's nine lives, and what do you have? Thirteen."

Walter seemed as impatient with Jerry's digression as I was. "Everybody who works for me loved the cat," he insisted.

"Do the owners of Band Wagon visit the backstretch often?"

Walter nodded. "What a bunch. If I didn't like their horse so much, I'd dump them in a minute. Old Preston Fremont is a mean bastard with a short temper and no real regard for horses. He'd run them into the ground if I'd let him. He's smart enough not to even try to do that to Band Wagon, though, and he certainly wouldn't have harmed the cat no matter how angry he was. He loves the money Band Wagon makes him too much.

"Then there's Millicent Fremont, his wife. Kids herself she can dress like a woman half her age, and every time she comes to the stable she seems to resent those filthy things you have to have around a barn—you know, dirt, dung, people. Imagines herself a horse-lover, though. Makes a big deal of feeding her horses carrots. I wonder how'd she'd react if one of them bit her polished nails!

"And the son is the prize of the lot. Young Delbert. Twenty-five and never did an honest day's work. Doesn't know one end of the horse from another but always has big plans for the stable. A terrible snob with all his other sterling qualities. It was his bright idea Band Wagon should prove his worth by racing in Europe next spring. Even had his old man half convinced it was a good plan. I told them it was impossible, and Preston understood, but the kid practically threw a tantrum."

"What relationship did the three owners have to the late Exterminator?" Jerry asked.

"Relationship with the cat? None at all, really. Preston understood why we had to keep him around, but I don't remember he ever came near him. Millicent would make a big fuss over him until he got pawprints over one of her thousand-dollar dresses one morning. Since then, she's kept her distance. Delbert's gone on record as hating all domestic animals, and I guess that includes horses as well as cats, though money-makers like Band Wagon he manages to take some interest in."

"Are any of *them* superstitious?"

"Just the opposite, if anything. You have to understand, Jerry, the role of Exterminator in that barn was not a matter of superstition. It was just the relationship he had with Band Wagon. They were pals. Mr. and Mrs. Fremont accepted that, but the son always figured it *was* superstition, and the idea drove him nuts."

"How frequently do you see the owners, Walter?"

"More than I want to. I sometimes think they're there every day, but it probably just seems that way."

Jerry nodded. "I think I know who killed the cat," he said, with the offhand casualness appropriate to a brilliant amateur. I'm sure he puts that on for my benefit. "Not that it will do you much good. Killing a domestic animal isn't nearly as serious a criminal offense as it ought to be, and knowing who did it won't help your problem with Band Wagon . . ."

Jerry shook his head solemnly and stared into the fire, letting his dramatic pause lengthen intolerably.

I cleared my throat. "Jerry, if you'll permit me, whodunits form a large part of my recreation. I still might like to know who the killer was."

"So would I," Walter said.

"Sure," Jerry said obligingly. "It has to be the son."

Walter wagged his head. "How on earth did you figure that out?"

"Go back a minute, Walter. You didn't say racing Band Wagon in Europe would be just a bad idea because he didn't like to run on grass or something. You said it would be impossible. Why impossible?"

Before Walter could answer, I belatedly caught on to Jerry's line of reasoning. "The quarantine! A domestic cat would probably have to be quarantined for months before he would be permitted in a European country. It wouldn't be possible for Band Wagon to travel with his pal. And without Exterminator's companionship, Band Wagon would have been useless on the track. So the idea really was impossible from your point of view, Walter."

Jerry nodded. "But young Delbert thought Exterminator's role was just superstitious nonsense. He thought if he killed the cat, and if Band Wagon then carried on his winning ways as before, his scenario of campaigning the horse over European tracks could be realized."

"I ought to have known!" Walter Cribbage exclaimed. "The last time Delbert visited the stable area he had a scratch on his face."

"Probably he got that on his first attempt, when he put the rubber band on Exterminator," Jerry said. He reached down to stroke Seabiscuit, who had fled my lap when the thrill of detection made me too animated.

So among the four of us we seemed to have solved the whodunit. But what good did that do Walter Cribbage, you ask, in his effort to restore Band Wagon to form? Jerry was able to offer him a small ray of hope. One of Regret's offspring, thus a nephew of Exterminator, was a backstretch resident at Santa Anita and might conceivably be available as a new companion for Band Wagon. If bloodlines meant anything at all, Jerry argued, why not give him a try?

I remained dubious about the probable success of a surrogate, but when I heard the cat's name, I felt it was a good omen. It was Vengeful, after my late husband's best runner.

Band Wagon did win the Surfside Handicap, but Delbert Fremont wasn't around to see it. Died of an infected cat scratch, poor lad.

Well, I wouldn't have told you the story if it didn't have a happy ending.

The Beast Within

Margaret Maron

EARLY SUMMER TWILIGHT HAD BEGUN to soften the city's harsh outlines as Tessa pushed aside the sliding glass doors and stepped out onto the terrace. Up here on the twenty-sixth floor, dusk blurred the sharp ugly planes of surrounding buildings and even brought an eerie beauty to the skeletal girders of the new skyscraper going up next door.

Gray-haired, middle-aged and emotionally drained by her last confrontation with Clarence, Tessa leaned heavily fleshed arms on the railing of their penthouse terrace and let the warm night air enfold her.

From the street far, far below, muffled sounds of evening traffic floated up to her and for a moment she considered jumping. To end it all in one brief instant of broken flesh while ambulances screamed and the curious stared—what real difference would it make to her, to Clarence, to anyone, if she lived another day or year or twenty years?

Nevertheless, she stepped back from the railing unconsciously, the habit of life too deeply rooted in her psyche. With a few cruel and indifferent words, Clarence had destroyed her world; but he had not destroyed her will to live. Not yet.

She glanced across the narrow space to the uncompleted building. The workmen who filled the daylight hours with a cacophony of rivets and protesting winches were gone now, leaving behind, for safety, hundreds of small bare light bulbs. In the mild breeze, they swung on their wires like chained fireflies in the dusk.

Tessa smiled at the thought. How long had it been since she had seen real fireflies drift through summer twilight? Surely not more than half a dozen times since marrying Clarence all those years ago—God! Was it really almost forty years now? She no longer hated the city, but she had never forgiven it for not having fireflies—nor for blocking out the Milky Way with its star-quenching skyscrapers.

When he first brought her away from the country, Clarence had probably loved her as much as he was capable of loving anyone; yet even then he hadn't understood her unease at living in a place so eternally and brilliantly lit. When his friends complimented them on the penthouse and marveled at the size of their terrace (enormous even by those booming postwar standards of the fifties), he would laugh and say, "I bought it for Tessa. Can't fence in a country girl. They need 'land, lots of land 'neath the starry skies above!' "

It hadn't taken her long to realize he'd bought the penthouse to feed his own vanity, not to still her unspoken needs. Eventually, she stopped caring. If this terrace wasn't high enough above the neon glare to see her favorite stars, it at least provided as much quiet as one could expect in a city. She could always lie back on one of the cushioned chaises and remember how the Milky Way swirled in and out of the constellations; remember the dainty charm of the Pleiades tucked away in Taurus the Bull.

But not tonight. Instead of star-studded skies, memory forced her to relive the past hour in every humiliating and painful detail.

She was long since reconciled to the fact that Clarence did not love her; but after years of trying to mold herself to his standards, she had thought that he was comfortable with her and that she was necessary to him in all the other spheres that hold a marriage together after passion fades away.

Tonight, Clarence had made it brutally clear: not only was she *not* necessary, she was a boring encumbrance. Further, the woman she'd become, in her efforts to please him, was the antithesis of the woman he'd chosen as her replacement.

Tessa had followed him through their apartment in a daze as he packed his suitcases to leave. Mechanically, she had handed him clean shirts and underwear; then, seeing what a mess he was making of those perfectly tailored suits, she had taken over the actual packing as she always did when he went away on business trips. Only this time, he was going farther away than he ever had before, to a midtown hotel, out of her life.

"But why?" she asked, smoothing a crease in his gray slacks.

They had met Lynn Herrick at one of his sister-in-law's parties. Aggressive and uninhibited, her dress was blatantly sexual and her long black hair frizzed in a cloud around her bare shoulders. Tessa had thought the young woman brittle and obvious, hardly Clarence's type, and she had been amused by Ms. Herrick's brazenly flirtatious approach.

"Why this one?" she demanded again, knowing there had been other, more suitable women over the years.

A fatuous expression spread across Clarence's face, a blend of pride, sheepishness and defiance. "Because she's going to bear my child," he said pompously.

It was the ultimate blow. For years Tessa had pleaded for a child, only to have Clarence take every precaution to prevent one.

"You've always loathed children. You said they were whining, slobbering nuisances!"

"It wasn't my fault," Clarence protested. "Accidents happen."

"I'll bet!" Tessa muttered crudely, knowing that nothing accidental ever happens to the Lynn Herricks of the world.

Clarence chose to ignore her remark. "Now that it's happened, Lynn's made me see how much I owe it to myself. And to the company. Another Loughlin to carry our name into the next century since it doesn't look as if Richard and Alison will ever produce an heir."

Richard Loughlin was Clarence's much younger brother and only living relative. Together they had inherited control of a prosperous chain of department stores begun by their grandfather. Although Tessa had heard Richard remark wistfully that a child might be fun, his wife Alison shared Clarence's previous attitude toward offspring; and her distaste was strengthened by the fear of what a child might do to her size-eight figure.

With Clarence reveling in the newfound joys of prospective fatherhood, Tessa had snapped shut the final suitcase. Still in a daze, she stared at her reflection in the mirror over his dresser and was appalled.

In her conscious mind, she had known that she was past fifty, that her hair was gray, her figure no longer slim; and she had known that Clarence would never let her have children—but deep inside, down at the primal core of her being, a young, half-wild girl cried out in protest at the old and barren woman she had become.

The siren of a fire engine on the street far below drew Tessa to the edge of the terrace again. Night had fallen completely and traffic was thin now. The sidewalks were nearly deserted.

She still felt outraged at being cast aside so summarily—as if a pat on the shoulder, the promise of lavish alimony, and an "I told Lynn you'd be sensible about everything" were enough to compensate for thirty-six years of her life—but at least her brief urge toward self-destruction had dissipated.

She stared again at the bobbing safety lights of the uncompleted building and remembered that the last time she'd seen fireflies had been six years ago, after Richard and Alison returned from their honeymoon. She and Clarence had gone down to Pennsylvania to help warm the old farmhouse Richard had bought as a wedding surprise for Alison.

The hundred and thirty acres of overgrown fields and woodlands had indeed been a surprise to that urban young woman. Alison's idea of a suitable weekend retreat was a modern beach house on Martha's Vineyard.

Tessa had loved it and had tramped the woods with Richard,

windblown and exhilarated, while Alison and Clarence complained about mosquitoes and dredged up pressing reasons to cut short their stay. Although Alison had been charming and had assured Richard that she was delighted with his gift, she found excellent excuses not to accompany him on his infrequent trips to the farm.

Remembering its isolation, Tessa wondered if Richard would mind if she buried herself there for a while. Perhaps in the country she could sort things out and grope her way back to the wild freedom she had known all those years ago, before Clarence took her to the city and "housebroke" her, as he'd expressed it in the early years of their marriage.

A cat's terrified yowl caught her attention. She looked up and saw it running along one of the steel girders that stuck out several feet from a higher level of the new building. The cat raced out as if pursued by the three-headed Hound of Hell, and its momentum was too great to stop when it realized the danger.

It soared off the end of the girder and landed with a sickening thump on the terrace awning. With an awkward twist of its furry body, the cat leaped to the terrace floor and cowered under one of the chaises, quivering with panic.

Tessa watched the end of the girder, expecting to see a battle-scarred tom spoiling for a fight. Although cats seldom made it up this high, it was not unusual to see one taking a shortcut across her terrace from one rooftop to another, up and down fire escapes.

When no other cat appeared, Tessa turned her attention to the frightened animal. The night air had roused that touch of arthritis that had begun to bother her this year, and it was an effort to bend down beside the lounge chair. She tried to coax the cat out, but it shrank away from her hand.

"Here, kitty, kitty," she murmured. "It's all right. There's no one chasing you now."

She had always liked cats and, for that reason, refused to own one. It was too easy to let a small animal become a proxy child. She sympathized with Richard's mild disapproval whenever Alison called their dachshund "baby."

Patiently, she waited for the cat to stop trembling and to sniff her outstretched hand; but even though she kept her voice low and soothing, it would not abandon its shelter. Tessa's calcified joints protested against her crouch and creaked as she straightened up and stepped back a few feet.

The cat edged out then, suspiciously poised for flight. From the living-room lamps beyond the glass doors, light fell across it and revealed a young female with crisp black-and-gray markings and white paws. Judging from its leggy thinness, it hadn't eaten in some time.

"You poor thing," Tessa said, moved by its uneasy trust. "I'll bet you're starving."

As if it understood Tessa meant no harm, the cat did not skitter aside when she moved past it into the apartment.

Soon she was back with a saucer of milk and a generous chunk of rare beef which she'd recklessly cut from the heart of their untouched dinner roast. "Better you than a garbage bag, kitty. No one else wants it."

Stiff-legged and wary, the young cat approached the food and sniffed; then, clumsily, it tore at the meat and almost choked in its haste.

"Slow down!" Tessa warned, and bent over heavily to pull the meat into smaller pieces. "You're an odd one. Didn't you ever eat meat before?" She tried to stroke the cat's thin back, but it quivered and slipped away from her plump hand. "Sorry, cat. I was just being friendly."

She sank down onto one of the chaises and watched the animal finish its meal. When the meat was gone, it turned to the saucer of milk and drank messily with much sneezing and shaking of its small head as it inadvertently got milk in its nose.

Tessa was amused but a bit puzzled. She'd never seen a cat so graceless and awkward. It acted almost like a young, untutored kitten; and when it finished eating and sat staring at her, Tessa couldn't help laughing aloud. "Didn't your mother teach you *any*thing, silly? You're supposed to wash your paws and whiskers now."

The cat moved from the patch of light where it had sat silhouetted, its face in darkness. With purposeful caution, it circled the chaise until Tessa was between it and the terrace doors. Light from the living room fell full in its eyes there and was caught and reflected with an eerie intensity.

Tessa shivered uneasily as the animal's luminous eyes met her own with unblinking steadiness. "Now I see why cats are always linked with the supernatu—"

Suddenly it was as if she were a rabbit frozen in the middle of a back-country road by the headlights of a speeding car. Those feral eyes bored into her brain with a spiraling vortex of blinding light. A roaring numbness gripped her. Her mind was assaulted—mauled and dragged down and under and through—existence without shape, time without boundaries.

It lasted forever; it was over in an instant; and somewhere amid the splintered, whirling clamor came an awareness of another's existence, a being formless and desperate and terrified beyond sanity.

There was mingling.

Tessa felt the other's panic.

There was passing.

Then fierce exultation.

There was a brief, weird sensation of being unbearably compacted and compressed; the universe seemed to tilt and swirl; then it was over. The light faded to normal city darkness, the roaring stopped, and she knew she was sprawled upon the cool flagstones of the terrace.

She tried to push herself up, but her body responded queerly. Dazed, she looked around and screamed at the madness of a world suddenly magnified in size—a scream which choked off as she caught sight of someone enormous sitting on the now-huge chaise.

A plump, middle-aged, gray-haired woman held her face between trembling hands and moaned, "Thank God! Thank God!"

Shocked, Tessa realized that she was seeing her own face for the first time without the reversing effect of a mirror. Her shock intensified as she looked down through slitted eyes and saw neat white paws instead of her own hands. With alien instinct, she felt the ridge of her spine quiver as fur stood on end. She tried to speak and was horrified to hear a feline yowl emerge.

The woman on the chaise—Tessa could no longer think of that body as herself—stopped moaning then and watched her warily. "You're not mad, if that's what you're wondering. Not yet, anyhow. Though you'll maybe go mad if you don't get out of that skin in time."

She snatched up a cushion and flung it at Tessa.

"Shoo! G'wan, scat!" she gibbered. "You can't make me look in your eyes. I'll never get caught again. Scat, damn you!"

Startled, Tessa sprang to the railing of the terrace and teetered there awkwardly. The body had begun to respond, but she wasn't sure how well she could control it, and twenty-six stories above street level was too high to allow for much error.

The woman who had stolen her body seemed afraid to come closer. "You might as well go!" she snarled at Tessa. She threw a calculating glance at the luxurious interior beyond the glass doors.

"It's a lousy body—too old and too fat—but it looks like a rich one and it's human and I'm keeping it, so *scat*!"

Tessa's new reflexes were quicker than those of her old body. Before the shoe even left the other's hand, she had dropped to the narrow ledge that circled the exterior of the penthouse. Residual instinct made her footing firm as she followed the ledge around the corner of the building to the fire escape for an easy climb to the roof. There, in comparative safety from flying shoes and incipient plunges to the street, Tessa drew up to consider the situation.

Cat's body or not, came the wry thought, *it's still my mind.*

Absently licking away the dried milk that stuck to her whiskers, she plumbed the sensations of her new body and discovered that vestigial traces of former identities clung to this brain. Mere wisps they were, like perfume hanging in a closed room, yet enough to piece together a picture of what had happened to her on the terrace below.

The one who had just stolen her body had been young and sly, but not overly bright. Judging from the terror and panic so freshly imprinted, she had fled through the city and taken the first body she could.

Behind those raw emotions lay a cooler, more calculating undertone and Tessa knew *that* one had been more mature; had chosen the girl's body deliberately and after much thought. Not for her the hasty grabbing of the first opportunity. Instead, she had stalked her prey with care, taking a body that was pretty, healthy and, above all, young.

Beyond those two, Tessa could not sort out the other personalities whose lingering traces she felt. Nor could she know who had been the first or how it had all started. Probing too deeply, she recoiled from the touch of a totally alien animal essence struggling for consciousness—the underlying basic *cat-ness* of this creature whose body she now inhabited.

Tessa clamped down ruthlessly on these primeval stirrings, forcing them back under. This must be what the girl meant about going mad. How long could a person stay in control?

The answer, of course, was to get back into a human body. Tessa pattered softly to the edge of the roof and peered down at the terrace. Below, the girl in her body still cowered on the chaise as if unable to walk into the apartment and assume possession. Her shoulders slumped and she looked old and defeated.

She's right, thought Tessa. *It is a lousy body. Let her keep it.*

At that moment, she could almost pity the young thief who had stolen her most personal possession; but the moment was short-lived. With spirits soaring, Tessa danced across the black-tarred roof on nimble paws. Joyfully she experimented with her new body and essayed small leaps into the night air. No more arthritis, no excess flab to make her gasp for breath. What bliss to *think* a motion and have lithe muscles respond!

Drunk with new physical prowess, she raced to the fire escape, leaped to the railing and recklessly threw herself out into space. There was one sickening moment when she felt she must have misjudged, then she caught herself on a jutting scaffold and scrambled onto it.

Adrenalin coursed in her veins and her confidence grew with each step that carried her farther and farther away from familiar haunts. She prowled the night streets boldly, recapturing memories and emotions almost forgotten in those air-conditioned, temperature-controlled, insulated years with Clarence. Never again, she vowed, would she settle for less than this.

Freed of her old woman's body, she felt a oneness again with—what? The world? Nature? God?

The name didn't matter, only the feeling. Even here in the city, in the heart of man's farthest retreat into artifice, she felt it, and a nameless longing welled within her.

What it must be to have a cat's body in the country! Yet even as the thought formed in her mind, Tessa shivered in sudden fear. It would be too much. To be in this body with grass and dirt underneath, surrounded by trees and bushes alive with small rustlings, with uncluttered sky overhead—a human mind might well go mad with so much sensory stimulation.

No, better the city with its concrete and cars and crush of people to remind her that she was human and that this body was only temporary.

Still, she thought, descending gracefully from the top of a shuttered newsstand, *how dangerous could a small taste be?*

She ran west along half-deserted streets, heading for the park. On the crosstown streets, traffic was light; but crossing the avenues scared her. The rumble and throb of all those motors, the many lights and impatient horns kept her fur on end. She had to force herself to step off the curb at Fifth Avenue; and as she darted across its wide expanse, she half expected to be crushed beneath a cab.

The park was a haven now. Gratefully she dived between its fence railings and melted into the safety of its dark bushes.

In the next few hours, Tessa shed the rest of the shackles of her life with Clarence, her years of thinking "What will Clarence say?" when she gave way to an impulsive act; the fear of being considered quaint by his friends if she spoke her inmost thoughts.

If Pan were a god, she truly worshiped him that night! Abandoning herself to instinctual joys, she raced headlong down grassy hills, rolled paws over tail-tip in the moonlight, chased a sleepy, crotchety squirrel through the treetops, then skimmed down to the duck pond to lap daintily at the water and dabble at goldfish turned silver in the moonbeams.

As the moon slid below the tall buildings west of the park, she ate flesh of her own killing. Later—behind the Mad Hatter's bronze toadstool—she crooned a voluptuous invitation and allowed the huge ginger male who had stalked her for an hour to approach her, to circle ever nearer . . .

As he grasped her by the scruff and began to mount, the alien animal consciousness below exploded into dominance, surging across her will in wave after roiling wave of raw sexuality with every pelvic thrust. Thrice more they coupled in excruciating ecstasy, and only when the ginger tom had spent himself into exhaustion was she able to reassert her will and force that embryonic consciousness back to submission.

Just before dawn, a neat feline head poked through the railing at Fifth and East Sixty-fourth Street and hesitated as it surveyed the deserted avenue, empty now of all traffic save an occasional bus.

Reassured, Tessa stepped out onto the sidewalk and sat on narrow haunches to smooth and groom her ruffled striped fur. She was shaken by the night's experiences, but complacently unrepentant. No matter what lay ahead, these last few hours were now part of her soul and worth any price she might yet have to pay.

Nevertheless, the strength of this body's true owner was growing and Tessa knew that another night would be a dangerous risk. She had to find another body, and soon.

Whose?

Lynn Herrick flashed to mind. How wickedly poetic it would be to take her rival's sexy young body, bear Clarence's child, and stick Lynn with a body which, after last night, would soon be producing offspring of its own. But she knew too little about that man-eating tramp to feel confident taking over that particular life.

No, she was limited to someone familiar, someone young, someone unpleasantly deserving and, above all, someone *close*.

She must be within transferring distance before the city's morning rush hour forced her back into the park until dark—an unthinkable risk.

The logical candidate sprang to mind.

Of course! she thought. *Keep it in the family.*

Angling across Fifth Avenue, she pattered north toward the luxurious building that housed the younger Loughlins. Her tail twitched jauntily as she scampered along the sidewalk and considered the potentials of Alison's body. For starters, it was almost thirty years younger.

The deception might be tricky at first, but she had met all of Alison's few near relatives. As for surface friends who filled the aimless rounds of her sister-in-law's social life, Tessa knew they could be dropped without causing a ripple of curiosity—especially if her life became filled with babies. That should please Richard. *Dear Richard!*

Dear Richard? Tessa was intrigued. When had her brother-in-law become so dear? Richard was a small boy when she and Clarence married, and she had always considered the tenderness he roused in her a sort of frustrated maternalism, especially since he was so comfortable to be with. Somewhere along the line, tender maternalism had apparently transmuted into something earthier; and all at once, wistful might-have-beens were suddenly exciting possibilities.

Behind the heavy bronze and glass doors of Richard's building, a sleepy doorman nodded on his feet. The sun was not yet high enough to lighten the doorway under its pink-and-gray striped awning, and deep shadows camouflaged her own stripes.

Keeping a low silhouette, she crouched outside and waited. When the doorman opened the door for an early-rising tenant, she darted inside and streaked across the lobby to hide behind a large marble ashstand beside the elevator.

The rest would be simple as the elevator was large, dimly lit, and paneled in dark mahogany. She would conceal herself under the pink velvet bench at the rear of the car and wait until it eventually stopped at Alison and Richard's floor.

Her tail twitched with impatience. When the elevator finally descended, she poised herself to spring.

The door slid back and bedlam broke loose in a welter of shrill barks, tangled leash and startled, angry exclamations. The dog was upon her, front and back, yipping and snapping before she knew what was happening.

Automatically, she spat and raked the dog's nose with her sharp claws, which set off a frenzy of jumping and straining against the leash and sent his master sprawling.

Tessa only had time to recognize that it was Richard, taking Liebchen out for a prebreakfast walk, before she felt herself being whacked by the elevator man's newspaper.

All avenues of escape were closed to her and she was given no time to think or gather her wits before the street doors were flung open and she was harried out onto the sidewalk.

Angry and disgusted with herself and the dog, Tessa checked her headlong flight some yards down the sidewalk and glared back at the entrance of the building where the dachshund smugly waddled down the shallow steps and pulled Richard off in the opposite direction.

So the front is out, thought Tessa. *I wonder if their flank is so well-guarded?*

It pleased her to discover that those years of easy compliance with Clarence's wishes had not blunted her initiative. She was not about to be thwarted now by any little canine frankfurter.

Halfway around the block, she found an alley that led to a small service court. From the top of a dumpster, she managed to spring to the first rung of a fire escape and scramble up.

As she climbed, the night's exertions began to pull at her physical reserves. Emotional exhaustion added its weight, too. Paw over paw, up and up, while every muscle begged for rest and her mind became a foggy treadmill able to hold but a single thought: paw in front of paw.

It seemed to take hours. Up thirteen steps to the landing, right turn; up thirteen steps to the landing, left turn, with such regular monotony that her mind became stupid with the endless repetition of black iron steps.

At the top landing, a ten-rung ladder rose straight to the

roof. Her body responded sluggishly to this final effort and she sank down upon the tarred rooftop in utter exhaustion. The sun was high in the sky now; and with the last dregs of energy, Tessa crept into the shade of an overhanging ledge and was instantly asleep.

When she awoke in the late afternoon, the last rays of sunlight were slanting across the city. Hunger and thirst she could ignore for the time, but what of the quickening excitement that twilight was bringing?

She crept to the roof's edge and peered down at the empty terrace overlooking the park. An ivied trellis offered easy descent and she crouched behind a potted shrub to look through the doors. On such a mild day, the glass doors had been left open behind their fine-meshed screens.

Inside, beyond an elegant living room, Alison's housekeeper set the table in the connecting dining room. There was no sign of Alison or Richard—or of Liebchen. Cautiously, Tessa pattered along the terrace to the screened doors of their bedroom, but it too was empty.

As she waited, darkness fell completely. From deep within she felt the impatient tail-flick of awareness. She felt it respond to a cat's guttural cry two rooftops away, felt it surfacing against her will, pulled by the promise of another night of dark paths and wild ecstasy.

Desperately, she struggled with that other ego, fought it blindly and knew that soon her strength would not be enough.

Suddenly the terrace was flooded with light as all the lamps inside the apartment were switched on. Startled, the other self retreated; and Tessa heard Alison's light voice tell the housekeeper, "Just leave dinner on the stove, Mitchum. You can clear away in the morning."

"Yes, Mrs. Loughlin, and I want you and Mr. Loughlin to know how sorry I am that—"

"Thank you, Mitchum," came Richard's voice, cutting her off.

Tessa sat motionless in the shadows outside and watched Liebchen trot across the room and scramble onto a low chair, unmindful of her nearness.

As Richard mixed drinks, Alison said, "It's so horrible. Poor Tessa. Those delusions that she's really a young girl—that she's never met Clarence or either of us. Do you suppose she's trying to fake a mental breakdown?"

"How can you say that? You saw her wretchedness. It wasn't an act."

"But—"

"What a shock it must have been to have him ask for a divorce after all these years. Did you know about it?" His voice was harsh with emotion. "You introduced Lynn to Clarence. Did you encourage them?"

"Honestly, darling," Alison said scornfully. "You act as if *Tessa's* been victimized."

"Maybe she has." Richard sounded tired now and infinitely sad. "In more ways than either of us can possibly know. You should have seen her when they were first married—so fresh and open and full of laughter. I was only a kid, but I remember. I'd never met an adult like her. All our stodgy relatives were snide to her. They thought she was a gold-digging country hick. *I* thought she was like an April breeze blowing through this family and I was proud of Clarence for breaking out of the mold."

He gazed bleakly into his glass. "After Father died, they sent me away to school and it was years before I really saw her again. I couldn't believe the change: all the laughter gone, her guarded words. Clarence did a thorough job of cramming both of them back into the Loughlin mold. First he kills her spirit and then he has the nerve to call her dull! No wonder she's retreated into her youth, to a time before she knew him. You heard the psychiatrist. He doesn't think she's faking."

"Perhaps not," Alison said coolly, "but you seem to keep forgetting: Clarence may have killed her spirit, but Tessa's killed *him*."

In the shadows outside the screen, Tessa quivered. So they had found Clarence's body! That poor thieving child! At the sight of Clarence lying on the bedroom floor with his head crushed in, she must have panicked again.

"I haven't forgotten," Richard said. "And I haven't forgotten

Lynn Herrick either. If what Clarence told me yesterday is true, I'll have to make some sort of arrangement for the child out of Clarence's estate."

"Don't be naive," said Alison. "I'm sure she merely let Clarence believe what he wanted. Trust me, darling. Lynn's far too clever to take on motherhood without a wedding ring and community property laws."

"You mean the divorce—his death—Tessa's insanity—all this was based on lies? And you knew it? You *did*! I can see it in your face!"

"Oh, please!" Alison snapped. She stood abruptly and stalked across the room. "Yes, I introduced them, but you can't blame me for your brother's stupidity. Clarence was sixty-three years old and Lynn made him feel like a young stud again. If Tessa couldn't hang on to him, why shouldn't Lynn have tried to land him?"

Richard stood, too, and freshened his drink. "Is that what marriage is to you? A hanging-on?"

But Alison had gone into the kitchen and appeared not to have heard when she returned with a large tray. As she began to arrange dishes and food on a low table in front of the couch, Liebchen put interested paws on the edge of the table, but Richard shoved him aside.

"There's no need to take it out on Liebchen," she said angrily. "Come along, baby. Mummy has something nice for you in the kitchen."

On little short legs, the dachshund trotted after Alison and disappeared into the kitchen. Relieved, Tessa moved nearer to the screen.

When Alison reentered the room, she left the kitchen door closed and her flash of anger had been replaced by a mask of solicitude. She brought silverware, poured hot tea and spoke in soothing tones.

Richard ate mechanically, then stood up and reached for his jacket.

"Must you really go out again tonight, darling? Can't things wait till morning?"

"You know lawyers," he sighed. "Everything's going to be doubly complicated by the way he died."

"That's right," Alison said thoughtfully. "Murderers can't inherit from their victims, can they? No, don't pull away from me like that, darling. I feel just as badly for Tessa as you do, but we have to face up to it. Insane or not, she did kill him."

"Sorry." Richard straightened his tie. "I guess I just can't take it all in yet."

He went down the hall to his study and came back with his briefcase. Alison remained on the couch with her back to him. As Richard sorted through some papers, she said with careful casualness, "If they decide poor Tessa did kill him while of unsound mind and she later snaps out of it, would she then be able to inherit?"

"Probably not legally," Richard answered absently, his mind on the papers. "Wouldn't matter though, since we'd feel morally obliged to see she's fairly provided for."

"Oh, of course," Alison agreed, but her eyes narrowed.

Richard leaned over the couch and kissed her cheek. "I don't know how long this will take. If you're tired, don't wait up."

Alison smiled up at him, but once he was gone and the outer door had latched shut, her smile faded and was replaced by a look of greedy calculation.

Lost in thought, she gazed blindly at the dark square of the screened doorway, unaware of someone watching. Slowly, slowly, Tessa eased up on narrow haunches until lamplight hit her eyes—eyes that were slitted and glowed with abnormal intensity . . .

It was after midnight before Richard came home again. Lying awake on that wide bed, she heard him drop his briefcase on the floor inside his study, then continue on down the hall to the dimly lit bedroom. She held her breath as he opened the door and whispered, "Alison?"

"I'm awake." She turned between the linen sheets. "Oh, Richard, you look absolutely drained. Come to bed."

When at last he lay beside her in the darkness, she touched him shyly and said, "All evening I've been thinking about Tessa and Clarence—about their life together. I've been as rotten to you as he was to Tessa."

Richard made a sound of protest, but she placed slim young fingers against his lips. "No, dearest, let me say it. I've been thinking how empty their marriage was and how ours would be the same if I didn't change. I want to become a whole new person. Will you let me? Let me pretend we just met and that I barely know you? Start new? Please?"

"Alison—"

"No, let me finish. As soon as the funeral's over—as soon as we've arranged for the best legal and medical care that we can give Tessa—could we go away to the farm for a few weeks? Just the two of us?"

Incredulous, Richard propped himself on one elbow and peered into her face. "Do you really mean that?"

She nodded solemnly and he gathered her into his arms, but before he could kiss her properly, the night was broken by an angry, hissing cry.

He sat up abruptly. "What the devil's that?"

"Just a stray cat. It's been out on the terrace all evening." With slender, eager arms, she pulled Richard back down to her, then pitched her voice just loud enough to carry through the screen to the terrace. "If it's still there in the morning, I'll call the animal shelter and have them take it away."

Reunification

Peter Crowther

JURGEN POLKE STARED OUT OF the *kaffeeklatsch* window at the concrete bust of Karl Marx and at the interminable stream of sad, aimless people killing time between sleepless nights.

The coming together of East and West at the end of 1990 had had little effect on industrial Chemnitz save to restore its original name. Known as Karl-Marx-Stadt since 1953, the city had kept the bust that still dominated the strasse as a reminder of the communist oppression that was spawned—at least in part—by the philosopher's theories.

Jurgen stubbed out his Marlboro and shook another out of the packet. He lit it from a match, blew out smoke and looked around.

At the table to his right, a small boy shook a box trying to get the tiny metal balls that it contained to drop into the recessed eye sockets of a monstrous gorilla. To his left, a woman sipped her coffee and stared into the unfathomable distance and the ethereal thoughts and dreams it contained. Her eyes seemed as empty and lifeless as those of the gorilla.

The woman reminded Jurgen Polke of his wife, Christa,

though he could not understand why. The woman's hair was dark and long, unlike Christa's blonde, almost boyish cut. And she had the flabby features of a poor diet—a common sight in Chemnitz, where one in three were unemployed—while around her left eye was what looked like the fading greeny purple stain of an aging bruise.

Christa, on the other hand, had had sharp features. Jurgen wondered if it were simply that the woman *was* a woman; if he were doomed to be reminded of Christa by all women for evermore.

It was almost two years since Christa had died. And though she was never far from his thoughts, maybe it was the woman's bruise that had brought the memory of her face back to him so strongly.

Christa had borne many bruises when she died, and her passing had left additional contusions on Jurgen's soul, bright, multi-colored weals that criss-crossed both heart and memory and tarnished everything he thought and felt.

Jurgen wanted to ask the woman—as he had asked Christa . . . his beautiful Christa—who had done that to her. Wanted to ask who could care so little for beauty that he—for surely no *woman* could be responsible—would so cruelly destroy it. But there was more than a simple act of violence responsible for the woman's condition. It was the Wall, just as it was the Wall that had caused all the suffering of all the people. Just as it was the Wall that had taken his love away.

Even though it was now gone these past four years, the thing hovered over all of their lives like a ghost. No matter how the authorities uprooted the fence posts and tore down the barbed wire and the lookout points; no matter how they hefted the huge chunks of stone and brick away and buried them in distant landfills, covering them over with virgin earth so that the sky could no longer look on such banal human folly, it was still constantly there, the collective cry of the separated echoing through the very fabric of the new nation's being. And now, paradoxically, now that they could see—*really* see—the West as it truly was, they were even more dissatisfied.

He blew out a thin column of smoke and suddenly realised

that he was staring at the woman. What was worse was that she had noticed. She leaned over towards him.

"Do I know you?" she asked.

Jurgen shook his head. "No, I don't think so."

"Ah," she nodded. "You stare at my injury." She lowered her face until it was staring straight down at the table, showing only the top of her head. Jurgen noticed that there were several bald patches showing through the carefully combed hair.

"No . . . well, yes. Perhaps I *was* staring." Jurgen shrugged and tapped his cigarette into the ashtray. "I'm sorry."

"There is no need to apologise," she said, gently swilling the contents of her cup around. "It is unsightly. But it was much worse. Now it is almost better."

He held out his hand, holding it low so that she might see it. "Jurgen, Jurgen Polke."

The woman raised her head and looked at the hand, then at him. She smiled widely and shook his hand. "Bianka Rapp. Are you—" She let the question hover a moment and then, seeming to steel herself, said, "May I join you?"

Jurgen waved expansively at his table. "Please do, please do."

The woman got to her feet and lifted up a bag that had been beneath the table. The bag seemed to move of its own accord. As she settled into the seat beside him, placing the suddenly mysterious bag firmly between her scuffed shoes, Jurgen noticed the boy at the other table pause in his deliberations, sensed him stare at the bag and he smiled inwardly as the boy got up from the table and backed across the floor to a man standing at the counter drinking a beer.

Jurgen nodded at the bag beneath the table. "What have you got there?"

At first, the woman seemed puzzled and then startled. She reached down for the bag and started to get up. Jurgen reached across the table and took hold of her arm.

"Don't go," he said. "Please."

Even he could hear the sincerity in his own voice. It sounded tired and lost, completely devoid of aggression or ulterior motive. It said, *Go if you must but if you would stay then your company would be appreciated.* And it said, *The decision is yours; I have neither the energy nor the inclination to plead.* It covered every syllable with loneliness, every nuance with failure, every consonant with regret. They ran across the words, these sentiments, like honey across bread.

For a moment, Bianka Rapp hovered above the abyss of decision, tottering the tightrope of uncertainty, and then she visibly relaxed. Pulling her chair in towards the table once more, she shook her head self-deprecatingly. "I'm sorry," she said at last.

Jurgen shrugged. "Why should you be sorry? It has nothing to do with me."

The woman frowned.

"The bag," he said. "Your bag and whatever is in it is of no concern of mine. Unless it is something good to eat or something warm to keep out the cold." He laughed.

Bianka Rapp allowed a small smile and shook her head again, this time in a single, sharp movement. "No, there is nothing in there to eat nor anything to wear. It is my good luck charm."

Jurgen nodded, taking in the woman's response while he studied her face more intently. "Good luck?"

"Yes. I have need of some, wouldn't you say?"

"Well—"

"A cat," she said, before he could finish. "A black cat."

Not sure whether to smile or frown—nor even whether he had heard the woman correctly—Jurgen felt himself nodding again, taking in the information and chewing it gently in his head. "A cat," he said at last.

The smile drifted self-consciously across her face, pulling the skin taught over her cheekbones. "Yes, a cat."

"I have heard of people carrying many strange things in these confusing times," Jurgen pointed out amiably, "but I have never heard of anyone carrying a pet around with them."

The woman shook her head. "No, you do not understand." A small tic rippled her left eye until she had to close it, blinking tightly, to make it stop. "This is not a *pet*—" She said the word sharply, almost spitting it out as though it were undercooked meat. "—it is a part of *me*."

Jurgen did not know what to say. He was considering either suggesting they had another drink—though he could scarcely afford one for himself, let alone one for a complete stranger— or standing up to leave, when the woman rested back on her chair, cocked her head on one side and clearly stared at him. He watched her eyes travel up and down his face.

"Do you believe in luck, Jurgen Polke?"

He shrugged. "If you mean to ask if I am superstitious then the answer must be *no*. I presume the concept of luck falls into the realm of superstition?"

"I suppose." She pouted her mouth and fluttered her eyes. "Perhaps you are fortunate."

"In what way?"

"Perhaps if you do not believe then they cannot touch you."

"They? Who cannot touch me? The cats?"

"No, not the cats. I don't know who . . . the fates, perhaps. Perhaps they can only torment those who subscribe to their theories."

"I'm afraid you're—"

"When I was a little girl, near Halle, my father brought a cat home. He gave the cat to my sister, Siglinde, and me. He said it would bring us luck.

"Have you ever been to Halle, Jurgen Polke?"

He shook his head.

"You have not missed anything. To those in the West it is synonymous with beautiful music—Handel was born there," she said, as though she had suddenly remembered. Jurgen nodded interestedly.

"But to those that live under the tyranny of its polluted skies it is akin to the dark ages. We lived in a village near Leipzig and, when I was very young, we would sit on the street in the early morning and watch the first strands of blackness from the chemical industries drift across the sun until it was like winter. A friend of my father's brother once visited with us and he remarked, while we were out one day, how surprised he was to see that there were no leaves on the trees and yet it was only

September. My father pointed out that the leaves are gone by midsummer and even that often happens overnight." She paused as though about to say something else, but then only frowned. "My sister went like one of those trees, overnight."

"Went? Where did she go?"

"Where did she *go?* She died. Siglinde died the night the cat did not return."

She turned to the window. "See the people in the colorful clothes out there?"

Jurgen followed her gaze. "Yes," he said.

"I never fail to be impressed by color. We never had color when I was a child. All we had was darkness, and black. Grey skies, grey clothes and grey faces. The children where we lived were never clean. There was no point in being clean when you would be dirty again in minutes." She turned back and clasped her hands on the table, watching them as though they were small animals, playfully wrapping their fingers around each other, fearful of separation.

"That was the first time," she said, softly.

Jurgen frowned and held the frown until Bianka Rapp looked at his face.

"The first time I encountered luck and the importance of a totem. I did not recognise it then, I don't think. Perhaps I didn't recognise until the second time or maybe even the third time." She looked up at him again and smiled tiredly. "I wonder . . . I wonder if I might have another coffee?"

"Of course." Jurgen turned and waved at the girl behind the counter. "Two coffees, please." The girl nodded.

"Thank you," said Bianka Rapp.

Jurgen waved away her thanks as though it were nothing. "What did she die of, your sister?"

"The Wall. Everyone died of the Wall. Many still do. They died of it when it was there and now they die of it because it is gone. It's a strange world."

"And what happened to the cat?"

She shook her head slowly. "We never found out. Ran away . . . killed . . . who can say. But the luck went with it."

"Did you get another cat?"

"No, not at first. We left Leipzig soon after Siglinde's death, moved to Bitterfeld where my father got a job making plastics. There were woods nearby, alongside the Mulde river, where the trees were permanently black skeletons. The only life in those woods is the larch bud moth." She laughed bitterly. "And the children. We used to make fun of the fact that we could walk alongside the river faster than the river itself could move, so full of poison and death it was.

"My father bought me another cat when we had been in Bitterfeld less than a year. The cat was killed by a truck either leaving or going to the complex. When it didn't come home in the evening, my mother and I walked out early the next morning and found it, still in the road. My father died four days later, when I was eleven. He was thirty one. My last memory of him is him lying on a table having liquid drained from his chest. Lung cancer."

Jurgen looked down at the table.

"That was when, I think, I first learned to believe in luck. So it *was* the second time." The girl from behind the counter arrived and placed two pots of steaming coffee in front of them. Jurgen thanked her and dropped a handful of small-denomination coins in her outstretched hand. He hoped it was enough. The girl nodded and walked away.

"I begged my mother to buy another cat but we did not have any money. We did not have money even for food." She lifted one of the pots to her lips and blew gently against the steam. "She left me when I was fourteen. I never saw her again." She sipped the coffee and returned her pot to the table. "Do you have a cigarette?"

"Of course." Jurgen fumbled the creased pack of Marlboro out of his shirt pocket and shook one out. She took the cigarette and tapped it on the table before accepting a light. Jurgen lit his own cigarette and flicked the match out, dropping it into the ashtray between them.

Bianka Rapp breathed in the smoke as though it were a fine perfume or the rarest of wines. Then she settled again and, running the tip of the cigarette against the ashtray in a circular motion, she resumed her story.

"I spent the next two years living with a friend and her parents. They were very good to me—as good as they could be—but my presence was a drain on their resources. When I was sixteen I left them and moved to Halle. I had it in mind to become a model.

"What do you think of that, Jurgen Polke?" she asked.

"What do I *think* of it?" He was surprised by the question. "Why, I think it must be a very exciting job."

"No, I mean about my wanting to become a model." She pulled back and turned her head first one way and then the other, showing him her profile. "Do you not find it hard to believe? Do you not find me singularly plain?"

He looked. And as he looked, it seemed that someone somewhere, somewhere high above them, lifted a veil from around the woman's face. The bruises seemed visibly to diminish while her features lightened, almost reforming and re-shaping themselves into something much more familiar than Bianka Rapp.

Oh, Christa, Jurgen Polke's heart whispered deep inside.

For just a moment, one of those all-powerful nano-seconds between slices of reality when anything may be possible, it seemed as though Bianka Rapp smiled a smile that belonged to Jurgen Polke's wife. But it was gone even as soon as it appeared.

"No," he said, after what seemed like an age, "No, I do not find you plain at all."

The woman seemed to find the answer satisfactory. She stubbed her cigarette out in the ashtray and said, "The people from the West interviewed me and told me I could become a successful model. But they asked me for 300 marks first. I got a job as a waitress and paid them the money. At the same time, I bought another cat. For the money, they had me attend some photo sessions and, at first, everything seemed to be going well. Then they asked me for more money. This, too, seemed to be okay. They said the money was for studio time. I paid it when they asked me.

"One day, I was looking out of my window and, on the street below, I saw Shatsi, my cat, go beneath the wheels of a car. When I got downstairs, the driver of the car had got out and was kneeling beside Shatsi. He was very apologetic. It wasn't his fault, of course. Just the way of things."

She took a deep breath and sipped her coffee.

"Shatsi wasn't dead but his body was crushed and there was a—" She shook her head and pointed to her eyebrow. "A piece of bone . . . it was . . . it was jutting—" Her voice faltered and Jurgen nodded.

"Anyway, I had to do something. The man got me a tire iron from the trunk of his car and I . . . I—"

"There was absolutely no alternative?" Jurgen asked, trying to break the course of her thoughts.

She regained her composure sufficiently to answer as she pulled a handkerchief out of her coat pocket. "No. No alternative. The man offered to do it for me but I would not let him. He was *my* cat.

"Later that day, I got a call from the people I was supposed to be doing the modelling for. They asked if I would be prepared to accompany a friend of their boss to a dinner engagement. He was visiting town and needed a consort. I thought about it for a few minutes and decided it would be in my best interests. I was 17 at the time, but I looked much older when I wore make-up."

The woman reached down and patted the bag between her feet.

"The man seemed nice at first but, as the evening wore on, his attitude changed. I should not have gone back to his hotel when he asked me to, but the people at the model agency promised the man would give me a good tip if I looked after him well." She shrugged. "What can I say? I have no excuse. I knew what he wanted me for but . . . well, I had to pay my bills. And I wanted to buy another cat. By this time, you see, I was convinced that my luck was tied up with these animals. I am still so convinced.

"But, of course, when I went up to his room, I did not own a cat." She lifted her pot and drained it in one fluid motion. Setting the pot back onto the table, she said, "The man was not a gentleman. He hurt me. Badly. And he did not give me any money. When I told him what the people at the model agency had said, he laughed at me. 'Model agency?' he said. '*Model* agency?' I can still hear him laughing some nights—" She tapped her temple with her forefinger. "—here in my head.

"The following day, I got a call from the model agency telling me that I had let them down and that they would no longer be able to help me." She sighed. "Could I have another cigarette?"

Jurgen lit her cigarette and sat back to listen to the rest of the woman's story.

"The next two years, I continued my job as waitress. It was not a nice job. The pay fell and my bills rose. And so, two years ago, I moved here, to Chemnitz, and took other work. They were bad years, years of pain and humiliation. I needed money and took it where I could—doing manual jobs, I mean. I did not go back to any of the so-called 'model agencies'. Then, a little over one month ago, I lost my job."

Jurgen leaned forward. "Did this tie in with the loss of another cat?"

"Oh, no." She breathed out a thick column of smoke and waved it away with her hand. "No, I have not had a cat these past four years."

The woman was only in her very early twenties. Jurgen was amazed. She looked so much older, so worn down and embattled. He tried not to show his surprise.

"And so, I lived out on the streets. I lay in doorways while drunken boys staggered by me, shouting . . . shouting things at me. And I saw many things—in only a few days—that I had not thought possible. Levels of human degradation that I could not have imagined once upon a time. Two men and a woman did this to me four days ago." She pulled her hair back from the sides of her face and showed Jurgen the full extent of the bruises. "They had no reason. They awoke me to do it." When she removed her hands and shook her hair back into place, it was an action of such pride and sadness that Jurgen felt a salty stinging sensation in the back of his throat. "I could not allow myself to become immersed in that life."

Jurgen frowned. "You could not allow yourself? I'm not sure that I—"

She raised her hands palm-up in a matter-of-fact way. "I could not afford to *buy* a cat and so I stole one."

"You stole a *cat*? From where?"

She shrugged and drew on her cigarette. "I don't know. A street. A house. I don't know. I found it."

"I don't think that is the answer, Bianka," Jurgen said. "Think of the sadness *you* felt when you lost *your* cats. And now you have sentenced another family to that same heartbreak."

Another shrug. "Maybe there is only so much happiness to go around. Maybe if someone has a piece of it then others must be sad. I am tired of being one of the sad ones." She reached down to the bag at her feet and lifted it onto her knee. "Here, let me show him to you."

Jurgen shuffled his chair around the table so that he could see into the bag on the woman's lap as she lifted a grey cat, no more than a year old, up onto the table. "I'm going to call her Gertraud," she said, "after my mother."

Jurgen stroked the animal and felt its *purr* resonating in its tiny body, a mixture of fear and affection. "You cannot do this," he said at last.

Without looking at Bianka, he felt rather than saw her nod her head. "I know," she said softly.

They both turned to face each other at the same time. "Will you go back with me?"

"You know where the cat belongs?"

As she nodded, a single tear fell onto her cheek. "Yes."

When Jurgen opened the *kaffeeklatsch* door the odour of approaching winter hit him in the face like a solid object, a singularly strange aroma of dying leaves, greatcoats and exhaust fumes.

Across the square they walked, striding with a renewed purpose neither of them had thought possible just an hour ago. As they walked they talked, observing passers-by and storefronts, Trabants and kindling-wood stacks by the score, and filling each other in on small remnants of their pasts.

Jurgen told Bianka Rapp all about Christa. It proved to be

less painful than he had imagined. More an epilogue than a catharsis.

The house where Bianka had stolen the cat was about ten minutes walk away, situated in a neat part of the town. Jurgen stepped through the gate and walked quickly to the door while Bianka Rapp held back. As he knocked loudly, he motioned her to join him.

Just five minutes later, they were walking back the way they had come, slower now.

The boy's name—the boy whose cat they had returned—was Günter, Günter Haube. He cried and laughed, spittle hanging between his lips like thick spider-webs and his eyes like pale-blue saucers, when Bianka held out Gertraud. The cat's name, it turned out, was Hilda.

The boy's father, a tall man with thinning hair and recessed eyes, came to the door when he heard his son's shouts and thanked them over and over again. They didn't know how pleased they all were, he told them. Didn't know how sad little Günter had been when the cat disappeared. They both nodded, anxious to be off, and Bianka said that, yes, perhaps they had realised. Nobody asked where the cat had been found nor how Bianka and Jurgen had known where it belonged. Sometimes fairy tales get cluttered up by information and lose their magic.

The boy and his father had remained at the door while Jurgen and Bianka, her bag now hanging limply by her side, turned out of the gate and along the street. When they turned for a final wave, the boy held up his cat's paw and waved it in their direction. Then they withdrew into the house and closed the door.

"Look on it like an early Christmas present," Jurgen told the silent Bianka. "You united a family—*re*-united them," he corrected himself.

There was no response.

"You know, I've been thinking about what you said . . . about luck and cats and so on."

He waited until she acknowledged his words this time. It came in the form of a half-hearted grunt, but it did come.

"If cats are supposed to be so lucky, then how come that

family got theirs returned—which has got to be good luck in anyone's judgement—when, according to your theory, they should have been doomed to nothing but bad luck? Them having lost their cat in the first place."

She shrugged but it was a thoughtful movement.

Jurgen suddenly wrapped his arm around her shoulders and squeezed her tightly. "Maybe we make our own luck. Maybe, just maybe, we get it only when our hearts are lifted and our spirits high." She turned her face towards him and the faint trace of a smile played at the corners of her mouth. "Maybe, like our own country's, *human* new beginnings take time to happen. And even then, only when we're ready." He smiled at her and hugged her even tighter. "What do you say?"

She nodded. "Maybe," she said. "Maybe you're right."

He faced forward into the late afternoon gloom and pulled his coat collar closed with his free hand. "Hell, right, wrong . . . who gives a damn. The whole *thing*'s guesswork."

And as they both started to laugh, Bianka Rapp threw out her right arm and pitched the empty bag over the fences, high into the night and forever out of sight.

I never thought to ask, I never knew;
But in my simple ignorance, suppose
The self-same Power that brought me there brought you.
   The Rhodora
   Ralph Waldo Emerson (1803–1882)

Cat Got Your Tongue

Barbara Collins
and
Max Allan Collins

THE WARM CALIFORNIA BREEZE PLAYED with Kelli's long blonde hair, which shimmered in the brilliant sun like threads of finely spun gold. Stretched out in a lounge chair by the pool—its water sparkling like diamonds, blinding her in spite of the Ray-Ban sunglasses—she looked like a goddess: long sleek curvy legs led to an even more curvaceous body that spilled over and out her bathing suit, as if resenting having to be clothed. Next to her, on a wrought-iron table, lay fruit, caviar and champagne. Her pouty-pink lips were fixed in a smug, satisfied smile. She was in heaven!

"Oh, poolboy!" she called out to the muscular, shirtless, sandy-haired man dragging a net across the back end of the swimming pool. "More champagne!" She waved an empty crystal goblet at him.

He ignored her.

So she stretched out even more in the lounge chair, moving seductively, suggestively. "I'll make it worth your while," she said, her tongue lingering on her lips.

Now he came to her, and looked down with mild disgust.

Sweat beaded his berry-brown body. "Put the stuff back, Kel. It's time to go."

"Just a little longer, Rick," she pleaded.

"It's *time*, Kel."

She sat up in the chair, swung both legs around, and stomped her feet to the ground. "How am *I* supposed to get a tan?" she whined.

He didn't answer but stood silently until she finally got up and picked up the fruit, caviar and champagne, and shuffled off to the house.

"Hurry it up!" he called after her. "They'll be home soon!"

Rick collected his gear, and after a few minutes Kelli returned, standing before him like a dutiful child.

"Everything put back?" he asked.

"Yes."

"And straightened up?"

"Yes."

"Do I have to check?"

"No."

As he turned away, she made a face and stuck out her tongue.

They left, out the patio's wooden gate, and down a winding cobblestone path that led through the gently sloping garden bursting with flowers.

"Why can't *we* live like this?" she complained.

He grunted, moving along. "Because I work for a pool cleaning company and you're on unemployment."

She sighed. "Life just isn't fair."

"Who said it was?"

They were at the street now, by his truck, a beat-up brown Chevy. He threw his gear into the back, then went around to the passenger side and opened the door for her.

"But this is *America*!" Kelli said, tossing her duffel bag inside. "Don't we have a right to *make* things fair?"

He looked at her funny.

"What?" she asked.

"Are those your sunglasses?"

"Yes, *those* are my sunglasses!" she replied indignantly. Anyway, they were now.

She got in the truck, and, while waiting for him to get in the other side, checked herself out in the visor mirror.

Now her hair looked like a cheap blonde wig, her bathing suit the bargain-basement Blue Light Special it was. She glanced down at her legs; they needed a shave. Cinderella, no longer at the palace, had turned back into a peasant!

"Where to?" she asked sullenly, pushing the mirror away.

Rick started the truck. "Samuel Winston's."

"Who the hell is he?" she exclaimed, scrunching up her face unattractively.

Rick didn't bother answering.

"Oh, why can't you clean Tom Cruise's pool or Johnny Depp's or something?"

"I can take you home."

"No." She pouted.

They rumbled off and rode in silence. Then Rick said, somewhat defensively, as he turned off La Brea onto Santa Monica Boulevard, "He's a retired actor."

She perked up a little. "Really?"

"Lives in Beverly Hills."

She perked up a lot. "Oh!" she said.

They rode some more in silence.

"With his wife?" she asked.

Rick looked at her sideways, suspiciously. "No, with his cat," he said.

Kelli smiled and settled back further in the seat.

"Isn't that nice," she purred. "I just love cats!"

With her looks, with her brains, Kelli knew she deserved better in life.

The only child of a commercial airline pilot and an elementary school teacher, she had it pretty easy as a kid, at least until the divorce. At Hollywood High, her good looks enabled her to run with a fast crowd; but it was hard to keep up, what with all their cars and money. Most of her friends had gone on to college; Kelli's terrible grades ruled that out.

She almost wished she had studied harder in school and paid more attention . . .

But what the hell: girls just want to have fun.

"Slow down, Rick!" Kelli said as the truck turned onto Roxbury Drive. She leaned forward intently, peering through the windshield, studying each mansion, every manicured lawn, as they drove by. She would live in a neighborhood like this someday, she just knew it!

The truck pulled into a circular drive.

"Here?" she asked.

Rick nodded and turned off the engine. They got out.

The mansion before them was a sprawling, pink stucco affair, its front mostly obscured by a jungle of foliage and trees that apparently had been left unattended for years. The main entrance didn't look like anybody used it. Kelli frowned, disappointed.

And yet, she thought, this *was* a house in Beverly Hills.

"This way," Rick said, arms loaded with his pool-cleaning gear. Duffel bag slung over her shoulder, she followed him around the side to an iron-scrolled gate.

"Good," Rick said, swinging the gate open.

"What?"

"He remembered to leave it unlocked. I'd hate to have to holler for him till he came and let us in."

Kelli smiled at what lay stretched before her: an Olympic-size swimming pool with an elaborate stone waterfall, a huge Jacuzzi nearby, and expensive-looking patio furniture poolside. And all around nestled exotic plants and flowers and trees, transforming the area into a tropical paradise. But her smile faded when she noticed the old man slumped in one of the chairs, head bowed, snoring. He had on a white terry-cloth robe. By his sandal-covered feet lay a shaggy black cat.

"That's Mr. Winston?" Kelli whispered to Rick.

He nodded, with just a hint of a smile.

Kelli put her hands on her hips. "Why, he's older than the Hollywood Hills!"

"You just be quiet." Rick approached the old man. "Good afternoon, Mr. Winston," he said loudly.

With a snore the old man jolted awake. He focused on them, momentarily confused.

He was a very old man, Kelli thought—somewhere between sixty and a hundred. His head was bald and pink but for some wisps of white, his eyes narrow-set and an almost pretty blue; his nose was hawklike, his lips thin and delicate.

"I'm here to clean the pool," Rick said and set some of his gear down.

The old man cleared his throat and sat up straighter in his chair. "Needs it," he said.

Rick gestured to Kelli. "Mr. Winston, this is my friend, Kelli. Is it all right if she stays while I work?"

The old man looked at her. "Of course." He pointed with a thin, bony finger to a nearby chair. "Have a seat, my dear."

Kelli sat down, crossing her legs.

"Kel, Mr. Winston worked in show business with a lot of famous people," he explained, "like Jack Benny and Houdini and Abbott and Costello . . ."

"Don't forget Bergen and McCarthy!" the old man said, suddenly irritable. He leaned forward and spat. "Bergen, that fraud—who *couldn't* be a ventriloquist on the radio?"

There was an awkward silence, and Kelli gave Rick a puzzled look.

Then Rick said, "Yes, well . . . I'd better get to work . . ." He gathered his things and left them.

Kelli smiled at the old man. "I didn't know Candice Bergen was on the radio," she said.

The old man laughed. And the laugh turned into a cough and he hacked and wheezed.

"Forgive me, my dear," he said when he had caught his breath. "I was referring to Edgar Bergen—her *father*. We were billed together at the Palace."

"The *Palace*!" Kelli said, wide-eyed.

"Ah, you've heard of it?"

"Yes, indeed," she said. She leaned eagerly toward him. "What was the queen like?"

"Not *Buckingham* Palace," he laughed, and wheezed again. "The Palace Theater in New York. Vaudeville. You're so charming, my dear . . . are you an *actress*, by any chance?"

She leaned back in her chair. "I wish!" she said breathlessly.

"Well, don't," he replied gruffly. "They're a sad, sorry lot." He studied her a moment. "I'm afraid, my dear, you belong on the arm of some wealthy man, or stretched out by a luxurious pool."

"That's what I think!" she said brightly, then clouded. "But I don't have one."

"One what, child? A rich man or pool?"

"Either!"

He smiled, just slightly. He bent down and picked up the cat and settled the creature on his lap. "You're welcome to use my pool anytime, my dear," he said.

"You mean it?"

"Most certainly." He drew the cat's face up to his. "We'd love the company, wouldn't we?" he asked it.

"Meow." Its tail swish, swished.

"How old is your cat?" Kelli asked.

Mr. Winston scratched the animal's ear. "Older than you, my dear," he said.

"You must love it."

"Like a child," he whispered, and kissed its head. "But of course, it's no substitute for the real thing."

"You never had any kids?"

"Never married, my dear. Show business is a harsh mistress."

"What was that word you used? Sounded like a town . . ."

"I don't follow you, child."

"Something-ville."

He smiled; his teeth were white and large and fake.

"Vaudeville! That was a form of theater, my dear. Something like the 'Ed Sullivan Show.' "

"What show?"

He smiled, shook his head. "You *are* a child. The Palace, which you inquired about, was only one of countless theaters in those days . . . the Colonial, the Hippodrome . . . but the Palace was the greatest vaudeville theater in America, if not the whole world!"

Kelli couldn't have cared less about any of this, but she wanted to seem interested. "What was vaudeville like, Mr. Winston?"

"One long, exciting roller-coaster ride . . . while it lasted. You see, vaudeville died in the late 1930s. A show would open with a minor act like acrobats or jugglers, because the audience was still finding their seats, you see. That's where I began, as an opening act . . . but not for long . . ."

He was lost in a smile of self-satisfaction.

"You were a big hit, huh, Mr. Winston?"

"Brought the house down, if you'll pardon my immodesty. Before long I was a top-billed act."

Gag me with a spoon, she thought. "That's so cool. What did you do in your act, Mr. Winston?"

He laughed and shook his head. "What *didn't* I do!" he said.

The old goat sure was full of himself.

"And that's how you got rich and famous, huh?"

His expression changed; it seemed sad, and something else. Bitter?

"I'm afraid I've not been as well remembered as some of my . . . lesser contemporaries have." His eyes hardened. "Sometimes when a person does *everything* well, he isn't remembered for anything."

"Oh, you shouldn't say that, Mr. Winston. Everybody remembers you!"

That melted the old boy. He leaned forward and patted her hand; his wrinkled flabby flesh gave her the creeps, but she just smiled at him.

"If only I could have had a child like you." He stroked the cat and it purred. "How much richer my life would've been."

"I'm lonely, too. My dad died before I was born."

"Oh . . . my dear. I'm so sorry. . . ."

He seemed genuinely touched by that b.s.

"Can I ask you a favor, Mr. Winston?"

"Anything, child."

"Could I come talk to you again, sometime? You know . . . when Rick comes to clean the pool."

His delicate lips were pressed into a smile; he stroked his cat. "I insist, my dear. I insist."

The sound of Rick clearing his throat announced that he had joined the little group; his body was glistening with sweat. He smiled at Mr. Winston, but his brow was furrowed.

"Almost done," he said.

Mr. Winston nodded and stood up, the animal in his arms; he scratched the cat's neck and it seemed to undulate, liking the attention. "Will you children excuse me? I'm going to put my little girl in the house where's it's cooler."

"Certainly," Kelli smiled, watching him go into the house through the glass door off the patio.

"I know what you're up to," Rick snapped in her ear.

She didn't reply.

"He's old enough to be your *great*-grandfather. And if he's interested in anyone, it'd be me!"

"What do you mean?"

"What do you *think?*" he smirked. "He's been a bachelor since like forever. Besides, he's no fool—he'd see through you before long."

"And if he didn't, you'd tell him, I suppose?"

"I might. Be satisfied with what you've got."

"You, you mean? A poolboy?"

"I put up with your lying ass, don't I?"

She felt her face flush and tried to think of something to say to that, but before she could, the patio door slid open and the old man stepped out.

Rick and Kelli smiled.

As Mr. Winston approached, Kelli asked, "May I use your bathroom?"

"Certainly, my dear. It's just to the left off the kitchen."

Kelli grabbed her duffel bag and headed for the patio door.

"Don't be long, Kel," said Rick behind her. She could feel his eyes boring into her back.

Inside she hesitated only a moment. She was in a knotty-pine TV room; the knickknacks looked pretty worthless, and the only stuff of value was too big to fit in her bag. She moved on, like a shopper searching bargains out in a department store,

moving down a narrow hallway to the kitchen. She stopped
and turned back. She plucked a small oil painting of a tiger off
the wall and started to drop it into her bag. But she changed
her mind and put it back; she wasn't nuts about the frame.

In the kitchen she turned to the right which opened into a
large, formal hallway. A wide staircase yawned upward, as she
stood in the shadow of an elaborate crystal chandelier. To one
side was a closed, heavy, dark wood door. She didn't have time
to go upstairs and track down the old man's pants and go
through the pockets, so she tried the door. It wasn't locked.

The room had stupid zebra-striped wallpaper like the rec
room at her drunken uncle Bob's; but there were also a lot of
plants, potted and hanging, only when she brushed against one,
she discovered all of them were plastic, and dusty. *Yuucch*, she
thought. A rich old guy like Winston ought to spring for a
damn housekeeper.

There was a fireplace with a lion's head over it—unlike the
plants, the lion seemed real, its fangs looking fierce. Big life-
size dolls or statues or something of other animals were standing on little platforms against the walls, here and there: a
monkey, a hyena, a coiled snake. *Ick!* The couch had a cover
that looked like a leopard's skin, and the zebra walls were cluttered with photos of people who must have been famous, because they had signed their names on themselves—she
recognized one as that old unfunny comedian Bob Hope. Others she didn't know: a spangly cowboy named Roy Rogers, a
guy with buggy eyes named Eddie Cantor. In some of the pictures Mr. Winston wore a weird hat that looked like something
out of a jungle movie.

"Koo-koo!"

The sound made her jump; she turned and saw, among the
wall clutter, a cuckoo clock. The little bird sticking its head out
said its name a few more times and went back inside.

She sighed with relief; but the relief was quickly replaced
with panic. She'd been gone too long! She must find something
of value, and soon.

She advanced to a desk almost as cluttered as the walls and
switched on the green-shaded lamp and rifled through papers,

letters mostly, and a stack of photos of Mr. Winston, younger and in the safari hat. Finding nothing that seemed worth anything, she looked around the room and then she saw it.

The cat!

Sleeping in a dark corner of the room, in a little wicker bed; dead to the world . . .

Quickly she went for it, duffel bag at the ready, hands outstretched.

"Nice kitty-kitty," she smiled. "You're coming with Kelli . . ."

"What the hell are you doing?"

A dark shape filled the doorway.

"Nothing!" she said, and the figure stepped into the light. Rick.

"Don't scare me like that," Kelli said crossly.

"You have no business being in here . . . this is Mr. Winston's private collection . . . things from his career."

"Sorry," she said, almost defiantly. "Can I help it if I took a wrong turn?"

"And what were you going to do with that cat?"

"What cat?"

"Come with me—*now!*" Rick growled. "Mr. Winston's an important account, and you're not screwing this up for me!"

"Okay," she said. She glanced back at the cat, who hadn't stirred. How *easy* it would have been. . . .

On the way out she waved at Mr. Winston like a little girl and he smiled at her impishly and waved back the same way.

"Get in the truck," Rick ordered.

"Oh! I forgot something—my new sunglasses!"

"Hurry up, then."

She hadn't forgotten them, of course; she wanted to go back to make sure the gate was left unlatched.

Larry Hackett had been in California only two days, but already he wanted to go home. The vacation—his first in L.A.—was a major disappointment, from the scuzzy streets of Hollywood to the expensive dress shops of Century City, where his wife, Millie, had insisted on going, though she certainly couldn't afford (let alone fit into) the youthful, glamorous clothes.

And their stay in Beverly Hills with his wife's aunt—a live-in housekeeper for some director off on location for the summer—was also a disappointment; not that Beverly Hills wasn't nice, but he felt like a hick putzing along in his Toyota, while Porsches and Jaguars honked and zoomed around him on the palm-lined streets.

He supposed he should just make the best of the trip; sit back and look at all the beautiful women—few of whom looked back, and when they did it was as if to say, "Are you kidding? Lose some weight!"

If truth be told, the thirty-five-year-old Larry was just plain homesick. He longed to be back in his office at the computer.

"Tell us, Aunt Katherine," said Millie, pouring some sugar into her coffee, "what famous people live nearby?" The three were seated in the spacious, sunny kitchen, at a round oak table, having a late-morning cup.

"Well, let's see," Millie's aunt said. She was a big woman with a stern face offset by gentle eyes. "Rosemary Clooney has a house just down the street. And Jimmy Stewart."

Millie clasped her hands together. "How thrilling!" she said. "I'd love to meet them."

"We don't intrude on our famous neighbors out here, dear," Aunt Katherine said patiently. "Besides, I'm just hired help, remember."

Millie frowned like a child denied a cookie.

Larry sipped his coffee.

"Well, who's next door in the Deco place?" Millie persisted.

"An Arab sheik."

"*No kidding!*" Millie exclaimed. "I'll bet some wild parties go on over there, don't you, Larry?" She elbowed her husband, trying to draw him into the conversation.

He smiled politely.

"Actually," Aunt Katherine replied, "the sheik is very reserved."

"And who lives on the other side of you, in the pink stucco house?" Millie persisted in her questioning.

Larry rolled his eyes.

"Oh, you probably wouldn't know him," her aunt said. "His name is Samuel Winston."

Now Millie smiled politely, but Larry sat up straight in his chair. "Who did you say?" he asked.

"Samuel Winston," Aunt Katherine repeated.

Larry, eyes wide, turned to his wife. "Do you know who that *is*?" he asked excitedly.

Millie shook her head.

"*You* know! From when we were kids!"

She looked at him blankly.

"Safari Sam!"

Millie continued her vacant stare.

Larry sighed in irritation. "Didn't you ever watch the 'Safari Sam and Pooky Show'?"

"Ohhh . . ." Millie said slowly, nodding her head, ". . . now I remember. I didn't like that show. I could never tell which animals were real and which weren't. And that Pooky scared me."

"Why would a puppet scare you?"

"It wasn't a puppet, it was a *real* cat!"

Larry leaned toward her. "How can a *real* cat play the violin?" he asked, then added dramatically, "Remember its eyes? You can always tell by the eyes."

Millie glared at him—she didn't like to be corrected—then asked innocently, "Didn't Safari Sam get his show cancelled because of cruelty to animals?"

Larry's face flushed. "That was just a vicious rumor!" he said. "Safari Sam loved those animals!"

"I know," Millie laughed, "maybe he *tortured* that cat until it played the violin!"

"Very funny . . ."

"After all," she said, continuing her verbal assault, "I heard he cut out that cat's voice box so he could pretend to talk for it!"

"He did not!" Larry shouted.

"Did too!" Millie shouted.

Aunt Katherine stood up from the table. "Larry! Millie!" she said. "Children, *please!*"

They stopped their bickering.

"Aunt Katherine," Larry said, "could you please introduce me to Mr. Winston? I'm his biggest fan."

"Well . . ."

"I know all about him . . . his career as a comedian, a magician, a ventriloquist . . ." Larry paused and stared out the window at the pink stucco house. ". . . Samuel Winston was a genius, a great man! He just never got his due. . . ."

Aunt Katherine smiled, but raised a lecturing finger. "Samuel Winston *is* a great man. He deserves respect—*and* to be allowed his privacy."

Reluctantly, Larry nodded. Millie looked sheepish.

Then Larry said, "You're right, Aunt Katherine. I'm sorry I asked."

But Larry knew he'd be asking again; they were staying all week, and he had time to work on her.

The gate creaked as Kelli swung it open; behind her Rick was shaking. The big chicken.

"I can't believe I let you talk me into this," he whispered.

It *had* taken some doing, particularly after he'd bawled her out about it in the truck when they left Winston's earlier that day.

"Jeez, Kel," he had said, the breeze riffling his hair, "if you want a goddamn cat, I'll buy you a goddamn cat!"

"But I want *that* cat!"

"Why?" he said, exasperated. "It's old, it's mangy . . ."

"It's worth a lot of money," she cut in.

She had explained on the waterbed in their tiny apartment off Melrose. He'd stared at her, shook his head. "You want to *kidnap* that cat and hold it for ransom?"

"I wouldn't do that!" she exclaimed, offended, covering her breasts modestly with the sheet.

"Then what? I can't wait to hear."

"I want to kidnap the cat and collect a *reward*."

"Oh, swell," Rick jeered, "well, that's different. A reward as in somehow the cat got out and we found it and took it home, then saw the ad in the paper?"

"Exactly."

He had looked at her dazed, as if struck by a stick; but then his eyes had tightened.

"The old man *is* worth a lot of money . . . and it's just a cat."

"Just a cat," she said, stroking him, "just a silly old cat."

The full moon reflected on the shimmering surface of the pool; it was the only light on the patio. The lights in the big pink house were off.

"You got that screwdriver?" she whispered.

Rick, dressed all in black as she was, swallowed and nodded.

But they didn't have to pry the patio door open; it, too, was unlocked. They moved through the house slowly, quietly, and the sound of their footsteps was something even they couldn't detect, let alone some deaf old man.

Soon they stood in the safari room; Kelli turned on the green-shaded desk lamp. The mounted lion's head and the animal shapes and the plastic plants threw distorted shadows.

"It's in the corner," Kelli said.

"You get it. You wanted it."

"It might *scratch* me!"

"It might scratch *me!*"

"Children, don't fight," said Samuel Winston, his voice kindly; but an elephant gun in his hands was pointed right at them. He had plucked it from the gun rack just inside the door.

Kelli jumped behind Rick, who put both hands out in a "stop" motion. "Whoa, Mr. Winston," he said, "don't do anything rash . . ."

The old man moved closer. "Aren't you children the ones behaving rashly? Trying to steal my little girl away from me? If you needed money, all you had to do was ask!"

"Please, Mr. Winston," Rick pleaded. "Don't call the cops. We were wrong to break in . . ."

"Very wrong, Rick. I'm disappointed. I thought you were a nice young man . . . and you, Kelli. How very sad."

Kelli didn't know what to say; she'd only been caught stealing twice in her life, and both times she'd wormed her way out—once by crying, and once with sex. Neither seemed applicable here.

"Rick can give you free pool service for a year!" she blurted. "Please don't call the police, Mr. Winston!"

"I have no intention of calling the police," the old man said.

Rick backed up with Kelli clinging to him. Seconds seemed like minutes.

Then the old man lowered the gun. "Don't worry," he said, almost wearily. "I'm not going to shoot you, either."

Rick sighed; Kelli relaxed her grip on him.

The old man turned away from them and put the gun back in its rack. "I know what it's like to live in a town where everyone else seems to have everything."

He faced them.

"The only thing worse is to finally *have* everything, and no one to share it with."

Something in the old man's voice told Kelli she was out of danger; smiling a little, she stepped out from behind Rick.

"That is sad, Mr. Winston. I wish we could make this up to you somehow . . ."

His pretty blue eyes brightened. "Perhaps you could! How would you like to live here and share in my wealth? To be my son and daughter?"

Rick was stunned. Kelli's smile froze.

"What's the matter?" the old man chuckled. "Cat got your tongue?"

Rick stuttered, "Well, I . . . we . . ."

But Kelli rushed forward, arms outstretched.

"Daddy!" she cried.

"Koo-koo! Koo-koo!" went the clock, high on the cluttered wall.

"Ah, two o'clock," the old man said. "Shall we discuss this further over a hot cup of cocoa? Perhaps you could heat some milk for Pooky, my dear."

"Pooky?" Kelli asked.

"That's my little girl's name. My cat you were so interested in. . . ."

And with Kelli on his arm, Winston walked out of the den, patting the girl's hand soothingly, a bewildered Rick trailing behind. Kelli glanced over her shoulder and grinned at him like the cat that ate the canary.

The warm California breeze played with Kelli's long blonde hair, which shimmered in the brilliant sun like threads of finely spun gold. Stretched out in a lounge chair by the pool, she looked like a goddess in her white bathing suit and Ray-Ban sunglasses. Next to her on a wrought-iron table lay fruit, caviar and champagne. Her pouty-pink lips were fixed in a smug, satisfied smile. She was in heaven.

"More champagne, my dear?" asked Samuel Winston, who stood next to her in a terry-cloth robe worn loosely over swimming trunks.

"Yes, please!"

He filled the empty goblet she held in one hand.

"Another beer, Rick?" Samuel called out.

Rick, in a purple polo shirt, white Bermuda shorts and wraparound sunglasses, sat a few yards away, beneath the umbrella, a can of Bud Lite by his feet.

"No thanks, Sam . . . haven't finished this one."

Samuel returned to his chair, next to Kelli. He looked at her, studying her, and frowned. "You'd better put on more sunscreen, my dear," he advised.

"Am I red?"

Samuel nodded.

"Well, I don't feel it . . . Rick! Do I look red?"

"Not that I can see."

Samuel stood up. "Let me get your back for you," he said.

"Would you? I can't do it myself."

Samuel took the tube of sunscreen off her towel and squeezed some out on his hands. He spread it gently on her back. "Does that hurt?" he asked.

"Not a bit."

When Samuel had finished, he wiped his hands on the towel, then he went over to the cat, which lay on the patio in the shade of the umbrella, and picked it up. He went back to his chair, sat and stroked the animal's fur.

"Are you happy?" he asked it.

"Meow." Its tail swish, swished.

"Me, too, Pooky," Samuel said. He peered skyward. "Such a beautiful day. Don't you think?"

"I'll say!" the cat said.

"Oh, *yoo-hoo!*" came a grating voice from the gate.

Samuel looked sharply toward it. "Hell and damnation!" he said. "It's that woman next door. That housekeeper. And who's that with her?" He squinted to make out the forms. "Tweedledee and Tweedledum. Don't worry, my pets, I'll get rid of them."

He waved one hand half-heartedly.

The trio pushed through the gate, the housekeeper marching in the lead, the man and woman trailing timidly behind.

Samuel groaned behind his grin. He put down the cat and stood to greet them.

"Ah, madam," he said, "it's so nice to see you."

"I hope we're not interrupting anything," the housekeeper said with a silly little laugh.

"Not at all."

"I don't make a habit out of intruding . . ."

"Think nothing of it."

"But I'd like to introduce you to my niece Millie, and nephew Larry—Larry is your biggest fan."

Samuel smiled politely at the two. "It's a pleasure to meet you," he said.

The niece had a blank expression, but the nephew looked like an eager puppy-dog, beads of sweat forming on his brow. The boy rushed forward and grabbed one of Samuel's hands, pumping it vigorously.

"Mr. Winston," he gushed, "you don't know how much the 'Safari Sam and Pooky Show' meant to a little kid with asthma in Akron, Ohio!"

Now Samuel smiled genuinely. "Why, thank you," he said, "That's very gratifying."

Suddenly Larry clutched his heart, mouth gasping, eyes bugging.

"Is anything wrong?" Samuel asked, alarmed.

"Pooky!" Larry cried, pointing a wavering finger at the cat that lay a few yards away on the ground. "It's Pooky!"

The pudgy boy-man ran to it, and fell on his knees, palms outspread as if worshiping.

Reverently, he looked up at Samuel. "May I?" he asked.

Samuel nodded.

Gingerly, tenderly, Larry picked up the cat. It lay limp in his hands. "It's so well preserved," he said in awe.

"I did it myself."

"Really!"

"Taxidermy has long been an avocation of mine. Have you ever been out to the Roy Rogers Museum?"

"You didn't do . . . *Trigger!*" Larry gasped.

Samuel merely smiled.

Larry seemed spellbound by Pooky. "There's a place for your hand . . . he's real *and* a puppet! So that's your secret!"

"One of them."

Larry gave his wife a withering look. "I told you he was a genius!"

The plump little wife, however, only looked sickened.

Larry handed the cat back to Samuel. "Could you have Pooky sing the 'Pooky Song'?" he asked.

"I'd rather not," the old man answered.

"Oh, please!" Larry pleaded, his chubby hands pressed together, prayerlike.

Samuel sighed. "Well, all right," he said, but irritated.

"And do the Pooky dance . . . ?"

Samuel glared, then nodded, grudgingly.

". . . while you drink a glass of water?"

"I don't *have* a glass of water!"

"I could get you one," Larry offered.

"No!" Samuel snapped. "Never mind. Just hand me that champagne."

Samuel stuck his hand inside the cat, slung the bottle to his lips and drank it, while Pooky, his legs and tail flapping in a crazy jig, sang in a high-pitched voice.

"I'm Pooky, a little kooky, it's kind of spooky . . ."

Larry, with joy on his face and tears in his eyes, applauded wildly. So did the housekeeper. But the niece stood frozen, horrified.

"That was just like the show!" Larry exclaimed.

"Thank you," Samuel said tersely. "Now, if you don't mind, you must go . . . I need my rest."

The housekeeper stepped toward him. "We were just wondering," she said, "if you could join us for lunch."

"I've just had brunch, thank you."

"Well, what about your guests?" the housekeeper pressed.

"My guests?" Samuel asked, annoyed, frowning. He turned and looked at the lounging Kelli and Rick nearby; the two had their backs to Samuel's unwanted company.

"Oh, I've been rude," Samuel said. "I didn't introduce my son and daughter . . . they're on an extended visit . . ."

"We'd love to have all three of you for lunch," the stupid woman persisted.

"Well, I'll have to decline," he said, then added with a wicked little smile, "but of course, I shouldn't speak for Kelli and Rick . . ."

"Oh, I'm not hungry," Rick said.

Though the trio of intruders didn't notice, the lips of Samuel's children didn't move when they spoke, nor did Samuel's— for he was no radio ventriloquist.

"Me neither," Kelli said. "We couldn't possibly eat. We're just stuffed!"

Sax and the Single Cat

Carole Nelson Douglas

THE DAY I GET THE call, I am lounging on Miss Temple Barr's patio at the Circle Ritz condominiums in Las Vegas, trying to soak up what little January sunshine deigns to shed some pallid photosynthesis on my roommate's potted oleanders.

Next thing I know, some strange Tom in a marmalade-striped T-shirt is over the marble-faced wall and in my own face.

It is not hard to catch Midnight Louie napping these days, but I am on my feet and bristling the hair on my muscular nineteen-pound-plus frame before you can say "Muhammad Ali." My butterfly-dancing days may be on hold, but I still carry a full set of bee-stingers on every extremity.

Calm down, the intruder advises in a throaty tone I do not like. He is only a messenger, he tells me next; Ingram wants to see me.

This I take exception to. Ingram is one of my local sources, and usually the sock is on the other foot: I want to see Ingram. When I do, I trot up to the Thrill 'n' Quill bookstore on Charleston to accomplish this dubious pleasure in person.

I look over my yellow-coated visitor and ask, "Since when has Ingram used Western Union?"

Since, says the dude with a snarl, he has a message for me from Kitty Kong. The intruder then leaps back from whence he came—Gehenna, I hope, but the city pound will do—and is as gone as a catnip dream.

A shiver plays arpeggios on my spine, which does nothing to restore my ruffled body hair.

This Kitty Kong is nobody to mess with, having an ancestry that predates saber-toothed tigers, who are really nothing to mess with. They would make Siegfried and Roy's menagerie at the Mirage Hotel look like animated powder-room rugs.

Though the designated titleholder changes, there is always a Kitty Kong. Long ago and far away, in Europe in pre-New World days, this character was known as the King of Cats, but modern times have caught up even with such a venerable institution. Nowadays Kitty Kong can as easily be a she as a he, or even an it. Nobody knows who or what, but the word gets out.

Supposedly, a Kitty Kong rules on every continent, the seven-plus seas being the only deterrent to rapid communication. Even today, dudes and dolls of my ilk hate to get their feet wet. If the aforementioned saber-tooths had been as particular, they would have avoided a lot of tar pits, but these awesome types are legend and long gone. Only Midnight Louie remains to do the really tough jobs, and at least I resemble an escapee from a tar pit.

I follow my late visitor over the edge to the street two stories below and am soon padding the cold Las Vegas pavement. Nobody much notices me—except the occasional cooing female, whom I nimbly evade—which is the way I like it.

Ingram you cannot miss. He is usually to be found snoozing amongst the murder and mayhem displayed in the window of the Thrill 'n' Quill. Today is different. He is waiting on the stoop.

"You are late, Louie," he sniffs.

Such criticism coming from someone who never has to go anywhere but the vet's does not sit well. I give the rabies tags on his collar a warning tap, then ask for the straight poop.

"And vulgar," he comments, but out it comes. A problem of national significance to catkind has developed and Kitty Kong wants me in Washington to help.

No wonder Ingram is snottier than usual; he is jealous. But his long, languorous days give him plenty of time to keep up with current events.

I am not a political animal by nature, but even I have noticed that the new Democratic administration in Washington means the White House will be blessed with the first dude of my ilk in a long, long time, one Socks (somehow that name always makes my nose wrinkle like it had been stuffed in a dirty laundry basket). However, I am not so socially apathetic as to avoid a thrill of satisfaction that one of Our Own is back in power after a long period when the position of presidential pet had gone to the dogs.

This First Feline, as the press so nauseatingly tagged the poor dude, is not the first of his kind to pussyfoot around the national premises. I recall that a polytoed type named Slippers was FDR's house cat and the White House's most recent First Adolescent, Amy Carter, had a Siamese named Misty Malarky Ying Yang. Come to think of it, Socks is not such a bad moniker at that.

Anyway, Ingram says the inauguration is only two days away and a revolting development has occurred: The President's cat is missing; slipped out of the First Lady's Oldsmobile near the White House that very morning. We cannot have our national icon (Ingram uses phrases like that) going AWOL (he does not use expressions like that, but I do) at so elevated an occasion. The mission, should I choose to accept it (and there is nil choice when Kitty Kong calls): find this Socks character and get him back on the White House lawn doing his do-do where he is supposed to do it.

The reason Midnight Louie is regarded as a one-dude detection service is some modest fame I have in the missing-persons department. A while back I hit the papers for finding a dead body at the American Booksellers convention, but I also solved the kidnapping of a couple of corporate kitties named Baker and Taylor. Things like that get back to Kitty Kong.

You would be surprised to know how fast cats like us can communicate. Fax machines may be zippy, but MCI (Multiple Cat Intelligence) can cross the country in a flash through a secret network of telecats who happen to look innocent and wear a lot of fur. These telecats are rare, but you can bet that they are well looked out for. I have never met one myself, but then I have never met a First Cat, either, and it looks like I will be doing that shortly.

After I leave Ingram, I ponder how to get to Washington, D.C. I could walk (and hitch a few rides along the way), but that is a dangerous and time-consuming trek. I prefer the direct route when possible.

Do I know anyone invited to the shindig? Not likely. Miss Temple Barr and her associates are nice folk but neither high nor low enough to come to this particular party. I doubt any of the Fifty Faces of America hails from Las Vegas (though several million such faces pass through here every year). I would have had better odds with the other guy and his "Thousand Points of Light."

But *que será, será*, and by the time I look up my feet have done their duty and taken me just where I need to be: Earl E. Byrd's Reprise storefront, a haven for secondhand instruments of a musical nature and Earl E. himself.

If anyone from my neck of the wilderness is going to Washington, it will be Earl E., owing to his sideline. I scratch at the door until he opens it. Earl E. stocks a great supply of meaty tidbits, for good reason, and I am a regular.

Of course, when I visit Earl E., I have to put up with Nose E.

I do not quite know how to describe this individual, and I am seldom at a loss for words. Nose E. resembles the product of an ill-advised mating between a goat-hair rug and a permanent-wave machine of the old school. Imagine a white angora dust mop with a hyperactive hamster inside and a rakish red bow over one long, floppy ear. Say it tips the scale at four pounds, is purportedly male and canine. There you have

Nose E., one of the primo dope-and-bomb-sniffing types in Las Vegas, even the U.S. You figure it.

Earl E. has a secret, and lucrative, sideline in playing with bands at celebrity dos all over the country. The lucrative part is that Nose E. goes along in some undercover cop's grip, ready to squeal on any activities of an illegal nature among the guests, including those so rude as to disrupt the doings with an incendiary device.

Dudes and dolls of my particular persuasion are barred from this cushy job for moral reasons. Our well-known weakness for a bit of nip now and then supposedly makes us unreliable.

Oh. Did I mention Earl E.'s instrument of choice? Tenor sax. Will Earl E. be at the inauguration? As sure as it rains cats and dogs (that *look* like dogs) in Arkansas.

Commercial airliners are not my favorite form of travel, but with Earl E., I and Nose E. get separate but equal cardboard boxes and a seat in first-class. (Actually, my box is bigger than Nose E.'s, since I outweigh this dust-mop dude almost five to one.)

Getting here is not hard—after I gnaw on the heavy cream parchment of Earl E.'s invitation for a few minutes he gets the idea and says, "What is happenin', Louie? You want to go to D.C. today with Nose E. and me and boogie?"

I look as adorable as a guy of my age and weight can stomach, and wait.

"All right. I am paying for an extra seat anyway for the sax and Nose E. A formerly homeless black cat like you should have a chance to see history made."

See it? I make it. But that is my little secret.

As per the usual, there is little room at the inn in D.C., but Earl E. has connections due to his vocations of music and marijuana sniffing. My carrier converts into a litter box for a few days in a motel room not too far from the Capitol with a king-size bed I much approve and promptly fall asleep on for the night, despite the company. I also plan to use most of my facilities outdoors, reconnoitering.

Naturally, Earl E. has no intentions of letting me out unchaperoned, though he takes that miserable Nose E. everywhere. Imagine a Hostess coconut cupcake sitting on some dude's elbow and squeaking every now and then. But there is not a hotel maid alive who can see past her ankles fast enough to contain Midnight Louie when he is doing a cha-cha between the door and a service cart.

I am a bit hazy on dates when denied access to the Daily Doormat—otherwise known as the morning paper—but I discover later that we arrived on the day before the inauguration.

Washington in January is snowless, but my horizon is an expanse of gray pavement and looming white monuments, so the effect is wintry despite a delicate dome of blue backdropping it all.

I stroll past the White House unobserved except by a pair of German shepherds, whose handlers curb them swiftly when they bay and lunge at me.

"It is just a cat," one cop says in a tone of disgust, but the dogs know better. Luckily, nobody has much listened to dogs since Lassie was a TV star.

Socks is not officially resident at the Big White until after the swearing in, so I do not expect to find any clue in the vicinity. What I do expect is to be found. When I am, it is a most unexpectedly pleasant experience.

I am near the Justice Building when I hear my name whispered from the shade of a Dumpster. I whirl to see a figure stalking out of the shadow—a slim Havana Brown of impeccable ancestry.

"You the out-of-town muscle?" she asks, eyeing me backwards and forwards with a dismaying amount of doubt.

"My best muscle is not visible," I tell her smugly.

"Oh?" Her supple rear extremity arches into an insulting question mark.

I sit down and stroke my whiskers into place. "In my head."

That stops her. She circles me, pausing to sniff my whiskers, a greeting that need not be intimate but often is. Then she sits in front of me and curls her tail around her sleek little brown toes, paired as tightly as a set of chocolate suede pumps in Miss Temple Barr's closet.

"You know my name," I tell her. "What is yours?"

"You could not pronounce my full, formal name," she informs me with a superior sniff. "My human companions call me Cheetah Habanera for short."

Cheetah, huh? She does look fast, but a bit effete for the undercover game.

"You sure you are not a Havana Red?" I growl.

She shrugs prettily. "Please. My people fled Cuba more than thirty years ago with my grandmother twelve-times removed. I am a citizen, and more than that, my family has been in government work ever since. What have you done to serve your country lately?"

Disdain definitely glimmers in those round orbs the color of old gold.

"They also serve who stand and wait," I quip. An apt quote often stands a fellow in good stead with the opposite sex. Not now.

She eyes my midsection. "More like sit and eat. But you managed to get here quickly, and that is something. Do you know the background of the subject?"

"What has grammar got to do with it?"

"The subject," she says with a bigger sigh, "Socks, is a domestic shorthair, about two years old; nine to ten pounds, slender and supple build." She eyes me again with less than enchantment. "He has yellow eyes; wears black with a white shirtfront, a black face-mask, and, of course, white socks."

"Yeah, yeah. I know the type. A Uni-Que."

"Uni-Que? I never heard of that breed."

"It is not one," I inform her brusquely, "just a common type. That is what I call them. Street name is 'magpie.' I know a hundred guys who look like that. If this Socks wants to lose himself in a crowd, he picked the right color scheme for the job. You, on the other hand—"

"Stick to business," she spits, ruffling her neck fur into a flattering, chocolate brown frill.

I refrain from telling her that she looks beautiful when she is angry. The female of my species is a hard sell who requires convincing even when in the grip of raging hormonal imbalance, and I do mean moan. This one is as cold as the Washington Monument.

"Fixed?" I ask.

"Do you mean has he had a politically correct procedure? Of course," she answers, "is not everybody 'fixed' these days?"

"Not everybody," I say. "What is the dude's routine?"

"He is not a performing cat—"

"I mean where does he hang out, what jerks his harness?"

"Oh. Squirrels."

"Squirrels?"

"He is from Arkansas. They must have simpler sports there."

"Nothing wrong with a good squirrel chase," I say in the absent dude's defense, "though I myself prefer lizards."

Her nose wrinkles derisively. "We D.C. cats have more serious races on our minds than with squirrels and lizards. Do you know how vital to our cause it is that an intelligent, independent, dignified cat with integrity inhabit the White House, rather than a drooling, run-in-all-directions dog, for the first time in years? The four major animal-protection organizations have named 1993 the Year of the Cat, and the year is off to a disastrous start if Socks does not take residence ASAP."

"Huh? What is ASAP, some political interest group?"

Her lush-lashed eyes shudder shut. "Short for 'As Soon As Possible.' Do Las Vegans know nothing?"

"Only odds, and it looks like Washington, D.C., is odder than anything on the Las Vegas Strip, and that is going some. Okay. We got a late-adolescent ex-tom who is a little squirrelly. Any skeletons in the closet?"

"Like what?"

"Insanity in the family?"

For the first time she is silent, and idly paws the concrete, all the better to exhibit a slim foreleg. I cannot tell if she is merely scratching her dainty pads, or thinking.

"Family unknown," she confesses. "Could be a plant by a foreign government. Odd how neatly he became First Cat of Arkansas. The Clintons had lost their dog Zeke to an auto accident—"

I nod soberly. "It happens, even to cats."

"The First Offspring, Chelsea, saw two orphaned kittens outside the house where she took piano lessons and begged for the one with white socks. The President and his wife are allergic to cats, but okayed Chelsea taking the male."

"Now that is the most encouraging sign of presidential timber I have seen yet," I could not help noting. "Ask not what you can sacrifice for your country when your own president and spouse will suffer stuffy noses so their little girl can take in a homeless dude. Kind of makes your eyes water."

"Mine are bone dry," Cheetah answers with enough ice in her tone to frost her brown whiskers white.

"What about the female?" I ask next.

"What female?"

"You said 'the male.' There were two orphans. Ergo, the other must be female."

She blinks, impressed by my faultless logic and investigative instincts, no doubt. Then she sighs.

"Taken in too, by a friend of the piano teacher who read about Socks and also had lost a pet dog. A Republican lady." She sniffs, whether at the political or former pet leanings of the other kit's adoptive family, I cannot tell.

"Another Uni-Que?" I ask.

"No." Cheetah Habanera is proving oddly reluctant to reveal Socks's family connections. I soon discover why. "Jet black. All over. Now called 'Midnight.' "

All right! Methinks a small detour to Arkansas on the way home might become necessary. I am not politically prejudiced. Republican cats are still superior to Democratic dogs. Midnight, huh. Nice name. At least Little Miss Midnight is not missing.

"She is also fixed?" I inquire.

"Who knows? Or cares? Listen, Mr. Midnight, better keep your nose to business. Without Socks found by tomorrow, your name will by *Mudd*night Louie. I do not know why Kitty Kong wanted out-of-town help anyway."

"To catch a thief, send a thief. To find a disoriented, disaffected out-of-towner—"

"Right. If you get a lead on Socks, you can find me here."

She sidles back into the Dumpster shadow like she was born there, and I start looking around Washington. My plan is serendipitous, which is to say, nonexistent.

I pace the terrain, sniff the chill winter air and generally observe how this place would strike a fellow from the country's heartland. Like a monumental chip off the big cold white berg on an iceman's truck.

Miles of hard pavement and towering buildings as white and bland as the grave markers in the National Cemetery would not seem welcoming to a junior good ole boy squirrel-chaser from Little Rock.

One other thing is clear. Not many cats hang out in these sterile public corridors. Even a down-home Uni-Que would stick out like a sore throat.

Naturally, I do not expect to stumble over the absent Socks on my first tour of the place, so I amble over to the Arkansas Ball hotel for some forced-air heat and human company.

The place is a mess of activity, a snarl of hotel minions and party organizers in both senses of the word, a veritable snake pit of electrical cables and audiovisual equipment. Even the Secret Service wouldn't notice a stray cat in this mayhem and I make sure I am not noticeable when I want to be.

Earl E. is jamming onstage with the other boys in the band. (How come there are never girls? Even we cats make our night music coed.) He is rehearsing for the big Arkansas Ball tonight, where you can bet Clinton, Inc. will be even if Socks is missing.

Nose E., wearing a Scotch-plaid vest to protect him from the winter chill, is lying like a discarded powder puff near the Earl E.'s open burgundy-velvet-lined instrument case, eyes the usual coal black glint behind the haystack hairdo, and black nose pillowed on furry toes. I presume the thing has toes.

I have been out pounding pavement all morning while this fluffpuff has been supine posing for a Johnnie Walker Red ad.

Nose E. gives an obligatory growl of greeting, then admits that he has nothing to do. It seems that Earl E. and his buddies are too busy jiving and massaging their glittering brass saxes onstage to pay Nose E. any mind. Or is that saxi?

That is the trouble with a prima donna dog, whatever the

gender: they get addicted to being the center of attention. So would I if I were carried everywhere, wore bows on my ears and was called "Sweetie Pie" by celebrities who never would dream that I am really a cross between a bodyguard and a snitch. Me, I like being Mr. Anonymous and underestimated.

Nose E.'s litany of ills goes on. Nothing is doing until six o'clock or so, he says. He has met his handler of the evening, and it is not the usual scintillating doll in rhinestones, but a former football player who holds him like a dumbbell, with one hammy hand around his rib cage.

Besides, Nose E. notes morosely, so many federal security types decorate the building, and indeed the entire town—they even seal the manholes along the Inauguration parade route—that not even a speck of fairy dust could escape notice. Nose E., in short, is redundant. For such a spoiled squirt, that is indeed hard to take.

So sunk is Nose E. in his imagined troubles that he does not think to ask about my mission; besides, to a dude after cocaine and TNT, normal, ordinary canine pursuits, such as finding and harassing cats, is low priority.

This is fine, for my observations during my meander, in which I have seen Socks's puss peeking out from every newspaper-dispensing machine, has given me an idea—not that anybody outside the Clinton inner circle knows that Socks is missing.

What is obvious, if not the whereabouts of Socks, is that this dude's overnight fame has made him a hard slice of salami to hide, no matter how commonplace his appearance. Now I know where to look.

I wander toward the river. I am not much for rivers, but I avoid the public portions bordered by leafless trees and bare expanses of brown green lawn, heading for the fringes where I know I can find a population that inhabits every city—the homeless.

Even the homeless are hard to find in D.C. right now. Panhandlers know better than to haunt the populated areas when a major network event is unfolding; besides, half of them are dressing and duding up like the rest of the inauguration influx, to play Cinderella and Prince Charming-for-a-day at the Homeless Ball.

At last I find a motley group wearing their designer hand-me-downs from Salvatore Arme. In their battered trench coats and tattered sweaters and mufflers, they resemble a huddle of war correspondents.

I do not expect any revelations as to the whereabouts of the missing Socks from these folks, but where the homeless gather, so do their animal companions of choice: dogs. And no one on the city streets knows the scuttlebutt like a dog that associates with a transient person.

Sure enough, I spot a Hispanic man in a cap with numerous news clips safety-pinned to it, surrounded by a bark of dogs, doing same. I look for the unseated Millie of White House fame among them, but these dogs' only visible pedigree is by purée. They are as awkward a conjunction of mutts as I have ever seen, and are barking and milling and twining their leashes until they resemble one of those seven-headed monsters of antiquity, but they are at least talkative and really rev up when I stroll into view.

I sit down, making clear that I will not depart without information. The people present view me with alarm, but I am used to being considered unlucky and even dog bait. Besides, should the pack lose their leashes, I have already spied the tree I would climb like a berserk staple gun.

"Cat," these morons yap at me and each other, growing evermore excited. (I do not speak street dog, a debased and monosyllabic language, but I understand enough to get by.)

"Yeah," I growl back, "I suppose you are not used to seeing such fine specimens of felinity."

They claw turf as their whines go up a register. The poor dude in the cap now has his arms twisted straitjacket-style as he tries to control his entourage, all the while yelling, "Scat!"—only he pronounces it "Escat!"

The other homeless watch in hopes of some action entertainment shortly.

"Black cat," the dogs carol in chorus after rubbing their joint brain cell together.

"Bingo." I yawn. "See any black and white cats lately?"

They go berserk, baying out cats of all colors that they have seen and pursued. Not one is a magpie.

After a few more seconds of abuse, I am convinced that the street dogs have not sniffed hide nor hair of Socks, luckily for him. Further, I also learn that the humans present are not as ignorant of Socks's newfound celebrity as I had hoped.

A woman with a face as cracked as last year's mud edges toward me, a bare hand stretched out in the chill. "Here, Kitty. Stay away from those dogs. Come on. If you walked through whitewash you'd even look like that there Socks. Here, Kitty," she croons in that seductive tone of entrapment used upon my ancestors for millennia, "I got some food."

I remain amazed that people who have nothing, not even the basic fur coat my kind take for granted, are so eager to take kindred wanderers under their wings.

These homeless individuals may be sad, or deficient in some social or mental way, but they share a certain shrewd survival instinct and camaraderie also found among the legion of homeless of the feline and canine kind. Of course we all need and want a home, but most are not destined for such bounty and are not above appealing to the guilt of the more fortunate in making our lot more palatable. At least the homeless of the human kind are not corralled into the experimental laboratories or the animal-processing pounds that ultimately offer little more than the lethal injection or the gas chamber in the name of mercy.

So I look upon this sweet old doll with fond regret, but I am a free spirit on a mission, and too well-fed (if not well-bred) to take advantage of a kind face despite the temptation of a free meal. I scamper away, leaving the battlefield to the dogs, and trudge back downtown, much dispirited.

If even the homeless have seen enough discarded newspapers to know about Socks, it will prove harder than I thought to turn up the little runaway. Will Socks vanish into the legions of homeless felines from which he came? Will the country and the Clintons survive such a tragic turn of events? Will Midnight Louie strike out?

I picture Cheetah Habanera's piquant but triumphant face as I trot back to Hoopla Central. The sun is shining; the brisk air hovers pleasantly above freezing. For some reason mobs of people are thronging down Pennsylvania Avenue. I manage to thread my way through a berserk bunch performing calisthenics with lawn chairs. People do the strangest things.

Still distracted, I return to the hotel that will host the Clintons' triumphant Arkansas Ball. Everybody in this town has something to celebrate, except for Socks and me.

The stage area is temporarily deserted; even Nose E. is gone, and I shudder to find that I miss the little snitch's foolish face. Earl E.'s instrument case is still cracked open like a fresh clam. I curl up on the burgundy velvet lining—an excellent background for one of my midnight-black leanings—and lose myself in a catnap. Maybe something will come to me in a dream.

The next thing I know, I am being shaken out of my cushy bed like a cockroach out of a shoe.

Earl E. Byrd is leaning over me, his longish locks pomaded into Michael Jackson tendrils and his best diamond earring glittering in one ear. I take in the white shirtfront and the jazzy black leather bolo tie with the real live dead scorpion embedded in acrylic in the slide. Earl E. looks snazzy, but a little shook up.

"The case is for the instrument, dude," he thunders, brushing a few handsome black hairs from the soft velvet. "Behave yourself or you will be ejected from the ball. How did you get here, anyway?"

Of course I am not talking, and I can see by the way the lights, camera, action and musicians are revving up that Earl E. has no time to escort me elsewhere. He has other things on his mind as he lays his precious sax back in *my* bed. Does a sax feel? Does a sax need shut-eye? Is a sax on a mission to save the First Feline? Is there no justice?

Nose E. comes up to sniff at me in sneering rectitude, and I know that the last question was exceedingly foolish. Before Nose E. can really rub it in, a humongous man in a structurally challenged tuxedo swoops up the little dust bunny and moves into a room that has now filled with women in glitz and glitter and men in my classy colors—black with a touch of white about the face.

Let the ball begin.

Earl E. and the boys swing out. Although Earl E. is essaying the licorice stick at the moment, several musicians bear saxophones that shine brassy gold in the spotlights and wail, I'll admit, like the Forlorn Feline Choir in the darkest, bluesiest, funkiest alley on the planet. Folks foxtrot. The hip . . . hop. I settle grumpily next to the sax case from which I was so rudely evicted. All is lost. On the morrow the nation will wake to the news that it has a new president and a former First Feline. Bast knows—Bast is the Egyptian cat deity and my purrsonal favorite—what Kitty Kong will do.

While I am drowsing morosely, I start when the case beside me jolts. A burp of excitement bubbles just offstage. Someone knocks into Earl E.'s sax. So what. A pair of anonymous hands rights the big, shiny loudmouth thing. I see enough black wing-tips to shoe a centipede cluster onto the stage from the wings. When the phalanx of footwear suddenly parts, the First Couple stands there like a King and Queen in a Disney animated feature—Bill and Hillary dancing.

No doubt this is a festive and triumphal scene, and the First Lady's hair is rolled into a snazzy Ginger Rogers do, and they got rhythm and all's right with the world and I could go out in the garden and eat worms . . .

As my bleary eyes balefully regard the hated sax that has usurped my spot, I spy an odd thing. Inside the deep, dark mouth of the instrument something shines—not bright and gold—but whitish silver.

A snake of suspicion stirs in my entrails until it stings my brain fully awake. Why is Earl E. not playing the sax, when he brought it especially for that purpose?

Even as I speculate, Earl E. slips offstage and heads toward me. I expect another ejection, but he ignores me and reaches for the sax, his eyes on the stage where the First Couple has stopped dancing. The President is edging over to the band and microphone. He's going to talk, that is what presidents do, only when they do it, it is an address. He's going to address the crowd . . . my big green eyes flash to the approaching Earl E. The President is going to talk, then Earl E. is going to give him the sax and the President is going to *play it!*

The President is going to play a doctored sax in front of millions of TV-watching citizens.

Even as Earl E. grabs the sax I leap up, all sixteen claws full out, and sink them into his arm.

He jumps back and mouths an expression that luckily is drowned out by all the bebopping going on, but it rhymes with "rich" if that word had a male offspring.

I can tell I drew blood, because Earl E. drops his precious sax and it hits the case sideways and something falls out of the mouth like a stale wad of gum.

Earl E.'s eyes get wide and worried. He whirls back to the stage, runs over to appropriate a sax from a startled fellow player and hands it to the President with a flourish.

Everybody plays. Saxophones wail in concert. Everybody laughs and applauds. Something rustles behind me. The Meat Locker has returned Nose E. to the vicinity. The creature stiffens on its tiny fuzzy legs as its nose gives several wild twitches. Nose E. rushes toward the fallen sax, sits up and cocks an adorable paw as he tilts his inquisitive little noggin one way, then the other.

Earl E. is over in a flash. This nauseating behavior is Nose E.'s signal that he has smelled a rat. Being an undercover canine, he can resort to nothing obvious like barking. (Besides, he squeaks like a castrated seal.)

Then Earl E. upends the sax to shake out a windfall of plastic baggies containing a substance that much resembles desiccated catnip. I come closer for a look-see, but am rudely shoved aside.

"Good dog," Earl E. croons several sickening times.

What about my early warning system? Except for rubbing a hand on his forearm, he seems to have forgotten my pivotal role in exposing the perfidy. Probably puts it down to mysterious feline behavior.

Two of the wingtips come to crouch beside Earl E., taking

custody of the bags, the sax and the case. There goes beddy-bye.

"Marijuana. Whoever did this," one comments softly, "wanted to make sure that this time the President would inhale."

"Saxophones don't work that way."

"Does not matter," the other wingtip says. "The idea was to embarrass the President. The dog yours?"

"Yeah," Earl E. says modestly.

"Sharp pup." The wingtip pats Nose E. on the cherry red bow.

Sure, the dogs always get the credit.

So I sit there, overlooked and ignored and Sockless, as the party goes on. The President surrenders the sax and the stage and leaves for another inaugural ball. I cannot even get excited at this one when Carole King comes on to sing "You've Got a Friend." Name one.

The band plays on. I recognize a couple tunes, like the ever tasteful "Your Mama Don't Dance and Your Daddy Don't Rock and Roll," and the ever inspirational "Amazing Grace."

I'll say inspirational. I rise amid the postinaugural hubbub and make my silent retreat. Nobody notices.

Outside it is dark, but I have already reconnoitered the city and I know where I am going. There is only one place in town where a dude as overpublicized as Socks Clinton could hang out and be overlooked.

"I once was blind but now I see." I see like a cat in the dark, and I see my unimpeded way to a certain street on which stands a certain civic building. Around back is the obligatory Dumpster.

I wait.

Soon a curious pair of electric green eyes catches a stray beam of sodium iodide street light. The dude's white shirtfront and feet look pretty silly tinted mercurochrome pink as he steps out into the sliver of light. He looks okay, for a Uni-Que.

"Why did you do it?" I ask.

"How did you find me?" he retorts instead of answering. Then I realize that the poor dude *has* answered me.

"I figured out that there was only one place you could hang out and beg tidbits without being recognized: The Society for the Blind. Midnight Louie always gets his dude. You have to go back."

"Where? Home? I live in Little Rock."

"Not any more. You are a citizen of the nation now."

"I didn't ask to be First Cat."

I search through my memory bank of clichés but only find "Life is no bed of Rose's." (I do not know who this Rose individual was, but apparently she knew how to take a snooze, and that I can endorse.) I decide to appeal to his emotions.

"It seems to me that your human companion, Miss Chelsea Clinton, faces the same dislocation," I point out. "I would hate to see my delightful roommate, Miss Temple Barr, face a barrage of public curiosity and a new and demanding role in life without my stalwart presence at her side."

"You would move here?" Socks asks incredulously. "Where are you from?"

"Las Vegas."

"Oh," he nods, as if that explains a lot. "I bet you do not even chase squirrels. Did you know the White House squirrels may be . . . rabid?" he adds morosely.

"No!" I respond in horror. There is nothing worse than tainted grub. Poor little guy . . . no wonder he split.

"And," Socks adds in the same spiritless monotone, "you have not had the press shooting pictures down your tonsils for weeks, or getting you high on nip so you'll spill your guts to the press and embarrass your family. Then they dug up some rumor that my father was a notorious tomcat—"

"Shocking! But so was my old man."

"You are not First Feline," he spat glumly. "There's that instant book about me by that name, and all those T-shirts, then menu items named after me in places where I would not even be allowed to lap water. Can you believe that a local hotel concocted a Knock Your Socks Off drink?"

"Sounds like incitement to riot to me. What is in it?"

"Frangelico, Grand Marnier, half-and-half and crème de cacao."

"Does not sound half bad."

"I do not even know what most of those ingredients are. Now if they had made it from Dairy Queen ice cream—"

"Forget Dairy Queens. You are on a faster track now."

"I guess. They dug up some love letters I scratched in the sand to a certain lady named Fleur before I was fixed; I'm only an adolescent, for Morris's sake—I should be allowed some privacy."

"Sacrifice of privacy is a small price to pay considering what you can do for the country and your kind. We need a good role model in a prominent position. You owe your little doll and cats everywhere to stick in there for four years."

"Eight," Socks says, a combative gleam dawning in his yellow eyes.

I swallow a smile (my kind are not supposed to smile or laugh, and I like to keep up appearances) and trot out my more grandiose sentiments. I begin to see that what this dude needs is a campaign speech.

"Remember, Socks, you represent millions of homeless cats, crowded masses yearning to breathe free of the pounds and the lethal streets. We are a transient kind in a world that little notes nor long remembers our welfare. You may not have chosen prominence, but now you can use it to do good. Some are born great," I add, preening, "others have greatness thrust upon them by circumstance. You are one of these . . . circumstantial dudes. Do you want to drive your little doll into such loneliness at your defection that the First Kid goes turncoat and gets a dog to replace you? Do you want to be known as the first First Feline in history to abdicate?"

"No-o-o."

I have him. I brush near, give him a big brotherly tap of the tail on his shoulder. "What is really troubling you, kid? What made you snap and take off just as you got into town?"

Socks sighed. "I have been offered a book contract."

"Hey! That is good. I dabble in that pursuit myself."

"The book is to be called *Socks: The Untold Story.*"

I am nudging him down the alleyway and into the full glare of the street light. The bustle of inaugural traffic rumbles in the distance along with faint sounds of revelry. D.C. could be the Big Easy tonight.

"What is so bad about that?" I ask.

Sock stops. "There is nothing untold left to tell! The press has squeezed every bit of juice out of my own life. I have nothing to say."

"Is that all? Big-time celebrity authors do not let that stop them from penning shoo-in bestsellers. You just think you are not interesting. What you need, my lad, is what they call a 'ghost writer'—someone discreet and more experienced who can help you bring out the most interesting facets of your life."

"Squirrels?"

"No. We must create a feline 'Roots.' We can call it 'Claws.' What do you know about your mom and dad? All cats in this country are descended from the Great Mayflower Mama, of course, but I have heard on good authority that your forebears were mousers around Mount Vernon. Did not Martha Washington herself have a cat-door installed there for somebody's ancestors? Why not yours? Obviously, there is a long tradition of presidential association in your family . . . speaking of which, how about your sister, Midnight—nice name—where in Little Rock did you say she hung out?"

By now I have the dude heavily investing in his new career as raconteur and idol of his race. We reach the White House in no time, and I push him in. He admits that he could use the litter box in the engineering room. Aside from a few distraught aides—and aides are used to being distraught—no one need know of Socks's little escapade.

I trot back to my hotel, anticipating informing that snippy Cheetah Habanera of my success, and contemplating the fifty-fifty book deal I have just cut with Socks. Somebody has got to look out for a naive young dude in this cruel world.

Even though it is late, I have to wait outside the motel room door for at least an hour before Earl E. and Nose E. arrive, both a bit tipsy: Earl E. high on jamming and celebrity, Nose E. on all that marijuana he sniffed out.

I am in like Flynn and ensconced on the king-size before either of them gets a chance at it. Earl E. phones home before he retires, with news of his big adventure, which is how I learn who planted the weed in the presidential saxophone.

"PUFF," Earl E. explains to a benighted buddy on the phone while Nose E., half zonked, tries to curl up near me. I cuff the little spotlight-stealer away. "They called to claim responsibility. Can you believe it, man? PUFF is a radical wing of the pro-smoking types. I do not know what it stands for—People United For Fumes? Whatever, they were ticked off when Clinton made such a big deal about not inhaling once long ago and far away! They think it is un-American and namby-pamby to smoke anything without inhaling. Weird. We have had a weird time in this burg, man. What a gig. I cannot wait to get back to someplace normal like Las Vegas."

Amen.

Fat Cat

Nancy Pickard

"ZEKE, HAVE A HEART. HOW would it *look?*"

My friend, the Mt. Floresta chief of police, Jamison Grant, screwed up his face into what he apparently thought was a pleading expression. The effect produced among the deep, tanned wrinkles of his fifty-six years was unnervingly grotesque.

"So that's how you get criminals to confess." I grimaced back at him. Not the same effect, though, me being thirty years younger. "No need to beat it out of them. Just pull a face like that and they'll say anything."

Having thrown himself on my mercy and found it wanting, Jamison resorted to his own particular brand of subtlety. "Now listen, you harebrain." He sucked in his stomach behind his massive brass belt buckle and pulled his gargantuan frame upward until his face hovered several inches above my own six feet. From up there, like a great blue bald-headed eagle, he loomed. I was not intimidated. Insulted, maybe, but not intimidated. The legal eagle squawked: "Now this may be a small town, and we may not get reams of rapes and murders to keep us busy, but that does not mean I am free to go chasing some old lady's damn cat!"

"It's more than one cat and more than one old lady," I informed him. "And they're not all old. The ladies, I mean. I can name you at least one who's young and pretty."

"Do not interrupt me when I am being officious," Jamison said sternly. He grabbed a sheaf of paperwork from the in-basket on his desk and fanned the air in front of my nose with it. "Do you see these papers? *All* these papers? If you were to examine them closely, you would see there are blanks on them. I have to fill out those blanks, Zeke. And I have two thefts to investigate, one mayor to meet, the owner of a health spa to placate, three trials to attend in Gunnison, and a hell of a lot of other *important* work to do."

"The cats are important to their owners," I protested.

As owner, manager and general runabout for our town's animal shelter, I know a priority when I see one. It was quickly evident, however, that my priorities were not necessarily those of the Mt. Floresta, Colorado, police force.

"I don't even *like* cats," the bald eagle reminded me. Under the fluorescent light, his shiny pate gleamed. "Cats are sneaky, like thieves in the night and some young friends I could mention."

I decided it was the better part of caution not to argue with him. When you're an animal freak, as I am, sometimes you forget all the world does not love a cat. So I said in my best martyr's tone, "Okay, okay. I don't know what's become of the police in this town. Used to be they'd come help you get a kitten out of a tree, just one little kitten—"

"That was the firemen, Ezekiel."

"But now—" I waved my arms to encompass the entire one-room police station. "But now, I can't even get your attention when fifteen cats vanish."

"You exaggerate."

"No way, Jamison. I swear to God, fifteen cats have disappeared from this town in the last two months. And there may be more, for all I know."

"They got run over."

"Nope. No bodies, no squashed cat bodies lying around the streets. And don't tell me they ran away from home. These are pets, gorgeous cats, mama's little darlings."

"Zeke." Jamison's voice dripped compassion. "Old pal, friend of my own son, I would love to help you. You know I'd do anything if I could—"

"Yeah, right!"

"—but you are a fanatic when it comes to animals. And fanatics cannot see the forest for the aspens, the glacier for the ice. Just trust me on this one. There is no mystery. There is no problem. Cats come, cats go. Like tourists. And, like tourists, not soon enough, in my opinion."

I squinted my eyes like an angry tom. "You forgetting the cat lobby, Jamison?"

"The what?" He looked suspiciously on the verge of laughing.

I yelled at my friend the political appointee, "Cat owners vote, you know!" I let the door slam behind me when I stomped out of the station.

Outside, the crisp mountain air cooled me off as it always does. There's something about living in the mountains, at 10,000 feet above sea level, that puts things in perspective, or so the tourists say. I wouldn't know. Having lived in Mt. Floresta all my life, I have no perspective on that. Maybe Jamison was right, I thought, maybe I have blown this out of proportion. I snapped my ski vest shut against the fall wind and hiked up my jeans. Worry makes me lose weight, and I'd been getting real concerned about the increasing number of lost-cat reports coming into my office from distraught cat owners.

"Mr. Ezekiel Leonard?" That's how many of the calls began. The really older ladies called me by my full name and mister. It made me feel older than my twenty-six years, and smarter, which is possibly what they hoped I was. Like most of the cat owners, they sounded nervous, timorous, hesitant to bother me, and sad. "Mr. Leonard," they'd say, "my Snowflake has disappeared." Or Big Boy or Thomasina or Annabelle. "He's (she's) never done this before, and I just don't know what to think. I've looked everywhere, and I've asked everybody I know. But nobody has seen my Big Boy (or Thomasina or Snowflake) since Tuesday."

At first, I didn't attach any significance to the calls. I just searched our pens for a feline of the right description and then assured the caller I'd keep an eye out for kitty. Then I'd add kitty's name and phone number to my "missing" list.

It took me a while to notice how long that list was getting. And how few names I was crossing off. Oh, I found Mrs. McCarty's Siamese and returned him. And I had to break the news to Bobby Henderson after I saw his calico lying by the side of the highway. But by the end of September, the obvious was becoming just that: seventeen pet cats had been declared missing since August and I'd found only two of them. I was sure somebody was stealing them. But what the hell would somebody want with fifteen very spoiled cats? There wasn't any animal experimentation lab in the county, or anywhere else nearby that I knew of. And I made it my business to know such things. I just couldn't figure it out.

I broke off my reverie on the steps of the police station and headed down Silverado Street toward the office of the *Lode*, which passes for a newspaper in our town. "Get a Lode of This!" is their motto, which actually appears above the masthead. I guess everything's a lot more casual up here in the mountains, where everybody wears blue jeans and nobody ever wears a suit, except maybe visiting bank examiners.

Mt. Floresta is an old mining center turned chic: we're about as "in" as a ski resort can get and still stand itself. We have your restored Victorian buildings, we have your ugly new condos, we have your charming gas streetlights and your café au laits, we have your lift tickets and your gourmet restaurants, we have your drunk tourists and your inflated prices. We also have a lot of great big dogs—Malamutes, Samoyeds, huskies, and the like—that people who move here think they just have to have along with a nice cat to sit by the fire at their rental hearth. And then, when they move out after getting a taste of one whole cold long snowy winter season, they sometimes abandon those poor creatures, and that's where I come in, at the Mt. Floresta Animal Shelter located on the edge of town just around the corner of the closest mountain.

As I walked, I ducked my head, but not against the wind or the tourists. The longer I went without finding those cats, the harder it was to face the cat lovers in town. I knew if I encountered the lugubrious eyes of Miss Emily Parson one more time I'd go jump in Spirit Lake. Miss Parson's great black Angora, Puddy, was among the missing.

I was so intent on making like a turtle that I nearly collided with the current love of my life.

"Hello, Atlas," she said. "World a little heavy on those shoulders?"

"Hi, Abby." I leaned down and kissed her cheek, which was soft and downy and well shaped like the rest of her. Abigail Frances, late of New York, was by far the best of the current crop of easterners to have fallen in love with our town and decided to grace us with their permanent presence. If I sound cynical, it's because in a resort town, *permanent* has a shelf life of about nine months. I've gotten leery of making new friends and weary of farewell parties.

"No luck with the police?"

There was sympathy in her soft voice, but I thought I detected an edge to it that had nothing to do with her New York accent. If I was a fanatic, Abby was a flaming zealot when it came to cats and, as I knew only too well, she was one of the grieving and aggrieved cat owners whose baby was missing. In fact, she and I had met over the report of her lost cat, a magnificent—to judge by the pictures she showed me—Himalayan, name of Fantasia.

Like Atlas, I shrugged. But I didn't feel any burdens roll off. I took Abby's arm and turned her around.

"Come spend your lunch hour with me," I said. Abby, who didn't need the money, worked hard at the gift shop she bought when she moved to Mt. Floresta. "We're going to give the *Lode* a front-page story."

"Classifieds, Zeke, that's where missing cats go."

"But, Ginny," I protested to my friend, the editor of the

Lode, "that's where they've been going for two months! Aren't your classifieds getting a little full by now? I'll bet you've got more missing cats than you do skis for sale—"

"I doubt *that*."

"Well, I'm telling you this is a bona-fide front-page story, a *scoop*."

Ginny Pursell cast her navy-blue eyes skyward. "Dear Ezekiel, darling Zeke, whom I have loved more or less like a brother since grade school, in your business you may know all there is to know about *scoops*. But let me tell you a thing or two about front-page stories."

By my side, Abby cracked a knuckle ominously. It's a disgusting habit she likes to indulge in when she really wants to annoy somebody—like a local who makes it clear who is the newcomer to town and who is not. I did think Ginny's comment about grade school was a shade gratuitous.

"A front-page story," she lectured us, "is our cretinous mayor making an ass of himself in front of the White House in a protest against oil-shale development. No," Ginny held up a forestalling hand, "we shall not argue politics. I have my editorial stance and I shall keep it. What's good for oil-shale development is good for Mt. Floresta."

More knuckles. Mine. I am about as much in favor of digging into our mountains as I am of vivisection. Besides, the mayor's also a friend of mine. But Ginny's an anomaly—a conservative Republican journalist in a liberal Democratic county. As a newspaper editor and publisher, she's the only game in town, however, so we have to swallow her opinions along with the news.

"A front-page story is the hassle I'm getting from Larry Fremont—"

"You too?" I recalled the chief's gripe about having to "placate" the owner of a health spa. "Hell, I never thought ol' Larry would give this town anything, not even so much as a hassle or a hard time."

"What do you mean, 'you too'?"

"I think he's bugging Jamison Grant about something."

"Oh, lord." Ginny groaned. "He'll try anything to keep my

story out of print." Like Jamison before her, she picked up some papers and waved them at me. I was rapidly tiring of the gesture. "I had this article practically written. All about trash disposal and what we're going to do about it in the future. It's a major problem, you know, because we need places to toss our garbage and the environmentalists won't let us put a dump near any place that's practical or economical."

"Like right beside Spirit Lake? Good for them."

"Who's Larry Fremont?" Abby asked, bravely asserting her ignorance.

Ginny threw me a knowing look, local-to-local, as it were, whereupon Abby's knuckles cracked resoundingly. I hurried to explain. Larry, I told her, was a local boy made good. So good he wouldn't have anything to do with us anymore. He was the founder of La Floresta, the combination health spa/dude ranch down in the valley. It was one of those resorts where rich ladies paid thousands of dollars to get a few pounds beaten and starved out of them.

"They all look the same to me when they come out," said Ginny, who has nothing to worry about herself when it comes to the slim-and-trim department. She also has lots of curly black hair—like a standard poodle, I tell her, which always makes her reach for a comb immediately, to my regret—and one of those tanned mountain faces in which blue eyes stand out like beacons. "Except they look like they go in fat and unhappy and they come out fat and happy."

At first *everybody* was happy about Larry's success, I told Abby, particularly since he was generous with jobs. But in the last year he'd started firing everybody from around here. Not that he made it so obvious; it happened little by little, person by person. Before we knew it, there wasn't one person from Mt. Floresta left on his payroll. Instead, he was hiring folks from further down the valley. And he took on a lot of college kids looking for resort work.

"Since then," I said, "nobody from Mt. Floresta cares much for Larry Fremont. We call him Fremont the Freeloader. He trades on our famous name without giving anything back to our economy. The S.O.B. even banks in Denver." I turned to

Ginny. Her office cat, a stray she'd picked up from my shelter, jumped on her desk and made pet-me sounds. "What if Tiger was one of the cats that was missing?" I reached over to stroke his ugly yellow head. "Then how would you feel?"

"Why is Fremont hassling you about trash dumps?" Abby asked. She sticks to a subject better than I do.

"Because La Floresta sits on a landfill," Ginny told her. "Remember, Zeke? That was the old county dump for fifty years. God knows how many secrets are buried there. They filled it in just before Larry bought the land and built his spa.

"And he doesn't want me to say so in my article," she went on. "I have to mention it because it's such a good example of a landfill. Shows how the land can be reclaimed successfully. But he's afraid for his image. Can you believe it? He doesn't want his precious customers to know La Floresta sits on a trash heap!" Ginny shook her head in apparent dismay over the sorry state of progressive conservatives in the United States. "So I can't help you, Zeke. I've got more on my mind than cats. If you want a front-page story, give me something with blood and guts. Like a good juicy murder."

She smirked. We left.

Knowing Ginny, I'm sure she regretted that smirk the next day when she had to write the story of Rooney Bowers' death. OIL SHALE ENGINEER VICTIM OF HIT AND RUN, her headline told me. The story said that Rooney Bowers, associate professor of petroleum engineering at the university, had been bowled down in front of his house in the frosty hours of the morning. Whatever hit him threw him fifty feet across Mabel Langdon's holly hedge and into her front yard. Mabel found him a few hours later when she went out to get the paper.

"It was awful," she allowed herself to be quoted as saying. "There he was dead as a smelt and him such a nice quiet neighbor and all." Mabel sometimes has a colorful way of putting things.

I called Chief Jamison Grant immediately.

"It's Zeke." I got right to the point. "Where is Rooney Bowers' cat?"

"Honest to God, Ezekiel, you have the most one-track mind of anyone I ever knew." Jamison sounded harried. "The man gets killed and all you can think of is his damn cat. I don't know where it is. Maybe the neighbors have it, maybe—"

"It's a long-haired silver tabby. It wasn't in the house when you got there?"

"No, it wasn't in the house or around the house and I didn't even know Rooney had a cat and will you please stop bugging me about cats? Look, we'll get the cat to you. You know we will. Nobody's going to let the darned thing starve. But I got a hit-and-run to solve, Zeke. The cat's got to wait."

"Wait, Jamison, listen to me. I know Rooney pretty well, I mean, I knew him. We used to get together for a beer, he and the mayor and I, and we'd argue about oil shale."

"Zeke, please—"

"But the last time we didn't talk about oil, Jamison. We talked about cats. I told him all about the missing cats and how I thought somebody was stealing them."

"So?"

"So Rooney always gets—got—up real early to start his research. About four in the morning. And that's when he let his cat out, Jamison. He used to joke about it. Said his Tom was the only one he ever knew who liked it better in the morning than at night. Like some women he knew, he said."

"I repeat: so?"

"So . . ." Suddenly I knew how foolish I sounded. "So maybe it's got something to do with his death, that's all. I mean maybe all the missing cats are some kind of clue or something." It has been pointed out to me more than once that the less I know the more inarticulate I get.

"Thank you so much, Zeke," Jamison said heavily. "I'll certainly think on it."

I hung up quickly while we were still friends.

Abby thought I was crazy, too.

"But what if somebody was stealing Rooney's cat and Rooney saw him do it?" I said, expressing my theory in the sparsity of its fullness.

"Well, I seriously doubt they'd kill him over it," she said. We were sitting in my office trying to talk over the cacophony coming from the pens. I'd just put a new dog out there and he was getting quite a greeting. "I mean, don't you think you're being just a bit melodramatic? I'm as upset as you about the cats, but still—murder?"

She took a careful sip of the truly awful coffee I had brewed in my brand-new machine. "You know, if you put a lot of sugar in this, you might cover the taste of the plastic."

"Sugar rots teeth," I said righteously.

"These missing cats are rotting your brain. Zeke, I've shown cats before. I know that competition at cat shows is killing, and there are a few cat owners I could easily have murdered when their mangy beasts placed higher than my own Fantasia. But that's all hyperbole. We wouldn't really kill each other. We love our cats, but not that much."

"So?" I demanded in good cop form.

"So I can't believe anybody wants these cats badly enough to kill for them."

She had me there. I love cats, too, but murder?

I tried it from another angle: "Okay, then where is Rooney's cat? What if it doesn't show up? Will you say that's just co-incidence, just another missing cat?"

"It'll show up," my lady love assured me. When she thought I wasn't looking, she poured her coffee into the litter box I keep in the corner.

It didn't show up, not hide nor long hair of it.

Abby drove out to my office on the Saturday morning after the hit-and-run, which was still unsolved.

"Wake up, Zeke!" She lifted one cat off my stomach, pushed another aside and sat down beside my sleeping body on the overstuffed couch I keep for the convenience of visitors, human and un-. "*I believe!*" she said, like one born again. "Rooney's missing cat is one too many coincidences, I agree. Let's talk." She tickled my ear with a strand of her long silky blonde hair. I loved the hair, hated the technique. Like a cranky old dog, I barked at her: "Dammit, Abigail, don't do that! Can't a man get a little catnap?"

Her lovely gray eyes widened. Her delicate jaw dropped. She looked like a woman who's seen the truth. I panicked, shot up in bed, grabbed and hugged her. "Abby! I'm sorry! I'm a grouch in the—"

"Catnap," she said breathily into my left ear, so that it sent nice little electric shivers down my side, and I didn't for a moment catch on that she wasn't whispering sweet nothings to me. "That's it, Zeke! Catnap, catnip, *kidnap*—that's how we need to think about this business. Like a kidnapping!"

Distracted as I was by kissing her neck, I said, "What?"

She pushed me away. "What if it weren't cats that were missing?" she enunciated with a clarity that was just this side of insulting. "What if they were *people?*"

I leaned toward her. "Um?"

"Well, how would the police investigate their disappearances? However *they'd* do it, that's how *we* should do it."

"How would they do it?"

"Oh, honestly, Zeke. Well, let's think about it. I mean, wouldn't they want to figure out why these particular people were kidnapped?"

"Yeah." Finally, I got excited about something besides her proximity. "What do these people—cats—have in common that might attract a kidnapper?"

"Good, Zeke!" She was no longer condescending. Unfortunately, she was also no longer within reach, having stood up and started to pace. "Maybe they'd look at the times and days the kidnappings took place."

"And where, to see if that had anything to do with it."

"And method."

"And motive." I picked up a cat and tucked him under my arm. "Come on, Abs, let's look at my list of missing cats."

We looked.

"So what *do* they have in common?" Abby demanded. "I don't know them, and you do."

I squinted at the list until something hit me.

"Geez, Abby, they're all long-hairs."

"Really?" She was excited, too. "What does that mean?"

"I don't know," I confessed.

We stared at each other in frustration.

"Find me another clue," she demanded.

I did, but it took a while. First we considered the ages of the cats, but that was no good because they ranged from a few months to seventeen years. Sex was no good, either, so to speak, as they were males, females and "other." Nor could we find any common denominators in their owners, other than the fact that they all lived around Mt. Floresta and they were mighty upset with my lack of efficiency. But then Abby raised the question of breeds. And it turned out that all but two were purebreds—Angora, Himalayan, Persian and other classy cats. There were two mixed breeds, which stumped us until Abby asked me if they *looked* like purebreds.

"Yes," I decided. "If you didn't know cats, you'd think they were Persians."

"So maybe our catnapper doesn't know cats?"

"Maybe." I was doubtful. "But he knows them well enough to know he wants only long-haired cats that are purebreds or look as if they are."

As I summed up, Abby jotted down key words on the chalk board I use for messages. She scrawled *long hair* and *purebred*. Then she added *elegant* and *beautiful*.

"Maybe that doesn't have anything to do with it," she said defensively in the face of my skepticism. "But those are other qualities all the cats share. What if a lot of women were kidnapped, and they all happened to be young and beautiful? Don't you think the police would call that a clue?"

I guessed so. But then we ran up against the problem of motive. People kidnap other people for money, sex, revenge, power or leverage. Why cats? It obviously wasn't for ransom, since none had been demanded. And Abby didn't think the catnapper was selling them, because if he were he'd have snatched some valuable short-hairs, as well. I'd already eliminated lab experiments, I told Abby, unless she wanted to consider the possibility of a mad scientist working in a secret mountain cave, conducting weird tests on long cat hair. She thought we were pretty safe in eliminating that.

"Maybe the tourists are taking them," I offered.

"Have you ever tried to get a cat in a suitcase?" But then, as though inspired, she pronounced: "Oil shale! Maybe they didn't kill Rooney because he saw them take the cat. Maybe they killed him and took the cats because of something to do with the oil-shale controversy."

"Come on, Abby." I felt tired and crabby again. "What do you think, that they've discovered a way to get oil out of cats?"

She withdrew into a dignified and injured silence to my coffee pot. I knew she must be really mad if she was going to drink that stuff, but I was too frustrated to be contrite.

"Maybe we're getting the wrong answers because we're asking the wrong questions," I said into the chilly silence.

Being of a basically forgiving nature, she looked at me with interest.

"Maybe we're getting too fancy by asking what's the motive," I suggested. "Maybe the question is real simple. Like, what's a cat for?"

"Rats!" said my lady love, and I knew it wasn't because she'd spilled the coffee. "*Rats*, Zeke!"

My legs being longer than hers, by all rights I should have beat her to the car. But she was already in the driver's seat by the time I got in and slammed the door.

"So sorry, but only guests are admitted to La Floresta."

We got that maddening response at two out of the three gates of the walled compound of the health spa. Having raced five miles as fast as Abby's specially-calibrated-for-high-altitude Jag would scream, and gotten ourselves wound to a fever pitch of resolve, it was infuriating to be so easily halted by an upturned hand.

A snooty upturned hand.

"Maybe it's me," I suggested, humbly, after the second rejection. "Maybe I don't look the part. You try it alone next time. You look like trust funds."

"So kind," she said through gritted teeth. She didn't like to be reminded of her inherited wealth. I always told her if she felt so guilty about it, she could assuage that guilt by sharing the loot with poor folks like me. "The only reason you don't look the part is because you've let yourself get so skinny. On the other hand, as it were, if you let your fingernails grow, maybe they'd think you were Howard Hughes."

"Touché," I said, wounded. I'm told I can dish it out, but I can't take it, a piece of criticism I resent very much. "I mean it, though. I'll stay back in the bushes, and you try the next gate by yourself."

It didn't work. Abby's name wasn't on their list and she didn't have the gold membership card they so tactfully demanded. Perhaps the young lady would like to call and make a reservation? Perhaps they'd like to go to hell, the young lady said to me upon arriving back at my bush.

We thought it best to wait until dark before launching our assault on the elegant buff walls. When we left Mt. Floresta the second time, we packed a ladder into Abby's precious Jaguar. "You scratch that paint and I'll kill you," she said sweetly. I'd heard that Jags get something like seventeen hundred coats of hand-rubbed lacquer on them. I told her she would never miss one little coat of paint in one little spot. "I won't miss *you*, either," she said. I took the hint and stowed the ladder without damage to the car or the relationship.

So getting in was no problem.

"It's awfully dark," she said, as we crouched on our respective haunches in the well-pruned shrubbery. In the dark, the bushes looked like fat ladies squatting.

"It's awfully big," I rejoined. Across a lawn like a cemetery, the administration building rose white against the night. All around in the darkness we could hear the sounds of guests moving from their cabins to other parts of the compound. A splash to the right alerted us to the location of one of the swimming pools, presumably heated for cold fall nights like this one. Like spies in a B movie, we scuttled across the grass to the shelter of an enormous fir tree.

"Zeke, I just thought of something." Abby sounded less sure of herself than usual.

"I wish you wouldn't say things like that at a time like this," I whined.

"No, listen," she whispered. "I've been thinking about how Rooney Bowers died. If you're letting your cat out of the house, all you do is open the door, right? And the same thing when you let him in. I mean, you don't have to step outside with him. You don't *walk* a cat."

"Few do."

"Yes, well, how come Rooney was out there in the street where he could get hit? Zeke, I think he opened the door to call his cat in, and that's when he saw somebody grab the cat. If it were you, what would you do?"

"I'd go chasing and yelling after the son of a—"

"Right, and that would put you in the street. But, Ezekiel, if somebody were stealing a cat, they'd have to slow down to do it. So when Rooney saw them, they couldn't have been going fast enough to hit him as hard as they did."

"Oh, God." Gooseflesh crawled down my arms.

"Yes," Abby whispered in a curiously vibrating voice. "And that means they saw *him* when he saw *them*. So they came back around to kill him. They had to speed up to do it."

We stared at each other.

Premeditated murder? Even if it was only premeditated by a few seconds?

We stared at Larry Fremont's million-dollar administration building.

"What is important enough for premeditated murder?" I asked, appalled at the idea we had formed. A hit-and-run was one thing, and plenty bad enough, but this . . . "Abby, we should go back out the way we came in. We should drive back to town and call Jamison."

She told me what she thought of those cowardly ideas by scooting across the lawn to a stand of pines further inside the compound. I thought of all the times my mother told me not to cross the street without looking both ways, and I ran after her. She had slipped into the shadows, so I couldn't see her, when she suddenly called my name. Just as I was ready to shush her, she grasped my elbow. Or, at least I thought she did. I was certainly surprised when the person attached to that grasp turned out to be good ol' Larry Fremont himself.

"Zeke Leonard," he said in a less-than-welcoming tone of voice. In the years since the high school football team, Zeke had not lost muscle, he'd added it—on his fancy spa weight-lifting equipment, no doubt. If he'd looked then like he looked now, we'd have won every game for the Mt. Floresta Mountain Lions. "And friend."

"Long time no see, Larry," I babbled. "I'd like you to meet my good friend Tanya Smith. Tanya is staying up at Mt. Floresta and she indicated an interest in your beautiful place, so I said, well, Tanya, I'll take you down and introduce you to ol' Larry himself."

Ol' Larry himself proved there is such a thing as a cold smile.

Abby moved out of the shadows and looked at me as if I were the resident fool of the mountains.

"That's thoughtful of you, Zeke," he said. "And I'd show your friend, uh, Tanya, around, but as you can see, it's rather dark for show and tell. So I think I'll just escort you to the gate."

Instead of releasing my elbow, he added another to his collection. From Abby's wince, I could tell his grip of her was every bit as firm as the one he had on me. But it wasn't so strong I couldn't break away when I saw a black cat stroll by about three steps ahead of me.

"Zeke, it's Fantas—" Abby cried.

I didn't look to find out why her last syllables were cut off. I just threw myself on the bundle of soft fur as if it were an opposing lineman, and held on for dear life. The cat, unclear as to my intentions, returned my embrace—with claws. I swore loudly. Which is probably why I didn't know Larry had come up behind me until his head hit me in the middle of the small of my back. In high school, he and I had played on the same team, so I never knew how much damage he could do with his famous illegal tackles. As I collapsed, the cat jumped over my shoulder, landing with all four clawed paws on Larry's head. His attention having been thus nicely distracted, I turned and threw a tackle of my own. I didn't grieve when his head hit an imitation Greek sculpture like a football hitting a goal post.

Fremont the Freeloader lay on the ground, out cold.

But the hollering from cats and people had switched on a lot of lights in the compound. I sat on Larry and took the petrified cat in my arms. He held still, probably paralyzed by fright, like me.

"Zeke, Zeke, are you okay?" Abby ran up out of the dark where Larry had thrown her into the bushes in his chase after me. "Zeke, is it Fantasia? Is it my Fantasia?"

Her voice was full of tears and hope.

"No," I said gently. "It's not."

She sank to her knees. I saw the light go out of her face.

"It's not Fantasia," I said quickly. "It's Puddy! It's Miss Emily Parson's cat, Puddy."

Hope returned to Abby's eyes just as the guests and employees merged on our mangled scene.

"Call the police!" someone yelled.

"Yes," I agreed, "do that. Ask for the chief. Tell him I told him so."

"We smell more than a rat," Jamison told us the next day in his office. "Larry confessed to Rooney's hit-and-run. When Rooney saw him grab the cat, he went racing out to Larry's car, accusing him of stealing all those other cats. And that was enough to panic Larry. He knew if that got out, everything else would too."

"*What* else?" Abby looked up from a chair in the corner where her hands were occupied in petting Fantasia. The Himalayan purred and blinked smugly at me as if to re-establish squatter's rights to that lovely blue-jeaned lap.

"Fraud," Jamison announced. "All kinds of consumer fraud." He glanced at the intrepid editor busily scribbling notes. "Ready, Ginny?"

"Go," she commanded, pencil poised.

"It's almost funny." Jamison was seated on a corner of his desk, and now he folded his arms over his stomach. "It seems that Larry got himself financially overextended, so he started cutting corners to save money. For one thing, the food at La Floresta is not exactly what their menus say it is. They've been altering the recipes with cheaper, more fattening ingredients—using starches for fillers and sugar for taste, for instance, instead of all those expensive herbs and spices they advertise."

"But don't the guests get weighed?" I asked.

"They fixed the scales!" Jamison hooted with laughter. "And they made sure the guests got plenty of exercise to burn up some of those calories they didn't know they were eating. Plus, nobody stayed long enough to gain much. Most of them just went out weighing the same as when they went in. Gives a whole new meaning to the phrase, 'fat farm,' wouldn't you say?"

"But they'd find out the truth when they got home," Ginny said.

"Nope." The bald eagle preened on his exclusive information. "Larry told them they could expect to gain back some water weight as soon as they started to eat regularly again."

"Diabolical," Abby hissed. "Not to mention mean and lousy."

Jamison said, "It wasn't just the food, either. The doctor was a quack, the physical therapists were phonies, the dietitian was just an amateur cook, and the European chefs were ordinary restaurant cooks from Denver; not even the aerobics instructors had the experience the advertising says they did. Almost nobody was quite what they claimed to be, and so they could be paid a lot less. It was all a joke to most of them, but it meant serious money in the bank to Larry. Now we know why he fired everybody from Mt. Floresta. His original employees from up here knew how things were supposed to be. They wouldn't have stood for his cheating."

"He didn't want any of us to know." I shook my head over the greed of my old teammate. "I bet that's why he took all his business away. It was safer to deal with out-of-town banks and suppliers. They weren't close enough to catch him at his shell game."

"But the cats," Ginny interrupted. "Why the cats?"

Abby and I traded supercilious smiles.

"Remember your story about landfills?" I asked Ginny. "The one Larry didn't want you to run? That was our best clue. We thought of all the reasons somebody might want a cat and came up with the oldest reason of all: to kill rats. And where in this wide valley might there be a problem with rats?"

"At a landfill over a garbage dump!" Ginny exclaimed.

"Right. Larry saw big fat ugly rats invading his precious gold mine. He had to get rid of them. Poison was dangerous because some of the guests bring their dogs to stay with them. And dead dogs are bad for business. Live cats was the answer."

"But not just any cats." Abby giggled and held Fantasia aloft. "They had to fit the 'ambiance.' They had to be beautiful, elegant cats, so the guests would not object."

"And they had to be long-haired," I added. "Because Larry wasn't going to feed them much. He wanted them hungry so they'd kill rats. And a long-haired cat always looks fatter than a short-hair. So nobody would notice if the cats lost weight."

"But why so many?" Ginny persisted.

"It's a big place," was my simple explanation.

"Beast," Abby said, and she didn't mean cats.

"It was all a matter of appearances," I continued, taking the opportunity to philosophize grandly. The others exchanged tolerant glances, but I ignored them. "That's what La Floresta was all about anyway, wasn't it? Appearances. Larry stole the cats and killed Rooney to keep up appearances."

I stood up and stretched carefully. My kidneys still hurt where Larry's head had dented them. "Glad to be of help, Jamison," I said graciously. "But Abby and I must be off. Miss Emily Parson is serving tea in our honor."

I looked into his amused, craggy face.

"You wanna come, too?"

"A cop having tea?" He recoiled in mock horror. "Have a heart, Zeke. How would it *look?*"

The Christmas Kitten

Ed Gorman

1.

"SHE IN A GOOD MOOD?" I said.

The lovely and elegant Pamela Forrest looked up at me as if I'd suggested that there really *was* a Santa Claus.

"Now why would she go and do a foolish thing like that, McCain?" She smiled.

"Oh, I guess because—"

"Because it's the Christmas season, and most people are in good moods?"

"Yeah, something like that."

"Well, not our Judge Whitney."

"At least she's consistent," I said.

I had been summoned, as usual, from my law practice, where I'd been working the phones, trying to get my few clients to pay their bills. I had a 1951 Ford ragtop to support. And dreams of taking the beautiful Pamela Forrest to see the Platters concert when they were in Des Moines next month.

"You thought any more about the Platters concert?" I said.

"Oh, McCain, now why'd you have to go and bring *that* up?"

"I just thought—"

"You know how much I love the Platters. But I really don't think it's a good idea for the two of us to go out again." She gave me a melancholy little smile. "Now I probably went and ruined your holidays and I'm sorry. You know I like you, Cody, it's just—Stew."

This was Christmas 1959 and I'd been trying since at least Christmas 1957 to get Pamela to go out with me. But we had a problem—while I loved Pamela, Pamela loved Stewart, and Stewart happened to be not only a former football star at the university but also the heir to the town's third biggest fortune.

Her intercom buzzed. "Is he out there pestering you again, Pamela?"

"No, Your Honor."

"Tell him to get his butt in here."

"Yes, Your Honor."

"And call my cousin John and tell him I'll be there around three this afternoon."

"Yes, Your Honor."

"And remind me to pick up my dry cleaning."

"Yes, Your Honor."

"And tell McCain to get his butt in here. Or did I already say that?"

"You already said that, Your Honor."

I bade goodbye to the lovely and elegant Pamela Forrest and went in to meet my master.

"You know what he did this time?" Judge Eleanor Whitney said three seconds after I crossed her threshold.

The "he" could only refer to one person in the town of Black River Falls, Iowa. And that would be our esteemed chief of police, Cliff Sykes, Jr., who has this terrible habit of arresting people for murders they didn't commit and giving Judge Whitney the pleasure of pointing out the error of his ways.

A little over a hundred years ago, Judge Whitney's family

dragged a lot of money out here from the East and founded this town. They pretty much ran it until World War II, a catastrophic event that helped make Cliff Sykes, Sr., a rich and powerful man in the local wartime construction business. Sykes, Sr., used his money to put his own members on the town council, just the way the Whitneys had always done. He also started to bribe and coerce the rest of the town into doing things his way. Judge Whitney saw him as a crude outlander, of course. Where her family was conversant with Verdi, Vermeer, and Tolstoy, the Sykes family took as cultural icons Ma and Pa Kettle and Francis the Talking Mule, the same characters I go to see at the drive-in whenever possible.

Anyway, the one bit of town management the Sykes family couldn't get to was Judge Whitney's court. Every time Cliff Sykes, Jr., arrested somebody for murder, the judge called me up and put me to work. In addition to being an attorney, I'm taking extension courses in criminology. The judge thinks this qualifies me as her very own staff private investigator, so whenever she wants something looked into, she calls me. And I'm glad she does. She's my only source of steady income.

"He arrested my cousin John's son, Rick. Charged him with murdering his girlfriend. That stupid ass."

Now in a world of seventh-ton crime-solving geniuses, and lady owners of investigative firms who go two hundred pounds and are as bristly as barbed wire, Judge Eleanor Whitney is actually a small, trim, and very handsome woman. And she knows how to dress herself. Today she wore a brown suede blazer, a crisp button-down, white-collar shirt, and dark fitted slacks. Inside the open collar of the shirt was a green silk scarf that complemented the green of her eyes perfectly.

She was hiked on the edge of the desk, right next to an ample supply of rubber bands.

"Sit down, McCain."

"He didn't do it."

"I said sit down. You know I hate it when you stand."

I sat down.

"He didn't do it," I said.

"Exactly. He didn't do it."

"You know, one of these times you're bound to be wrong. I mean, just by the odds, Sykes is bound to be right."

Which is what I say every time she gives me an assignment.

"Well, he isn't right this time."

Which is what she says every time I say the thing about the odds.

"His girlfriend was Linda Palmer, I take it."

"Right."

"The one found in her apartment?"

She nodded.

"What's Sykes's evidence?"

"Three neighbors saw Rick running away from the apartment house the night before last."

She launched one of her rubber bands at me, thumb and forefinger style, like a pistol. She likes to see if I'll flinch when the rubber band comes within an eighth of an inch of my ear. I try never to give her that satisfaction.

"He examine Rick's car and clothes?"

"You mean fibers and blood, things like that?"

"Yeah."

She smirked. "You think Sykes would be smart enough to do something like that?"

"I guess you've got a point."

She stood up and started to pace.

You'll note that I am not permitted this luxury, standing and pacing, but for her it is fine. She is, after all, mistress of the universe.

"I just keep thinking of John. The poor guy. He's a very good man."

"I know."

"And it's going to be a pretty bleak Christmas without Rick there. I'll have to invite him out to the house."

Which was not an invitation I usually wanted. The judge kept a considerable number of rattlesnakes in glass cages on the first floor of her house. I was always waiting for one of them to get loose.

I stood up. "I'll get right on it." I couldn't recall ever seeing the judge in such a pensive mood. Usually, when she's going to war with Cliff Sykes, Jr., she's positively ecstatic.

But when her cousin was involved, and first cousin at that, I supposed even Judge Whitney—a woman who had buried three husbands, and who frequently golfed with President Eisenhower when he was in the Midwest, and who had been ogled by Khrushchev when he visited a nearby Iowa farm—I supposed even Judge Whitney had her melancholy moments.

She came back to her desk, perched on the edge of it, loaded up another rubber band, and shot it at me.

"Your nerves are getting better, McCain," she said. "You don't twitch as much as you used to."

"I'll take that as an example of your Christmas cheer," I said. "You noting that I don't twitch as much as I used to, I mean."

Then she glowered at me. "Nail his butt to the wall, McCain. My family's honor is at stake here. Rick's a hothead but he's not a killer. He cares too much about the family name to soil it that way."

Thus basking in the glow of Christmas spirit, not to mention a wee bit of patrician hubris, I took my leave of the handsome Judge Whitney.

2.

Red Ford ragtops can get a little cold around Christmas time. I had everything buttoned down but winter winds still whacked the car every few yards or so.

The city park was filled with snowmen and Christmas angels as Bing Crosby and Perry Como and Johnny Mathis sang holiday songs over the loudspeakers lining the merchant blocks. I could remember being a kid in the holiday concerts in the park. People stood there in the glow of Christmas-tree lights listening to us sing for a good hour. I always kept warm by staring at the girl I had a crush on that particular year. Even back then, I gravitated toward the ones who didn't want me. I guess that's why my favorite holiday song is "Blue Christmas" by Elvis. It's really depressing, which gives it a certain honesty for romantics like myself.

I pulled in the drive of Linda Palmer's apartment house. It

was a box with two apartments up, two down. There was a gravel parking lot in the rear. The front door was hung with holly and a plastic bust of Santa Claus.

Inside, in the vestibule area with the mailboxes, I heard Patti Page singing a Christmas song, and I got sentimental about Pamela Forrest again. During one of the times that she'd given up on good old Stewart, she'd gone out with me a few times. The dates hadn't meant much to her, but I looked back on them as the halcyon period of my entire life, when giants walked the earth and you could cut off slices of sunbeams and sell them as gold.

"Hi," I said as soon as the music was turned down and the door opened up.

The young woman who answered the bell to the apartment opposite Linda Palmer's was cute in a dungaree-doll sort of way—ponytail and Pat Boone sweatshirt and jeans rolled up to mid calf. "Hi."

"My name's McCain."

"I'm Bobbi Thomas. Aren't you Judge Whitney's assistant?"

"Well, sort of."

"So you're here about—"

"Linda Palmer."

"Poor Linda," she said, and made a sad face. "It's scary living here now. I mean, if it can happen to Linda—"

She was about to finish her sentence when two things happened at once. A tiny calico kitten came charging out of her apartment between her legs, and a tall man in a gray uniform with DERBY CLEANERS sewn on his cap walked in and handed her a package wrapped in clear plastic. Inside was a shaggy gray throw rug and a shaggy white one and a shaggy fawn-colored one.

"Appreciate your business, miss," the DERBY man said, and left.

I mostly watched the kitten. She was a sweetie. She walked straight over to the door facing Bobbi's. The card in the slot still read LINDA PALMER.

"You mind picking her up and bringing her in? I just need to put this dry cleaning away."

*   *   *

Ten minutes later, the three of us sat in her living room. I say three because the kitten, who'd been introduced to me as Sophia, sat in my lap and sniffed my coffee cup whenever I raised it to drink. The apartment was small but nicely kept. The floors were oak and not spoiled by wall-to-wall carpeting. She took the throw rugs from the plastic dry-cleaning wrap and spread them in front of the fireplace.

"They get so dirty," she explained as she straightened the rugs, then walked over and sat down.

Then she nodded to the kitten. "We just found her downstairs in the laundry room one day. There's a small TV down there and Linda and I liked to sit down there and smoke cigarettes and drink Cokes and watch *Bandstand*. Do you think Dick Clark's a crook? My boyfriend does." She shrugged. "Ex boyfriend. We broke up." She tried again: "So do you think Dick Clark's a crook?"

A disc jockey named Alan Freed was in trouble with federal authorities for allegedly taking bribes to play certain songs on his radio show. Freed didn't have enough power to make a hit record and people felt he was being used as a scapegoat. On the other hand, Dick Clark *did* have the power to make or break a hit record (Lord, did he, with *American Bandstand* on ninety minutes several afternoons a week), but the feds had rather curiously avoided investigating him in any serious way.

"Could be," I said. "But I guess I'd rather talk about Linda."

She looked sad again. "I guess that's why I was talking about Dick Clark. So we wouldn't *have* to talk about Linda."

"I'm sorry."

She sighed. "I just have to get used to it, I guess." Then she looked at Sophia. "Isn't she sweet? We called her our Christmas kitten."

"She sure is."

"That's what I started to tell you. One day Linda and I were downstairs and there Sophia was. Just this little lost kitten. So we both sort of adopted her. We'd leave our doors open so Sophia could just wander back and forth between apartments. Sometimes she slept here, sometimes she slept over there." She raised her eyes from the kitten and looked at me. "He killed her."

"Rick?"

"Uh-huh."

"Why do you say that?"

"Why do I say that? Are you kidding? You should've seen the arguments they had."

"He ever hit her?"

"Not that I know of."

"He ever *threaten* her?"

"All the time."

"You know why?" I said.

"Because he was so jealous of her. He used to sit across the street at night and just watch her front window. He'd sit there for hours."

"Would she be in there at the time?"

"Oh, sure. He always claimed she had this big dating life on the side but she never did."

"Anything special happen lately between them?"

"You mean you don't know?"

"I guess not."

"She gave him back his engagement ring."

"And that—"

"He smashed out her bedroom window with his fist. This was in the middle of the night and he was really drunk. I called the police on him. Just because he's a Whitney doesn't mean he can break the rules anytime he feels like it."

I'd been going to ask her if she was from around here but the resentment in her voice about the Whitneys answered my question. The Whitneys had been the valley's most imperious family for a little more than a century now.

"Did the police come?"

"Sykes himself."

"And he did what?"

"Arrested him. Took him in." She gave me a significant look with her deep blue eyes. "He was relishing every minute, too. A Sykes arresting a Whitney, I mean. He was having a blast."

So then I asked her about the night of the murder. We spent

twenty minutes on the subject but I didn't learn much. She'd
been in her apartment all night watching TV and hadn't heard
anything untoward. But when she got up to go to work in the
morning and didn't hear Linda moving around in her apartment, she knocked, and, when there wasn't any answer, went
in. Linda lay dead, the left side of her head smashed in,
sprawled in a white bra and half-slip in front of the fireplace
that was just like Bobbi's.

"Maybe I had my TV up too loud," Bobbi said. "I love
westerns and it was *Gunsmoke* night. It was a good one, too.
But I keep thinking that maybe if I hadn't played the TV so
loud, I could've heard her—"

I shook my head. "Don't start doing that to yourself, Bobbi,
or it'll never end. If only I'd done this, if only I'd done that.
You did everything you could."

She sighed. "I guess you're right."

"Mind one more question?"

She shrugged and smiled. "You can see I've got a pretty busy
social calendar."

"I want to try and take Rick out of the picture for a minute.
Will you try?"

"You mean as a suspect?"

"Right."

"I'll try."

"All right. Now, who are three people who had something
against Linda—or Rick?"

"Why Rick?"

"Because maybe the killer wanted to make it *look* as if Rick
did it."

"Oh, I see." Then: "I'd have to say Gwen. Gwen Dawes. She
was Rick's former girlfriend. She always blamed Linda for taking him away. You know, they hadn't been going together all
that long, Rick and Linda, I mean. Gwen would still kind of
pick arguments with her when she'd see them in public places."

"Gwen ever come over here and pick an argument?"

"Once, I guess."

"Remember when?"

"Couple months ago, maybe."

"What happened?"

"Nothing much. She and a couple of girlfriends were pretty drunk, and they came up on the front porch and started writing things on the wall. It was juvenile stuff. Most of us graduated from high school two years ago but we're still all kids, if you see what I mean."

I wrote Gwen's name down and said, "Anybody else who bothered Linda?"

"Paul Walters, for sure."

"Paul Walters?"

"*Her* old boyfriend. He used to wait until Rick left at night and then he'd come over and pick a fight with her."

"Would she let him in?"

"Sometimes. Then there was Millie Styles. The wife of the man Linda worked for."

"Why didn't she like Linda?"

"She accused Linda of trying to steal her husband."

"Was she?"

"You had to know Linda."

"I see."

"She wasn't a rip or anything."

"Rip?"

"You know, whore."

"But she—"

"—could be very flirtatious."

"More than flirtatious?"

She shrugged. "Sometimes."

"Maybe with Mr. Styles?"

"Maybe. He's an awfully handsome guy. He looks like Fabian."

She wasn't kidding. They weren't very far out of high school.

That was when I felt a scratching on my chin and I looked straight down into the eager, earnest, and heartbreakingly sweet face of Sophia.

"She likes to kiss noses the way Eskimos do," Bobbi said.

We kissed noses.

Then I set Sophia down and she promptly put a paw in my coffee cup.

"Sophia!" Bobbi said. "She's always putting her paw in wet things. She's obsessed, the little devil."

Sophia paid us no attention. Tail switching, she walked across the coffee table, her left front paw leaving coffee imprints on the surface.

I stood up. "I appreciate this, Bobbi."

"You can save yourself some work."

"How would I do that?"

"There's a skating party tonight. Everybody we've talked about is going to be there." She gave me another one of her significant looks. "Including me."

"Then I guess that's a pretty good reason to go, isn't it?" I said.

"Starts at six-thirty. It'll be very dark by then. You know how to skate?"

I smiled. "I wouldn't exactly call it skating."

"Then what would you call it?"

"Falling down is the term that comes to mind," I said.

3.

Rick Whitney was even harder to love than his aunt.

"When I get out of this place, I'm going to take that hillbilly and push him off Indian Cliff."

In the past five minutes, Rick Whitney, of the long blond locks and relentlessly arrogant blue-eyed good looks, had also threatened to shoot, stab, and set fire to our beloved chief of police, Cliff Sykes, Jr. As an attorney, I wouldn't advise any of my clients to express such thoughts, especially when they were in custody, being held for premeditated murder (or as my doctor friend Stan Greenbaum likes to say, "pre-medicated murder"). "Rick, we're not getting anywhere."

He turned on me again. He'd turned on me three or four times already, pushing his face at me, jabbing his finger at me.

"Do you know what it's like for a Whitney to be in jail? Why, if my grandfather were still alive, he'd come down here and shoot Sykes right on the spot."

"Rick?"

"What?"

"Sit down and shut up."

"You're telling me to shut up?"

"Uh-huh. And to sit down."

"I don't take orders from people like you."

I stood up. "Fine. Then I'll leave."

He started to say something nasty, but just then a cloud passed over the sun and the six cells on the second floor of the police station got darker.

He said, "I'll sit down."

"And shut up?"

It was a difficult moment for a Whitney. Humility is even tougher for them than having a tooth pulled. "And shut up."

So we sat down, him on the wobbly cot across from my wobbly cot, and we talked as two drunks three cells away pretended they weren't listening to us.

"A Mrs. Mawbry who lives across the street saw you running out to your car about eleven P.M. the night of the murder. Dr. Mattingly puts the time of death at right around that time."

"She's lying."

"You know better than that."

"They just hate me because I'm a Whitney."

It's not easy going through life being of a superior species, especially when all the little people hate you for it.

"You've got fifteen seconds," I said.

"For what?"

"To stop stalling and tell me the truth. You went to the apartment and found her dead, didn't you? And then you ran away."

I watched the faces of the two eavesdropping winos. It was either stay up here in the cells, or use the room downstairs that I was sure Cliff Sykes, Jr., had bugged.

"Ten seconds."

He sighed and said, "Yeah, I found her. But I didn't kill her."

"You sure of that?"

He looked startled. "What the hell's that supposed to mean?"

"It means were you drinking that evening, and did you have

any sort of alcoholic blackout? You've been known to tip a few."

"I had a couple beers earlier. That was it. No alcoholic blackout."

"All right," I said. "Now tell me the rest of it."

"Wonder if the state'll pass that new law," Chief Cliff Sykes, Jr., said to me as I was leaving the police station by the back door.

"I didn't know that you kept up on the law, Cliff, Jr."

He hated it when I added the Jr. to his name, but since he was about to do a little picking on me, I decided to do a little picking on him. With too much Brylcreem—Cliff, Jr., apparently never heard the part of the jingle that goes "A little dab'll do ya"—and his wiry moustache, he looks like a bar rat all duded up for Saturday night. He wears a khaki uniform that Warner Brothers must have rejected for an Errol Flynn western. The epaulets alone must weigh twenty-five pounds each.

"Yep, next year they're goin' to start fryin' convicts instead of hanging them."

The past few years in Iowa, we'd been debating which was the more humane way to shuffle off this mortal coil. At least when the state decides to be the shuffler and make you the shufflee.

"And I'll bet you think that Rick Whitney is going to be one of the first to sit in the electric chair, right?"

He smiled his rat smile, sucked his toothpick a little deeper into his mouth. "You said it, I didn't."

There's a saying around town that money didn't change the Sykes family any—they're still the same mean, stupid, dishonest, and uncouth people they've always been.

"Well, I hate to spoil your fun, Cliff, Jr., but he's going to be out of here by tomorrow night."

He sucked on his toothpick some more. "You and what army is gonna take him out of here?"

"Won't take an army, Cliff, Jr., I'll just find the guilty party and Rick'll walk right out of here."

He shook his head. "He thinks his piss don't stink because he's a Whitney. This time he's wrong."

4.

The way I figure it, any idiot can learn to skate standing up. It takes a lot more creativity and perseverance to skate on your knees and your butt and your back.

I was putting on quite a show. Even five-year-olds were pointing at me and giggling. One of them had an adult face pasted on his tiny body. I wanted to give him the finger but I figured that probably wouldn't look quite right, me being twenty-six and an attorney and all.

Everything looked pretty tonight, gray smoke curling from the big log cabin where people hung out putting on skates and drinking hot cider and warming themselves in front of the fireplace. Christmas music played over the loudspeakers, and every few minutes you'd see a dog come skidding across the ice to meet up with its owners. Tots in snowsuits looking like Martians toddled across the ice in the wake of their parents.

The skaters seemed to come in four types: the competitive skaters who were just out tonight to hone their skills; the show-offs who kept holding their girlfriends over their heads; the lovers who were melting the ice with their scorching looks; and the junior-high kids who kept trying to knock everybody down accidentally. I guess I should add the seniors; they were the most fun to watch, all gray hair and dignity as they made their way across the ice arm in arm. They probably came here thirty or forty years ago when Model-Ts had lined the parking area, and when the music had been supplied by Rudy Vallee. They were elegant and touching to watch here on the skating rink tonight.

I stayed to the outside of the rink. I kept moving because it was at most ten above zero. Falling down kept me pretty warm, too.

I was just getting up from a spill when I saw a Levi'd leg— two Levi'd legs—standing behind me. My eyes followed the line of legs upwards and there she was. It was sort of like a dream, actually, a slightly painful one because I'd dreamt it so often and so uselessly.

There stood the beautiful and elegant Pamela Forrest. In her white woolen beret, red cable-knit sweater, and jeans, she was the embodiment of every silly and precious holiday feeling. She was even smiling.

"Well, I'm sure glad you're here," she said.

"You mean because you want to go out?"

"No, I mean because I'm glad there's somebody who's even a worse skater than I am."

"Oh," I said.

She put out a hand and helped me up. I brushed the flesh of her arm—and let my nostrils be filled with the scent of her perfume—and I got so weak momentarily I was afraid I was going to fall right back down.

"You have a date?"

I shook my head. "Still doing some work for Judge Whitney."

She gave my arm a squeeze. "Just between you and me, McCain, I hope you solve one of these cases yourself someday."

She was referring to the fact that in every case I'd worked on, Judge Whitney always seemed to solve it just as I was starting to figure out who the actual culprit was. I had a feeling, though, that this case I'd figure out all by my lonesome.

"I don't think I've ever seen Judge Whitney as upset as she was today," I said.

"I'm worried about her. This thing with Rick, I mean. It isn't just going up against the Sykes family this time. The family honor's at stake."

I looked at her. "You have a date?"

And then she looked sad, and I knew what her answer was going to be.

"Not exactly."

"Ah. But Stewart's going to be here."

"I think so. I'm told he comes here sometimes."

"Boy, you're just as pathetic as I am."

"Well, that's a nice thing to say."

"You can't have him any more than I can have you. But neither one of us can give it up, can we?"

I took her arm and we skated. We actually did a lot better as a team than we did individually. I was going to mention that to her but I figured she would think I was just being corny and coming on to her in my usual clumsy way. If only I were as slick as Elvis in those movies of his where he sings a couple of songs and beats the crap out of every bad guy in town, working in a few lip locks with nubile females in the interim.

I didn't recognize them at first. Their skating costumes, so dark and tight and severe, gave them the aspect of Russian ballet artists. People whispered at them as they soared past, and it was whispers they wanted.

David and Millie Styles were the town's "artistic fugitives," as one of the purpler of the paper's writers wrote once. Twice a year they ventured to New York to bring radical new items back to their interior decorating "salon," as they called it, and they usually brought back a lot of even more radical attitudes and poses. Millie had once been quoted in the paper as saying that we should have an "All Nude Day" twice a year in town; and David was always standing on the library steps waving copies of banned books in the air and demanding that they be returned to library shelves. The thing was, I agreed with the message, it was the messengers I didn't care for. They were wealthy, attractive dabblers who loved to outrage and shock. In a big city, nobody would've paid them any attention. Out here, they were celebrities.

"God, they look great, don't they?" Pamela said.

"If you like the style."

"Skin-tight, all-black skating outfits. Who else would've thought of something like that?"

"You look a lot better."

She favored me with a forehead kiss. "Oh God, McCain, I sure wish I could fall in love with you."

"I wish you could, too."

"But the heart has its own logic."

"That sounds familiar."

"Peyton Place."

"That's right."

Peyton Place had swept through town two years ago like an army bent on destroying everything in its path. The fundamentalists not only tried to get it out of the library, they tried to ban its sale in paperback. The town literary lions, such as the Styleses, were strangely moot. They did not want to be seen defending something as plebeian as Grace Metalious's book. I was in a minority. I not only liked it, I thought it was a good book. A true one, as Hemingway often said.

On the far side of the rink, I saw David Styles skate away from his wife and head for the warming cabin.

She skated on alone.

"Excuse me. I'll be back," I said.

It took me two spills and three near-spills to reach Millie Styles.

"Evening," I said.

"Oh," she said, staring at me. "You." Apparently I looked like something her dog had just dragged in from the backyard. Something not quite dead yet.

"I wondered if we could talk."

"What in God's name would you and I have to talk about, McCain?"

"Why you killed Linda Palmer the other night."

She tried to slap me but fortunately I was going into one of my periodic dives so her slap missed me by half a foot.

I did reach out and grab her arm to steady myself, however.

"Leave me alone," she said.

"Did you find out that Linda and David were sleeping together?"

From the look in her eyes, I could see that she had. I kept thinking about what Bobbi Thomas had said, how Linda was flirtatious.

And for the first time, I felt something human for the striking if not quite pretty woman wearing too much makeup and way too many New York poses. Pain showed in her eyes. I actually felt a smidge of pity for her.

Her husband appeared magically. "Is something wrong?" Seeing the hurt in his wife's eyes, he had only scorn for me. He put a tender arm around her. "You get the hell out of here, McCain." He sounded almost paternal, he was so protective of her.

"And leave me alone," she said again, and skated away so quickly that there was no way I could possibly catch her.

Then Pamela was there again, sliding her arm through mine. "You have to help me, McCain," she said.

"Help you what?"

"Help me look like I'm having a wonderful time."

Then I saw Stew McGinley, former college football star and idle rich boy, skating around the rink with his girlfriend, the relentlessly cheery and relentlessly gorgeous Cindy Parkhurst, who had been a cheerleader at State the same year Stew was All Big-Eight.

This was the eternal triangle: I was in love with Pamela; Pamela was in love with Stew; and Stew was in love with Cindy, who not only came from the same class—right below the Whitneys—but had even more money than Stew did, and not only that but had twice done the unthinkable. She'd broken up with Stew and started dating somebody else. This was something Stew wasn't used to. *He* was supposed to do the breaking up. Stew was hooked, he was.

They were both dressed in white costumes tonight, and looked as if they would soon be on *The Ed Sullivan Show* for no other reason than simply existing.

"I guess I don't know how to do that," I said.

"How to do what?"

"How to help you look like you're having a wonderful time."

"I'm going to say something and then you throw your head back and break out laughing." She looked at me. "Ready?"

"Ready."

She said something I couldn't hear and then I threw my head back and pantomimed laughing.

I had the sense that I actually did it pretty well—after watching all those Tony Curtis movies at the drive-in, I was bound to pick up at least a few pointers about acting—but the whole thing was moot because Stew and Cindy were gazing into each other's eyes and paying no attention to us whatsoever.

"There goes my Academy Award," I said.

We tried skating again, both of us wobbling and waffling along, when I saw Paul Walters standing by the warming house smoking a cigarette. He was apparently one of those guys who didn't skate but liked to come to the rink and look at all the participants so he could feel superior to them. A sissy sport, I could hear him thinking.

"I'll be back," I said.

By the time I got to the warming house, Paul Walters had been joined by Gwen Dawes. Just as Paul was the dead girl's old boyfriend, Gwen was the suspect's old girlfriend. Those little towns in Kentucky where sisters marry brothers had nothing on our own cozy little community.

Just as I reached them, Gwen, an appealing if slightly overweight redhead, pulled Paul's face down to hers and kissed him. He kissed her right back.

"Hi," I said, as they started to separate.

They both looked at me as if I had just dropped down from a UFO.

"Oh, you're Cody McCain," Walters said. He was tall, sinewy, and wore the official uniform of juvenile delinquents everywhere—leather jacket, jeans, engineering boots. He put his Elvis sneer on right after he brushed his teeth in the morning.

"Right. I wondered if we could maybe talk a little."

" 'We'?" he said.

"Yeah. The three of us."

"About what?"

I looked around. I didn't want eavesdroppers.

"About Linda Palmer."

"My one night off a week and I have to put up with this crap," he said.

"She was a bitch," Gwen Dawes said.

"Hey, c'mon, she's dead," Walters said.

"Yeah, and that's just what she deserved, too."

"You wouldn't happened to have killed her, would you, Gwen?" I said.

"That's why he's here, Paul. He thinks we did it."

"Right now," I said, "I'd be more inclined to say *you* did it."

"He works for Whitney," Walters said. "I forgot that. He's some kind of investigator."

She said, "He's trying to prove that Rick didn't kill her. That's why he's here."

"You two can account for yourselves between the hours of ten and midnight the night of the murder?"

Gwen eased her arm around his waist. "I sure can. He was at my place."

I looked right at her. "He just said this was his only night off. Where do you work, Paul?"

Now that I'd caught them in a lie, he'd lost some of his poise. "Over at the tire factory."

"You were there the night of the murder?"

"I was—sick."

I watched his face.

"Were you with Gwen?"

"No—I was just riding around."

"And maybe stopped over at Linda's the way you sometimes did?"

He looked at Gwen then back at me.

"No, I—I was just riding around."

He was as bad a liar as Gwen was.

"And I was home," Gwen said, "in case you're interested."

"Nobody with you?"

She gave Walters another squeeze.

"The only person I want with me is Paul."

She took his hand, held it tight. She was protecting him the way Mr. Styles had just protected Mrs. Styles. And as I watched her now, it gave me an idea about how I could smoke out the real killer. I wouldn't go directly for the killer—I'd go for the protector.

"Excuse us," Gwen said, and pushed past me, tugging Paul along in her wake.

I spent the next few minutes looking for Pamela. I finally found her sitting over in the empty bleachers that are used for speed-skating fans every Sunday when the ice is hard enough for competition.

"You okay?"

She looked up at me with those eyes and I nearly went over backwards. She has that effect on me, much as I sometimes wished she didn't.

"You know something, McCain?" she said.

"What?"

"There's a good chance that Stew is never going to change his mind and fall in love with me."

"And there's a good chance that *you're* never going to change *your* mind and fall in love with *me*."

"Oh, McCain," she said, and stood up, the whole lithe, elegant length of her. She slipped her arm in mine again and said, "Let's not talk anymore, all right? Let's just skate."

And skate we did.

5.

When I got home that night, I called Judge Whitney and told her everything I'd learned, from my meeting with Bobbi Thomas to meeting the two couples at the ice rink tonight.

As usual, she made me go over everything to the point that it got irritating. I pictured her on the other end of the phone, sitting there in her dressing gown and shooting rubber bands at an imaginary me across from her.

"Get some rest, McCain," she said. "You sound like you need it."

It was true. I was tired and I probably sounded tired. I tried watching TV. *Mike Hammer* was on at 10:30. I buy all the Mickey Spillane books as soon as they come out. I think Darren McGavin does a great job with Hammer. But tonight the show couldn't quite hold my interest.

I kept thinking about my plan—

What if I actually went through with it?

If the judge found out, she'd probably say it was corny, like something out of a Miss Marple movie. (The only mysteries the judge likes are by Rex Stout and Margery Allingham.)

But so what if it was corny—if it turned up the actual culprit?

I spent the next two hours sitting at my desk in my underwear typing up notes.

Some of them were too cute, some of them were too long, some of them didn't make a hell of a lot of sense.

Finally, I settled on:

If only you really love you-know-who, then you'll meet me in Linda Palmer's apt. tonight at 9:00 o'clock.

A Friend

Then I addressed two envelopes, one to David Styles and one to Gwen Dawes, for delivery tomorrow.

I figured that they each suspected their mates of committing the murder, and therefore whoever showed up tomorrow night had to answer some hard questions.

It was going to feel good, to actually beat Judge Whitney to the solution of a murder. I mean, I don't have that big an ego, I really don't, but I'd worked on ten cases for her now, and she'd solved each one.

6.

I dropped off the notes in the proper mailboxes before going to work, then I spent the remainder of the day calling clients to remind them that they, ahem, owed me money. They had a lot of wonderful excuses for not paying me. Several of them could have great careers as science fiction novelists if they'd only give it half a chance.

I called Pamela three times, pretending I wanted to speak to Judge Whitney.

"She wrapped up court early this morning," Pamela told me on the second call. "Since then, she's been barricaded in her chambers. She sent me out the first time for lunch—a ham-and-cheese on rye with very hot mustard—and the second time for rubber bands. She ran out."

"Why doesn't she just pick them up off the floor?"

"She doesn't like to reuse them."

"Ah."

"Says it's not the same."

After work, I stopped by the A&W for a burger, fries, and root-beer float. Another well-balanced Cody McCain meal.

Dusk was purple and lingering and chill, clear pure Midwestern stars suddenly filling the sky.

Before breaking the seal and the lock on Linda Palmer's door, I went over and said hello to Bobbi Thomas.

She came to the door with the kitten in her arms. She wore a white sweater that I found it difficult to keep my eyes off of, and a pair of dark slacks.

"Oh, hi, Cody."

"Hi."

She raised one of the kitten's paws and waggled it at me. "She says 'hi' too."

"Hi, honey." I nodded to the door behind me. "Can I trust you?"

"Sure, Cody. What's up?"

"I'm going to break into Linda's apartment."

"You're kidding."

"You'll probably hear some noises—people in the hallway and stuff—but please don't call the police. All right?"

For the first time, she looked uncertain. "Couldn't we get in trouble?"

"I suppose."

"And aren't you an officer of the court or whatever you call it?"

"Yeah," I said guiltily.

"Then maybe you shouldn't—"

"I want to catch the killer, Bobbi, and this is the only way I'll do it."

"Well—" she started to say.

Her phone rang behind her. "I guess I'd better get that, Cody."

"Just don't call the police."

She looked at me a long moment. "Okay, Cody. I just hope we don't get into any trouble."

She took herself, her kitten, and her wonderful sweater back inside her apartment.

7.

I kind of felt like Alan Ladd.

I saw a great crime movie once where he was sitting in the shadowy apartment of the woman who'd betrayed him. You know how a scene like that works. There's this lonely wailing sax music and Alan is smoking one butt after another (no wonder he was so short, probably stunted his growth smoking back when he was in junior high or something), and you could just feel how terrible and empty and sad he felt.

Here I was sitting in an armchair, smoking one Pall Mall after another, and if I wasn't feeling quite terrible and empty, I was at least feeling sort of sorry for myself. It was way past time that I show the judge that I could figure out one of these cases for myself.

When the knock came, it startled me, and for the first time I felt self-conscious about what I was doing.

I'd tricked four people into coming here without having any proof that any of them had had anything to do with Linda Palmer's murder at all. What would happen when I opened the door and actually faced them?

I was about to find out.

Leaving the lights off, I walked over to the door, eased it open, and stared into the faces of David and Millie Styles. They both wore black—black turtlenecks; a black peacoat for him; a black suede car coat for her; and black slacks for both of them—and they both looked extremely unhappy.

"Come in and sit down," I said.

They exchanged disgusted looks and followed me into the apartment.

"Take a seat," I said.

"I just want to find out why you sent us that ridiculous note," David Styles said.

"If it's so ridiculous, why did you come here?" I said.

As he looked at his wife again, I heard a knock on the back door. I walked through the shadowy apartment—somehow, I

felt that lights-out would be more conducive to the killer blub-
bering a confession—and peeked out through the curtains near
the stove: Gwen and Paul, neither of them looking happy.

I unlocked the door and let them in.

Before I could say anything, Gwen glared at me. "I'll swear
under oath that Paul was with me the whole time the night she
was murdered."

Suspects in Order of Likelihood

1. Millie
2. Gwen
3. David
4. Paul

That was before Gwen had offered herself as an alibi. Now
Paul went to number one, with her right behind.

I followed them into the living room, where the Styleses were
still standing.

I went over to the fireplace and leaned on the mantel and
said, "One of us in this room is a murderer."

Millie Styles snorted. "This is just like a Charlie Chan
movie."

"I'm serious," I said.

"So am I," she said.

"Each of you had a good reason to kill Linda Palmer," I
said.

"I didn't," David Styles said.

"Neither did I," said Paul.

I moved away from the mantel, starting to walk around the
room, but never taking my eyes off them.

"You could save all of us a lot of time and trouble by just
confessing," I said.

"Which one of us are you talking to?" Gwen said. "I can't
see your eyes in the dark."

"I'm talking to the real killer," I said.

"Maybe you killed her," David Styles said, "and you're trying to frame one of us."

This was pretty much how it went for the next fifteen minutes, me getting closer and closer to the real killer, making him or her really sweat it out, while I continued to pace and throw out accusations.

I guess the thing that spoiled it was the blood-red splash of light in the front window, Cliff Sykes, Jr.'s, personal patrol car pulling up to the curb, and then Cliff Sykes, Jr., racing out of his car, gun drawn.

I heard him on the porch, I heard him in the hall, I heard him at the door across the hall.

Moments after the door opened, Bobbi Thomas wailed, "All right! I killed her! I killed her! I caught her sleeping with my boyfriend!"

I opened the door and looked out into the hall.

Judge Whitney stood next to Cliff Sykes, Jr., and said, "There's your killer, Sykes. Now you get down to that jail and let my nephew go!"

And with that, she turned and stalked out of the apartment house.

Then I noticed the Christmas kitten in Bobbi Thomas's arms. "What's gonna happen to the kitty if I go to prison?" she sobbed.

"Probably put her to sleep," the ever-sensitive Cliff Sykes, Jr., said.

At which point, Bobbi Thomas became semihysterical.

"I'll take her, Bobbi," I said, and reached over and picked up the kitten.

"Thanks," Bobbi said over her shoulder as Sykes led her out to his car.

Each of the people in Linda Palmer's apartment took a turn at glowering at me as he walked into the hall and out the front door.

"See you, Miss Marple," said David Styles.

"So long, Sherlock," smirked Gwen Dawes.

Her boyfriend said something that I can't repeat here.

And Millie Styles said, "Charlie Chan does it a lot better, McCain."

*   *   *

When Sophie (I'm an informal kind of guy, and Sophia is a very formal kind of name) and I got back to my little apartment over a store that Jesse James had actually shot up one time, we both got a surprise.

A Christmas tree stood in the corner resplendent with green and yellow and red lights, and long shining strands of silver icing, and a sweet little angel right at the very tip-top of the tree.

And next to the tree stood the beautiful and elegant Pamela Forrest, gorgeous in a red sweater and jeans. Now, in the Shell Scott novels I read, Pamela would be completely naked and beckoning to me with a curling, seductive finger.

But I was happy to see her just as she was.

"Judge Whitney was afraid you'd be kind of down about not solving the case, so she asked me to buy you a tree and set it up for you."

"Yeah," I said. "I didn't even have Bobbi on my list of suspects. How'd she figure it out anyway?"

Pamela immediately lifted Sophie from my arms and started doing Eskimo noses with her. "Well, first of all, she called the cleaners and asked if any of the rugs that Bobbi had had cleaned had had red stains on it—blood, in other words, meaning that she'd probably killed Linda in her apartment and then dragged her back across to Linda's apartment. The blood came from Sophia's paws most likely, when she walked on the white throw rug." She paused long enough to do some more Eskimo nosing. "Then second, Bobbi told you that she'd stayed home and watched *Gunsmoke*. But *Gunsmoke* had been preempted for a Christmas special and wasn't on that night. And third—" By now she was rocking Sophie in the cradle of her arm. "Third, she found out that the boyfriend that Bobbi had only mentioned briefly to you had fallen under Linda's spell. Bobbi came home and actually found them in bed together—he hadn't even been gentleman enough to take it across the hall to Linda's apartment." Then: "Gosh, McCain, this is one of the cutest little kittens I've ever seen."

"Makes me wish I was a kitten," I said. "Or Sherlock Holmes. She sure figured it out, didn't she?"

Pamela carried Sophie over to me and said, "I think your daddy needs a kiss, young lady."

And I have to admit, it was pretty nice at that moment, Pamela Forrest in my apartment for the very first time, and Sophie's sweet little sandpaper tongue giving me a lot of sweet little kitty kisses.

Long Live the Queen

Ruth Rendell

IT WAS OVER IN AN instant. A flash of orange out of the green hedge, a streak across the road, a thud. The impact was felt as a surprisingly heavy jarring. There was no cry. Anna had braked, but too late and the car had been going fast. She pulled in to the side of the road, got out, walked back.

An effort was needed before she could look. The cat had been flung against the grass verge which separated road from narrow walkway. It was dead. She knew before she knelt down and felt its side that it was dead. A little blood came from its mouth. Its eyes were already glazing. It had been a fine cat of the kind called marmalade because the color is two-tone, the stripes like dark slices of peel among the clear orange. Paws, chest, and part of its face were white, the eyes gooseberry green.

It was an unfamiliar road, one she had only taken to avoid roadworks on the bridge. Anna thought, I was going too fast. There is no speed limit here but it's a country road with cottages and I shouldn't have been going so fast. The poor cat. Now she must go and admit what she had done, confront an

310

angry or distressed owner, an owner who presumably lived in the house behind that hedge.

She opened the gate and went up the path. It was a cottage, but not a pretty one: of red brick with a low slate roof, bay windows downstairs with a green front door between them. In each bay window sat a cat, one black, one orange and white like the cat which had run in front of her car. They stared at her, unblinking, inscrutable, as if they did not see her, as if she was not there. She could still see the black one when she was at the front door. When she put her finger to the bell and rang it, the cat did not move, nor even blink its eyes.

No one came to the door. She rang the bell again. It occurred to her that the owner might be in the back garden and she walked round the side of the house. It wasn't really a garden but a wilderness of long grass and tall weeds and wild trees. There was no one. She looked through a window into a kitchen where a tortoiseshell cat sat on top of the fridge in the sphinx position and on the floor, on a strip of matting, a brown tabby rolled sensuously, its striped paws stroking the air.

There were no cats outside as far as she could see, not living ones at least. In the left-hand corner, past a kind of lean-to coalshed and a clump of bushes, three small wooden crosses were just visible among the long grass. Anna had no doubt they were cat graves.

She looked in her bag and, finding a hairdresser's appointment card, wrote on the blank back of it her name, her parents' address and their phone number, and added, *Your cat ran out in front of my car. I'm sorry, I'm sure death was instantaneous.* Back at the front door, the black cat and the orange-and-white cat still staring out, she put the card through the letter box.

It was then that she looked in the window where the black cat was sitting. Inside was a small overfurnished living room which looked as if it smelt. Two cats lay on the hearthrug, two more were curled up together in an armchair. At either end of the mantelpiece sat a china cat, white and red with gilt whiskers. Anna thought there ought to have been another one between them, in the center of the shelf, because this was the only clear space in the room, every other corner and surface being crowded with objects, many of which had some association with the feline: cat ashtrays, cat vases, photographs of cats in silver frames, postcards of cats, mugs with cat faces on them, and ceramic, brass, silver, and glass kittens. Above the fireplace was a portrait of a marmalade-and-white cat done in oils and on the wall to the left hung a cat calendar.

Anna had an uneasy feeling that the cat in the portrait was the one that lay dead in the road. At any rate, it was very like. She could not leave the dead cat where it was. In the boot of her car were two plastic carrier bags, some sheets of newspaper, and a blanket she sometimes used for padding things she didn't want to strike against each other while she was driving. As wrapping for the cat's body, the plastic bags would look callous, the newspapers worse. She would sacrifice the blanket. It was a clean dark-blue blanket, single size, quite decent and decorous.

The cat's body wrapped in this blanket, she carried it up the path. The black cat had moved from the lefthand bay and had taken up a similar position in one of the upstairs windows. Anna took another look into the living room. A second examination of the portrait confirmed her guess that its subject was the one she was carrying. She backed away. The black cat stared down at her, turned its head, and yawned hugely. Of course it did not know she carried one of its companions, dead and now cold, wrapped in an old car blanket, having met a violent death. She had an uncomfortable feeling, a ridiculous feeling, that it would have behaved in precisely the same way if it had known.

She laid the cat's body on the roof of the coalshed. As she came back round the house, she saw a woman in the garden next door. This was a neat and tidy garden with flowers and a lawn. The woman was in her fifties, white-haired, slim, wearing a twin set.

"One of the cats ran out in front of my car," Anna said. "I'm afraid it's dead."

"Oh, dear."

"I've put the—body, the body on the coalshed. Do you know when they'll be back?"

"It's just her," the woman said. "It's just her on her own."

"Oh, well. I've written a note for her. With my name and address."

The woman was giving her an odd look. "You're very honest. Most would have just driven on. You don't have to report running over a cat, you know. It's not the same as a dog."

"I couldn't have just gone on."

"If I were you, I'd tear that note up. You can leave it to me, I'll tell her I saw you."

"I've already put it through the door," said Anna.

She said goodbye to the woman and got back into her car. She was on her way to her parents' house, where she would be staying for the next two weeks. Anna had a flat on the other side of the town, but she had promised to look after her parents' house while they were away on holiday, and—it now seemed a curious irony—her parents' cat.

If her journey had gone according to plan, if she had not been delayed for half an hour by the accident and the cat's death, she would have been in time to see her mother and father before they left for the airport. But when she got there, they had gone. On the hall table was a note for her in her mother's hand to say that they had had to leave, the cat had been fed, and there was a cold roast chicken in the fridge for Anna's supper. The cat would probably like some, too, to comfort it for missing them.

Anna did not think her mother's cat, a huge fluffy creature of a ghostly whitish-grey tabbyness named Griselda, was capable of missing anyone. She couldn't believe it had affections. It seemed to her without personality or charm, to lack endearing ways. To her knowledge, it had never uttered beyond giving an occasional thin squeak that signified hunger. It had never been known to rub its body against human legs, or even against the legs of the furniture. Anna knew that it was absurd to call an animal selfish—an animal naturally put its survival first, self-preservation being its prime instinct—yet she thought of Griselda as deeply, intensely, callously selfish. When it was not eating, it slept, and it slept in those most comfortable places where the people that owned it would have liked to sit but from which they could not bring themselves to dislodge it. At night it lay on their bed and, if they moved, dug its long sharp claws through the bedclothes into their legs.

Anna's mother didn't like hearing Griselda referred to as "it." She corrected Anna and stroked Griselda's head. Griselda, who purred a lot when recently fed and ensconced among cushions, always stopped purring at the touch of a human hand. This would have amused Anna if she had not seen that her mother seemed hurt by it, withdrew her hand and gave an unhappy little laugh.

When she had unpacked the case she brought with her, had prepared and eaten her meal and given Griselda a chicken leg, she began to wonder if the owner of the cat she had run over would phone. The owner might feel, as people bereaved in great or small ways sometimes did feel, that nothing could bring back the dead. Discussion was useless, and so, certainly, was recrimination. It had not in fact been her fault. She had been driving fast, but not *illegally* fast, and even if she had been driving at thirty miles an hour she doubted if she could have avoided the cat which streaked so swiftly out of the hedge.

It would be better to stop thinking about it. A night's sleep, a day at work, and the memory of it would recede. She had done all she could. She was very glad she had not just driven on as the next-door neighbor had seemed to advocate. It had been some consolation to know that the woman had many cats, not just the one, so that perhaps losing one would be less of a blow.

When she had washed the dishes and phoned her friend Kate, wondered if Richard, the man who had taken her out three times and to whom she had given this number, would phone and had decided he would not, she sat down beside Griselda—not *with* Griselda but on the same sofa as she was on—and watched television. It got to ten and she thought it unlikely the cat woman—she had begun thinking of her as that—would phone now.

There was a phone extension in her parents' room but not

in the spare room where she would be sleeping. It was nearly eleven-thirty and she was getting into bed when the phone rang. The chance of its being Richard, who was capable of phoning late, especially if he thought she was alone, made her go into her parents' bedroom and answer it.

A voice that sounded strange, thin, and cracked said what sounded like "Maria Yackle."

"Yes?" Anna said.

"This is Maria Yackle. It was my cat that you killed."

Anna swallowed. "Yes. I'm glad you found my note. I'm very sorry, I'm very sorry. It was an accident. The cat ran out in front of my car."

"You were going too fast."

It was a blunt statement, harshly made. Anna could not refute it. She said, "I'm very sorry about your cat."

"They don't go out much, they're happier indoors. It was a chance in a million. I should like to see you. I think you should make amends. It wouldn't be right for you just to get away with it."

Anna was very taken aback. Up till then the woman's remarks had seemed reasonable. She didn't know what to say.

"I think you should compensate me, don't you? I loved her, I love all my cats. I expect you thought that because I had so many cats it wouldn't hurt me so much to lose one."

That was so near what Anna had thought that she felt a kind of shock, as if this Maria Yackle or whatever she was called had read her mind. "I've told you I'm sorry. I am sorry, I was very upset, I *hated* it happening. I don't know what more I can say."

"We must meet."

"What would be the use of that?" Anna knew she sounded rude, but she was shaken by the woman's tone, her blunt, direct sentences.

There was a break in the voice, something very like a sob. "It would be of use to me."

The phone went down. Anna could hardly believe it. She had heard it go down but still she said several times over, "Hallo? Hallo?" and "Are you still there?"

She went downstairs and found the telephone directory for the area and looked up Yackle. It wasn't there. She sat down and worked her way through all the Ys. There weren't many pages of Ys, apart from Youngs, but there was no one with a name beginning with Y at that address on the rustic road among the cottages.

She couldn't get to sleep. She expected the phone to ring again, Maria Yackle to ring back. After a while, she put the bedlamp on and lay there in the light. It must have been three, and still she had not slept, when Griselda came in, got on the bed, and stretched her length along Anna's legs. She put out the light, deciding not to answer the phone if it did ring, to relax, forget the run-over cat, concentrate on nice things. As she turned face-downward and stretched her body straight, she felt Griselda's claws prickle her calves. As she shrank away from contact, curled up her legs, and left Griselda a good half of the bed, a thick rough purring began.

The first thing she thought of when she woke up was how upset that poor cat woman had been. She expected her to phone back at breakfast time but nothing happened. Anna fed Griselda, left her to her house, her cat flap, her garden and wider territory, and drove to work. Richard phoned as soon as she got in. Could they meet the following evening? She agreed, obscurely wishing he had said that night, suggesting that evening herself only to be told he had to work late, had a dinner with a client.

She had been home for ten minutes when a car drew up outside. It was an old car, at least ten years old, and not only dented and scratched but with some of the worst scars painted or sprayed over in a different shade of red. Anna, who saw it arrive from a front window, watched the woman get out of it and approach the house. She was old, or at least elderly—is elderly older than old or old older than elderly?—but dressed like a teenager. Anna got a closer look at her clothes, her hair, and her face when she opened the front door.

It was a wrinkled face, the color and texture of a chicken's wattles. Small blue eyes were buried somewhere in the strawberry redness. The bright white hair next to it was as much of a contrast as snow against scarlet cloth. She wore tight jeans with socks pulled up over the bottoms of them, dirty white trainers, and a big loose sweatshirt with a cat's face on it, a painted smiling bewhiskered mask, orange and white and green-eyed.

Anna had read somewhere the comment made by a young girl on an older woman's boast that she could wear a miniskirt because she had good legs: "It's not your legs, it's your face." She thought of this as she looked at Maria Yackle, but that was the last time for a long while she thought of anything like that.

"I've come early because we shall have a lot to talk about," Maria Yackle said and walked in. She did this in such a way as to compel Anna to open the door farther and stand aside.

"This is *your* house?"

She might have meant because Anna was so young or perhaps there was some more offensive reason for asking.

"My parents.' I'm just staying here."

"Is it this room?" She was already on the threshold of Anna's mother's living room.

Anna nodded. She had been taken aback but only for a moment. It was best to get this over. But she did not care to be dictated to. "You could have let me know. I might not have been here."

There was no reply because Maria Yackle had seen Griselda.

The cat had been sitting on the back of a wing chair between the wings, an apparently uncomfortable place though a favorite, but at sight of the newcomer had stretched, got down, and was walking toward her. Maria Yackle put out her hand. It was a horrible hand, large and red with ropelike blue veins standing out above the bones, the palm calloused, the nails black and broken and the sides of the forefinger and thumb ingrained with brownish dirt. Griselda approached and put her smoky whitish muzzle and pink nose into this hand.

"I shouldn't," Anna said rather sharply, for Maria Yackle was bending over to pick the cat up. "She isn't very nice. She doesn't like people."

"She'll like me."

And the amazing thing was that Griselda did. Maria Yackle sat down and Griselda sat on her lap. Griselda the unfriendly, the cold-hearted, the cat who purred when alone and who ceased to purr when touched, the ice-eyed, the standoffish walker-by-herself, settled down on this unknown, untried lap, having first climbed up Maria Yackle's chest and onto her shoulders and rubbed her ears and plump furry cheeks against the sweatshirt with the painted cat face.

"You seem surprised."

Anna said, "You could say that."

"There's no mystery. The explanation's simple." It was a shrill, harsh voice, cracked by the onset of old age, articulate, the usage grammatical but the accent raw cockney. "You and your mum and dad, too, no doubt, you all think you smell very nice and pretty. You have your bath every morning with bath essence and scented soap. You put talcum powder on and spray stuff in your armpits, you rub cream on your bodies and squirt on perfume. Maybe you've washed your hair, too, with shampoo and conditioner and—what-do-they-call-it?—mousse. You clean your teeth and wash your mouth, put a drop more perfume behind your ears, paint your faces—well, I daresay your dad doesn't paint his face, but he shaves, doesn't he? More mousse and then aftershave.

"You put on your clothes. All of them clean, spotless. They've either just come back from the drycleaners or else out of the washing machine with biological soap and spring-fresh fabric softener. Oh, I know, I may not do it myself but I see it on the TV.

"It all smells very fine to you, but it doesn't to her. Oh, no. To her it's just chemicals, like gas might be to you or paraffin. A nasty strong chemical smell that puts her right off and makes her shrink up in her furry skin. What's her name?"

This question was uttered on a sharp bark. "Griselda," said Anna, and, "How did you know it's a she?"

"Face," said Maria Yackle. "Look—see her little nose. See her smiley mouth and her little nose and her fat cheeks? Tomcats got a big nose, got a long muzzle. Never mind if he's been neutered, still got a big nose."

"What did you come here to say to me?" said Anna.

Griselda had curled up on the cat woman's lap, burying her head, slightly upward turned, in the crease between stomach and thigh. "I don't go in for all that stuff, you see." The big red hand stroked Griselda's head, the stripy bit between her ears. "Cat likes the smell of me because I haven't got my clothes in soapy water every day, I have a bath once a week, always have and always shall, and I don't waste my money on odorizers and deodorizers. I wash my hands when I get up in the morning and that's enough for me."

At the mention of the weekly bath, Anna had reacted instinctively and edged her chair a little farther away. Maria Yackle saw, Anna was sure she saw, but her response to this recoil was to begin on what she had in fact come about: her compensation.

"The cat you killed, she was five years old and the queen of the cats, her name was Melusina. I always have a queen. The one before was Juliana and she lived to be twelve. I wept, I mourned her, but life has to go on. 'The queen is dead,' I said, 'long live the queen!' I never promote one, I always get a new kitten. Some cats are queens, you see, and some are not. Melusina was eight weeks old when I got her from the Animal Rescue people, and I gave them a donation of twenty pounds. The vet charged me twenty-seven pounds fifty for her injections—all my cats are immunized against feline enteritis and leptospirosis—so that makes forty-seven pounds fifty. And she had her booster at age two, which was another twenty-seven fifty. I can show you the receipted bills, I always keep everything, and that makes seventy-five pounds. Then there was my petrol getting her to the vet—we'll say a straight five pounds, though it was more—and then we come to the crunch, her food. She was a good little trencherwoman."

Anna would have been inclined to laugh at this ridiculous word, but she saw to her horror that the tears were running down Maria Yackle's cheeks. They were running unchecked out of her eyes, over the rough red wrinkled skin, and one dripped unheeded onto Griselda's silvery fur.

"Take no notice. I do cry whenever I have to talk about her.

I loved that cat. She was the queen of the cats. She had her own place, her throne—she used to sit in the middle of the mantelpiece with her two china ladies-in-waiting on each side of her. You'll see one day, when you come to my house.

"But we were talking about her food. She ate a large can a day—it was too much, more than she should have had, but she loved her food, she was a good little eater. Well, cat food's gone up over the years, of course, what hasn't, and I'm paying fifty pee a can now, but I reckon it'd be fair to average it out at forty pee. She was eight weeks old when I got her, so we can't say five times three hundred and sixty-five. We'll say five times three fifty-five and that's doing you a favor. I've already worked it out at home, I'm not that much of a wizard at mental arithmetic. Five three-hundred and fifty-fives are one thousand, seven hundred and seventy five, which multiplied by forty makes seventy-one thousand pee or seven hundred and ten pounds. Add to that the seventy-five plus the vet's bill of fourteen pounds when she had a tapeworm and we get a final figure of seven hundred and ninety-nine pounds."

Anna stared at her. "You're asking me to give you nearly eight hundred pounds?"

"That's right. Of course, we'll write it down and do it properly."

"Because your cat ran under the wheels of my car?"

"You murdered her," said Maria Yackle.

"That's absurd. Of course I didn't murder her." On shaky ground, she said, "You can't murder an animal."

"You did. You said you were going too fast."

Had she? She had been, but had she said so?

Maria Yackle got up, still holding Griselda, cuddling Griselda, who nestled purring in her arms. Anna watched with distaste. You thought of cats as fastidious creatures but they were not. Only something insensitive and undiscerning would put its face against that face, nuzzle those rough grimy hands. The black fingernails brought to mind a phrase, now unpleasantly appropriate, that her grandmother had used to children with dirty hands: in mourning for the cat.

"I don't expect you to give me a check now. Is that what

you thought I meant? I don't suppose you have that amount in your current account. I'll come back tomorrow or the next day."

"I'm not going to give you eight hundred pounds," said Anna.

She might as well not have spoken.

"I won't come back tomorrow, I'll come back on Wednesday." Griselda was tenderly placed on the seat of an armchair. The tears had dried on Maria's Yackle's face, leaving salt trails. She took herself out into the hall and to the front door. "You'll have thought about it by then. Anyway, I hope you'll come to the funeral. I hope there won't be any hard feelings."

That was when Anna decided Maria Yackle was mad. In one way, this was disquieting—in another, a comfort. It meant she wasn't serious about the compensation, the seven hundred and ninety-nine pounds. Sane people don't invite you to their cat's funeral. Mad people do not sue you for compensation.

"No, I shouldn't think she'd do that," said Richard when they were having dinner together. He wasn't a lawyer but had studied law. "You didn't admit you were exceeding the speed limit, did you?"

"I don't remember."

"At any rate, you didn't admit it in front of witnesses. You say she didn't threaten you?"

"Oh, no. She wasn't unpleasant. She cried, poor thing."

"Well, let's forget her, shall we, and have a nice time?"

Although no note awaited her on the doorstep, no letter came, and there were no phone calls, Anna knew the cat woman would come back on the following evening. Richard had advised her to go to the police if any threats were made. There would be no need to tell them she had been driving very fast. Anna thought the whole idea of going to the police bizarre. She rang up her friend Kate and told her all about it and Kate agreed that telling the police would be going too far.

* * *

The battered red car arrived at seven. Maria Yackle was dressed as she had been for her previous visit, but, because it was rather cold, wore a jacket made of synthetic fur as well. From its harsh, too-shiny texture there was no doubt it was synthetic, but from a distance it looked like a black cat's pelt.

She had brought an album of photographs of her cats for Anna to see. Anna looked through it—what else could she do? Some were recognizably of those she had seen through the windows. Those that were not, she supposed might be of animals now at rest under the wooden crosses in Maria Yackle's back garden. While she was looking at the pictures, Griselda came in and jumped onto the cat woman's lap.

"They're very nice, very interesting," Anna said. "I can see you're devoted to your cats."

"They're my life."

A little humoring might be in order. "When is the funeral to be?"

"I thought on Friday. Two o'clock on Friday. My sister will be there with her two. Cat's don't usually take to car travel, that's why I don't often take any of mine with me, and shutting them up in cages goes against the grain—but my sister's two Burmese love the car, they'll go and sit in the car when it's parked. My friend from the Animal Rescue will come if she can get away and I've asked our vet, but I don't hold out much hope there. He has his goat clinic on Fridays. I hope you'll come along."

"I'm afraid I'll be at work."

"It's no flowers by request. Donations to the Cat's Protection League instead. Any sum, no matter how small, gratefully received. Which brings me to money. You've got a check for me."

"No, I haven't, Mrs. Yackle.'

"Miss. And it's Yakop. J-A-K-O-B. You've got a check for me for seven hundred and ninety-nine pounds."

"I'm not giving you any money, Miss Jakob. I'm very, very sorry about your cat, about Melusina, I know how fond you were of her, but giving you compensation is out of the question. I'm sorry."

The tears had come once more into Maria Jakob's eyes, had

spilled over. Her face contorted with misery. It was the mention of the wretched thing's name, Anna thought. That was the trigger that started the weeping. A tear splashed onto one of the coarse red hands. Griselda opened her eyes and licked up the tear.

Maria Jakob pushed her other hand across her eyes. She blinked. "We'll have to think of something else then," she said.

"I beg your pardon?" Anna wondered if she had really heard. Things couldn't be solved so simply.

"We shall have to think of something else. A way for you to make up to me for murder."

"Look, I will give a donation to the Cats' Protection League. I'm quite prepared to give them—say, twenty pounds." Richard would be furious, but perhaps she wouldn't tell Richard. "I'll give it to you, shall I, and then you can pass it on to them?"

"I certainly hope you will. Especially if you can't come to the funeral."

That was the end of it, then. Anna felt a great sense of relief. It was only now that it was over that she realized quite how it had got to her. It had actually kept her from sleeping properly. She phoned Kate and told her about the funeral and the goat clinic, and Kate laughed and said Poor old thing. Anna slept so well that night that she didn't notice the arrival of Griselda who, when she woke, was asleep on the pillow next to her face but out of touching distance.

Richard phoned and she told him about it, omitting the part about her offer of a donation. He told her that being firm, sticking to one's guns in situations of this kind, always paid off. In the evening, she wrote a check for twenty pounds but, instead of the Cats' Protection League, made it out to Maria Jakob. If the cat woman quietly held onto it, no harm would be done. Anna went down the road to post her letter, for she had written a letter to accompany the check, in which she reiterated her sorrow about the death of the cat and added that if there was anything she could do Miss Jakob had only to let her know. Richard would have been furious.

*   *   *

Unlike the Jakob cats, Griselda spent a good deal of time out of doors. She was often out all evening and did not reappear until the small hours, so that it was not until the next day, not until the next evening, that Anna began to be alarmed at her absence. As far as she knew, Griselda had never been away so long before. For herself, she was unconcerned—she had never liked the cat, did not particularly like any cats, and found this one obnoxiously self-centered and cold. It was for her mother, who unaccountably loved the creature, that she was worried. She walked up and down the street calling Griselda, though the cat had never been known to come when it was called.

It did not come now. Anna walked up and down the next street, calling, and around the block and farther afield. She half expected to find Griselda's body, guessing that it might have met the same fate as Melusina. Hadn't she read somewhere that nearly forty thousand cats are killed on British roads annually?

On Saturday morning, she wrote one of those melancholy lost-cat notices and attached it to a lamp standard, wishing she had a photograph. But her mother had taken no photographs of Griselda.

Richard took her to a friend's party and afterward, when they were driving home, he said, "You know what's happened, don't you? It's been killed by that old mad woman. An eye for an eye, a cat for a cat."

"Oh, no, she wouldn't do that. She loves cats."

"Murderers love people. They just don't love the people they murder."

"I'm sure you're wrong," said Anna, but she remembered how Maria Jakob had said that if the money was not forthcoming, she must think of something else—a way to make up to her for Melusina's death. And she had not meant a donation to the Cats' Protection League.

"What shall I do?"

"I don't see that you can do anything. It's most unlikely you could prove it, she'll have seen to that. You can look at this way—she's had her pound of flesh."

"Fifteen pounds of flesh," said Anna. Griselda had been a large, heavy cat.

"Okay, fifteen pounds. She's had that, she's had her revenge. It hasn't actually caused you any grief—you'll just have to make up some story for your mother."

Anna's mother was upset, but nowhere near as upset as Maria Jakob had been over the death of Melusina. To avoid too much fuss, Anna had gone further than she intended, told her mother that she had seen Griselda's corpse and talked to the offending motorist, who had been very distressed.

A month or so later, Anna's mother got a kitten, a grey tabby tomkitten, who was very affectionate from the start, sat on her lap, purred loudly when stroked, and snuggled up in her arms, though Anna was sure her mother had not stopped having baths or using perfume. So much for the Jakob theories.

Nearly a year had gone by before she again drove down the road where Maria Jakob's house was. She had not intended to go that way. Directions had been given her to a smallholding where they sold early strawberries on a roadside stall but she must have missed her way, taken a wrong turning, and come out here.

If Maria Jakob's car had been parked in the front, she would not have stopped. There was no garage for it to be in and it was not outside, therefore the cat woman must be out. Anna thought of the funeral she had not been to—she had often thought about it, the strange people and strange cats who had attended it.

In each of the bay windows sat a cat, a tortoiseshell and a brown tabby. The black cat was eyeing her from upstairs. Anna didn't go to the front door but round the back. There, among the long grass, as she had expected, were four graves instead of three, four wooden crosses, and on the fourth was printed in black gloss paint: MELUSINA, THE QUEEN OF THE CATS. MURDERED IN HER SIXTH YEAR. RIP.

That "murdered" did not please Anna. It brought back all the resentment at the unjust accusations of eleven months before. She felt much older, she felt wiser. One thing was certain, ethics or no ethics, if she ever ran over a cat again she'd drive on—the last thing she'd do was go and confess.

She came round the side of the house and looked in at the bay window. If the tortoiseshell had still been on the windowsill, she probably would not have looked in, but the tortoiseshell had removed itself to the hearthrug.

A white cat and the marmalade-and-white lay curled up side by side in an armchair. The portrait of Melusina hung above the fireplace and this year's cat calendar was up on the left-hand wall. Light gleamed on the china cats' gilt whiskers—and between them, in the empty space that was no longer vacant, sat Griselda.

Griselda was sitting in the queen's place in the middle of the mantelpiece. She sat in the sphinx position with her eyes closed. Anna tapped on the glass and Griselda opened her eyes, stared with cold indifference, and closed them again.

The queen is dead, long live the queen!

Animals

Clark Howard

As NED PRICE GOT OFF the city bus at the corner of his block, he saw that Monty and his gang of troublemakers were, as usual, loitering in front of Shavelson's Drugstore. A large portable radio—they called it their "ghetto blaster"—was sitting atop a newspaper vending machine, playing very loud acid rock. The gang, six of them, all in their late teens, appeared to be arguing over the contents of a magazine that was circulating among them.

Ned started down the sidewalk. An arthritic limp made him favor his right leg. That, coupled with lumbago and sixty-two years of less than easy living, gave him an overall stooped, tired look. A thrift-shop sportcoat slightly too large didn't help matters. Ned could have crossed the street and gone around Monty and his friends, but he lived on this side of the street so he would just have to cross back again farther down the block. It was difficult enough to get around these days without taking extra steps. Besides, he figured he had at least as much right to walk down the sidewalk as they did to obstruct it.

When Ned got closer, he saw the magazine the gang was

327

passing around was *Ring* and that their argument had to do with the relative merits of two boxers named Hector "Macho" Camacho and Ray "Boom Boom" Mancini. Maybe they'd be too caught up in their argument to hassle him today. That would be a welcome change. A day without having to match wits with this year's version of the Sharks.

But no such luck.

"Hey, old man, where you been?" Monty asked as Ned approached. "Down to pick up your check?" He stepped in the middle of the sidewalk and blocked the way.

Ned stopped. "Yes," he said, "I've been down to pick up my check."

"You're one of those old people who don't let the mailman bring their check, huh?" Monty asked with a smile. "You know there's too many crooks in this neighborhood. You're smart, huh?"

"No, just careful," Ned said. If I was smart, he thought, I would have crossed the street.

"Hey, lemme ask you something," Monty said with mock seriousness. "I seen on a TV special where some old people don't get enough pension to live on an' they eat dogfood and catfood. Do you do that, old man?"

"No, I don't," Ned replied. There was a slight edge to his answer this time. He knew several people who *did* resort to the means Monty had just described.

"Listen, old man, I think you're lying," Monty said without rancor. "I myself have seen you in Jamail's Grocery buying catfood."

"That's because I have a cat." Ned tried to step around Monty but the youth moved and blocked his way again.

"You got a cat, old man? Ain't that nice?" Monty feigned interest. "Wha' kind of cat you got, old man?"

"Just an ordinary cat," Ned said. "Nothing special."

"Not a Persian or a Siamese or one of them expensive cats?"

"No. Just an ordinary cat. A tabby, I think it's called."

"A tabby! Hey, tha's really nice."

"Can I go now?" Ned asked.

"Sure!" Monty said, shrugging elaborately. "Who's stopping you, old man?"

Ned stepped around him and this time the youth did not interfere with him. As he walked away, Ned heard Monty say something in Spanish and the others laughed.

A regular Freddie Prinze, Ned thought.

As Ned entered his third-floor-rear kitchenette, he said, "Molly, I'm back." Double-locking the door securely behind him, he hung his coat on a wooden wall peg and limped into a tiny cluttered living room. "Molly!" he called again. Then he stood still and a cold feeling came over him that he was alone in the apartment. "Molly?"

He stuck his head in the narrow Pullman kitchen, then pushed back a curtain that concealed a tiny sleeping alcove.

"Molly, where are you?"

Even as he asked the question one last time, Ned knew he would not find her. He hurried into the bathroom. The window was open about three inches. Ned raised it all the way and stuck his head out. Three stories below, in the alley, some kids were playing Kick-the-Can. A ledge ran from the window to a backstairs landing.

"Molly!" Ned called several times.

Moments later, he was out in front looking up and down the street. Monty and his friends, seeing him, sauntered down to where he stood.

"What's the matter, old man?" Monty asked. "You lose something?"

"My cat," Ned said. He turned suspicious eyes on Monty and his friends. "You wouldn't have seen her, by any chance, would you?"

"Is there a reward?" Monty inquired.

Ned gave the question quick consideration. There was an old watch of his late wife's he could probably sell. "There might be, if the cat isn't harmed. Do you know where she is?"

Monty turned to the others. "Anybody see this old man's cat?" he asked with a total absence of concern. When they all shrugged and declared ignorance, he said to Ned, "Sorry, old man. If you'd let the mailman deliver your check, you'd have been home to look after your cat. See the price you pay for being greedy?" He strutted off down the street, his followers in his wake. Feeling ill, Ned watched them all the way to the corner, where they turned out of sight. Pain from an old ulcer began as acid churned in his stomach.

"Molly!" he called and started walking down the block. "Molly! Here, kitty, kitty."

He searched for her until well after dark.

Ned was up early the next morning and back outside looking. He scoured the block all the way to the corner, then came back the other way. In front of the drugstore, he encountered Monty again. The youth was alone this time, leaning up against the building, eating a jelly doughnut and drinking milk from a pint carton.

"You still looking for that cat, old man?" Monty asked, his tone a mixture of incredulity and irritation.

"Yes."

"Man, why don't you go in the alley and get another one? There mus' be a dozen cats back there."

"I want this cat. It belonged to my wife when she was alive."

"Hell, man, a cat's a cat," Monty said.

Shavelson, the drugstore owner, came out, broom in hand. "Want to make half a buck sweeping the sidewalk?" he asked Monty, who looked at him as if he were an imbecile, then turned away disdainfully, not even dignifying the question with an answer. Shavelson shrugged and began sweeping debris toward the curb himself. "You're out early," he said to Ned.

"My cat's lost," Ned said. "She may have got out the bathroom window while I was downtown yesterday."

"Why don't you go back in the alley—"

Ned was already shaking his head. "I want *this* cat."

"Maybe the pound got her," Shavelson suggested. "Their truck was all over this neighborhood yesterday."

The storekeeper's words sent a chill along Ned's spine. "The pound?"

"Yeah. You know, the city animal shelter. They have a truck comes around—"

"It was here yesterday? On this block?"

"Yeah."

"Where do they take the animals they catch?" Ned asked out of a rapidly drying mouth.

"The animal shelter over on Twelfth Street, I think. They have to hold them there seventy-two hours to see if anybody claims them."

Too distressed by the thought to thank Shavelson, Ned hurried back up the street and into his building. Five minutes later, he emerged again, wearing a coat, his city bus pass in one hand. Crossing the street, he went to the bus stop and stood peering down the street, as if by sheer will he could make a bus appear.

Monty, having finished his doughnut and milk, sat on the curb in front of Shavelson's, smoking a cigarette and reading one of the morning editions from the drugstore's sidewalk newspaper rack. From time to time he glanced over at Ned, wondering at his concern over a cat. Monty knew a few back yards in the neighborhood that were knee-deep in cats.

Presently it began to sprinkle light rain. Monty stood up, folding the newspaper, and handed it to Shavelson as the storekeeper came out to move his papers inside.

"You sure you're through with it?" Shavelson asked. "Any coupons or anything you'd like to tear out?"

Monty's eyes narrowed a fraction. "Someday, man, you're gonna say the wrong thing to me," he warned. "Then you're gonna come to open up your store and you gonna find a pile of ashes."

"You'd do that for *me*?" Shavelson retorted.

The sprinkle escalated to a drizzle as the storekeeper went back inside. From the doorway, Monty looked over at the bus stop again. Ned was still standing there, his only concession to the rain being a turned-up collar. I don't believe this old fool, Monty thought. He goes to more trouble for this cat than most people do for their kids.

Tossing his cigarette into the gutter, he trotted down the

block and got into an old Chevy that had a pair of oversize velvet dice dangling from the rearview mirror. Revving the engine a little, he listened with satisfaction to the rumble of the car's gutted muffler, then made a U-turn from the curb and drove to the bus stop.

"Get in, old man," he said, leaning over to the passenger window. "I'm going past Twelfth Street—I'll give you a lift."

Ned eyed him suspiciously. "No, thanks. I'll wait for the bus."

"Hey, man, waiting for a bus in this city at your age ain't too smart. An old lady over on Bates Street *died* at a bus stop last week, she was there so long. Besides, in case you ain't noticed, it's raining." Monty's voice softened a touch. "Come on, get in."

Ned glanced up the street one last time, saw that there was still no bus in sight, thought of Molly caged up at the pound, and got in.

As they rode along, Monty lighted another cigarette and glanced over at his passenger. "You thought me and my boys did something with your cat, didn't you?"

"The thought did cross my mind," Ned admitted.

"Listen, I got better things to do with my time than mess with some cat. You know, for an old guy you ain't very smart."

Ned grunted softly. "I won't argue with you there," he said.

On Twelfth, Monty pulled to the curb in front of the animal shelter. "I got to go see a guy near here, take me about fifteen minutes. I'll come back and pick you up after you get your cat."

Ned studied him for a moment. "Is there some kind of Teenager of the Year award I don't know about?"

"Very funny, man. You're a regular, what's-his-name, Jack Albertson, ain't you?"

At the information counter in the animal shelter a woman with tightly styled hair and a superior attitude asked, "Was the animal wearing a license tag on its collar?"

"No, she—"

"Was the animal wearing an ID tag on its collar?"

"No, she wasn't wearing a collar. She's really an apartment cat, you see—"

"Sir," the woman said, "our animal enforcement officers don't go into apartments and take animals."

"I think she got out the bathroom window."

"That makes her a street animal, unlicensed and unidentifiable."

"Oh, I can identify her," Ned assured the woman. "And she'll come to me when I call her. If you'll just let me see the cats you picked up yesterday—"

"Sir, do you have any idea how many stray animals are picked up by our trucks every day?"

"Why, no, I never gave—"

"*Hundreds*," he was told. "Only the ones with license tags or ID tags are kept at the shelter."

"I thought all animals had to be kept here for three days to give their owners time to claim them," Ned said, remembering what Shavelson had told him.

"You're not listening, sir. Only the animals with license or ID tags are kept at the shelter for the legally required seventy-two hours. Those without tags are taken directly to the disposal pound."

Ned turned white. "Is that where they—where they—?" The words would not form.

"Yes, that is where stray animals are put to sleep." She paused a beat. "Either that or sold."

Ned frowned. "Sold."

"Yes, sir. To laboratories. To help offset the overhead of operating our department." Her eyes flicked over Ned's shabby clothing. "Tax dollars don't pay for *everything*, you know." But she had unknowingly given Ned an ember of hope.

"Can you give me the address of this—disposal place?"

The woman scribbled an address on a slip of paper and pushed it across the counter to him. "Your cat might still be there," she allowed, "if it was picked up late yesterday. Disposal hours for cats are from one to three. If it was a dog you'd be out of luck. They do dogs at night, eight to eleven, because

there are more of them. That's because they're easier to catch.
They trust people. Cats, they don't trust—"

She was still talking as Ned snatched up the address and
hurried out.

Monty was waiting at the curb.

"I didn't think you'd be back this quick," Ned said, getting
into the car.

"The guy I went to see wasn't there," Monty told him. It
was a lie. All he had done was drive around the block.

"They've taken my cat to be gassed," Ned said urgently,
"but if I can get there in time I might be able to save her." He
handed Monty the slip of paper. "This is the address. It's way
out at the edge of town, but if you'll take me there I'll pay
you." He pulled out a pathetically worn billfold, the old-
fashioned kind that zipped around three sides. When he opened
it, Monty could see several faded cellophane inserts with photographs in them. The photographs were old, all in black-and-
white except for a paper picture of June Allyson that had come
with the billfold.

From the currency pocket Ned extracted some bills, all of
them singles. "I don't have much because I haven't cashed my
check yet. But I can at least buy you some gas."

Monty pushed away the hand with the money and started
the car. "I don't *buy* gas, man," he scoffed, "I quit buying it
when it got to a dollar a gallon."

"Where do you get it?" Ned asked.

"I siphon it. From police cars parked behind the precinct
station. It's the only place where cars are left on a lot un-
guarded." He flashed a smile at Ned. "That's because nobody
would *dare* siphon gas from a cop car, you know what I
mean?"

They got on one of the expressways and drove toward the
edge of the city. As Monty drove, he smoked and kept time to
rock music from the radio by drumming his fingers on the steering wheel. Ned glanced at a scar down the youth's right cheek.
Thin and straight, almost surgical in appearance, it had probably been put there by a straight razor. Ned had been curious

about the scar for a long time. Now would be an opportune time to ask how he got it, but Ned was too concerned about Molly. She was such an old cat, nearly fourteen. He hoped she hadn't died of a stroke from the trauma of being captured and caged. If she was still alive, she was going to be so glad to see him Ned doubted she would ever climb out the bathroom window again.

After half an hour on the expressway, Monty exited and drove them to a large warehouselike building at the edge of the city's water-treatment center. A sign above the entrance read simply: *Animal Shelter—Unit F.*

F for final, Ned thought. He was already opening his door as Monty brought the car to a full stop.

"Want me to come in with you?" Monty asked.

"What for?" Ned wanted to know, frowning.

The younger man shrugged. "So's they don't push you around. Sometimes people push old guys around."

"Really?" Ned asked wryly.

Monty looked off at nothing. "You want me to come in or not?"

"I can handle things myself," Ned told him gruffly.

The clerk at this counter, a thin gum-chewing young man with half a dozen ballpoints in a plastic holder in his shirt pocket, checked a clipboard on the wall and said, "Nope, you're too late. That whole bunch from yesterday was shipped out to one of our lab customers early this morning."

Ned felt warm and slightly nauseated. "Do you think they might sell my cat back to me?" he asked. "If I went over there?"

"You can't go over there," the clerk said. "We're not allowed to divulge the name or address of any of our lab customers."

"Oh." Ned wet his lips. "Do you suppose you could call them for me? Tell them I'd like to make some kind of arrangements to buy back my cat?"

The clerk was already shaking his head. "I don't have time to do things like that, mister."

"A simple phone call," Ned pleaded. "It'll only take—"

"Look, mister, I said no. I'm a very busy person."

Just then someone stepped up to the counter next to Ned. Surprised, Ned saw that it was Monty. He had his hands on the counter, palms down, and was smiling at the clerk.

"What time you get off work, Very Busy Person?" he asked.

The clerk blinked rapidly. "Uh, why do you want to know?"

"I'm jus' interested in what kind of hours a Very Busy Person like you keeps." Monty's smile faded and his stare grew cold. "You don't have to tell me if you don't want to. I can wait outside and find out for myself."

The clerk stopped chewing his gum; the color disappeared from his face, leaving him sickly pale. "Why, uh—why would you do that?"

" 'Cause I ain't got nothing better to do," Monty replied. "I *was* gonna take this old man here to that lab to try and get his cat back. But if he don't know where it is, I can't do that. So I'll just hang around here." He winked at the clerk without smiling. "See you later, man."

Monty took Ned's arm and started him toward the door.

"Just—wait a minute," the clerk said.

Monty and Ned turned back to see him rummaging in a drawer under the counter. He found a sheet of paper with three names and addresses mimeographed on it. With a ballpoint from the selection in his shirt pocket, he circled one of the addresses. Monty stepped back to the counter and took the sheet of paper.

"If it turns out they're expecting us," Monty said, "I'll know who warned them. You take my meaning, man?"

The clerk nodded. He swallowed dryly and his gum was gone.

At the door, looking at the address circled on the paper, Monty said, "Come on, old man. This here place is clear across town. You positive one of them cats in the alley wouldn't do you?"

On their way to the lab, Ned asked, "Why are you helping me like this?"

Monty shrugged. "It's a slow Wednesday, man."

Ned studied the younger man for a time, then observed, "You're different when your gang's not around."

Monty tossed him a smirk. "You gonna, what do you call it, analyze me, old man? You gonna tell me I got 'redeeming social values' or something like that?"

"I wouldn't go quite that far," Ned said dryly. "Anyway, sounds to me like you've *been* analyzed."

"Lots of times," Monty told him. "When they took me away from my old lady because it was an 'unfit environment,' they had some shrink analyze me then. When I ran away from the foster homes I was put in, other shrinks analyzed me. After I was arrested and was waiting trial in juvenile court for some burglaries, I was analyzed again. When they sent me downstate to the reformatory, I was analyzed. They're very big on analyzing in this state."

"They ever tell you the results of all that analyzing?"

"Sure. I'm incorrigible. And someday I'm supposed to develop into a sociopath. You know what that is?"

"Not exactly," Ned admitted.

Monty shrugged. "Me neither. I guess I'll find out when I become one."

They rode in silence for a few moments and then Ned said, "Well, anyway, I appreciate you helping me."

"Forget it," Monty said. He would not look at Ned; his eyes were straight ahead on the road. After several seconds, he added, "Jus' don't go telling nobody about it."

"All right, I won't," Ned agreed.

Their destination on the other side of the city was a large square two-story building on the edge of a forest preserve. It was surrounded by a chain-link fence with an entrance gate manned by a security guard. A sign on the gate read: *Consumer Evaluation Laboratory.*

Monty parked outside the gate and followed Ned over to the security-guard post. Ned explained what he wanted. The security guard took off his cap and scratched his head. "I don't

know. This isn't covered in my guard manual. I'll have to call
and find out if they sell animals back."

Ned and Monty waited while the guard telephoned. He
talked to one person, was transferred to another, then had to
repeat his story to still a third before he finally hung up and
said, "Mr. Hartley of Public Relations is coming out to talk to
you."

Mr. Hartley was a pleasant but firmly uncooperative man.
"I'm sorry, but we can't help you," he said when Ned had told
him of Molly's plight. "We have at least a hundred small animals in there—cats, dogs, rabbits, guinea pigs—all of them un-
dergoing scientific tests. Even the shipment we received this
morning has already been processed into a testing phase. We
simply can't interrupt the procedure to find one particular cat."

"But it's *my* cat," Ned insisted. "She's not homeless or a
stray. She belonged to my late wife—"

"I understand that, Mr. Price," Hartley interrupted, "but the
animal *was* outside with no license or ID tag around its neck.
It was apprehended legally and sold to us legally. I'm afraid
it's just too late."

As they were talking, a bus pulled up to the gate. Hartley
waved at the driver, then turned to the security guard. "These
are the people from Diamonds-and-Pearls Cosmetics, Fred. Pass
them through and then call Mr. Draper. He's conducting a tour
for them."

As the bus passed through, Hartley turned back to resume
the argument with Ned, but Monty stepped forward to inter-
cede.

"We understand, Mr. Hartley," Monty said in a remarkably
civil tone. "We're sure you'd help us if you could. Please accept
our apology for taking up your time." Monty offered his hand.

"Quite all right," Hartley said, shaking hands.

Ned was staring incredulously at Monty. Macho had suddenly become Milquetoast.

"Come along, old fellow," Monty said, putting an arm
around Ned's shoulders. "We'll go to a pet store and buy you
a new kitty."

Ned allowed himself to be led back to the car, then demanded, "What the hell's got into you?"

"You're wasting your time with that joker," Monty said. "He's been programmed to smile and say no to whatever you want. We got to find some other way to get your cat."

"What other way?"

Monty grinned. "Like using the back door, man."

Driving away from the front gate, Monty found a gravel road and slowly circled the fenced-in area of the Consumer Evaluation Laboratory. On each side of the facility, beyond its fence, were several warehouses and small plants. In front, beyond a feeder road, was a state highway. Growing right up to its rear fence was the forest preserve: a state-protected wooded area.

Monty made one full circuit of the complex occupied by the laboratory and its neighbors, then said, "I think the best plan is to park in the woods, get past the fence in back, and sneak in that way."

"You mean slip in and *steal* my cat?" Ned asked.

Monty shrugged. "They stole her from you," he said.

Ned stared at him. "I'm sixty-two years old," he said. "I've never broken the law in my life."

"So?" said Monty, frowning. He did not see any relevance. The two men, one young, one old, each so different from the other, locked eyes in a silent stare for what seemed like a long time.

They were parked on the shoulder of the gravel road, the car windows down. The air coming into the car was fresh from the morning rain. Ned detected the scent of wet earth. Some movement a few yards up the road caught his eye and he turned his attention away from Monty. The movement was a gray squirrel scurrying across the road to the safety of the nearby woods. Watching the little animal, wild and free, made Ned think of the animals in the laboratory that were not free—the dogs and rabbits and guinea pigs.

And cats.

"All right," he told Monty. "Let's go in the back way."

* * *

Monty parked in one of the public picnic areas. From the
trunk, he removed a pair of chain cutters and held them under
his jacket with one hand.

"What do you carry those things for?" Ned asked, and realized at once that his question was naive.

"To clip coupons with, man," Monty replied. "Coupons
save you money on everyday necessities."

The two men made their way through the trees to the rear
of the laboratory's chain-link fence. Crouching, they scrutinized
the back of the complex. Monty's eyes settled immediately on
a loading dock served by a single-lane driveway coming around
one side of the building. "We can go in there," he said. "Over-
hang doors are no sweat to open. But first let's see if there's
any juice in this fence." Keeping his hands well on the rubber-
covered handles, he gently touched the metal fence with the tip
of the chain cutters. The contact drew no sparks. "Nothing on
the surface," he said. "Let's see if there's anything inside. Some
of these newer chain-links have an insulated circuit running
through them." Quickly and expertly, he spread the cutters and
snipped one link of the metal. Again there were no sparks.
"This is going to be a breeze."

With a practiced eye, he determined his pattern and quickly
snipped exactly the number of links necessary to create an
opening large enough for them to get through. Then he gripped
the cut section and bent it open, like a door, about eight inches.
The chain cutters he hid nearby in some weeds.

"Now here's our story," he said to Ned. "We was walking
through the public woods here and saw this hole cut in the
fence, see? We thought it was our civic duty to tell somebody
about it, so we came inside looking for somebody. If we get
caught, stick to that story. Got it?"

"Got it," Ned confirmed.

Monty winked approval. "Let's do it, old man."

They eased through the opening and Monty bent the cut
section back into place. Then they started toward the loading
dock, walking upright with no attempt at hurrying or hiding.
Ned was nervous but Monty remained very cool; he even whis-

tled a soft little tune. When he sensed Ned's anxiety, he threw him a grin.

"Relax, old man. It'll take us forty, maybe fifty seconds to reach that dock. The chances of somebody seeing us in that little bit of time are so tiny, man. And even if they do, so what? We got our story, right?"

"Yeah, right," Ned replied, trying to sound confident.

But as Monty predicted, they reached the loading dock unobserved and unchallenged. Once up on the dock, Monty peered through a small window in one of the doors. "Just a big room with a lot of work tables," he said quietly. "Don't look like nobody's around. Hey, this service door's unlocked. Come on."

They moved inside into a large room equipped with butcher-block tables fixed to a tile floor. A number of hoses hung over each table, connected to the ceiling. As the two men stood scrutinizing the room, they suddenly heard a voice approaching. Quickly they ducked behind one of the tables.

An inner door opened and a man led a group of people into the room, saying, "This is our receiving area, ladies and gentlemen. The animals we purchase are delivered here and our laboratory technicians use these tables to wash and delouse them. They are then taken into our testing laboratory next door, which I will show you next. If you would, please take a smock from the pile there, to protect your clothes from possible contact with any of the substances we use in there."

Peering around the table, Ned and Monty watched as the people put on smocks and regrouped at the door. As they were filing out, Ned nudged Monty and said, "Come on."

Monty grinned. "You catching on, old man."

The two put on smocks and fell in at the rear of the group. They followed along as it was led through the hall and into a much larger room. This one was set up with a series of aisles formed by long work counters on which stood wire-grille cages of various sizes. Each cage was numbered and had a small slot containing a white card on its door. In each cage was a live animal.

"Our testing facility, we feel, is the best of its kind currently in existence," the tour guide said. "As you can see, we have a variety of test animals: cats, dogs, rabbits, guinea pigs. We also have access to larger animals, if a particular test requires it. Our testing procedures can be in any form. We can force-feed the test substance, introduce it by forced inhalation, reduce it to a dermal form and apply it directly to an animal's shaved skin, or inject it intravenously. Over here, for instance, are rabbits being given what is known as a Draize test. A new hairspray is being sprayed into their very sensitive eyes in order to gauge its irritancy level. Just behind the rabbits you see a group of puppies having dishwashing detergent introduced directly into their stomachs by a syringe with a tube attached to a hand pump. This is called an Internal LD-50 test; the LD stands for lethal dose and the number fifty represents one-half of a group of one hundred animals on which the test will be conducted. When half of the test group has died, we will have an accurate measurement of the toxity level of this product. This will provide the company marketing the product with evidence of safety testing in case it is later sued because some child swallows the detergent and dies. During the course of the testing, we also learn exactly how a particular substance will affect a living body, by observing whatever symptoms the animal exhibits: convulsions, paralysis, tremors, inability to breathe, blindness as in the case of the rabbits there—"

Ned was staring at the scene around him. As he looked at the helpless, caged, tortured animals, he felt his skin crawl. Which were the animals, the ones in the cages, or the ones outside the cages? Glancing at Monty, he saw the younger man reacting the same way—his eyes were wide, his expression incredulous, and his hands were curled into fists.

"We can test virtually any substance or product there is," the guide continued. "We test all forms of cosmetics and beauty aids, all varieties of detergents and other cleaning products, every food additive, coloring, and preservative, any new chemical or drug product—you name it. In addition to servicing private business, we test pesticides for the Environmental Protection Agency, synthetic substances for the Food and Drug Administration, and a variety of products for the Consumer Product Safety Commission. Our facility is set up so that almost no lead time is required to service our customers. As an example of this, a dozen cats brought in this morning are already in a testing phase over here—"

Ned and Monty followed the group to another aisle where the guide pointed out the newly arrived cats and explained the test being applied to them. Ned strained to see beyond the people in front of him, trying to locate Molly.

Finally the tour guide said, "Now, ladies and gentlemen, if you'll follow me, I'll take you to our cafeteria, where you can enjoy some refreshments while our testing personnel answer any questions you have about how we can help Diamonds-and-Pearls Cosmetics keep its products free of costly lawsuits. Just drop your smocks on the table outside the door."

Again Ned and Monty ducked down behind a workbench to conceal themselves as the people filed out of the room. When the door closed behind the group, Ned rose and hurried to the cat cages. Monty went over to lock the laboratory door.

Ned found Molly in one of the top cages. She was lying on her side, eyes wide, staring into space. The back part of her body had been shaved and three intravenous needles were stuck in her skin and held in place by tape. The tubes attached to the needles ran out the grille and up to three small bottles suspended above the cage. They were labeled: FRAGRANCE, DYE, and POLYSORBATE 93.

Ned wiped his eyes with the heel of one hand. Unlatching the grille door, he reached in and stroked Molly. "Hello, old girl," he said. Molly opened her mouth to meow, but no sound came.

"Dirty bastards," Ned heard Monty whisper. Turning, he saw the younger man reading the card on the front of Molly's cage. "This is some stuff that's going to be used in a hair tint," he said. "This test is to see if the cat can stay alive five hours with this combination of stuff in her."

"I can answer that," Ned said. "She won't. She's barely alive now."

"If we can get her to a vet, maybe we can save her," Monty suggested. "Pump her stomach or something." He bobbed his chin at the back wall. "We can get out through one of those windows—they face our hole in the fence."

"Get one open," Ned said. "I'll take Molly out."

Monty hurried over to the window while Ned gently unfastened the tape and pulled the hypodermic needles out of Molly's flesh. Once again the old cat looked at him and tried to make a sound, but she was too weak and too near death. "I know, old girl," Ned said softly. "I know it hurts."

Near the window, after opening it, Monty noticed several cages containing puppies that were up and moving around, some of them barking and wagging their tails. Monty quickly opened their cages, scooped them out two at a time, and dropped them out the window.

"Lead these pups to the fence, old man," he said as Ned came over with Molly.

"Right," Ned replied. He let Monty hold the dying cat as he painfully got his arthritic legs over the ledge and lowered himself to the ground. "What about you?" he asked as Monty handed down the cat.

"I'm gonna turn a few more pups loose, an' maybe some of those rabbits they're blinding. You head for the fence—I'll catch up."

Ned limped away from the building, calling the pups to follow him. He led them to the fence, bent the cut section open again, and let them scurry through. As he went through himself, he could feel Molly becoming ever more limp in his hands. By the time he got into the cover of the trees, her eyes had closed, her mouth had opened, and she was dead. Tears coming again, he knelt and put the cat up against a tree trunk and covered her with an old red bandanna he pulled out of his back pocket.

Looking through the fence, he saw that Monty was still putting animals out the window. Two dozen cats, dogs, rabbits, and guinea pigs were moving around tentatively on the grass behind the laboratory. He's got to get out of there or he'll get caught, Ned thought. Returning through the opening in the fence, he hurried back to the window.

"Come on," he urged as the younger man came to the window with a kitten in each hand.

"No—" Monty tossed the kittens to the ground "—I'm going to turn loose every animal that can stand!"

Old man and young man fixed eyes on each other as every difference there had ever been between them faded.

"Give me a hand up, then," Ned said.

Monty reached down and pulled him back up through the window.

As they worked furiously to open more cages and move their captives out the window, they became aware of someone trying the lab door and finding it locked. Several moments later, someone tried it again. A voice outside the door mentioned a key. The two inside the lab worked all the faster. Finally, a sweating Monty said, "I think that's all we can let go. The rest are too near dead. Let's get out of here!"

"I'm going to do one more thing first," Ned growled.

Poised by the open window, Monty asked, "What?"

Ned walked toward a shelf on which stood several plastic gallon jugs of isopropyl alcohol. "I'm going to burn this son-of-a-bitch down."

Monty rushed over to him. "What about the other animals?"

"You said yourself they were almost dead. At least this will put them out of their misery without any more torture." He opened a jug and started pouring alcohol around the room. After a moment of indecision, Monty joined him.

Five minutes later, just as someone in the hall got the lab door open and several people entered, Ned and Monty dropped out the open window and tossed a lighted book of matches back inside.

The laboratory became a ball of flame.

While the fire spread and the building burned, Ned and Monty managed to get the released animals through the fence and into the woods. Sirens of fire and police emergency vehicles pierced the quiet afternoon. There were screams and shouts as the burning building was evacuated. Monty retrieved the chain cutters and ran toward the car. Ned limped hurriedly after him, but stopped when he got to where Molly was lying under the red bandanna. I can't leave her like that, he thought. She had been a good, loving pet to Ned's wife, then to Ned after his wife died. She deserved to be buried, not left to rot next to a tree. Dropping to his knees, he began to dig a grave with his hands.

Monty rushed back and saw what he was doing. "They gonna catch you, old man!" he warned.

"I don't care."

Ned kept digging as Monty hurried away.

He had barely finished burying Molly a few minutes later when the police found him.

Ned's sentence, because he was a first offender and no one had been hurt in the fire, was three years. He served fourteen months. Monty was waiting for him the day he came back to the block.

"Hey, old man, ex-cons give a neighborhood a bad reputation," Monty chided.

"You ought to know," Ned said gruffly.

"You get the Vienna sausages and crackers and stuff I had sent from the commissary?"

"Yeah." He did not bother to thank Monty; he knew it would only embarrass him.

"So how you like the joint, old man?"

Ned shrugged. "It could have been worse. A sixty-two-year-old man with a game leg, there's not much they could do to me. I worked in the library, checking books out. Did a lot of reading in between. Mostly about animals."

"No kidding?" Monty's eyebrows went up. "I been learning a little bit about animals, too. I'm a, what do you call it, volunteer down at the A.S.P.C.A. That's American Society for the Prevention of Cruelty to Animals."

"I know what it is," said Ned. "Good organization. Say, did that Consumer Evaluation Laboratory ever rebuild?"

"Nope," Monty replied. "You put 'em out of business for good, old man."

"Animal shelter still selling to those other two labs?"

"Far as I know."
"Still got their addresses?"
Monty smiled. "You bet."
"Good," Ned said, nodding. Then he smiled, too.

Notes On the Authors

Lilian Jackson Braun wrote the first three books in *The Cat Who* . . . series back in the late 1960s, but it wasn't until she revived Jim Qwilleran and his cats Koko and Yum Yum in 1986 for the Edgar-nominated *The Cat Who Saw Red* that the cat-mystery craze was officially launched. A former writer for the *Detroit Free-Press*, she, her husband and their two cats divide their time between Michigan and North Carolina.

Peter Lovesey is well known to mystery readers the world over as the creator of Victorian age police officers Sergeant Cribb and Constable Thackeray. Other creations include using King Edward VII as a sleuth in another take on the Victorian age. In between these series he has also written dozens of short stories, as well as several television plays. A winner of both the Silver and Gold Dagger awards from the Crime Writers Association, he recently added another laurel to his list of honors by winning the Mystery Writers of America story contest with his short story "The Pushover."

Sharyn McCrumb is a *New York Times* Best-Selling author whose critically-acclaimed success in Southern fiction has been both scholarly as well as popular. Her novels are studied in universities throughout the world, translated into German, Dutch, Japanese, French, Greek, Czech, Russian, Danish, Spanish, and Italian, in addition to being national bestsellers in the

U.S. She has won more awards in crime fiction than any other author, including all of the major U.S. awards in the field, although critics and scholars are now recognizing her as an author of serious, non-mystery fiction. She has been awarded the Edgar, two Anthony awards, two Macavity Awards, three Agatha awards, and the Nero. She is the author of fourteen novels including the "Ballad Books," consisting of *If I Ever Return Pretty Peggy O* and *The Hangman's Beautiful Daughter*, and the *New York Times* Best Sellers *She Walks These Hills* and *The Rosewood Casket*, all of which were named *New York Times* or *Los Angeles Times* Notable Books.

One of the most memorable figures in modern crime fiction is that of the Nameless Detective. Just like his title, he is a man about whom the reader knows everything but his identity. Even more incredible is the fact that Nameless has appeared in over a dozen more novels since his first, *The Snatch*, in 1969. Despite his lack of a first name, Nameless is as endearing a character as has ever been created. But strong writing is not the only thing his creator, **Bill Pronzini**, is known for. He has also co-edited over 50 anthologies in the western, horror, and mystery genres and written dozens of excellent short stories.

Joan Hess first started out writing romances, but switched to mysteries on the advice of her agent, and has never looked back. Her novels, usually set in small Arkansas towns, have won the Agatha, American Mystery and Macavity awards. Her shorter fiction has appeared in *Cat Crimes* and *Crimes of Passion*. Recently she edited a collection of humorous fiction, *Funny Bones*, along the lines of her own fiction.

Bruce Holland Rogers is not a stranger to anthologies, having appeared in *Feline and Famous, Danger in D.C.*, and *Cat Crimes Takes a Vacation*. When he not plotting feline felonies, he's writing excellent fantasy stories for such collections as *Enchanted Forests, The Fortune Teller*, and *Monster Brigade 3000*. He lives in Eugene, Oregon.

Bill Crider won the Anthony award for his first novel in the Sheriff Dan Rhodes series. His first novel in the Truman Smith series was nominated for a Shamus Award, and a third series features college English professor Carl Burns. His short stories have appeared in numerous anthologies, including past *Cat Crimes 11* and *III*, *Celebrity Vampires*, *Once Upon a Crime*, and *Werewolves*. His recent work includes collaborating on a series of cozy mysteries with television personality Willard Scott. The first novel, *Blue Skies*, was published in 1997.

Mat Coward is a British writer better known in his native country than over here. Hopefully the stories he sends across the water will change all that. He brings a special sardonic touch to his crime fiction, a touch that can sometimes sting with fury and other times touch with unexpected sentiment. Other fiction by him appears in *The Year's 25 Finest Crime and Mystery Stories, 3rd edition* and *Once Upon a Crime*.

Larry Segriff is an author and editor working in the science fiction, fantasy, and mystery fields. His recent novels include *The Four Magics* (co-authored with William R. Forstchen) and *Spacer Dreams*, with the sequel, *Alien Dreams*, recently published. He has also co-edited several anthologies, including *Murder Most Irish* and *Cat Crimes at the Holidays*. He currently lives in Green Bay, Wisconsin, with his wife and two daughters.

Michael Stotter held a wide variety of jobs before turning to writing, among them bus conductor, bank messenger and film clerk for the British Broadcasting Company. He is primarily known as a western writer, garnering critical acclaim for his first novel, *McKinney's Revenge*. He was an editor for *The Westerner* magazine and a consultant and co-founder of *The Western Magazine*. He currently lives with his family in Essex, England.

B. J. Mull is a pseudonym for a short story writer whose work has appeared in numerous anthologies including *Night*

Screams, Celebrity Vampires, and *Love Kills.* She is currently writing her first novel for a major paperback publisher.

Richard T. Chizmar's fiction has been called "always effective, notable for its clarity of style and originality of concept." and "[his work] should concern anyone interested in exceptional writing talent." Some of his over 40 published short stories appear in *Frankenstein: The Monster Wakes, White House Horrors,* and his own collection, *Midnight Promises,* published in 1996.

Jon L. Breen has written six mystery novels; most recently *Hot Air* (1991), and over seventy short stories; contributes review columns to *Ellery Queen's Mystery Magazine* and *The Armchair Detective*; was shortlisted for the Dagger Awards for his novel *Touch of the Past* (1988); and has won two Edgars, two Anthonys, a Macavity, and an American Mystery Award for his critical writing.

Margaret Maron first made a large splash in the mystery field when her 1992 novel *Bootlegger's Daughter,* featuring North Carolina judge Deborah Knott, won the Agatha, Anthony, Edgar, and Macavity awards. The next two novels in the series were equally well-received, with *Southern Discomfort* nominated for the Agatha and the Anthony. A former president of Sisters in Crime, she remains active in the Carolina Crime Writers Association and Mystery Writers of America.

Since the World and British Fantasy Award-nominated *Narrow Houses* (1992), **Peter Crowther** has edited or co-edited eight further anthologies, continued to produce reviews and interviews for a variety of publications on both sides of the Atlantic, sold some of 50 of his own short stories, and completed *Escardy Gap,* a collaborative novel with James Lovegrove due out in September 1996 from Tor Books. A solo novel, a short story collection, more anthologies and *Escardy Gap II* are all currently underway.

Max Allan Collins writes hard-edged historical detective fiction that bears more than a trace of Hammett and Chandler. Rather that just pay homage to these pulp greats, however, he puts his own indelible spin on the noir tale, with incredibly effective results. More of his short fiction can be found in *Murder is My Business, Werewolves,* and *Vampire Detectives.* His current novel series features Nate Heller, a private-eye in the 1940s.

Barbara Collins other short fiction can be found in *Marilyn: Shades of Blonde, Till Death Do Us Part, and The Year's 25 Finest Crime and Mystery Stories, 3rd Edition.* Adept at many forms of mystery fiction, she lives in Muscatine, Iowa, with her husband, novelist Max Allan Collins and their son Nathan.

Carole Nelson Douglas is the author of over 30 novels, covering such diverse genres as mainstream, historical, mystery, and science fiction. Her rise in the mystery field began with her quartet of historical mysteries, featuring Irene Adler, the female counterpoint to Sherlock Holmes, and the only character to outwit him. Her series character, Midnight Louie, is once again on the prowl, solving a case in the nation's capitol.

Nancy Pickard is a Macavity, Agatha, and Anthony-award winning author who just seems to get better with every story she writes. Her long running novel series features Jenny Cain, director of a philanthropic organization in a small New England town trapped in a recession. She is a past president of Sisters in Crime, and her short fiction also appears in *Careless Whispers, Murder, She Wrote,* and past *Year's 25 Finest Crime and Mystery* volumes.

Ed Gorman has written virtually every type of crime novel. Called "one of the world's great storytellers" by Britain's *Million* magazine, he is at his best when he is at his most ironic. Recent novels include *Cold Blue Midnight* and the suspense-horror novel *Cage of Night,* and short stories in *Once Upon a Crime* and *Guilty as Charged.*

Ruth Rendell's stories of psychological suspense always reveal a new twist in the human psyche that seemed to be just waiting for an author like her to reveal it. The author of over twenty novels and innumerable short stories, she explores the dark recesses of the mind that make men and women do unexplainable things. Recent novels include *Bloodlines, Keys to the Street, The Reason Why*, and her most recent, *Road Rage*.

California writer **Clark Howard** has been nominated for the Edgar award for his short fiction five times, and won it in 1980 for his story "Horn Man." He's been writing for the past forty years, with dozens of short stories sold to magazines such as *Alfred Hitchcock's Mystery Magazine* and *Ellery Queen's Mystery Magazine*. His stories are often focused on people living on the fringes of society. He has also written more than a dozen suspense novels and non-fiction books on such varied topics as Alcatraz prison and the murder of militant activist George Jackson.